FINAL SCREAM

Angie's lungs were on fire as she made her way toward the back rooms, where the trapped smoke had collected.

There had to be another way out of here. Had to!

Think, Angie, think . . . you don't have time for this.

Coughing, gasping, stumbling, she moved deeper into the building, through smaller rooms that had once been offices. Where were the windows?

She saw none and she was panting now, terrified beyond belief.

Where was the door?

Then she saw it. Through the smoke . . . a change in the wall. Thank God! She threw herself at the old panels, found the knob. Her fingers burned as she turned the brass fixture and she yanked with all her might.

Nothing happened.

She tried again, threw all her weight into pulling the damned thing open.

It didn't budge.

"Help!" she cried, coughing, banging on the door, hearing the first sounds of sirens in the air. "Help me!"

The heat was so intense, she had to fight from blacking out . . . she lifted a fist. Pounded again and noticed the flames, licking across the floor, creeping around her, circling that little spot where she stood.

"No!" she screamed as she struggled for a last, searing breath and realized with horrifying certainty that she was going to die . . .

Books by Lisa Jackson

Published by Zebra Books

LISA JACKSON

FINAL SCREAM

ZEBRA BOOKS
KENSINGTON PUBLISHING CORP.
http://www.zebrabooks.com

ZEBRA BOOKS are published by

Kensington Publishing Corp.
850 Third Avenue
New York, NY 10022

All Kensington titles, imprints and distributed lines are available at special quantity discounts for bulk purchases for sales
promotion, premiums, fund-raising, educational or institutional
use.

Special book excerpts or customized printings can also be
created to fit specific needs. For details, write or phone the
office of the Kensington Special Sales Manager: Kensington
Publishing Corp., 850 Third Avenue, New York, NY 10022.
Attn. Special Sales Department. Phone: 1-800-221-2647.

Zebra and the Z logo Reg. U.S. Pat. & TM Off.

First Printing: August 2005
10 9 8 7 6 5 4 3 2 1

Printed in the United States of America

Acknowledgments

Special thanks to Nancy Bush, Marilyn Katcher, Jack and Betty Pedersen, Sally Peters, and Debbie Todd for their help and encouragement with this book.

Prologue

Prosperity, Oregon
1977

I imagined her death.

Not a quick, easy giving up of the ghost, but a slow, torturous passing from this world to the next where, I was certain, she'd meet Lucifer at hell's gate. Which was perfect and, I figured, long overdue.

I felt a little thrill. A tingle of anticipation as I double-checked the locks of the old mill, then saw again the thin, nearly invisible filament that I had stretched between the detonation device and the pile of oily rags near the only route of escape, the doorway from the parking lot, the one she'd use to enter.

Yes, yes, yes!

I envisioned her walking through the cobwebs that draped over the doorway and into this gargantuan room, the heart of the hundred-year-old behemoth of a building that was in a sorry state of decay. Slated for a renovation that would never come.

So intent on her purpose, to meet a lover who would never show, she wouldn't notice that overhead, the metal roof gaped, creaking in the hot summer wind. Nor would she see the owl in the rafters as he flapped his wings before taking flight. She'd ignore the scent of dust and the old, unmistakable odor of sweat from a century of men who had toiled here.

Blind as she was to everything except herself, she'd miss the fact that the entire building had been wired to go up in the worst conflagration this sorry little town had ever seen.

Perfect.

I licked my lips in anticipation; tasted the salt from sweat pouring off my skin. Fingered the padlock in my jacket pocket; the one I'd removed from the back exit. *Burn, you sorry little bitch,* I thought and smiled to myself at how clever I was and how no one would ever suspect me. I'd already been pegged, typecast by this pathetic, small-minded community as one who didn't have the brains or wherewithal for something as complicated as murder.

Little did they know.

Just wait, I thought and trembled in eager anticipation.

In my mind's eye, I witnessed her walking through the doorway in expensive shoes—probably those high-heeled slip-ons she liked, as they showed off the perfect curve of her calves and gave her a few extra inches from which she could look down her straight nose. Then she would make her way toward the back of the building to a private room that had once been a windowless office.

I nearly fumbled with the detonator as I considered how she'd first understand what was about to happen.

She might catch a whiff of smoke in the stale air, but she'd think it was only the strike of a match as a cigarette was lit; that her lover had gotten to their tryst a few minutes before she had.

That would please her.

She *loved* to make an entrance.

The goddamned whore!

She was so damned predictable.

She'd call out and wait, hoping to hear him respond, and when he didn't she wouldn't worry, just think he was playing a seductive game of hide-and-seek as he lurked in the shadows. Waiting for her. Lusting after her. His cock rock-hard with need.

She'd smile seductively. Lift a dark, inquisitive eyebrow. Unbutton her blouse to show off her cleavage on this hot, breathless night and wind her long hair into a knot that she'd hold over her head, pushing those beautiful breasts forward. Oh, she understood how to play the game. How well I knew.

My hands were slippery in my gloves as I fantasized about how she, in that low, throaty voice, would call out to him again, saying something naughty. Dirty. Maybe she'd take off a high heel and playfully let it dangle from her fingers.

But the smell of smoke would be stronger by then and she'd start to wonder, perhaps feel that first little niggle of fear slide down her spine.

I smiled at that thought, tamped down the rage that burned through me at the thought of her seductive games. Jesus, I hoped she'd experience real, gut-wrenching, piss-your-pants terror tonight.

That's what it was all about.

That, and getting rid of her.

Forever.

In my vision, I saw her, dark hair intentionally mussed. Disturbed, even a little frightened, she'd yell his name more loudly. Anxiously. She would be getting angry. Worried. She'd warn him that she was in no mood for jokes and this wasn't funny anyway. She'd even turn petulantly, offering him a view of her rounded little ass.

Because she knew it was flawless and, oh, so inviting.

But by that time it would be too late.

She'd take one step toward the door and . . .

Bam!

The gunpowder would explode.

She'd be thrown off her feet.

She'd land with a bone-rattling smack onto the hard wood floor.

Her head would crack on the oily planks.

The building would shudder.

A ball of fire would spew sparks and flames to the ceiling.

Tinder-dry walls would ignite, fire climbing up to the rafters, sparks raining down, catching in her hair, burning her clothes, sizzling against her skin.

And she'd scream . . . oh, how she'd scream.

I quivered with the thrill of my fantasy, so close at hand. Raw panic would surge through her. She'd be frantic.

Realize that she was about to die in a horrible oven from which there would be no escape.

I felt another shiver of exhilaration zing through my blood, and the sound of Jim Morrison's voice echoed through my head as the vision became more distinct. More real.

"Try to set the night on fi—re," I whispered, as I, through the projector of my mind, watched what was to come.

The old timbers of this mill would quake, burn hot, groan eerily and tumble down, breaking into hundreds of flaming chunks as the fiery walls began to collapse and the roof gave way.

Dazed, blinded by smoke, she'd feel horrifying fear. She'd cough and gasp. Crying, begging for someone to save her, she'd crawl on bloodied knees to the back door—her only hope of escape. But it would be shut forever. The padlock that I'd opened earlier for my escape, firmly back in place.

Black smoke would fill her lungs. She'd cough. Gag. Scream. Pound on the old door.

But no one would hear her.

No one would come.

The smoke and heat would be terrifying.

And she would be trapped. That was the best part. Those last, brutal minutes of her life. Would she wail and keen? Pray wildly to a deaf god? See her life flash behind her eyes and regret all her sins?

In a matter of seconds, the entire building would be engulfed in intense, hellish flames.

Her lungs would feel as if they were being seared.

Flames would lick her bare flesh.

Pain would tear through every inch of her.

Her skin would begin to peel from her body.

And she'd know, in those last desperate moments, that she'd been condemned to hell.

But she wouldn't know who had done this to her.

Nor would she know why.

Not that it mattered.

Because *I* would know.

Finally, she would have gotten what she'd deserved.

Excited, barely able to think beyond what was about to happen, I lingered in the darkened building, near the back wall of the large room that had been the receiving area. Waiting. Heart pounding. Feeling sweat run down my back.

Where was she?

I glanced at my watch, then through the dirty windows where I saw the streetlights of town giving off a dull blue light. Few cars passed this way.

She was already five minutes late.

"Come on, come on," I whispered.

Relax. She's never on time. You know that.

My nerves were jumping. What if something went wrong? What if she didn't show up?

Don't worry. She'll be here . . . don't panic . . . do not panic.

Slowly, I let out my breath. Rested my head against the wall. Closed my eyes for what seemed an eternity. Then I checked my watch again. Nearly ten minutes had passed since the meeting time. Shit! What if she'd decided to let him wait? What if they'd had a fight? What if she'd called him to confirm and realized that she'd been set up? What if she'd called the police . . . no, no, she wouldn't. There was no reason. And yet my pulse was jumping erratically.

My fists clenched. She had to come here tonight.

She *had* to!

All this planning couldn't be just a waste of time.

She had to die.

Tonight.

Five more agonizing minutes passed, and she was now fifteen minutes late.

Son of a bitch, son of a goddamned bitch! I pounded my gloved fist against the wall. I had to leave soon. Before anyone noticed the truck parked in an alley a few blocks north.

This was all a waste of time, a big pain in the ass!

Headlights flashed against the windows; the sound of a car's engine cut through the night.

Finally.

All my muscles racheted up a notch. I glanced through the window again but only caught a glimpse of a dark vehicle as it flew into the parking lot.

Tires crunched on the sparse gravel.

She was here!

It was now or never.

Fingers shaking, the gloves hampering me, I set the timer . . . I had three minutes to get away from the building and into the truck. It would take me two minutes to sprint to the alley, and that was if I ran fast and didn't encounter any problems. I should leave right now; but I couldn't. Not quite yet. I was too fascinated by what was to come.

I heard footsteps and then a hesitation at the doorway.

Silence . . . as if she sensed something was wrong.

I held my breath. Told myself that she was just pausing to primp—to touch up her lipstick or finger-comb her hair, do a little something to ensure that she looked perfect.

Christ, what a slut!

I was nearly jumping out of my skin.

Get the hell in here!

But the seconds kept ticking down. Thirty gone. Now thirty-five.

Come on. Come on, you bitch. Don't make me drag you!

I held my breath and waited in the darkness. The timer was a simple device; I couldn't stop it. Once it was set, it would count off the remaining seconds then detonate. There was no fail-safe on the damned thing.

I had to leave. Now.

But I had to be sure. Certain she would die.

For God's sake, come the hell in!

Still the door from the parking lot didn't creak open.

You should have waited to set the timer until she entered. To make sure that she got into this place and allow yourself enough time to get out. Now you're trapped!

Sweat was running into my eyes. Adrenaline shooting through my blood. I'd have to do something. And fast.

My heart was pumping wildly, pounding in my ears.

I eased my way through the dark hallway to the back door.

Come on, you bitch! Get inside!

Finally the footsteps resumed.

I smiled. All was not lost after all.

The lock on the door rattled.

I slipped out the hallway to the back exit. A rush of dry summer wind hit me full in the face.

The footsteps behind me were louder.

Heavy.

Too heavy.

Damn!

Panic rifled through me.

"Are you here?" a deep male voice called, echoing through the empty building.

A man?

Son of a bitch!

It wasn't her.

Disappointment ripped through me.

All of my planning for nothing.

"Hey! Where are you?" A pause, then a knowing little snigger and the sound of a lighter clicking as he lit a cigarette. "So you want to play games, huh? Okay by me. Come out, come out, wherever you are."

I recognized the voice. Thought I'd be sick at the realization that I was going to kill him. But it was too late. I could not wait. I'd already lost a full minute. I had to leave now or I'd be caught. Detained. Questioned by the police.

I could yell and warn him. Risk being exposed.

But then I'd lose my next chance to kill her.

No way.

I slipped the padlock from my pocket, snapped it through the metal brackets and turned the dial. I gave the lock a tug. It didn't release.

And then I ran.

Part I

1977

One

So this was how the other half lived.

Brig McKenzie threw his denim jacket over the seat of his beat-up old Harley-Davidson. Squinting against the harsh sunlight, he glared at the groomed lawn that rose in tiered layers to the monstrosity of a house mounted upon the crest of a small hill. Rock walls supported each layer of clipped grass, and roses heavy with bloom splashed the grounds with color and scented the air. No dandelion or blossom of clover or thistle dared interrupt the thick green carpet of Buchanan grass.

This ranch—if that's what you'd call it—was a far cry from his own home, the single-wide trailer he'd shared with his mother and brother for most of his life. An orange crate shored up with two-by-fours sufficed as the front step, and dry weeds and crabgrass choked the gravel walkway. A metal sign, rusted with age, swung near the screened front window and boasted palm readings and psychic consultations by Sister Sunny. His ma. Part Cherokee and part Gypsy and the best damned mother a kid could ask for.

Gazing at the Buchanan house, he felt none of the jealousy that consumed his older brother, Chase.

"Christ, Brig, you should see that place," Chase had said on more than one occasion. "It's a mansion. A goddamned mansion complete with maids and cooks and even a chauffeur. Can you believe it? In Prosperity, Oregon, which is Hicksville, U.S.A., an honest-to-goodness chauffeur. Man, what a life." Chase had leaned across the scratched Formica table in the trailer's kitchen and whispered, "You know, I'd kill for a place like that!"

Brig wasn't all that impressed. He figured old man Buchanan had his own demons to deal with.

Now, he stared at the massive gray stone and cedar structure that was Rex Buchanan's home. Three rambling stories with gabled roofs, arched windows, decorative shutters and more chimneys than Brig cared to count. A monument built to a timber king.

Buchanan owned nearly everything and everyone in town, and to hear Brig's mother tell it, old Rex was practically a god on earth, but then his mother said a lot of things—strange, psychic things that bothered Brig. He didn't believe in all that astrological crap, and yet Sunny McKenzie had scored big-time on more than one of her predictions. It was spooky—gave him the creeps.

He didn't want to think of his beautiful mother, whose husband had walked out on her soon after Brig was born. Instead he concentrated on the vast acres of land that belonged to the Buchanans. Fences, painted stark white, split the countryside into smaller fields where expensive horses—mostly quarter horses from the looks of them—grazed on the dry summer grass. Sleek coats gleamed in the late afternoon light—brown, black, sorrel and bay—as the animals swatted flies with their tails. Gangly-legged half-grown foals tried to mimic their mothers and pick at the sun-bleached grass.

The ranch seemed to go on for miles, acre after acre of dry fields that rolled upward to the foothills, where thick stands of fir and cedar, the backbone of Buchanan's business, waited to be felled by the logger's ax. The timber on this spread alone was worth a fortune.

Yep, Rex Buchanan was one rich son of a bitch.

"You McKenzie?"

Brig glanced over his shoulder and found a tall man with weathered skin, sharp nose and deep-set gray eyes. Dressed as if he planned to do a little rodeo riding, one thumb hooked on a tattered belt loop of his dusty jeans, the man stepped out of the doorway of the stable and crossed the yard. "I'm Mac." He shoved his Stetson back on his head. Sweat ran down from his forehead. "The boss said you'd be showin' up." Mac's expression, one of silent distrust, didn't alter. He offered Brig a callused hand with a firm shake, but didn't let go. "I'm the foreman and I'll be watchin' you." His grip tightened just a fraction, squeezing Brig's hand to the point of pain. "I don't want no trouble here, boy." Finally, he released the vise of his fingers. "You got yourself a reputation in town; don't pretend that you don't know about it. The boss, well, he's into charitable causes and hard-luck cases, but I'm not. Either you pull your own weight around here and do as you're told or you're out. Got it?"

"Got it," Brig said, bristling under his work shirt. He should find it amusing, he supposed, the way everyone assumed that he was up to no good, but he didn't. Not today. He didn't like the idea of working for Buchanan, but in a town the size of Prosperity, he had little choice and he'd lost more than his share of decent jobs already. At nineteen he was nearly out of options. He gritted his teeth and told himself that he was lucky to be here, but a part of him, an inner rebellion that he couldn't quite tamp down, told him that working for Rex Buchanan was going to be the worst mistake of his life.

"Good." Mac clapped him on the shoulder. "Then we understand each other. Now, come on, I'll show you where you can start." He headed off for the stable, Brig at his heels. "I expect you here at five-thirty every morning and sometimes we'll work until it gets dark, at nine—ten o'clock. You'll get overtime. The boss is death on payin' a man his fair share, but you'll be expected to stay until whatever job we're doin' is done. Okay?"

"No problem." Brig couldn't hide the sarcasm in his voice and Mac stopped dead in his tracks.

"I'm not talkin' about just occasionally. In the summer we work nearly 'round the clock and you won't have much time for drinkin' or women." He threw open the door to the stable. Dust swirled in air thick with the smells of horses, dung, and urine. Flies buzzed against grimy windows and the temperature in the stable seemed to rise another five degrees. "Let's cut the crap, okay?" Facing Brig again, he jabbed a long, bony finger at Brig's chest. "I know about you, McKenzie. Heard all the stories. If it ain't stealin', it's booze, and if it ain't booze, it's women."

Brig's shoulder muscles bunched and his fingers coiled into fists, but he didn't say a word, just held the bastard's hard gaze.

"The women around here, they're ladies, and they don't need no riffraff from the wrong side of the tracks sniffin' at their skirts. One thing that's sure to piss off the old man is some randy young buck tryin' to get into his daughters' panties. And that doesn't begin to say what their older brother would do. Derrick's not someone you want to mess with; he's got a mean streak in him that runs real deep. He's on the possessive side and he won't take kindly to anyone tryin' to feel up his sisters. Miss Angela and Miss Cassidy, they're off limits, y'hear?"

"Loud and clear," Brig replied with a sneer. As if he'd want one of Buchanan's uppity daughters. He'd seen the older one in town, a flirt who knew she was drop-dead gorgeous and toyed with the randy boys that hung out at the Burger Shed. The younger girl wasn't near as pretty as her half sister, but she could look right through a man. Rumor had it she was a tomboy, liked horses more than she did boys, and couldn't control her sharp tongue. She was too young anyway, barely sixteen. Brig wasn't interested.

He hadn't had much contact with the Buchanan girls. The dark-haired tease had been shipped off to a Catholic school in Portland—St. Something-or-other—boarding there during the week, coming home only on the weekends to show off for the boys, and Cassidy was just too damned young and headstrong. Neither one was Brig's kind of woman. He liked them sexy but honest, horny but clever, with no plans for a future with him. He wasn't interested in rich women; they just spelled trouble. He'd leave the wealthy girls who were looking for a good time with the wrong kind of guy to his brother.

Chase had a lust for wealth, expensive cars and rich women. Brig just didn't give a damn.

Mac was explaining what his responsibilities were: ". . . as well as hauling hay and helping with the combining. We'll be puttin' up fence over by Lost Dog Creek where it borders the Caldwell place and then you can work with the horses. From what I hear, you're supposed to know how to handle even the meanest of the lot." They walked through the back doors to stand in the shade of the building.

In the next paddock a spirited two-year-old colt was holding court. His head was high, nostrils quivering in the dry wind that swept through the valley, ears pricked forward to the east where a herd of fillies was grazing. The colt pawed the dry ground, threw his head back and let out a high whistle, then ran from one end of the paddock to the other, his tail streaming behind him like a red banner. "That there's Remmington . . . well, Sir George Remmington the Third or some such shit. 'Sposed to be Miss Cassidy's horse, but he's just too damned headstrong. Threw her off two weeks ago, nearly caused her shoulder to separate, and yet she still insists she's gonna break him."

Mac patted his breast pocket, found a crumpled pack of Marlboros. "I don't know who's more stubborn, the horse or the gal. Anyway, Remmington will be your first project." The Marlboro wedged between his teeth, he slid a glance toward Brig and lit up. Smoke drifted out of Mac's nostrils. "You make sure that he's under control before Miss Cassidy tries to ride him again."

"I'm supposed to stop her if she tries?"

Grinning, Mac drew hard on his cigarette. "Ain't no one gonna stop her if she tries, but she had a bad fall. She ain't stupid. She'll wait."

The colt, as if sensing he had an audience, galloped to the far end of the paddock, where he kicked up a cloud of dust and reared, his front legs pawing the air.

Mac's eyes thinned. "He's a damned devil."

"I can handle him."

"Good." Mac looked skeptical but Brig would prove him

wrong. He'd grown up around horses, hanging out at his Uncle Luke's ranch. Luke had let him learn the trade but had to sell out. Since then Brig had worked on a couple of other places and ended up being fired from each, not because he didn't do a decent job, but because he couldn't control his temper and let his fists do the talking. The last job, only two weeks before at the Jefferson place, was the worst. He'd ended up with a broken nose and bruised fist. The other guy, the one who had made the mistake of calling him the son of a "cheap Indian whore" before throwing a punch that Brig had sidestepped, was feeling the pain of Brig's wrath every time he took a breath, compliments of two broken ribs. No charges had been filed. Enough ranch hands had seen the fight to know that Brig wasn't to blame.

"Okay, so that's it." Mac crushed his cigarette beneath the toe of a scuffed cowboy boot, reached inside the door of the stable and dragged out a shovel. "You can start today by cleaning the stalls." A spark of malevolence gleamed in Mac's eyes as he tossed the shovel to Brig, who snatched it quickly out of the air. "As long as you do as I say, things'll be fine, but if I ever find out that you crossed me, you're out."

He turned to walk into the stable, but a man barely out of his teens, about the same age as Brig, blocked his path. Tall and muscular with suspicious blue eyes, he just stared at Mac. "Oh, this here's Willie. He can help you with the shovelin'."

Brig knew all about Willie Ventura. The town half-wit. A retarded boy whom Rex Buchanan had decided to take in and offer a job. Willie wasn't bad-looking, but his hair was always mussed, his shirt dirty, his mouth slack a lot of the time. He hung out in town drinking sodas at the Burger Shed or playing some kind of pool at Burley's—a local striptease joint.

"Willie," Mac said, "you'll be workin' with Brig from now on."

Willie's mouth worked a bit and his eyebrows drew over his eyes in a worried scowl. "Trouble," he said, motioning quickly in Brig's direction and avoiding his eyes.

"No, he's workin' here now. Boss's orders."

Willie wasn't happy. His thick lips pulled into a puckered little frown. "Big trouble."

Mac rubbed his chin and eyed Brig again. "Yeah, well," he said, "nothin' I can do about that."

Cassidy's shoulder throbbed, but she wasn't going to let any stubborn mule of a horse beat her. She downed two aspirins with a swallow of water, then dashed out of the bathroom, her boots ringing loudly on the bare steps of the back staircase. She was out the screen door before her mother could catch her. Racing down the hill to the stable, she ignored the fact that it was twilight, nearly dark. Night or day, it was time to teach that damned colt a lesson.

Sweat beaded on her forehead—the heat of the afternoon still lingering like a curse. Even the faint breeze had little effect on the temperature, which had been hovering near a hundred for most of the afternoon. The roses had begun to wilt in the heat despite the sprinklers that were pumping well water onto the dry beds. Yellow jackets, thirsty and mean, hovered near the sprinkler heads.

At the stable, she didn't bother with the lights; she could still see well enough and there was no reason to let her mother know what she was up to. Dena Buchanan would have a fit if she knew Cassidy was deliberately disobeying her. Again. Though she'd never said it, Cassidy was sure that her mother wanted her to be more like Angie, her half sister. Beautiful, boy-crazy Angela, who dieted to keep her waist tiny and brushed her long black hair until it gleamed. Her clothes came from the finest stores in Portland, Seattle and San Francisco, where sometimes she'd been asked to model. With flawless skin, high cheekbones, pouty lips and eyes as blue as a summer sky, Angie Buchanan was, without a doubt, the most beautiful girl in all of Prosperity.

The boys were crazy for her and she teased them mercilessly, reveling in their adoration, lust and sexual frustration. Even Derrick seemed mesmerized around his sister.

It was enough to make Cassidy sick.

She yanked a bridle off a hook in the tack room and found Remmington in his stall. In the half-light his liquid eyes held a tiny spark of fire. Yep, this one liked a challenge. Well, so did she. "Okay, you mean old jackass," she said in her most coaxing tone, "it's time for you to learn a thing or two."

She slipped through the gate to the stall, stepped inside and sensed the tension in the air. The colt pawed the straw and snorted, the whites of his eyes showing in the darkness.

"You'll be all right," she said, slipping the bridle over his head and feeling his tense muscles quiver as she fiddled with the buckle. "We'll just take a nice little ride—"

A hand clamped over her forearm.

She yelped. Her heart nearly stopped. Spinning around, she started to scream before she recognized Brig McKenzie. Her father's latest acquisition. That thought bothered her. She'd heard stories about Brig and had admired his irreverent streak, never once believing that he, like everyone else in town, would eventually become a Buchanan possession.

Tall, broad-shouldered, with tanned skin and a nose that had been broken more than once, he glared down at her as if *she'd* done something wrong.

"What the hell do you think you're doing?" she demanded, trying to yank back her arm and failing.

"You know, that's exactly what I was gonna ask you." Furious blue eyes assessed her. Thin, nearly cruel lips drew flat over his teeth. She knew in a split second why so many girls in town found him dangerously sexy.

"I came here to get my horse and ride—"

"No way."

"You think you can stop me?" she scoffed, unsettled by the way he was holding her, furious that he would try to tell her what to do. Truth to tell, she was more than a little embarrassed that he'd sneaked up on her without her hearing him, but she wasn't going to let that side of her show.

"It's my job."

"Remmington's *your* job? Since when?"

"Yesterday." His voice was rough and close, his breath much too warm as it whispered across her face. "Your dad hired me to train your horse."

"My dad hired you to work in the fields."

"And with this colt."

"I don't need any help."

"That's not the way I heard it."

"Then you heard wrong." She wrenched her arm away and winced as pain burned through her shoulder. "This is my horse and I'll do what I please with him."

A derisive snort. "The way I heard it, he does what he pleases with you."

"Get out of my way—" she warned, and to her mortification he laughed, low and sexy and without much real emotion. But he didn't move, just stood between her and the animal, looking for all the world like a range-tough cowboy, determined to have his way. His chin was hard and set, his eyes narrowed obstinately. He smelled of sweat, horses and leather along with the faint undercurrent of smoke.

Her heartbeat quickened a bit and she saw his gaze shift to her throat, where she felt her pulse throb angrily. For some reason it seemed as if the stable was fading away, that suddenly she and he were the only two people in the universe. Aware that her chest was rising and falling much too quickly, she wished it wasn't so damned hot. Hot enough for perspiration to soak the back of her shirt.

"Why are you here so late?" Time to put him on the defensive.

"Just puttin' things away." He unbuckled the bridle with ease, as if he'd done it a thousand times. The bit jangled as he slipped the leather straps off the colt, and Remmington tossed his great head.

"Then you'll be leaving soon."

Again that humorless laugh. "Don't count on it." He walked through the gate and held it open for Cassidy. She had no choice but to follow him through. "I might just spend the night here," he said, ramming the bolt into place.

"You wouldn't."

"Try me." His voice was challenging. Firm. She would have liked nothing better than to get the best of him right then and there, but she didn't know how. If, as he said, he'd been hired by her father, he had every right to be in the stable. If he was lying . . . well, he wasn't. No one could be that stupid. She'd heard a lot of stories about Brig McKenzie. Some wild, others downright nasty, but no one had ever accused him of being a fool. Oh, he'd done some stupid things, but only when he was drunk or involved with a woman.

The thought of him lying with a woman, making love to her with his tough, sinewy body, did strange things to Cassidy's insides, caused her stomach to flutter and a rush of warm blood to invade her face. She closed her mind to those kinds of thoughts.

Lately, ever since Rusty Calhoun had kissed her behind the football stadium, pressing her back against the rough cement wall, she'd been thinking too much about men and women and the kinds of things they did behind closed doors. Rusty had even reached up and opened her blouse, clumsily sticking his hand into her bra and trying to fondle her before she'd torn away from him. Kissing him hadn't been all that unpleasant, even if they'd both been bumbling teenagers, but doing anything else was a little frightening. Tempting but scary. Rusty had called every night since, but she hadn't gone out with him again. She wasn't ready for the kind of fun he expected of her. And she suspected he was just using her to get closer to Angie.

All the boys wanted Angie.

So why was she thinking such forbidden thoughts about Brig McKenzie?

He was a hired hand. He couldn't tell her what to do, but she was all too aware of his eyes following her as she marched rigidly back to the house.

Once on the back porch, she kicked off her boots and sneaked up the back stairs to her room. She heard music drifting from the radio in the kitchen, and the smooth voice of a news anchorman blared from the television in the den. Somehow she'd find a way to get around Brig McKenzie. He couldn't stand guard over Remmington day and night. Or could he?

Heart pumping more wildly than it should have been, she locked her door, then stole across her room without bothering with the light. At the open window she paused and looked over the stable yard. Dusk had colored the fields with deep purple shadows, and only a few dark shapes, the horses allowed to stay out at night, spotted the dry, sun-dried fields. But Brig was there. Leaning against the fence, staring up at her window. He struck a match and his face was illuminated in the twilight for just a second. Chiseled, rugged features, all sharp angles and planes, thick black eyebrows and eyes a mystical shade of blue didn't waver as he stared up at her and lit his cigarette, then deliberately waved out his match.

Her throat went dry and she held on to the window casing with rigid fingers. Biting her lip, she stared outside where the lone figure leaned against the white boards. The tip of his cigarette glowed red, and the thin, acrid smell of smoke wafted upward, past the aromas of freshly mown grass, dry roses and dust. Insects hummed in the warm night, and Brig silently smoked, a dark sentinel intent on having his way. As stubborn as the colt she intended to break.

Well, he couldn't stay here forever. She'd just have to outwait and outwit him. Turning from the window, she heard his laughter again, low and mocking, seeming to ricochet off the distant hills.

Two

Jed Baker rapped his fingers on the hot steering wheel of his new Corvette. Parked at the Burger Shed, he left the keys in the ignition and let the radio play as he sipped his Coke and gazed past the small restaurant to the picnic area where a few tables were clustered in the shade of three giant fir trees. Angie Buchanan and her best friend, Felicity Caldwell, were seated there, sucking the catsup off fries and lazily drinking soda, as if they didn't know he and Bobby were in the convertible, staring at them. "Hotel California" by the Eagles was playing, the familiar notes rolling out of the Corvette's speakers, but he barely heard. Squinting against the sun, he said, "She doesn't know it yet, but I'm gonna be the one to bust Angie Buchanan's cherry." His eyes slit in delicious consideration as he swirled the shaved ice in his Coke.

"Yeah, and I'm the pope," Bobby Alonzo replied with a sneer. He finished his chocolate shake in one swallow and stared through the windshield, his gaze never moving from Angie.

Angie and Felicity. What a pair. The older daughter of the richest man in town and the only child of one of the most prominent judges in the county. The girls laughed and talked together, whispering secrets, giggling in naughty-girl sniggers and placing their pink lips lovingly around the straws of their drinks.

Jed got hard just looking at Angie, and he could almost taste her. Bobby might not believe him, but he wasn't lying.

Before the end of the summer, Jed planned to make it with Angie.

"If you ask me, she's already done it," Bobby said, tossing his cup out the window and hitting the trash can. Syrup ran down the sides of the plastic container and bees and flies swarmed over the remnants of food.

Jed's fingers clamped over the steering wheel. "With who?"

"I dunno, but she just looks . . . so hot." Bobby licked the remnants of his milk shake from his lips. "She can't be a virgin."

"A lot you know about it." Jed couldn't hide his irritation. The thought of anyone else touching her made him see red. She was everything he wanted in a woman. Good looks, sexy smile, big tits and lots and lots of money. The favorite of Rex Buchanan's children, she was sure to inherit a fortune when the old man kicked off, and even if she didn't, she was one helluva woman.

A napkin caught in the breeze, floating off her table, and Angie bent over to pick it up. Her short pink skirt shimmied up thighs that were meant to squeeze a man's ribs to the breaking point. The pink fabric stretched beguilingly over her rump, and Jed caught just a glimpse of lace—either her slip or panties, and that one flash of heaven made him groan. "She's mine," he muttered under his breath. His throat was suddenly parched, and he swilled back the final gulp of his drink. He was so horny he thought he would bust, but he didn't want anyone but Angie. There were other girls—plenty of 'em—who would do it with him, but they weren't good enough. Easy lays. Willing bodies.

As he turned on the ignition, and the engine of his powerful car roared to life, he imagined what it would be like to press Angie back against a bed, her black hair fanned out like a cloud of dark silk, her eyes slumberous and blue, her pink lips whispering his name in anxious abandon. He fantasized about how she would writhe beneath him, begging for more, offering to do things to him he'd only dreamed about.

The tires squealed as he pulled out of the lot, and he

caught her looking at him when he checked his rearview mirror. Yeah, she was interested all right. And he couldn't wait to give it to her.

"You're dreaming," Bobby told him as Jed ground through the gears and sped through town.

"Wanna bet?"

Old stores with the false fronts of the 1800s swept by. A light turned yellow and Jed tromped on the accelerator. The car lurched forward, passing through the intersection as amber switched to red. The old gristmill, a relic that was owned by the Buchanans, passed by in a blur.

Bobby laughed. "You're a maniac, but I'll take that bet." He grinned, showing off straight white teeth. "You're on. How much?"

"Twenty bucks."

"Fifty."

Jed didn't miss a beat. "Sure."

"But I have to have proof."

"Like what?"

"A picture of her naked."

"Aw, come on—"

"Or she could tell me herself." Bobby grinned wickedly, and Jed had the sinking sensation that his best friend wanted Angie, too.

Glancing down at the gearshift, Jed let his eyes wander to Bobby's crotch. Sure enough, Bobby had a hard-on that pressed against his jeans. Hell. They passed the sign welcoming tourists to the town.

"Maybe we could make this a little more interesting," Bobby suggested with a leer that had set many a coed's heart soaring. "How about whoever makes it with her first, wins the bet?"

Jed stood on the brakes. The car shuddered. Expensive tires screamed as the Corvette slid to the gravel shoulder of the county road.

A pickup that had been tailgating the faster car swerved into the oncoming lane. The truck's horn blared. The red-faced driver swore from his open window as the truck skidded back into the right lane, avoiding oncoming traffic, but Jed barely heard the oath. His head was still pounding with Bobby's lewd suggestion. "Don't mess with me on this," Jed warned, his jaw so tight it ached as he scowled at his friend. He felt the edges of his nostrils flare and quiver in rage. "She's mine. This is no joke." Jed grabbed the front of Bobby's T-shirt. The soft cotton crumpled in his meaty fingers. "You got it? No one else touches her. No one! I'm not only gonna score with her, but I'm gonna make her my wife."

Bobby had the audacity to laugh. "Oh shit, man, you *are* crazy."

Jed shook him hard, but Bobby wasn't scared. Even though Jed was bigger, Bobby was an athlete, the star running back for last year's football team and the best wrestler in his weight in the district. Jed's extra thirty pounds wouldn't help him because Bobby was so damned agile—got himself a wrestling scholarship to Washington State. If it came to blows, Bobby would have an edge, but Jed didn't care. He'd give as good as he got. "She's mine," Jed declared again. "She just doesn't know it yet."

"When you plannin' on givin' her the news? Before or after you pop her cherry?" Bobby's dark eyes turned up at the corners. He was laughing, but this was no joke.

For once, Jed was dead serious. He'd spent the last two months considering what he wanted from Angela Marie Buchanan. The answer was, everything. He loved her. "Soon. I'm gonna tell her soon." Jed let go of Bobby's shirt, and his rage dissipated in the sweltering heat that seemed to pound down from the sun.

Bobby snorted. "Ever think she might laugh in your face? That she might move on? I hear she's goin' to some fancy Ivy League school back East. What was the name of that school in the movie out a few years ago—*Love Story*—wasn't it Radcliffe or some such shit? She might have other plans."

Jed's smile was slow and wicked. "Then she'll just have to change them, won't she?"

* * *

"Jed's got the hots for you," Felicity drawled as Angie parked her sporty Datsun near the garage.

"So what else is new?"

Lifting her heavy mane of straight red hair off her nape, Felicity shook her head and glanced at her friend. "He's so horny he can't stand it."

Angie wasn't interested. Jed Baker was an oaf. A big, overgrown ox of a boy.

They climbed out of the air-conditioned interior of the silver car, and Angie felt the late afternoon heat sear her skin. God, it was hot. Her blouse was sticking to her, her hair was wet where it met her scalp, and she didn't care one way or the other about Jed Baker. He was just a kid. Nineteen. Same as her.

"I think he's in love with you," Felicity continued as she slammed the Datsun's passenger door shut and scanned the parking area near the garage.

Felicity was obviously looking for Derrick's truck, but his black pickup wasn't in sight and the corners of Felicity's mouth tightened a bit. For a second she looked desperate. It was an emotion Angie understood all too well. She recognized it each time she looked in the mirror. But she didn't want to think about it—not now.

"Jed Baker loves poker. He loves booze. But he doesn't love me," Angie said, trying to keep her mind on the conversation. "Besides I don't want a boy." She glanced around the stable yard, searching until her gaze settled on the bare back of Brig McKenzie. He was working with one of the horses and the animal was fighting him. The colt's eyes were blazing, his massive head pulling hard at the lead, trying to free himself of the stubborn man. Brig's boot heels were dug into the dust, and the more the horse resisted, the more he worked the lead rope, his shoulder muscles gleaming with sweat, his face set in determination. It was as if he didn't notice anyone or anything but the animal, and Angie felt a fluttering in her stomach. She wondered what it would be like if Brig looked at her like that, with that same gleam of reckless stamina that he forced on the wayward animal. Though he wasn't much older than she, Brig McKenzie seemed to have years of experience on the other boys in town. He could give her what she wanted. What she needed.

Tossing her hair away from her face, she crossed the hot asphalt and leaned against the fence, content to watch the play of sinew and muscle in his shoulders and forearms.

The horse tried to back up and Brig talked to him, low and soft, a rough whisper that caused Angie's scalp to tingle.

"What's he doing here?" Felicity asked, catching up with her.

"Dad hired him last week."

"Why?"

"Ranch work." Angie was irritated by Felicity's questions and the snooty tone of her voice. There was a lot that bothered her about Felicity these days, but then, Angie hadn't been her usually lighthearted self the past few weeks. "He's supposed to be the best horseman in the county."

"Yeah, when he's not in jail," Felicity said under her breath. "Or sleeping with someone's wife."

"He's never been booked," Angie whispered hotly, surprised at how much she knew of Brig McKenzie and disturbed by the fact that she felt compelled to defend him. "And that womanizing bit . . . it's probably exaggerated." She let her gaze wander down the cleft of his spine, past the smooth curve of his waist. His belt was thick rough leather that rested low on his hips. The denim was thin and pale across his butt, and one frayed hole showed off an inch of muscular thigh. Her insides trembled then twisted into a knot, and she found it suddenly hard to breathe. "You know," she said under her breath, so that only Felicity could hear, "he's not half bad."

"If you're into slumming."

As if he'd heard her, Brig turned, and his eyes, a lazy shade of blue, seemed to burn right into her. "Somethin' I can do for you?" he asked. His voice, so steady with the colt, was now impatient.

"We're just watching you," Angie said with a smile that usually melted boys' hearts.

"Like what you see?"

She couldn't help but lick her lips. "It's all right. I've seen better."

One black dark brow arched, and he slanted her a knowing, cocksure grin that silently called her a liar. "Then you don't need to be starin' now, do ya?" With that he turned back to the horse, and Angie felt a slow-growing burn climb up the back of her neck.

Felicity couldn't swallow her grin fast enough, and Angie turned on her heel, stalking across the pavement, her heart throbbing in her flushed cheeks. "Insolent bastard," she spat as she ran up the sweeping flagstone path that curved toward the wide front porch. Mortified, she threw open the front door and stormed through the foyer. How *dare* he insult her! He was a nobody. Rumored to be illegitimate. Oh God, she was beginning to sound as snobbish as Felicity.

She stopped in the bathroom, splashed water on her face, then joined Felicity in the kitchen. Her best friend's green eyes were glinting with humor at Angie's expense, but she had the good sense not to tease Angie right now.

"You want somethin' to drink?" Mary asked. A heavy woman who liked her own fare, Mary had cooked for the Buchanan family for years and had been hired long before Angie's mother had died and her father had married Dena. Angie frowned at the thought of her stepmother—so pale and lifeless compared to the first Mrs. Rex Buchanan. "I've got iced tea. Or lemonade." Mary was already reaching into the refrigerator, pulling out two chilled pitchers.

"Tea," Felicity said.

"Sounds good," Angie agreed as she glanced out the bay window and looked to the side of the house. She caught a glimpse of the stable and the paddock where Brig was still working with the stubborn horse. His black hair gleamed in the sunlight and his skin still shone with sweat. From a purely sensual and animal point of view, he was perfect. Toned, firm muscles, tight butt, square jaw and eyes that seemed to look right through her. A challenge. With a bad reputation already firmly established. The natural choice. A man unafraid to call her bluff. Someone her father, despite all his ridiculous philanthropy, could hate.

Mary, intent on pounding every ounce of toughness out of a huge piece of flank steak, left two iced glasses on the counter and turned back to her cutting board. Her spiked wooden hammer started slapping against the raw meat as Angie grabbed her glass and stepped outside.

"When will Derrick be back?" Felicity asked casually though there was a hint of worry in her voice. They followed a brick and stone path past Dena's flower gardens and through the rose arbor to the pool.

Angie shrugged and felt a twinge of sadness for her friend. Derrick had lost interest in Felicity months ago. He only saw her to keep her strung along. She was, after all, the judge's daughter and she was willing to sleep with him despite the way he treated her.

"Who knows?" Slipping a pair of sunglasses onto the bridge of her nose, Angie settled into a lounge chair near a large terra-cotta planter filled with fuchsias. Purple and pink blossoms dripped from leafy stems. She sipped thoughtfully from her drink and watched the ice cubes melt around a single slice of lemon. "If I were you and I wanted Derrick," she said, sensing her friend bristle a little, "I'd play hard to get."

"It's a little late for that," Felicity said.

"It's never too late." Angie studied the sunlight rippling on the pool's clear surface. From the corner of her eye, she spied Willie hovering in the thick rhododendrons on the far side of the pool. She gritted her teeth. The retard was always around, spying, looking like he might drool at any minute. "I hate the way he hovers," she said, inclining her head to the shadows where Willie pretended to be busy spreading bark dust. "It gives me the creeps even though he's harmless."

Felicity leaned back in the chair. "Is he? Maybe we should give him something to gawk at."

"What do ya mean?" Angie asked, but felt a tingle of excitement. Felicity had an outlandish side—one that would turn her father, the judge's, gray hair white.

With a naughty little laugh, Felicity yanked her T-shirt

over her head. Her bra was cut low and lacy over her white breasts. Her tan line was visible and the sheer lace was stretched tight, barely hiding the rosy disks that were her nipples. "This." She lifted her arms over her head, pushing her breasts together and creating a lot of cleavage where there had been none. "Want to go skinny-dipping?" She reached for the zipper of her cutoffs.

"Stop it! What if Dena shows up? She's always prowling around the house!" Biting her lip, Angie glanced up to the master bedroom window and was relieved to find that her stepmother wasn't peeking through the blinds.

Felicity sighed, blowing her bangs from her eyes before tugging the T-shirt back over her head. "I just wanted to see what the moron would do if he saw a real woman."

"What did you think?" Angie turned her gaze back to the shadowed spot where Willie had been keeping his vigil, but he was gone. Only the leaves of the rhododendrons moved in his wake as he made his hasty retreat. "Stop playing games with him."

Felicity giggled and pulled her hair through the neck of her T-shirt. "So what were you doing with Jed and Bobby?"

"That's different."

"Why? Because they have an IQ over twenty?"

"Says who?" Angie said with a smile as she thought back to the Burger Shed and Jed's searing gaze.

"Either one would do anything you wanted, you know." Felicity's words held just a touch of jealousy.

"You think?" The idea had possibilities.

Pressing her lips to the glass, Felicity nodded. *"Any*thing."

"Too bad I don't want them," Angie said, nudging one sandal off with the toe of her other foot as she leaned back against the orange cushions of the lounge.

"Why not?"

"Got my eye on someone else." May as well plant the seeds of doubt now. Her lips curved into a thoughtful smile.

"Who?" Felicity asked.

Angie paused a beat, watching her friend squirm. "Brig McKenzie."

"No!"

"Why not?"

"A million reasons why not!" Felicity whispered, though her mouth curved into a smile. "First of all he's trouble and . . . well, I think he could be dangerous."

"Maybe I like trouble and danger."

"For God's sake, he lives in a trailer and his mother is some kind of a witch or something."

"A psychic."

Felicity's patrician nose wrinkled in distaste. "She's part Indian and some kind of Gypsy. That makes him—"

"Interesting," Angie said, warming to the idea forming in her mind. "And I bet he'd be a great lover. You said he'd been with a lot of women."

"And you said it was probably rumors."

"Maybe I should find out," Angie teased.

"Oh, God . . ." But Felicity's breath caught a little and she swallowed hard. "You're not thinking . . ."

"Why not?" Angie tossed her hair out of her face and felt the warmth of the sun caress her cheeks. "I think Brig McKenzie is just the right man to make me a woman."

Three

"That's right," Angie said in a whisper that floated in the hot summer air. "I'm gonna see if all those rumors about Brig McKenzie are true."

The words whispered through the gardens, and Cassidy, hidden by the rose arbor as she carried her towel and radio, nearly stumbled on the path. Catching herself, she stopped before her sister and friend could catch a glimpse of her. *What rumors?* There seemed to be a new one about the McKenzie boys every day.

Felicity's laugh was nasty. "It had better be worth it, 'cause if your daddy found out you were going to seduce one of the hired hands—"

"Hey, wait a minute. You've got it all wrong," Angie said. *"He's* gonna seduce me. He just hasn't figured it out yet."

"Well, what can you expect? He's probably all brawn and no brain."

Cassidy couldn't believe it. What was Angie thinking? She was actually planning to *do it? With Brig?* The idea made her sick, but it wasn't because Brig was an employee; it was the fact that his life was being planned—manipulated—and he didn't have a clue. Maybe it didn't matter. He was a surly one anyway, but the thought of Angie and him kissing and touching and getting all sweaty turned her stomach.

"When?" Felicity asked, leaning closer.

"Soon."

Felicity's smile stretched wide and catlike. She nearly purred, "He'll never know what hit him."

Cassidy had heard enough. Coughing loudly, she walked through the arbor, her bare feet suddenly seeming to smack against the flagstones.

Conversation stopped. Angie and Felicity exchanged smirking glances. "What're you doing sneaking around here?" Angie asked as she picked up her drink and scowled at the melting ice cubes.

"What's it look like? I thought I'd go for a swim."

"Don't you think you should shower first?" Angie's nose wrinkled slightly at the dust that clung to her younger sister's skin.

"I'm okay." Cassidy wasn't going to get into an argument with her sister. At least not now when her ears were ringing with Angie's announcement.

Felicity slid a look up Cassidy's body—her cutoff jeans, frayed around the edges, the smudges on her legs, the red blouse that was opened to reveal the top of her two-piece. Cassidy nearly blushed. She knew she wasn't as endowed as either of the two older girls; in fact, she'd been waiting for her breasts to grow for the last couple of years. It seemed as if they barely got started, then stopped completely. "Be careful," Felicity warned. "Good ol' Willie has been sneaking around here trying to get a free peek."

"I told you, he's harmless." Angie swirled her drink.

Rolling her eyes, Felicity said, "He's a grown man with the brain of a ten-year-old. Hardly harmless."

Cassidy wasn't worried about Willie. She stripped off her blouse and cutoffs, scraped her hair back and snapped it into a ponytail, then dived quickly into the water. She'd never liked Felicity Caldwell and didn't know what Angie saw in the redhead. Felicity wasn't quite as pretty as Angie, but she was the daughter of Judge Caldwell, who was a good friend of their father's. Rex and The Judge—his real name was Ira but everyone called him The Judge—played golf together, hunted together and drank together. They'd known each other all their lives, and Felicity and Angie had grown up together. For as long as Cassidy could remember, Felicity had had her eyes and heart set on Derrick.

Cassidy surfaced, shook the water from her hair and began swimming laps. Felicity and Angie left. Well, good; Cassidy didn't want to think any more of Brig and Angie and what they would do together if Angie got her way. And what would stop them? Nothing. The stories about Brig McKenzie were legendary; even Cassidy had heard a few. If you could believe all the town gossip, Brig McKenzie had warmed more beds than all the electric blankets in Prosperity put together. Cassidy didn't know if she trusted the rumors, but she couldn't deny that she, herself, had noticed he was sexy in a rough-and-tumble, I-don't-give-a-damn sort of way. A few people even considered him dangerous and his past was black enough to prove it. Some women seemed to like to flirt with danger—like sticking their toe into a deep, unfathomable lake, without really jumping in. While some bored women appeared to be turned on by money, others liked a challenge—someone who made them feel a little bit naughty. Cassidy suspected that Brig McKenzie was a man who would make a woman feel downright indecent.

She felt a tingling against her skin that had nothing to do with the temperature and, angry with herself, stroked all the harder, knifing through the water, swimming each lap as if it were the last in a swim meet until, gasping for breath, she touched the side of the pool on the deep end, pulling herself up to lie half-in and half-out of the water.

Then she saw him.

Sitting on the edge of a brick planter, a profusion of red and white petunias looking out of place against his grimy, tanned skin and hard male muscles, Brig was watching her intently. His clothes were stained from hours of work—dirty jeans and a plaid shirt with the sleeves rolled up, the buttons undone.

She wanted to die. To cover up. To avoid those mocking blue eyes.

"Thought you might want to hear how it's going with your horse," he drawled.

Her mouth turned to sand. Heart pumping stupidly, she climbed out of the pool with as much dignity as she could muster and stood dripping in front of him. "Let me dry off first."

With a shrug of indifference, Brig watched as she walked to the far end of the pool, where she toweled off, slipped her arms through the sleeves of her blouse and knotted her shirttails beneath her small breasts. Quickly she yanked on her pair of dusty cutoff jeans. He couldn't help but smile at the angle of her chin, all proud and militant, as if he were the enemy. He wondered what she'd heard about him, decided he didn't really give a damn, and waited until she turned. All legs, this one was, unlike her sister, who was shorter, rounder, and seemed to be proud as a peacock of curves that wouldn't quit.

"The horse is trained, right?" she said, approaching him again, her face flushed from the exertion of her swim. The freckles usually bridging her nose seemed to have faded a bit, and her wide eyes, a whiskey-gold color, blinked against drops of water still clinging to her lashes.

"Not quite. You got yourself a hellion in that one."

"It's been a week—"

"Five days," Brig corrected her. "It'll take a few more. At least."

"Why? Don't you know how to break him?"

She watched as a lazy, taunting smile slid from one side of his beard-stubbled jaw to the other. "Some things take time," he said, his gaze penetrating. "They can't be rushed, if you want to do 'em right."

Her stomach curled in on itself, and in her mind's eye she saw him making love to Angie, so slowly that Angie was writhing and desperate for the want of him. Cassidy swallowed hard, then cleared her throat. "Seems to me if you know what you're doing—"

"I do."

"Then you could speed things up."

"What's the rush?" he asked, leaning back a little and squinting up at her.

She didn't know what to say. "Summer's . . . summer's almost over. I want to spend as much time . . ." She sounded silly, like a whining, spoiled rich girl anxious to get her way. "I just planned to do a lot of riding, that's all."

"Your dad's got other horses. Lots of 'em."

"This one's special," she said.

"Why's that?"

Again, she felt stupid and young, but there was no use lying to him. She suspected he could tell if she veered too far from the truth. "Dad knew I was horse crazy and he wanted to give me one—a special one; so he let me pick the mare and the stallion—it was a birthday gift."

Brig snorted and shook his head, as if he couldn't, for the life of him, understand rich people.

"I picked the smartest mare and the wildest stallion."

"Well, hell, that explains it." Casting her a mocking glance, Brig reached into his pocket for his pack of cigarettes. "Don't tell me, the old man let you watch while the horses went at it."

"It wasn't a big deal," she lied, remembering that fierce coupling, how the stallion, eager and volatile at being with a mare in season, thrashed in his stall at the scent of her and then bit the back of the mare's neck as he'd mounted her. Primal, rough, raw sex. She cleared her throat. "We raise horses here. It happens all the time."

"And you watch?" He lit up and smoke curled from the tip of his cigarette.

"Sometimes."

"Jesus!" Taking a long drag, he climbed to his feet and started down the gravel path leading through the trees and around the house. Over his shoulder, he said, "Stay away from Remmington for another week or so; by that time he should be ready."

"I don't want his spirit broken."

"What?" Brig turned and blew a plume of smoke from the corner of his mouth.

"Don't make him into a merry-go-round pony, okay? I picked his dam and sire for a reason and I got what I wanted. So don't foul it up. I want more than a show pony."

She heard him swear under his breath before disappearing around the corner of the house.

Closing her eyes and tracing the lines of the large woman's hand with the tip of her finger, Sunny McKenzie shivered slightly. Belva Cunningham's fleshy palms gave out no feeling, yet the woman was worried sick.

"Jest let me know if we're gonna make it," Belva was saying, destroying Sunny's concentration. "I need to know if this year's herd will—"

"Shh!" Sunny's brows deepened and she felt a sadness, but not for the cattle that Belva was so worried about, no . . . the feeling was a distant little jarring in her brain. "You will have visitors . . . from far away. One speaks with an accent."

"That's Rosie and her new husband, Juan. He's a Mexican. She's always been wild, y'know; I never could hold her back. Anyway, she met Juan down in Juarez, got herself knocked up and brought him back to the States with her. They live in L.A. now and they're plannin' to come up here."

"But they bring with them trouble," Sunny said, feeling that cold little touch on her backbone.

"Trouble?" The word trembled in the air. "What kind of trouble? Oh, Lordy, it's not the baby—"

"No, this is different." Sunny concentrated. "There is a problem with the law."

"Oh, no, Juan is from a very good family. You know, one of them rich Mexicans, and it's a good thing, too, 'cause Rosie's dad ain't none too happy that she married him. But Juan's a good boy."

Good old-fashioned prejudice. Sunny knew only too well how it flourished and spread in a town the size of Prosperity.

Many times she'd wondered why she hadn't left this place with its small minds, but deep in her heart she knew. She wasn't a woman who lied to herself and she stayed because of one man—a man who had been good and kind to her. .

She concentrated on the few sensations she received from Belva's warm hand. "They are being hunted," she said, certain of the vision that was forming behind her closed eyelids, "by men with uniforms and guns . . . the government."

"Oh, Lordy," Belva whispered as Sunny opened her eyes. The big woman swallowed, and tiny lines appeared between her eyebrows. Sweat dripped down the side of her face. "You don't think they're hidin' out, that we'll have some U.S. Marshal beatin' down our door."

"I wish I could tell you. When Rosie calls, ask her."

"You bet I will. That girl's always been a handful. If she's in trouble, her pa will skin her alive. Now, you didn't have no kinda feelin' about the livestock?"

"None."

"Or Carl's prostate?"

"Nothing, but I would know better if I touched him or talked to him."

"Oh, gosh, no. If Carl knew I was usin' part of the grocery money on this, he'd kill me. I hate to say it, Sunny, 'cause you know I think the world of ya, but there's lots of people in town who think you're a fraud. Carl's one of 'em. So, I'd appreciate it if it didn't get out that I visit you."

Sunny smiled; she'd heard the speech before from most of her clients. Including Carl Cunningham. It had been Sunny who had first suggested he see the doctors, that there was a darkness within his organs that could spread. But Belva would never know why her husband of thirty years up and decided to have the first physical of his life this past spring.

Belva delved into her purse and left a twenty-dollar bill on the table. "I'll call you," she promised as she waddled, barely easing her wide hips through the open door of the old trailer. Though she was a heavyset woman, Belva was strong enough to run the farm while her husband worked for Rex Buchanan's logging operation.

Belva's wheezing two-toned Ford left a blue plume of exhaust and dust as it roared down the lane and disappeared through the thickets of oak and fir trees that sheltered this scrubby patch of property from the county road. Sunny had lived here most of her adult life, and though the old trailer was small, too small for the size of her family, she'd never left.

In the beginning, she'd had big dreams. She'd grown up on a dusty ranch outside of town. Her father, Isaac Roshak, had barely scratched out a living, and her mother, Lily, a beautiful woman who was half Cherokee Native American, had suffered the indignities of the tiny community. Isaac had married Lily for her earthy and exotic beauty, but he'd never respected her and, when drunk, had often called her a half-breed before dragging her into the bedroom and closing the door. The sounds that had drifted through the thin plywood—screams, moans and grunts of pleasure or pain—had scared Sunny, their only child.

From the age of three, Sunny had visions; dreams that oftentimes came true. Only her mother knew of her gift; Isaac had never been told. "You must keep what you see a secret," Lily had confided in her small daughter.

"But Papa—"

"Will only use you, honey. He'd make a sideshow out of you and have you talk to strangers for money." Lily had smiled then, a sad smile that never blossomed into happiness. "Some things must be kept close to your heart."

"Do you have secrets?" Sunny had asked.

"A few, little ones, but none to worry about."

In later years Sunny had discovered the secrets and they were simple. Isaac had always wanted a son and Lily, in her own discreet way, had denied him. There were no more children. Only Sunny.

Isaac assumed his wife had become barren and Lily let him believe that she could not conceive. Their arguments were bitter and he often accused her of not being a woman, calling her a dried-up old hag. No good to him. He needed sons and lots of them to help him with the ranch. If he wasn't a God-fearing Catholic, he would have divorced her in a minute and found a real woman, one who would bear him boys and quit staring at him with eyes that looked haunted.

But the truth of the matter was that Lily would not bring a son of Isaac's into the world.

In a cabinet that held makeup and nail polish and other "women things," Lily kept several vials and bottles of herbs, powders and potions that every so often she would use, mixing them to a foul-smelling concoction that she would drink. Within the day she would be sick and get her period. Sunny was never told, but she guessed much later in her life that, whatever it was her mother drank, it stopped her from having any more babies.

Isaac spent more and more time in town, drinking and whoring, coming home drunk and bragging about his conquests with women who enjoyed taking him to bed and didn't lie against the sheets frigidly like some goddamned statue! He'd rant and rave and eventually either drag his wife into the bedroom or pass out on the couch.

The little farmhouse was tense whenever he was home, but he made the mistake of striking his daughter only once, when she was five and had inadvertently spilled a bucket of milk that was to have been separated from the cream later. The pail had been sitting on the table when Sunny, chasing her cat, had tripped and fallen against the scarred old table. Sunny tried vainly to grab the pail, but it was too late. The bucket fell to the floor and milk, like the surf of the ocean, rolled in a huge wave that splashed over the cracked linoleum and ran in every direction.

Her father was smoking a cigarette in the living room and reading some hunting magazine. He heard the crash and her gasp. Already in a mean mood as one of his cattle had died, he took one look at the spillage and swore at the mess on the floor. "You little moron! What the hell did you think you were doing?"

"I'm sorry, Papa."

"Sorry doesn't count! That was the butter money and the cream and oh, for Christ's sake, clean it up," he raged, reaching for a bottle of whiskey he kept in the cupboard over the sink. His face was a mottled red as he tossed his cigarette into the drain and poured some of the liquor into a jelly glass.

Sunny had grabbed a rag, but she was small and all she succeeded in doing was spreading the milk in wider circles.

"Damn it, girl, you're just as bad as your ma." He walked to the porch and found a rag mop. "Now start over," he said, throwing the mop at her. She barely caught the long wooden handle in her small fingers. "And do it right. You cost me a bundle today, let me tell you."

Sunny's stomach trembled. She pushed the mop, but the strings were dry and the milk seeped everywhere, running under the table and along the old scratched baseboards.

"Don't you know nothin'?" Isaac yelled, cursing idiot daughters.

"Papa, I'm trying." Tears streamed down her cheeks.

"Well, try harder!" He drank from his glass, draining the amber liquid, and the look on his face was pure hatred. "I should never have married her, you know. But she was knocked up and I thought you were a boy." His lips curled into a sneer. "Instead you were a girl, and a useless one at that. Can't even mop a floor. Well, you'd better get used to it, Sunny, 'cause it's all you're ever gonna be good for. Women's work. Squaw labor. Jesus, I was a fool to marry her!" He tossed back his drink, and Sunny bit her lip to keep tears from raining from her eyes. Never had her father spoken so roughly to her. Many times he'd cursed his wife for being so beautiful, for tricking him into marriage, for being barren when it came to having more children. Sunny had heard their arguments, how he claimed that she'd wanted it before they were married, and how she'd screamed that he'd raped her and only married her to keep her father from cutting out his heart.

The arguments were ugly and vicious. Sunny had quivered in her small bed, holding her hands over her ears, feeling as if she were the cause of all the pain in the house. Her father hadn't wanted her, and her mother, though she loved her daughter, had been forced to live with a man she loathed.

Swallowing against the horrid lump in her throat, Sunny pushed the mop again, and her father laughed at her futile efforts, that wicked, ugly laugh he used whenever Mama tried to defy him. "You are useless," he said, shaking his head as the cat hopped down from the windowsill and began lapping the edges of the river of milk. Isaac muttered a curse and kicked hard.

"Don't!" Sunny yelled.

With a shrieking meow the tabby went flying, sailing over the table to thud against the wall. Hissing and growling, it slid to safety behind the wheezing refrigerator.

Isaac turned back to his daughter, who had dropped the mop to run after her pet. "Where do you think you're going?"

"Kitty—"

He grabbed at the collar of her dress. "It'll be fine," he growled, his breath hot with whiskey and smoke. "Now you just do what you're told and clean this mess, or I'll have to take a strap to you, ya hear?"

"No!" she cried and his smile twisted even more.

Sunny tried to scramble away, but her bare feet slipped on the wet linoleum. Her father didn't let go. Still holding her by the collar with one fist, he began to slowly unbuckle his belt.

"No! Papa, no!" Sunny cried.

"It's time you learned your place around here. Turn around!"

She shivered and tears filled her eyes. "Please, don't—"

"Believe me, girl, this will hurt me more than it does you." He slid the belt through his pants and Sunny noticed his eyes, dark and burning with an unholy light, spittle collected beneath his ragged moustache, and then . . . in a sudden vision, she saw him falling to the ground and clutching at his chest, his eyes rolling up in his head, his skin turning blue, and her mother standing over him, never bothering to reach for the phone, though he was gasping for breath and cursing her and telling her to call an ambulance. The vision was so clear that she forgot where she was until she felt the first bite of the belt slap hard against her rump. She screamed loudly as the vision faded in a ripple of pain. Her knees gave out, but he jerked her to her feet.

"Don't hit me!"

The belt bit through her shorts again. Pain ripped through her buttocks. "Papa, don't!" she screamed and sobbed and begged, but still he held her.

"Now you seem to be gettin' it!"

He raised up his right hand again, but stopped in midair when the screen door opened and banged hard against the wall. Lily, carrying a bucket of beans from the garden in one hand, a butcher knife in the other, glowered at him. Rage burned in her cheeks. Fury glowed in her dark eyes.

"Let her go," Lily ordered, her lips barely moving, her nostrils quivering in repressed violence.

He snorted. "You don't scare me!"

"Let her go." Lily's lips flattened and she glared at him with a hatred so intense that Sunny inwardly shrank away from both her parents though her father still held her so tightly she could barely breathe.

"She defied me. I'm just teaching her to obey."

"And I'm going to teach you not to hurt her ever again."

He laughed and his grip eased a little. Sunny squirmed, her feet gaining purchase. She twisted away from her father but slipped, falling facedown into the sticky mess.

Isaac's anger centered on his wife. "You're gonna pay for this!"

"What you do to me has nothing to do with her." Lily's pail slid to the floor, rolling and spilling long beans onto the already dirty floor, but the tanned fingers surrounding the knife never loosened their deathlike grip.

"I'll kill you." His lips curved into an evil smile "Then what will she do, eh?" He hooked a thumb at his daughter. "She'll have to take over for you, won't she? Do the squaw work around here. I'll marry myself a nice white woman, a young one who'll do what I say and give me sons, and your kid, she'll be our little slave."

Lily placed her other hand around the knife, curling her long fingers over the bone handle, and a blank look came over her face. She began saying things—over and over—chanting words that Sunny didn't understand, and the smirk on Isaac's face faded. He stepped backward, dropping his belt as the strange litany continued. The buckle banged against the floor.

Sunny's hand snaked forward and she grabbed the horrid strap of old leather.

"Don't you put no curse on me," he sputtered, backing away from his wife and stumbling against a chair.

The chanting continued, soft and low, but endless, rolling like thunder over the far hills.

"For the love of Mary! Woman, what are you doing to me?" As if struck by a force that couldn't be seen, Isaac jerked backward. His legs wobbled. With a horrid gasp, he clutched at his chest. "Oh, God," he whispered. "Sweet Jesus, she's crazy. Save me." His knees buckled and he fell to the milky floor, his face turning blue, his hand over his heart. "Call an ambulance!" he sputtered, but the chanting continued and Lily stepped forward, through the spilled milk, crushing the beans with her bare feet, the knife still held aloft, the intonation rhythmic and endless.

"Sunny—help me!" her father cried. "Damn you, help me!"

She couldn't stand there and watch him die. She ran to the phone and dialed for help. "My pa's dying," she screamed into the phone. "Please! Help us!" She was sobbing, her words garbled. "My pa's dying."

Lily didn't move to stop her, nor aid her, just watched as her husband struggled for his life.

"You did this," he cried. "You cursed me!"

By the time the volunteers from the fire department arrived in the red ambulance with its shrieking siren and flashing lights, Isaac was dead. No one could bring him back to life.

"He knew he had a weak heart," Lily said calmly, not even pretending grief as she held Sunny tightly, "but he was very upset today, he lost a cow and calf. When he came into the house, he became angry with Sunny for spilling a pail of milk—I was out in the garden at the time, picking beans, and he had the attack. We called immediately, but there was no way to revive him."

"Is that what happened?" a tall, thin man smoking a cigarette asked Sunny. Still crying, Sunny nodded, knowing that she was lying, knowing that God would probably strike her dead or make it so she couldn't talk ever again, but lying because she knew the men would send her mother to jail and she'd be all alone.

Lily's story never changed, and Isaac Roshak was laid to rest in the family plot three days later. But Sunny had never forgotten how powerful her mother had been, and from that point forward she'd held new respect for her visions, for the vials of powder in her mother's closet, and for her own Cherokee and Gypsy heritage. Because she knew, without a doubt, that her mother had killed her father—as surely as if she'd plunged that wicked knife through his failing heart.

Now, some forty-odd years later, as she stood in the sweltering trailer with only a small fan to move the hot air, she gazed through the windows to the heat shimmering against the trees.

Her heart pumped a little faster, her blood circulating to pound near her temples. She reached for the back of a chair to steady herself, and the vision she hadn't been able to see for Belva came clear to her.

But it wasn't a glimpse of Belva's daughter or failing crops; it was much more personal. And chilling.

The image before Sunny's eyes was of her own sons, naked as the day they were born. Their skin shimmered in the heat as they stood on a ledge of sheer granite cliffs, the path at their bare feet much too narrow to walk upon.

Yet they moved. Slowly. Rocks and stones falling into the dark, bottomless abyss below them. They constantly tried to find higher ground, to scale the rocky precipice, their fingers clawing, their hands and feet bloody, their bodies covered in dirt and sweat as they strained, helping each other, inching upward to a darkness they couldn't see, a danger that lurked . . . waiting.

Sunny's heart froze.

"Don't!" she tried to cry, but her voice was silent, her warning a whisper that they couldn't hear. Ever upward they moved, trying to scale the treacherous precipice, and the clouds above them turned dark and stormy, swirling with malevolence.

The ledge became mere inches and still they strained, reaching up, hands nearly reaching the crest.

The earth shuddered. Violently.

The darkness swirled angrily above them. Growing near, a faceless shadow that was death itself.

Sunny's heart stopped.

She saw herself, on the other side of the crevice, trying to call to them, to warn them, but her voice was silent. Impotent.

Fear screamed through her; her heart pounded in dread. *Be careful! Climb down!* But her voice was stilled, and she could only watch in mounting horror as their fingers scrabbled against the sheer cliff and their bloody toes tried to grip, slid, knocking away dirt and sand as they tried desperately— vainly—to gain purchase.

No, oh, God, no!

Muscles strained. They shouted to each other. Ignored her and the blackness that blocked the sun.

Help them. Please, please keep them safe, she silently prayed to whatever deity would listen.

The earth moved, the cliff shattered, the nightlike darkness became a whirling vortex of smoke. Coughing, she watched in horror as her boys fell, tumbling and screaming, arms and legs flailing as the darkness splintered into a blistering burst of flames.

Screams reverberated through her mind, and her sons, dark silhouettes against a backdrop of hot, hungry fire, disappeared before her.

"No!" her own voice echoed around her. She blinked and the vision disappeared, scattering away from the hot little trailer, but the sweat and fear still lingered. Her insides seemed to melt and she fell, gasping, into a kitchen chair. She couldn't shake the image that her children—her precious sons—would soon meet their ruin.

It wasn't the first time she'd seen this same terrifying image; the premonition had started appearing two weeks ago, creeping into her sleep, breaking out of her subconscious.

She checked the old calendar—the free one she'd been given from Al's Garage—that hung on the wall near the refrigerator. Running her finger along the appointments and cancellations, she finally stopped on the fourth, the day of her first vision—the very day after Brig had taken the job with Rex Buchanan.

Four

"What're you doin' in here?"

At the sound of Brig's voice, Cassidy nearly dropped the comb that she was dragging through Remmington's knotted mane. The colt snorted, rolling his eyes as he tossed his head.

"What does it look like?" she asked, feeling heat sear up her cheeks. She glanced over her shoulder and stared into eyes that seemed to smolder in the half-light of the stable.

"Botherin' the horse."

"He needs to be groomed," she replied tartly, then winced when she recognized the sound of a spoiled little rich girl's voice. Her voice. "I, uh, thought it would be a good idea."

"I thought you didn't want a show pony."

"I don't."

"But you think he gives a good goddamn whether his mane and tail lay straight?" He snorted and shook his head. "Hell, all he cares about is throwin' you out of the saddle, tryin' to take a nip out of my arm, and mountin' those mares up in the south paddock. You should see him show off for the ladies." His smile was crooked and cynical, his voice low with a sexy drawl. "Kinda reminds me of Jed Baker and Bobby Alonzo anytime your sister's around." With a knowing grin, Brig climbed up the metal rungs of the ladder to the hayloft. Within seconds bales of hay tumbled to the concrete floor.

Cassidy didn't want to be reminded of her half sister. For nearly two weeks she'd remembered Angie and Felicity's conversation by the pool, and she'd watched as Angie had set her plan into motion. It bothered her how Angie had begun hanging around the stable, talking and smiling at Brig as he worked, laughing with him, turning on the charm. Cassidy wanted to believe that Brig was just being polite to the boss's daughter, but it was more than that. He, like every other male in Prosperity, responded to Angie. Male to female. It wouldn't take long before he and she were making out and . . . the image of their two bodies, slick with sweat, panting and heaving, flitted through Cassidy's mind.

A sour taste rose in the back of her throat.

Brig didn't bother with the ladder, just swung down from the haymow and landed lightly on his booted feet.

"What about you?" she asked as he pulled out a pocket knife, leaned over and slit the twine that held the bale together.

"What about me what?"

"The way you act around Angie."

He snorted as he stepped over another bale and sliced through the twine. The bale split, sending up a tiny cloud of dust. "I don't 'act' around anyone, Cass. You should know that by now."

It rankled her how he shortened her name. Like she was just one of the hands. Or a kid. "Sure you do. Every guy does."

"Well, I'm not just like every guy, am I?" He clucked his tongue and, straddling the broken bale, stared up at her. His gaze touched hers and held, causing the back of her mouth to turn to dust. His slow-spreading smile was downright nasty. "You think I've got the hots for your sister?"

"I didn't say—"

"But that's what you meant." Making a sound of disgust in his throat, he clicked his knife shut. "Women," he muttered under his breath as he grabbed a pitchfork hanging on the wall and began pronging hay into the mangers.

Dropping the currycomb and brush into a bucket, she climbed over the top of the stall gate as Remmington began picking at the hay Brig had shaken into his stall. Brig didn't stop working, just kept forking split bale after split bale into the open mangers. Cassidy watched him walk—saunter, really, along the row of feeding bins. She noticed the way his thighs and butt tightened beneath his sun-bleached Levi's as he stopped, bent over, cut the twine, then tossed hay into the stalls. A restless man, he never seemed to stop moving, and her heart fluttered stupidly whenever he looked her way. Not that he did very often.

She waited, hanging around until he was finished and walked back to the door. "All done with him?" Brig asked, nodding toward Remmington's stall as he hung the pitchfork on its hook. "No bows or ribbons?"

Anger surged through her, but she managed to hang on to her temper. "Not today. Maybe Sunday."

He laughed as they stepped outside, where the summer sun was hanging lazily over the ridge of mountains to the west, and yellow jackets and wasps hovered at the spilled water near the trough. The day was without a breath of wind, and Cassidy's clothes felt sticky and damp from the heat.

"You should be able to ride your horse soon," Brig said as he reached into his pocket for his cigarettes. "I think I told you before, I like to take it slow."

"Slow?"

"So as not to break his spirit." Shaking out a Camel, he eyed the lowering sun, then jabbed the cigarette into the corner of his mouth.

"I want to ride him now."

Striking a match on the bottom of his boot, he said, "Be patient."

"He's mine."

"Haven't you heard that patience is a virtue?" With a half-smile, he lit up and stared at her through the thin veil of smoke. "Or is that the problem—that you're not into being virtuous?"

Again his eyes held hers and she felt her stomach turn over. "I just want to ride my horse."

"It'll happen. In time."

"I can't wait forever."

"Two weeks isn't forever." He sighed heavily and plucked a piece of tobacco from his tongue. "You know, Cass, the best things in life are worth waiting for. At least that's what my old man used to say before he took off. I never knew him, but Chase, he did, and he keeps spouting off these words of wisdom from a guy who decided he didn't want to stick around and take care of his kids and wife." He frowned as he drew hard on his cigarette, and lines etched between his black eyebrows. He stared at a solitary fir tree in a corner of the paddock, but Cassidy suspected he was miles away, thinking back to a childhood filled with poverty and pain. "Personally, I think anything Frank McKenzie said was a pile of shit, but Chase, he seems to think our father was God." He chuckled without a trace of mirth. "Chase, he's the optimist. Has an idea that someday he'll be rich as your old man. Own himself a house bigger than yours. Can you imagine?"

"Why not?" Cassidy said.

He turned to face her again, and this time there was no light in his eyes. He dropped his cigarette and squashed the butt with the heel of his boot. "Because there's a system. The haves and the have-nots. Chase just hasn't figured out where he stands. He's a dreamer."

"And you're not?"

"It's a waste of time, Cass." His lips were thin and harsh. "Well, break's over," he said, as if suddenly realizing he was talking to the boss's daughter. "Time to get back to work."

"Everybody dreams."

"Only fools."

She couldn't help herself. She reached out, grabbing his arm as if to keep him from stepping away from her. He glanced at her hand, then slowly lifted his head until his gaze touched hers. "You . . . you must have dreams," she said, unable to let go of the conversation, the intimacy, the feeling of dark want that had started to unwind deep in the very center of her.

His lips curled cynically. "Believe me, you don't want to know about the kind of dreams I have." His voice was barely a whisper.

Cassidy licked her lips. "I do. I want to know."

"Oh, Cass, give it up." Slowly he peeled her fingers from his arm, but his gaze still held hers, and for the first time she saw a glimmer of something—some deep emotion he hid— a flicker of desire in his dusky blue eyes. "Believe me, the less you know about me, the better."

Every muscle in Brig's body ached from five hours of stretching fence line and two hours of shoveling manure from the broodmare barn. He smelled bad, felt worse, and couldn't wait to get off work, though he looked forward to working with Cassidy's feisty colt. Remmington was ornery and mean, but was slowly coming around. In another week he'd be tame enough for Rex Buchanan's mule-headed daughter to ride. Then maybe she'd quit bugging him. Not that he minded all that much, but she was just a kid, barely sixteen, a tomboy who didn't know that she was becoming a woman. Gritting his teeth, he remembered the heat he'd felt in her fingertips when she'd touched him the other day, when he'd witnessed a shimmer of passion in her gold eyes. Funny, he'd never really looked into her eyes before, never realized that a spattering of freckles across a girl's nose could be sexy. For the love of Christ, what was he thinking? She was the boss's daughter. And only sixteen. Problem was he was horny as hell. Needed to get laid. Then he'd quit thinking about her.

Sure. Since when do you ever quit thinking about a woman? He'd been cursed from the age of fourteen, wanting sex all the time.

He took a break and lit up, drawing hard on his smoke and resting his shoulders against the rough bark of a single fir tree near the stable. He glanced up at the Buchanan house and snorted. A family of five, living like goddamned royalty in a mansion big enough for fifty.

"Well, fancy meeting you out here," a soft female voice intoned. Brig didn't have to look over his shoulder to know that Angie had found him again. Third time this week. She was gorgeous, he'd give her that, prettier than her little sister, but big trouble.

Still propped against the tree, he rotated and found her squinting up at him with those incredible blue eyes. Her white shorts rode high on her thighs, barely covering her crotch, and her breasts were squeezed into the top of a black two-piece swimming suit a couple of sizes too small.

"Somethin' I can do for you?" he drawled, dragging hard on his Camel.

The tip of her tongue flicked against her lips. "I could think of a lot of things." Her eyes twinkled with a naughty, you-can't-believe-what-you're-missing look. She tilted her head to one side and her black ponytail fell forward, the tip curling on the swell of one breast. "But right now Dena needs someone to bring up a ladder to the main house. There's a few bulbs out in the chandelier."

"You want me to bring in a ladder?" He nearly laughed because it seemed like such a lame excuse to make conversation with him.

She smiled. "Not me. My stepmother. And it doesn't matter if it's you or someone else. You're just the first hand I saw." She flipped her hair over her shoulder and glanced at his boots, covered with dirt and dung from the barn. "You might want to take those off before you go inside. Dena's a stickler for keeping things tidy." With a wink, she turned and strutted away, her hips swaying in perfect rhythm to the bob of her ponytail and the swing of her arms.

He found a tall stepladder in the garage and kicked off his boots before he climbed up the stairs of the back porch. Carefully he finagled the ladder through the kitchen and into the foyer, where a crystal and brass chandelier hung some fifteen feet above the polished marble floor.

Dena was fretting. Company was coming over and a few bulbs were dim or had flickered out altogether. "I don't know how this could have happened," Dena said, little lines of irritation forming around the corners of her mouth. "The cleaning service should have told me." She glanced at Brig and there was a faint flaring of her nostrils, the hint of disdain in her cool eyes as she slid her gaze down his body to land on his socks and the holes in the dingy white cotton.

Brig didn't let her snobbery affect him as he set up the ladder. Dena Miller came from poor roots herself, though she didn't have a Gypsy or a Native American in her bloodlines as far as he knew. But she'd been the daughter of a farmer and a seamstress and had put herself through business college. After graduation, she'd taken a job with Buchanan Logging and had been Rex's personal secretary for years. When Rex's adored first wife had died, Dena had been around to pick up the pieces of Rex Buchanan's shattered life. The old man had been a shambles. Dena had seen her opportunity and gone for it. They were married less than a year after Lucretia Buchanan had been buried, and barely eight months later, Cassidy had been born. Dena Miller had seen plenty of tattered socks in her life.

He changed the bulbs and was conscious of the women watching him. Dena with hardly suppressed contempt, Angie with interest, and Cassidy, who thought she was hidden on the second-floor landing, with curiosity. She'd been avoiding him for a couple of days, ever since their conversation near the stable and now, as he finished screwing in the final bulb, he tilted back his head, caught her surprised gaze and winked at her.

She swallowed hard, and though she looked as startled as a rabbit caught in the beams of headlights at night, she held his stare, refusing to ease back into the shadows.

She had pluck, he'd give her that.

He dropped back to the ground and snapped the ladder together. Angie, probably just to bother her stepmother, laid her hand on his arm. "Thanks," she said with a soft smile. "Maybe we should repay you with a cold drink. Coke? Or if you want something stronger, my dad keeps a stash of Coors in the refrigerator."

"Mr. McKenzie's still working."

He felt rather than saw Dena stiffen, but her words were meant to make him understand his station. He offered Angie a grin. "I think I'll pass. Work to do," he drawled, then glanced back at Dena. "Maybe I'll take a rain check."

Angie lifted an elegant eyebrow. "And I'll hold you to it," she said, touching the tip of her finger to the front of his shirt. Beneath the cotton his skin seemed to ignite by the gentle pressure of her flesh, so close to his. He wondered if Cassidy saw the display, decided he didn't care and carried the ladder out the back door. He couldn't help but notice the sleek Corvette parked near the garage. The car's red exterior looked liquid in the afternoon light, and two boys, Bobby Alonzo and Jed Baker, leaned against a fender, ankles crossed, butts propped on the shiny paint job, arms folded over their chests.

Brig didn't pay them any mind. Just slid into his boots and carried the ladder back to the garage. He heard quick little footsteps as Angie caught up with him. She slid her arm through his while he balanced the ladder on his opposite shoulder. "Thanks again," she said.

"No problem."

"Oh, it was a big problem. A catastrophe, really. Almost as critical as running out of matching silver or driving a car with mud splattered near the tires." She rolled her eyes. "With Dena it's always one disaster after another."

"Looks like you've got company."

She slid a glance toward the shiny car and the two boys staring at her. "Wonderful," she said, her voice dripping with sarcasm.

"Thought they were your friends."

She sighed. "Immature spoiled little boys," she said as Jed pushed his body from the car and waved at her. "Do you know what? They actually have a bet." Her pretty lips pulled into a scornful little knot and she didn't bother waving back.

"On what?"

"Well, that's the interesting part." She angled her head toward him and her eyes held his. "On which one of them will be the first to sleep with me."

"They *told* you?"

"Bobby did." She showed off a dimple. "I think he did it so that I would be too disgusted to do it with Jed. Can you imagine?"

Brig snorted as if he didn't care. "So who'll it be?"

"Neither one," she said with a toss of that glossy ponytail. "They don't seem to realize that when it comes time, *I'll* do the choosing. And it won't be with a couple of snot-nosed little boys who only think about sex, football, and cars. Do you know they're so crude that they actually call a woman's breasts headlights? *Headlights!*" She snorted in revulsion. "Little boys." Reluctantly she slid her hand away from his, her fingertips brushing the inside of his arm. "See ya," she said, with a flirty little wave of her fingers.

Brig watched as she slipped away from him and he had the distinct feeling that he should be relieved to see her go, but he was male enough to appreciate the swing of her hips, the curve of her calves, the nip of her waist, as well as the fleshy tops of her breasts that jiggled as she turned and smiled at him one last time. Headlights, eh? Well, she certainly had hers on high beam all the time. He didn't understand the game she was playing or why she was determined to make him a part of it, but he guessed that she wanted to tease him, a rich little girl used to male adoration. *Look what I've got and you can't have because you're from the wrong side of the tracks.*

Who needed it?

His brother, Chase, maybe. Chase liked money. And women. Rich women.

But then, Chase was an idiot. A good-hearted idiot who worked his butt off to better himself and take care of the family. Brig grimaced. If it weren't for Chase, Brig would have sole care of their mother and he wasn't much good at it. Never had been one to express his emotions.

Angie strolled up to Jed and Bobby. Brig couldn't hear their conversation, but he didn't need to. Angie, for all her big talk about not being interested in the "little boys," was showing off. She laughed and whispered with Jed, letting him touch her waist as she turned back to see if Brig was still watching.

He wasn't in the mood. There was a part of him that was interested in Angie—any man would be. But another side of him knew she was the worst kind of trouble a man could find, and that if he were smart, he'd stay away from her. She was too damned manipulative and she was playing Jed and Bobby like they were violins. Those boys were suckered in so badly they were nearly drooling and Angie was eating it up. Like a two-year-old with a forbidden bowl of ice cream.

He hung the ladder on its pegs. He heard the roar of a powerful engine, then the tinkling sound of Angie's laughter. Through the dusty window he watched them leave, Jed behind the wheel, Angie wedged between the two boys. She was laughing gaily, one arm slung around Bobby's neck, the other around Jed's shoulders.

Brig walked out of the garage and nearly stumbled over Willie Ventura, who was peering through the lacey branches of a row of arborvitae planted as a hedge between the house and garage.

"Angie—" Willie said, his lips moving, as he stared after the car.

"What about her?"

Willie visibly jumped and he looked at Brig as if he expected to be beaten. Swallowing hard, eyes darting away from Brig's intense stare, Willie trembled. "She . . . she gone."

"Yeah, with those two creeps. I know."

Willie's eyes quit moving so frantically. "You don't like Bobby?"

"Don't really know him. Don't want to."

"He's bad."

"Is he?" Brig wasn't really interested, but he kept the conversation going just because he thought Willie wanted to talk and that in and of itself was a breakthrough. Willie didn't speak much and usually avoided Brig.

Willie stared after the car. "Trouble."

"That's what you said about me when I first came."

Nodding, Willie watched the car roll out of sight. He didn't move until the dust kicked up by the Corvette's wide tires had settled back on the lane. "You're trouble, too," he said and sniffed. "But different." He glanced at Brig, seemed suddenly embarrassed, then found the riding mower. "Got to work."

"Yeah, you and me both."

Cassidy was bored. Her best friend, Elizabeth Tucker, was still away at camp, and she'd already spent more time than she wanted to in town with her mother. Dena, deciding that Cassidy needed to get away from the house and stable, had taken her into Portland, where they'd driven all over the city, poking around antique stores in Sellwood, nosing through shops downtown, and dropping into one store after another. They ate lunch in the dining room of the Hotel Danvers, then joined rush hour traffic for the drive home.

Now, hours later, Cassidy had the start of a headache. She felt sticky and tired and wished she could climb onto Remmington's broad back, take off over the fields and ride the trails of the foothills to Bottleneck Canyon, where a pool formed in the Clackamas River and she could strip off her clothes and dive into the clear cool depths.

She could ride another horse, she supposed, but it wouldn't be the same. The sun was setting over the western hills, long shadows stretching over the valley floor. Near the stable, half-grown foals scampered in a herd of mares, who busied themselves by switching flies away with their tails.

Most everyone had gone for the day; it was Friday and her mother and father had driven back to Portland for dinner and a play, Derrick was with Felicity and most of the hands had gone home. Except for Brig. He was still in a single paddock, astride Remmington, trying to get the stubborn colt to obey him. And Willie was probably lurking around somewhere, though she hadn't seen him all afternoon.

Cassidy walked up to the fence and climbed onto the top rail. Brig glanced up at the sight of her, nodded a quick greeting, then ignored the fact that she was staring at him.

He clucked his tongue and the horse responded, trotting forward for a second before he stopped dead in his tracks, legs stiff.

"Move it, you miserable piece of horseflesh."

Muscles quivered beneath Remmington's dusty sorrel coat. The colt's ears flicked and his eyes rolled.

"Don't even think about it," Brig warned.

Too late. Remmington grabbed the bit between his teeth, bowed his long neck and kicked up his heels. Dust flew. Birds scattered. Cassidy's stomach clenched. The horse snorted angrily as he bucked across the dry ground. Brig, swearing, muscles straining, held on.

Cassidy watched in fascination.

Remmington whirled and raced from one end of the paddock to the other. Brig held on tightly to the reins. Near the fence, under a lone cedar tree, the colt reared, tossing his giant head, and Brig's thighs clamped tight. The colt bucked forward again. Brig ducked.

Cassidy's fingers curled over the top rail as man and beast pitted will against will.

With a whistle of protest, Remmington bolted forward, stopped, then shot straight into the air. Brig hung on like a burr. Again the colt ran the length of the fence line, a lather worked into his gorgeous coat, sweat staining the back of Brig's shirt and running down his face. "Go ahead, try and throw me, you miserable son of a bitch," Brig growled and the horse threw back his head and stood stock-still.

Cassidy held her breath. The dust settled. Flies droned again. She didn't know whether to laugh or cry. Brig seemed to have won and that was good—she'd be able to ride her horse again soon. But would he be the same fiery colt she adored or just another mindless piece of horseflesh with a broken spirit? That thought settled like lead in the pit of her stomach.

"That's better," Brig said, relaxing and patting Remmington's red neck.

"Is it?"

"Hey, don't say anything, okay? We're working here."

Anger coursing through her blood, Cassidy jumped into the paddock. "I don't want him to act like some wimpy—"

"Get out of here," Brig ordered in an even tone meant to keep the horse calm. "What're you trying to do, get me fired?"

"From what I hear, you do a pretty good job of that yourself!"

"For the love of Jesus, leave, Cassidy. I've got a job to do and it's not safe while I'm working with him. Who knows what he'll do!"

She kept striding to the horse. "You can't order me around!" Noticing the lackluster look in Remmington's usually flashing eyes, she felt a horrible sense of disappointment. "Get off him!"

"Not yet, Cass—" He twisted in the saddle to see her more clearly. His mouth turned down at the corners.

"He's my horse and I said—"

A flash of red hide swirled before her. Remmington, sensing his enemy had been distracted, reared high into the air, forelegs pawing, his whole body shuddering, and Brig, still twisted in the saddle, tried to keep his balance, but it was too late. The colt landed on his front feet, kicked up his rear legs, and Brig went flying, soaring through the air to land with a sickening thud on the cracked earth near a pile of manure. "Son of a bitch!"

So he wasn't hurt. "Are you okay? I didn't mean—"

"Get out of here!" Brig roared at Cassidy, but she was swallowing a smile.

"Guess you're not finished with him yet, are you?"

Springing to his feet, Brig dusted his jeans and glared at the colt. "Leave us to our business, Cass."

"Give it up, McKenzie."

"Never." The fire in his blue eyes was as bright as the flame in Remmington's.

With a victorious squeal, Remmington spun and started running along the fence line, heading straight for her.

"Cassidy! Get out of the way!" Brig lunged forward. "Oh, shit—"

She jumped onto the fence as the horse barreled past, his

body brushing against her so hard that she lost her grip and fell back to the ground. Pain fired through her shoulder.

"For the love of Christ!"

She started to get back onto her feet, but Brig was at her side, and before she could say anything, he'd swung her into his arms and walked her to the gate, which he shoved open with a knee. Anger lined his dusty face, sweat dampened his hair, grime and dirt streaked his arms, and the cords in his neck bulged with fury.

Kicking the gate closed, he plopped her onto the ground. "Don't you ever—"

"You can't lecture me!" she said, cutting him off and wincing as she moved her arm. "This is my property and you're working with my horse."

"And you could have got yourself killed, trampled, knocked unconscious or all three."

"No way, I—"

"Bullshit!" His nostrils flared and he sniffed loudly. "Worse yet, you could have done the same to me." Pointing a stiff, determined finger at her breastbone, he added, "You stay away from me when I'm working with that damned colt!"

"Don't you ever tell me what to do."

Eyes locked and Cassidy could barely breathe. He reached upward, grabbed the chain around her neck and the St. Christopher's medal that was hidden in her shirt. Yanking slightly, he slid his fingers down the links so that the flat metal piece slipped into his palm, then he held it tight, pulling her face to within inches of his so that she could smell his angry smoke-laced breath and see the pores of his skin. For the first time she noticed that his intense blue eyes were flecked with tiny streaks of gray. "I've got a job to do, Princess," he growled, "and you can play high-and-mighty all you want, but if you get in my way, you could get hurt."

Her heart was thudding so loudly she was certain he and the rest of the county could hear it. "I'll take my chances."

"Wouldn't be smart." His lips barely moved.

She inched her chin up a notch. "I'm old enough to make my own decisions."

"You're playing with fire, Cass."

"Meaning?"

"Just stay away from me."

"Why?"

"I need to concentrate. I can't do it when I have to worry about some candy-assed little girl getting in my way."

"I'm not—"

"Leave." He dropped the chain suddenly and she nearly fell over, then he stalked toward the horse. His muscles were bunched and he looked as if he could strangle the colt. "Okay, you ornery bastard," he growled. "Let's try it again."

Five

Cassidy made a point of staying away from Brig for the next few days, but she couldn't help seeing him driving the tractor, or shoring up the fence, or cutting the herd, or working with Remmington. From the corner of her eye she watched as he talked, laughed and smoked with several of the other ranch hands, and she noticed that he didn't bother telling Angie to leave whenever she happened to run into him. Time and time again they were together, she smiling up at him, he being patient with her.

Cassidy couldn't imagine what they had to talk about. But with Angie, there didn't have to be any conversation. Men and boys alike vied for the honor of just standing close to her.

Nearly a week passed until Cassidy was alone again with time on her hands. She felt restless and bored and wondered why this summer was different from any other. Last year she'd still found a little fascination with the things she always had but this summer, with the weather so blasted hot . . . She glanced over to the paddock where Brig was working with Remmington. The colt seemed less prickly. Maybe Brig was making progress. Some men broke horses fast, in a matter of days, but Brig took his time working with an animal and, she supposed, she should be grateful for that. Still, she felt as if the whole family treated her like a little girl who couldn't do anything for herself—including ride her own horse.

She climbed over the fence and hiked down to the creek

where, as a girl, she'd caught crawdads and periwinkles and watched water skippers skim the ripples. She and Angie and Derrick had played down there years before, splashing each other and throwing mud, wading in the shallows. Derrick had been fun-loving then, laughing and pulling Cassidy's hair or trying to spatter his younger sisters with the muck he'd raked from the bottom of the creek. She and Angie had caught him smoking his first cigarette down there once, coughing up a storm, and another time she'd spied him with some dark-haired girl, kissing and rolling around in the shadows, sweating and panting. Cassidy had ducked away quickly, slipping back through the leafy curtain of willow branches before she recognized the girl who so willingly let him strip her of a scanty little training bra.

That's about the time things changed, when Derrick started being interested in girls. He started looking at her differently and didn't play their old games. He'd always had a streak of the devil, but he seemed to get meaner about the time his beard began to come in and his voice railed between low notes and screeches. He was frustrated and angry. Once he'd whipped a horse until it bled and shot a neighbor's cat for sport. In both instances, Rex had rebuked his son then marched him to the barn, where he'd forced the boy to lean over a sawhorse and used Derrick's whip on his butt. Derrick had screamed and yelled, swearing as he'd been struck, then marched back to the house red-faced and sweating, his eyes filled with hot tears of humiliation, the hard twist of his mouth set in angry defiance.

Rex had then driven him into town, made him talk to the priest, but no matter how many "Hail Marys" and "Our Fathers" Derrick was forced to utter, he just got meaner. Cassidy was sure he could have said the rosary over and over again, wearing the stones smooth, and still he wouldn't have bowed his head to his father's will.

No, something inside of Derrick had changed, but she didn't know what.

Now, she kicked off her boots and dug her toes into the mud near the water's edge. The stream was low, not much more than a trickle that gurgled and spit over time-worn stones.

Wrapping her arms over her knees, she felt restless again— the same unnerving energy that kept her up at night.

Plucking a piece of grass from the bank, she gasped as a shadow passed over her shoulders and spread on the ground before her.

"What're you doin' down here?"

Brig. She'd know his voice anywhere. Her heart slammed into her throat.

"Nothing." Turning, she tried not to notice that his shirt was open, the sleeves rolled up, his nearly threadbare jeans hanging so low over his slim hips that his navel and the dark hair around it were visible. A heady warmth invaded her blood as she tossed her hair over her shoulders and wished her feet weren't black with wet soil. "I was just wondering when I could ride my horse again."

"You sound like a broken record."

"Well?"

"Soon as he's docile as a puppy."

"If I'd wanted a dog," she said smartly, "I would've gone to the pound." Standing, she wiped her feet on the grass and tried to hide the fact that she was embarrassed. "I think you should stop working with Remmington. I like him the way he is."

"Ornery."

"Yeah, ornery."

He made a sound of disgust in the back of his throat.

"I already told you I like a colt with some fire, who has his own mind."

"Who throws you off and knocks you senseless?" he asked, fiddling with his pocketknife. He seemed taller standing in his cowboy boots when she was barefooted. The sunlight shifted through leaves that stirred with a breath of wind, causing shadows to move over his chiseled features. He snapped his knife shut.

"Seems to me he threw *you* off."

A twisted smile caressed his lips. He stuffed the jack

knife into his pocket. "Can't argue with that, but I hope you're not spreadin' it around. Wouldn't want the rest of the hands to get wind of it."

"It's our secret," she said with a smile.

"Is it?"

"Cross my heart and hope to die—" She made the childish gesture over her breastbone, then stopped when she noticed his gaze follow the movement. "Well, you know what I mean."

Lower lip thrust out, he nodded, the most agreeable she'd ever seen him.

"But I still think I should be able to ride him."

"You will," Brig promised. "Soon."

"I can control him."

"Then how do you explain this?" He touched her bruised shoulder, and she nearly jumped out of her skin.

Somewhere in the back of her mind she realized that being alone with him was flirting with a danger she really didn't understand. There was always something different in the air whenever she was around him—like the sharp electrical charge just before a thunderstorm hit.

She lifted the shoulder in question. "I made a mistake the last time I rode him."

"One your daddy doesn't want repeated."

"Maybe he doesn't know what's best for me."

"And you do?" A dark eyebrow shot skyward, and she realized he was laughing at her attempt at bravado.

"Why do you treat me like I'm a child?"

" 'Cause you are."

"You're not that much older."

"It's not the years, darlin'."

"Then what?" she asked, inching up her chin defiantly. "Your *experience?*"

A half-smile caressed his lips. "That's part of it."

Her heart was drumming wildly, and she noticed the dark hair on the back of his arms, the stubble on his chin, his attitude of insolence that she found both frightening and fascinating.

He reached forward, and she thought he might kiss her

for a timeless instant, but he touched the chain around her neck as he had before. The medal, dangling between her breasts, seemed to sear her skin. "You always wear this."

She nodded.

"Why?"

"I—I don't know."

"Some kind of commitment to your church? Or did some boy give it to you?"

"No boy gave it to me."

He dropped the chain, glanced away for a second, then sighed. "I followed you down here to apologize," he admitted. "I came on a little strong the other day."

"It's okay—"

"Nope. Let me do this. You, uh, caught me with my pants down, so to speak. I lost my concentration, the horse sensed it, and he threw me."

"But I distracted you." The air seemed heavy and she backed up a couple of steps, her buttocks making contact with the rough bark of the willow.

"I shouldn't have let you."

"Oh."

He glanced to the hollow of her throat, where her heart was thrumming wildly. In the span of a few seconds, only the soft gurgle of the stream broke the stillness. She sensed that he wanted to kiss her, that the reason his hands were curled into fists was that he was fighting a losing battle with himself. "I should go—"

"No!" she said quickly, then felt her cheeks burn. "I— uh—"

A muscle ticked in his jaw, counting off the heartbeats. His gaze collided with hers, and though no words were spoken, Cassidy knew that he felt it, too, that hot, anxious wanting that seemed to pulse in the air between them. She licked her lips. He let out a soft groan and when he spoke, his voice was dry and rough. "It would be better, for both of us, if you stayed away from me and the horse."

"I like being around you," she admitted and he squeezed his eyes shut, as if he could close off her image.

"Well, don't, Cass. Don't like me." When he opened his eyes again, he seemed to be in some sort of control and the veins didn't stand out so much in his arms and neck. "Believe me, girl, we'll all be a lot better off if you just stay the hell away."

"So what's it like working for the richest man in the county?" Chase pulled a bottle of beer from the refrigerator and offered one to Brig. Sawdust dusted Chase's hair and the shoulders of his work shirt.

"You tell me," Brig said, frustrated in the hot trailer. His mother's little fan was whirring loudly, in a vain attempt to keep the sweltering temperature below ninety. He swiped a hand over his sweaty forehead, then stripped out of his shirt, but the heat just stayed with him, like memories of the Buchanan girls, thoughts that played havoc with his mind. "You work for him, too."

"Along with half the town." Chase set the two bottles on the cluttered table, opened them both, then drained half of his. "But you, you have the privilege of seeing how they live, what they do . . ."

"I shovel shit." Brig took a long swallow. "It ain't all that glamorous."

"No? It has to beat standing on the green chain, pulling lumber until your gloves wear through and your hands bleed." Chase tossed a shock of black hair off his forehead, and his blue eyes, so like Brig's own, bored into him. No one would ever mistake them for strangers, they looked too much alike—the same size and build, dark hair and dusky blue eyes. The only difference was that Chase's features were a little more refined than Brig's. Brig had always accused his older brother of being prettier—and that usually set Chase off, starting a wrestling match which, until four years ago, Chase always won handily. Lately the tables had turned, and consequently they didn't take out their frustrations on each other—at least not physically.

"Okay," Chase said as he straddled a chair. "Tell me about

the house and the cars and the daughters." Chase's lips curved into a half-smile. "You like the women, don't you, Brig?"

"The girls are spoiled brats."

"You're not interested?" Chase asked, leaning both elbows on the table.

"No."

"Bullshit." He took another long swallow, his gaze holding his younger brother's. "I've been up there, to the house, when the old man asked me to sign papers for that loan. I got a good look at what he's got, and I swore to myself right then and there that I was in heaven. I'd find a way to have it all one day, the mansion facing the hills, another house in Portland, maybe even a beach cabin. I'll buy an airplane and invest in timber and the rock quarry and the sawmill. All I have to do is pay my dues, go to school and learn to kiss the right asses. Eventually, I'll be where old Rex is and I'll be the one passing out interest-free loans and being the richest damn bastard in the county. No more crawling on my knees."

It was a touchy subject. Chase hadn't wanted to borrow money to finish college, but hadn't had much of a choice. Rex Buchanan, in another benevolent gesture to the McKenzie clan had offered the loan.

"Yep, the old man knows how to live, and those daughters of his aren't hard to look at, are they?"

Brig wanted to say he hadn't noticed, but Chase would have accused him of the obvious lie.

"You know, it wouldn't be a bad plan to marry one of 'em and inherit a piece of the Buchanan estate."

"I thought you said to stay away from 'em. That Cassidy's jail-bait."

"She is, but she won't be forever. And Angie. Jeez, a man can get hard just thinking about her. I think she's old enough to know what she wants."

Brig didn't like the turn of his brother's thoughts. "What about Derrick?" Brig asked, not that he really cared. He never really gave Rex's son a second thought. "He's one mean son of a bitch and I don't think he'd take too kindly to you hornin' in on the family business."

"What about him? Just because he was born with a silver spoon rammed between his dentist-perfect teeth doesn't mean that the old man will give him everything. Besides, I'm smarter than he is."

"But his name is Buchanan."

Chase didn't subscribe to Brig's way of thinking. "The girls will get their due. Old Rex, he always tries to play fair—even if it's only to look good. So he'll take care of his daughters and his sons-in-law."

"You've got it all worked out." Brig didn't bother hiding his irritation.

"Damned right." With a grin, Chase took a long swig from his bottle, then pointed an accusing finger at his brother. "The trick is to treat those girls with respect. Hell, that's the only way to get anything in this world."

"By kissing ass, as you said."

Chase's jaw hardened. "I'm a realist, Brig. I'll do what I have to. You should take a lesson. Be careful."

"Not interested," he repeated, but his mind wandered to Cassidy—yep, a man could respect her. Angie was something else. "I'm not climbing onto this imaginary gravy train. It's all yours if you want it. But, believe me, you're setting yourself up for a fall. Derrick Buchanan isn't going to let you get one thin dime of what he thinks is his." Brig stared out the tiny window over the sink. "This is crazy talk anyway. We're both just working for the man."

"And we'd like to keep it that way, for a little while. So, I'm warning you, little brother. You're in heaven now working for the old man, but you'd better watch your step. You've really blown it in this town; you're nearly dead as far as work goes, and that little episode with Tamara Nichols was a nail in your coffin. You're lucky Rex Buchanan hired you, considering how he feels about his daughters."

Brig took a long pull on his beer and felt the cool liquid slide down his throat. Why Rex had hired him was a mystery, but then Rex Buchanan was into philanthropic causes, especially where the McKenzies were concerned. He'd come to their rescue a couple of times when Ma was in serious financial trouble. Rex's concern had generated more than a little gossip. Maybe old Rex did consider Brig a charity case. The thought grated on his nerves and he suddenly wanted a smoke.

"Why did Buchanan hire you anyway?" Chase asked, as if reading the questions running through his mind.

Brig propped the heel of his boot on the seat of the chair next to him. "Beats me," he said, then matched his brother's know-it-all smile with one of his own. "Must've been my charming personality."

"Yeah, right." Chase didn't bother hiding his sarcasm. "Just don't blow it. I've worked hard to start repaying Buchanan, and I don't want you to do anything that might make him think worse of me—or Mom."

"Don't worry," Brig said.

"Good." Chase leaned his head back and stared at the grimy ceiling. "It's sad to admit but I'd do anything to get a little closer to the Buchanan money."

"Would you?"

"Anything," Chase said, sighing as he grinned as if he were savoring a familiarly pleasant thought. Brig guessed he was dreaming again. "This is no way to live." Chase gestured around the old trailer house, hardly big enough for one person, and home to Sunny and her two grown boys.

Brig figured it was about time to move out, but Chase didn't have time or the money. Between a full-time job at the mill, and college, he barely had time to sleep. Living here was purely a matter of economics for Chase. As soon as he graduated from Portland State, he'd kiss his job at the mill good-bye and take off for the city—unless he found a shortcut to making big bucks here in Prosperity.

Prosperity. What a name for a town. A goddamned joke that's what it was, unless your name happened to be Buchanan, or Alonzo, or Baker, or Caldwell. Otherwise, the town could be named Poverty, or Kiss-Buchanan's-Ass, or some such drivel.

Brig told himself he stayed in the rust bucket of a trailer because, with Chase gone all the time, someone needed to stick around and watch the place. Their mother, with her claim of psychic powers, wasn't the most popular woman around. Several church groups were becoming vocal against her, claiming that she was communing with the devil or some such crap, and Reverend Spears had dropped by on more than one occasion suggesting that Sunny give up her heathen ways and start attending Christian services regularly on Sunday mornings.

The man was slick as snake oil and, Brig suspected, a hypocrite to boot. There were several preachers in Prosperity, and Spears was the most self-serving bastard of the lot.

Chase scooted his chair back and reached into the refrigerator for another beer. "So tell me about the girls—and not just that they're rich and spoiled. I know that much. Start with Angie."

Brig lifted a shoulder. He wasn't stupid. Obviously Angie was playing with him, teasing him, showing him just a little of what she had to offer just to get a reaction from him; well, he wasn't going to bite.

"Come on, I spend all day staring at Floyd Jones, John Anderson and Howard Springer's ugly mugs. I'd love to have a glimpse of Angie Buchanan instead. Of course, I'm afraid I'd get hard just lookin' at her."

"Why?" Brig asked, as if his cock hadn't sprung to attention at the sight of her lying in barely nothing and drizzled in suntan oil. " 'Cause she's good-lookin' or because she's rich?"

Chase leaned back in his chair. "Both. They're both turn-ons. *Big,* no, make that *massive* turn-ons."

"Well, you'll have to stand in line. She's already got a couple of guys who can't stay away, their tongues hangin' out so far they nearly lick the ground and their dicks so hard they can't breathe."

"Is one of those guys you?"

"No way."

Chase's eyes narrowed. He'd always been able to see past Brig's lies. "You're saying you don't want a piece of Angie Buchanan?"

"I'm saying she's too much trouble."

Chase thought for a second, then took a long swallow and rolled the brown bottle between his palms. "Just once I'd like to see what it's like to be with her . . . well, if not her, then that little sister of hers. When she grows up, she'll be—"

Brig's boots dropped down to the floor, and he felt his blood pound at his temples. He shot across the table in a second, his face just a fraction of an inch from his brother's. "Don't even think about it," he warned. "She's just a kid."

Chase's grin stretched wide and his eyes sparked. "Don't tell me you've got a thing for the tomboy." He chuckled. "Well, I'll be damned. You'd better be careful. Like I told you before, she's jailbait."

Brig grabbed the front of his brother's shirt. His elbow hit Chase's beer bottle and it fell to the floor, spraying foam. Brig ignored it. "That's why she's off-limits. Way off," he said.

"But you'd like to, wouldn't you? Christ, I can't believe it. She's cute enough, but she's hardly got any tits."

"Just leave her alone!"

"I told you, I like the older sister."

"Stay away from her, too." Brig unclenched his hands and straightened. He found a rag, wiped up the beer and dropped the bottle into a carton half-filled with empties. "I don't need any trouble with old man Buchanan or either of his daughters."

Six

Angie lay on the chaise barely noticing the heat. Absently she rubbed tanning oil on her arms and chest and legs, but her thoughts were far away. On Brig. She was running out of time. The Caldwells always threw a huge, end-of-the-summer barbecue at their home. Not only were The Judge's business associates from all over Clackamas County invited, but dignitaries from Portland, civic leaders and anyone worth their salt in Prosperity were on the guest list. It was, aside from Rex Buchanan's Christmas party, the event of the year.

Angie had been ducking offers from several boys including Bobby and Jed because she planned to go with Brig. Smiling, she thought of the tongues that would wag, the eyebrows that would rise, the shocked gasps that would be swiftly covered with hands when she showed up with her arm linked through Brig McKenzie's.

A lot of the women, whether they admitted it or not, would be jealous; others would be stunned. She would certainly be the center of attention, and everyone would assume that she'd been seeing Brig for weeks . . . just long enough. But she couldn't waste any more time.

She wiped off the excess tanning oil with a towel, then slid on a pair of shorts. Slipping her arms through a gauzy white blouse, she didn't bother with buttons, letting the front gape open, then rolled up her sleeves.

As she walked into a pair of flip-flops, she unsnapped the band holding her hair away from her face and gave the thick waves a toss so that ebony curls framed her eyes and cheeks and cascaded in tumbled disarray down the middle of her back.

She'd run out of excuses to hang out at the stable, and short of asking Brig for riding lessons, she didn't have a reason to loiter without looking too obvious. She couldn't appear desperate . . . just mildly interested.

She could ask him to take her into town, or fix the rattle in her car, or go riding with her . . .

Never in her life had she had so much trouble getting a man to notice her; usually she had the opposite problem, but Brig was different from any man she'd met in Prosperity. Or Portland, for that matter. Though she'd spent all four of her high school years boarding at St. Therese's, an all-girls Catholic school, she'd had ample opportunity to meet boys from Jesuit and Central Catholic as well as the male students who attended Portland State University, which was located a few blocks away from the hallowed brick halls of the all-girls school.

At the door of the stable she paused, dabbed at her lipstick and walked inside. Her nostrils curled at the harsh odors of urine and manure. And there was something else within the hot shadowy interior. Something out of place. Something that caused the hairs on the back of her neck to lift one by one.

"Brig?" she called out in the interior gloom. "Brig? You in here?" Sweat collected on her spine and she felt suddenly nervous. Edgy.

She strained to listen, but all she heard was quiet nickers and snorts and the rustle of hooves in straw. From the corner of her eye, she saw a movement. Her heart jumped. She stumbled back, nearly falling as she turned to find Willie standing near an open barrel of oats. He was holding a bridle and staring at her with unreadable blue eyes. "Jesus, Willie, you scared the hell out of me!"

He licked his lips nervously. "Sorry."

"You know where Brig is?" Angrily she dusted her hands.

His eyebrows drew together in concentration, and Angie wanted to shake him. Half the time he was dumb as a stone, stammering and avoiding answering questions and looking all embarrassed. Other times he seemed sharp as a tack, smarter than a lot of the ranch hands, and Angie wondered just how stupid he really was. It was almost as if he used his handicap to his advantage. But he couldn't, could he?

"Mac's out with the cows."

"I'm not interested in Mac. I asked about Brig."

Willie worried his lip and looked away. His hair was a deep shade of brown, but it was dull and unkempt and curled randomly. His eyes were an unsettling hue somewhere between gray and blue. "Brig's working."

"I know that."

"He don't like to be bothered."

"It's all right, Willie." Angie sighed inwardly and took a step closer to the half-wit. "I need to see him," she said in a soft, cajoling voice.

"Why?"

Damn, the big moron was irritating, but there was no reason she couldn't have a little fun with him. She placed her hands on her hips, outlining her small waist and thrusting out her chest. She saw the flicker of interest in Willie's eyes, how he glanced at her cleavage, then looked up at the rafters to avoid staring. She sauntered up to him. "Come on, Willie," she cooed. "I don't have all day. Now"—she touched his dirty shirt on the sleeve—"where's Brig?"

Willie's Adam's apple bobbed, and suddenly the stable seemed close and hot. He looked into her eyes, and she felt a little trill of fear and anticipation, for he didn't bother hiding his lust anymore and she wondered if this time she'd pushed him too far. He was, after all, a man, a young, physically strong and healthy man. From the darkness of beard shadow, the breadth of his shoulders and the curling hairs that sprang from beneath his work shirt, there was little doubt that he was a fully developed male.

"What do you want?" he said in a rasping whisper so low that Angie's heart began to knock. His eyes seemed suddenly unconfused and bright with challenge. She cleared her throat and stepped away from him, afraid of her own sexual power and his response—a response that would be purely animal and savage. Her mind clicked forward and she realized that Willie, poor, dumb Willie, just might be able to help her.

Thoughts like these were dangerous.

"I just need to talk to Brig."

"Then you find him." Willie, his breathing uneven, stepped away from her, his fingers curling over the bit of the bridle he'd been trying to fix. He walked quickly away, nearly stumbling on a rake, looking as if he was suddenly as scared as she was.

"Damn it," she muttered once he was gone. Sweat beaded across her brow and her hands shook. She'd have to be more careful in the future. Willie wasn't the silly innocent he seemed. She remembered the day by the pool, when Felicity had taken off her T-shirt and flashed Willie a glimpse of her breasts. The half-brain had gotten a good look. He'd probably hidden in the woods, closed his eyes and brought up the memory of Felicity's white skin and huge boobs and jacked himself off. Or had he been thinking of her?

Unable to shake the feeling that she'd inadvertently stepped over the threshold of a dangerous door that might never close again, she spent fifteen minutes searching the barns with renewed determination. She'd just about given up; Brig could be anywhere on the ranch, checking fence line or herding cattle acres away, clearing brush on the north side or with one of the hands in town picking up supplies.

Frustrated, Angie held her hair off her shoulders, hoping the breeze on her neck would cool her off. When she walked past the machine shed, she found Brig outside, twirling a tire in a trough of water, obviously searching for a leak in the thick black rubber. The trough was really an old oil barrel, cut in half and mounted on iron legs, the edges smoothed by a blowtorch, a pipe running from below to the drainage ditch, a hose hooked to an exterior faucet. Brig's sleeves were rolled to his elbows, his shirt open, his brows slammed together in concentration.

If he heard her approach, he didn't acknowledge it and only lifted his head when her shadow fell across the trough.

Air hissed from the tire and he marked the black rubber with chalk.

"I thought you were supposed to be working with the horses," she said, leaning her back against the brick wall of the shed. Heat from the sun had settled in the red bricks and then radiated outward to warm her skin.

"Didn't know you kept tabs on me."

Lifting a dismissive shoulder, she said, "I don't."

"Good." He turned back to his work and snagged a dirty rag from his back pocket. "Then you weren't looking for me."

"Not really."

He straightened and his cocky smile called her a liar. "Funny. I thought you were lookin' for somebody the way you were wanderin' through the barns and sheds. Thought it might be me."

"Don't flatter yourself."

He let out a deep chuckle that rankled her. "I never do." Swinging the tire over his shoulder, he headed into the interior of the machine shed and Angie, though she would have loved to toss her head and walk proudly away, followed him inside.

"Why do you hate me?" she asked, once they were alone in the building. She managed a petulant look as sunlight streamed through the doorway and a few small windows, but the hot interior was shaded and private. The smells of oil and grease lingered in the air.

Brig hauled the tire onto a workbench and was reaching for some kind of patch.

"Hate you?" he repeated, glancing over his shoulder. "Now what gave you that idea?"

"You avoid me."

"I have work to do."

"You talk to Cassidy."

"She's interested in the horses," he said quickly, but his jaw seemed to tighten a bit.

"Maybe she's interested in you."

"She's just a kid."

"Sixteen."

"As I said, a kid."

"Is that what you think of me?"

He let out a little laugh, and his gaze skated up the length of her, taking in her full hips, the feminine curve of her waist and the swell of her breasts straining beneath her open blouse as they pressed against the black top of her swimsuit. Sweat seemed to collect in that dusky hollow where Brig's cynical gaze lingered for an instant.

"No one would mistake you for a kid, Angie." He threw out a hip and reached in the pocket of his shirt for his pack of Camels. "Just what is it you want from me?" he asked, clicking his lighter and drawing a deep lungful of smoke.

She plucked the cigarette from his fingers and took a long drag herself, leaving a lipstick print on the white paper and letting smoke drift from her nostrils, the way she'd seen Bette Davis do in some old movie. "Why do you think I want something?" She tossed her hair and handed him the cigarette.

"It's in your nature."

"You don't know anything about me." She let her lower lip protrude just a fraction.

"I know enough."

Oh, God, he was shutting her down! No boy had ever shut her down. Most of them were panting after her and she, a tease and flirt by nature, loved the sick kind of desire that smoldered in their eyes. But Brig was different, and beneath her need to have him want her, anger sparkled through her blood. He, the son of a runaway sawmill worker and some crazy woman, had the nerve to act as if he didn't feel lust crawling through his blood. Well, she knew better. "Wouldn't you like to get to know me just a little better?" she asked, stepping close enough so that when he looked down at her, he had to see her cleavage.

With the cigarette burning from the corner of his mouth, he seemed almost unapproachable, like some hard-assed range cowboy. He squinted through the smoke, but he didn't back away.

"I've got a job to do. If you'll excuse me."

This wasn't working. He wasn't going to fall for blatant seduction, so she backed off quickly and turned around. "Look . . . I'm sorry," she said. "I didn't mean to . . . well, to look like I was coming on to you."

"Weren't you?"

When she turned around again, she'd changed her expression. "I . . . I want to be your friend. The boys my age bore me, and frankly, they're a pain in the backside." She looked up at him, and her eyes were no longer at half-mast. "I guess I thought acting like . . . well, like that was the way to get your attention. I, um, need someone like you."

He snorted and turned his eyes back to the tire.

"Jed and Bobby are giving me a hard time."

"They are?"

"I told you about the bet."

A look of contempt crossed Brig's handsome features. "I thought you were kidding."

"No," she sighed and ran her fingers through her hair. "I know that sometimes people think I'm . . . well, a flirt, and I suppose I am, but I don't sleep with boys, and because I'm who I am, you know, Rex Buchanan's daughter, I'm kind of a target, I guess. I've heard that the locker-room talk is who's going to do Angie Buchanan first. That's why my dad sent me to St. Therese's in Portland. At least one of the reasons. But now that I'm finished with high school and going on to college, the big talk in town is the same old disgusting question."

Brig's face remained impassive, almost as if he suspected she was lying.

"So anyway, I thought maybe I could become your friend, and because you're . . . well, a little bit . . . tougher, I guess is the right word . . . the other guys would back off."

He tossed his cigarette onto the floor and ground it out with his boot. "You know, Angie, not many women want me for their friend. Men and women . . . as friends . . . somehow it doesn't work out."

"Can't we rise above it?" she asked and impulsively stood on her tiptoes, brushing the side of his cheek with her lips. Without even seeing his reaction, she ran through the shed's open door and noticed a shadow move quickly around the side of the old brick building. Angie felt a coldness seep into her blood. Probably Willie again. God, that idiot was giving her the creeps. She shivered. She couldn't imagine why her father didn't just get rid of him.

But then her father was always partial to hard-luck stories, Brig McKenzie being a case in point.

I watched from the shadows.

Standing behind the Buchanan house, hidden by the thick cover of leafy shrubs and trees while twilight settled onto the huge home, I stared up at the windows, bright patches against a hot, dense night.

She was in the house, or so it appeared as her bedroom light was on . . . yes, I knew where all the rooms were and I glanced from the master bedroom with its bank of windows to the smaller dormers of the rooms that housed the members of their small, blended family.

Derrick's room was the farthest down the hall, and through the open blinds, I noticed posters of football players and long-legged, big-breasted models or porno stars, leaning over with their come-hither eyes and wet lips. A tight ball of disgust tightened in my gut as my gaze traveled to Cassidy's room, which was now dark, probably empty. I glanced around quickly because Cassidy was known to leave the house and hang out at the stable. My eyes searched the darkness, but I saw nothing. No movement. No sound of her quiet whistling under her breath. No sign of her.

Good.

My tense muscles relaxed a little until I looked up again and centered my attention on Angie's room. And there she was suddenly, seated on the window ledge and staring up at the sky, maybe watching the rising moon.

She was silhouetted by the light from her desk, a black, curvy shadow against a golden lamp. Her gaze lowered and she searched the darkness. As if sensing I was near.

My muscles tightened, and for a second I thought our gazes locked, mine desperate and determined from my hiding spot in the dense foliage, hers wide and wondering, a little suspicious as she eyed the shadows. I didn't breathe.

Go ahead and look, you bitch. Try and see me. Try to figure out what's going to happen.

Finally, she looked away. Closed the window. Pulled down the shade as if to keep my gaze from wandering where it shouldn't.

Which was stupid.

I took a chance.

Reached into my pocket and found my lighter. Then I held it to my nose and flicked it on, peering through the tiny flame, centering it on her window and the dusky silhouette beyond the shade.

Feel this, Angie?

Imagine it touching your skin, catching in your hair.

I smiled in the darkness, the flickering flame shifting before my eyes as I thought of her and what would happen to that beautiful, taut body.

Soon, it would be reduced to ashes.

Angie shivered and rubbed her arms despite the heat of the night. She glanced at the window, closed tight, shade drawn, and told herself she was being a ninny. A fool.

No one was watching her out there in the trees surrounding the lawn. *No one* was plotting to harm her. The worst thing that could have happened was that retard Willie was skulking about again.

She felt a twinge of regret at her unkind thoughts about him. It wasn't his fault that he was a few cards shy of a full deck. And hadn't she seen the way he'd looked at her the other day when she'd touched his sleeve? She'd had a glimmer that he wasn't as stupid as he let on, that he knew far more about what was going on at the Buchanan estate than anyone else, and that his dumb, poor town idiot routine might well be an act.

He was, after all, a man.

So she should be careful around him.

As should Cassidy and Felicity and even that witch Dena. Who knew what thoughts traveled through Willie's weak brain. She grinned at the thought of Willie and Dena, then shoved the ridiculous image aside.

She had more to worry about than creating her own personal boogeyman in the woods. Lots more. She had to concentrate.

Flopping onto her bed, she grabbed a heart-shaped pillow and held it tight to her breast. Tears threatened her eyes and she bit her lower lip. This was *not* the time to break down. She sighed and began putting the final touches on her plan and tamped down the rising sense of dread, the panic that was lately consuming her. Glancing at the calendar posted above her desk, she cringed.

She was running out of time.

Seven

— "I don't think it's right, that's all I'm saying, Rex." Dena looked at herself in the mirror over the sink in the master bedroom and frowned at the gray roots that were beginning to show starkly against her red hair. She had always been proud of her tresses, and now even they were beginning to turn on her, along with her face and neck, both of which showed far too many wrinkles and the bags under her eyes— well, it was small wonder she looked so strained, worried as she was about her daughters. How she'd be able to make herself radiant for the Caldwells' barbecue next weekend nagged at her. She needed a new dress, shoes and more than a little cosmetic surgery. She finished brushing her hair and picked up her pack of cigarettes. "Why you hired that riffraff is beyond me."

Rex stood behind the partially closed door to the walk-in closet. "Brig needed a job. He's damned good with the horses, and Cassidy's colt already threw her once. Didn't want to take another chance."

"But you don't mind taking a chance with that McKenzie boy. And with our girls." She saw him out of the corner of her eye, hanging up his robe. Standing in his boxer shorts, he was still an imposing man. Oh, he sagged a little around the middle, but his muscles still showed under his skin and his legs didn't have an ounce of fat thanks to hours spent on the golf course. His hair was snow white, in sharp contrast to his black eyebrows, and his face, tanned from his days on the links, was handsome, even chiseled, except for the line of his jaw where the beginnings of jowls had already made themselves evident. Aging was a bitch. She lit up and noticed the tiny lines surrounding her lips as she sucked on her cigarette.

"I'm not taking a chance on the girls. What're you talking about?" He threw on a pair of gray sweatpants and sweatshirt—the common locker-room garb instead of the burgundy velour jogging suit she'd bought him for their last anniversary. But she didn't have time to argue with him about that now; besides, no one would see him and she had other problems on her mind—big problems concerning Brig McKenzie. Sunny's wild boy.

Dena wouldn't have liked Rex hiring Chase, Sunny McKenzie's other son, but she could have understood it; Chase, from what the gossip mill churned out, was responsible, cared about his future, kept his nose clean and knew his station. At least he *tried* to do the right thing. He seemed a little more refined than his younger brother. But Brig—well, the common expression was that he was hell on wheels and had no respect for anything or anyone. He wore a leather jacket and rode a motorcycle, for God's sake, like some kind of hoodlum or Hell's Angel. She shuddered deep in the folds of her silk robe.

And Rex wasn't worried.

This was no time for delicacies. Sometimes the only way to get through to her bullheaded husband was to hit him over the head with a verbal baseball bat. "It was bad enough you hiring that half-wit. The way he drools over the girls—"

"Look, Dena, I'm a respected member in the community, one of the richest men in Prosperity, and as such I have responsibilities to do some things that might not be economically sound—goodwill gestures. Then there's the church. Father James seems to think that . . . oh, hell, you wouldn't understand. The bottom line is that no one else will hire him and Willie's a hard worker. Hasn't given me a lick of trouble." His jaw tightened stubbornly.

Rex was proud of his philanthropy, and when it came to Willie—the subject of firing him was and always would be taboo. Dena had learned that long ago when Rex had hired the moron. She'd had a fit then but her husband had been adamant. Several times since then, when tools or spare parts had been missing or stolen, she'd suggested Rex fire Willie, but the subject was always closed. Rex wasn't about to give in.

She drew on her cigarette, didn't like the looks of herself in the mirror and squashed the damned Viceroy out in the silver tray near the sink. She had to quit. The lines around her eyes from squinting through smoke were becoming too noticeable. "Brig McKenzie's got a reputation, you and I both know it. He drinks too much even though he's underage then gets into fights. He's been fired from God-only-knows how many jobs and beds any woman he can get his hands on."

"You don't know that. It's all small-town gossip."

"Where there's smoke, there's fire, Rex. Just remember his roots. He comes from trash."

"Sunny McKenzie—"

"Is trash and her husband, or ex-husband, wasn't much better. A drunk with a bad temper." She turned away from the sink and glared at her husband. "The more you do for that family, the more the rumors about you . . ." Her voice failed her, and she shuddered.

"Again, it's just gossip."

"That I hear over and over. At the country club, while playing bridge, when I get my hair done, even after mass. I'm telling you, Rex, you've got to stop bending over backward for Sunny and her boys!"

"I help other families as well. When husbands are out of work or little kids get sick—"

"—or nearly drown."

He stared at her hard "That was a long time ago," he warned. "Sunny needed help. Her husband walked out on her."

"I know and you know, but people still talk," she said, the ugly rumors always just under the surface of her consciousness. "It's bad enough you visit Lucretia's grave every week but—"

"Don't bring her into this," he commanded in the tone he reserved for her when he was particularly angry, a belittling tone.

She wouldn't push him about Lucretia, but she couldn't give up on the issue at hand. "Look, Rex, you and I both know that the only thing Brig McKenzie's got going for him is his good looks and the fact that he's shrewd as hell—he knows how to play people to get what he wants. Look how he played you."

"He didn't play me," Rex grumbled as he strode back to their bedroom.

She shot a look that silently called him a fool. "That boy knows exactly what he's doing, and mark my words, he's trouble, the likes of which we've never seen." She slid into her pink slippers and padded after him. He was already seated on his stationary bike, pedaling madly, sweat breaking out across his forehead. The armoire was open, displaying the television, where beautiful women in police uniforms were doing menial tasks. *Charlie's Angels,* one of Rex's favorite programs, was about to be aired. "I don't want Cassidy hanging around him. I think she's developing a crush on him."

"Cassidy? She's just a kid."

"Have you taken a good look at her lately, Rex?" Dena asked, a little wounded. In Rex's opinion Cassidy would never be anything more than his second daughter, second in line and second best. He never said as much, but it was obvious in the subtle little ways that Dena found so irritating and painful.

"She's not interested in boys."

"Not boys, just Brig. She can't stay away from him."

"That's because of her horse. It has nothing to do with McKenzie."

"Open your eyes, Rex. She's sixteen and . . . well, I remember how I was at that age."

"You can't stop her from hanging out at the stable."

Dena sighed. "No, but I can keep my eye on her and see that she stays away from that white trash. As for Angie, God knows I can't control her, she's *your* daughter, but if I were you, I'd forbid her to go anywhere near him."

"She doesn't."

Dena shook her head. "I've never thought of you as a fool, Rex, but maybe I was wrong." She settled onto the king-sized bed and plumped the pillows up against the headboard.

Dena usually didn't criticize Angie because Rex adored the girl and treated her as if she were royalty. He was more flagrantly devoted to Angie than he was to Cassidy; it was obvious to everyone in the house. Dena knew the reason why. Angie was Lucretia's daughter, and though his first wife had been dead for years, Rex still revered her—lit candles for her at mass, talked and acted as if she were some kind of saint.

The woman had taken her own life, for crying out loud, and everyone knew that suicide was a sin. But still Rex was faithful to Lucretia's memory and Dena was fairly certain, were she to die, Rex wouldn't go off lighting candles and saying prayers and worshipping her for nearly two decades.

"Angie's been at St. Therese's for four years, and the nuns have given her a good, strong moral education. Don't worry about her. Angie's a good girl." He was beginning to really sweat now, and the bicycle was whirring too loudly for him to hear the dialogue on the television. Before she could say a word, he clicked the remote and the television boomed a little louder through the bedroom.

"Is Derrick home yet?" Angie, wearing a swimsuit cover-up, her sandals dangling from her fingers, tiptoed through the door of Cassidy's room and plopped onto the corner of the bed.

Cassidy was leafing through a magazine. "Don't know."

"He's out with Felicity, isn't he?"

Cassidy lifted a shoulder. Ever since Angie had been on a campaign to win Brig's heart, Cassidy had found it difficult to be civil to her older sister. Not that Brig wasn't old enough to know better, and rumor had it that he'd known plenty of women. But none so pretty nor with such a high social station as Angie, Cassidy decided. Angie would be hard—make that nearly impossible—for any man to resist.

"Well, if he shows up here, will you cover for me?"

"Why?" Cassidy was instantly suspicious.

"He doesn't like me seeing Brig."

"Seeing Brig—as in dating?" Cassidy said, astounded. Sure, she'd known that Angie had been coming on to Brig, she'd even seen her older sister buzz a kiss across Brig's cheek, but she'd hardly call it *seeing* Brig.

"Well, not really *dating,* at least not yet. But soon. I'm gonna ask him to take me to the Caldwells' barbecue at the Country Club. Won't that tick a few people off?" She giggled and her eyes twinkled at that thought. "Anyway, I'm s'posed to meet him tonight down by the pool, and Mom and Dad, they'll be asleep as soon as the eleven o'clock news is over, so I shouldn't have to worry about them. The servants are all tucked away and you know what the deal is, so that only leaves Derrick."

"Have you already asked Brig to the barbecue?" Cassidy felt her stomach knot.

"No, not yet."

"But you think he'll go."

"Of course he'll go. It's one of the biggest events of the season, and the poor kids in town are all dying to be invited."

"It's hard to imagine that Brig would care."

Angie's eyebrows quirked. "What's this, Cass? A little jealousy?"

" 'Course not."

"Hmmm." Angie's full lips pulled into a knowing grin. "Well, he's got a brother, you know. Probably even more handsome than Brig. I know for a fact that Chase McKenzie would cut off his right arm for an invitation to the party."

"So why don't you ask him?"

"Because he's too hungry. Too anxious and eager. Kind of like Bobby and Jed. But Brig . . ." She stared through the open window and sighed loudly. "I guess I'm attracted to him because he's so cocky and self-assured. So strong. He does what he wants when he wants and doesn't give a damn about the circumstances." Her face clouded over and she bit into her lower lip. "In some ways we're a lot alike."

"You and Brig?" Cassidy snorted. "Give me a break."

Angie's touch of melancholy lasted only a second and was quickly replaced by a naughty smile that turned her sister's stomach.

Steaming inside, Cassidy aimed the remote control to the little television on her bureau. She needed noise—distraction— anything to keep her mind from running in the painfully familiar circles it took when she thought of Brig and Angie together.

"So run interference for me, will you? If Derrick—well, or anyone for that matter—starts asking questions, just turn on your desk lamp by the window and I'll get the message. Okay?"

"I don't know what good that will do."

"It's just a warning. Gives me time to head back to the house and come up with a logical story—you know, something about not being able to sleep and needing a midnight swim."

"Fine," Cassidy said without any inflection, though inside she was dying a thousand deaths.

Picking up her flip-flops, Angie slid off the bed and padded softly to the door. "Just remember the signal. That's all you have to do." She flashed Cassidy a brilliant smile. "I owe you one, Cass," she said, then opened the door so that it barely creaked. After checking the hallway, she disappeared and Cassidy was left with a feeling of incredible despair.

She flipped through the stations but didn't even see the images on the television screen. Instead, vivid pictures of Brig and Angie, their bodies wet from swimming naked in the pool, boiled through her mind.

She felt sick inside. Angie hadn't been kidding about Brig. She was going to seduce him. And Brig was eating it up!

Slamming her fist into her pillow, Cassidy stared out her open bedroom window to the dark sky, where stars winked in the dark heavens. A lazy half-moon hung low over the horizon. She rolled out of bed and gazed through the darkness. The breeze was warm though it was the coolest part of the day, and it whispered through her nightgown, pressing the soft cotton to her body.

She told herself it didn't matter, that what Brig did and with whom was none of her business, but she hadn't been able to stop herself from watching in horrified fascination as Angie set her plan into motion.

For the first time in her life Angie had taken an interest in the horses, and every time Brig was working with the stock, Angie found an excuse to hang around the stable and paddocks. She had learned to fold her arms over the top rail and talk to him, smile whenever he turned and faced her, as well as stand as close to him as possible without touching when a fence didn't separate them. She'd invited him swimming and riding, but he'd always declined, citing work, and secretly Cassidy had been triumphant. Maybe he wouldn't be tricked like all the other boys that seemed to swarm around the ranch like bothersome flies.

The closer it got to the end of the summer, the more the boys came, as if they knew Angie would be out of reach come the end of September when she went off to college.

Cassidy doubted that Brig McKenzie would be any different. Didn't he already have a reputation as a ladies' man, and didn't Angie always get what she wanted? She liked driving men to the point of distraction—Jed Baker and Bobby Alonzo were proof of her innate ability.

Glancing at the bed, Cassidy frowned. She couldn't sleep. It was too hot in her room, the bedsheets were cloying, her mind spinning with images of Brig and Angie. She had to do something, get out, away from the house.

Then she knew. It had been over three weeks since she'd been thrown from Remmington and her shoulder was nearly back to normal. Brig had no intention of ever letting her ride her horse again, so she'd just have to do it behind his back. Served him right, anyway. The way he looked at Angie!

And why should she stay and be lookout for her sister? Let her get caught for once. It was time their father, who worshipped the ground Angie walked on, knew the real story. If Rex caught her with Brig, maybe Angie wouldn't be such a goddess in his eyes. Not that it mattered. Cassidy would never have wanted the kind of attention her father lavished on Angie. She was content being who she was, doing what she did. She'd never once been jealous of Angie's position of princess—with the title came too much pressure. No, Cassidy was comfortable with her relationship with her father, though she wished her mother, who was always pushing her to be more like her older sister, would back off.

She threw on a pair of old jeans and a sweatshirt, snapped a rubber band around her wild, uncombed hair and, carrying an old pair of sneakers, slipped quietly from her room and down the back stairs. As Angie had predicted, no one was up.

Creeping softly through the back door, Cassidy cringed as the screen's hinges squeaked loudly, and Bones, her father's old border collie, lifted his head and gave one low, gruff bark.

"Shh. It's only me."

The dog wagged his tail, thumping it on the floorboards of the back porch. She thought of going directly to the stable, but paused in the shadows of a rhododendron.

She wondered if Angie was bluffing. Crossing her fingers, she crept around the corner of the house and silently along a flagstone path that weaved through the rose garden still fragrant with heavy blossoms. After ducking under the arbor and down a few terraced steps, she was near the pool.

The soft sound of a giggle rippled over the water, and as Cassidy's eyes adjusted to the darkness, she saw Angie swimming gracefully and completely naked. Her tanned body was white where her suit usually covered her, and her clothes had been left carelessly on the edge of the pool.

Cassidy's heart seemed to fall to the ground as Angie swam through the water, sleek and feminine, her nipples dark disks against the white skin of her breasts, a thatch of black hair visible at the apex of her legs. So feminine. So seductive.

Bile climbed up Cassidy's throat.

The scratch of a match being struck sizzled through the air, and she nearly jumped out of her skin.

The acrid scent of sparking phosphorous wafted on a slow-moving breeze, and she knew with sickening certainty that Brig hadn't been able to ignore Angie's attempts at seduction. He'd come and was here, watching her display.

She scanned the patio surrounding the pool and found him, standing near the diving board, the toes of his cowboy boots jutting over the water. The angles of his face were illuminated in gold as he bent down, cupped the end of his cigarette and lit up. Inhaling deeply, he waved out the match, and that tiny flame of light disappeared.

Angie broke the surface just beneath his feet. She tried to cover herself while treading water but it was impossible. Sexy glimpses of her rump and breasts escaped.

"I . . . I didn't expect you so early," she said, her voice a whisper.

He checked his watch but didn't say a word. Just smoked.

"Just give me a minute to get into my clothes." She swam to the side of the pool, hoisted herself out of the water, shook her hair and stepped quickly into her suit and cover-up, as if she were truly embarrassed.

Heart pounding, Cassidy watched as Angie walked back up to Brig and threw out a hip.

"What is it you want?" he asked.

Angie grinned up at him. "Lots of things." Bold enough to touch him on the forearm, she sighed.

He grabbed her quickly, holding her at arm's length as he glowered at her. "Maybe you'd better quit playing games. You said you wanted to meet me, that it was important."

"I need a date," she blurted out.

He snorted. "A date? You? You've got more dates than your old man has mill workers."

"I know, but this is special and I don't want to go with just anyone." Tossing her damp hair off her face, she stared up at him, her face nearly luminescent in the moonlight. "I want you to take me to the Caldwells' barbecue." She wound her arms around his neck and sighed. "It's a big deal and I can't stand the thought of going with one of the *boys*." She stood on her tiptoes, grabbed the cigarette from his lips and tossed it onto the wet cement surrounding the pool. The ashes sizzled before dying. Brushing her lips slowly over his, she said, "Come on, Brig. Wouldn't you love it? It would kind of be like crashing a party, and not just any party. This is a major social event."

"Except I'd be with you," he said warily.

Her smile flashed in the night. "Would that be so bad? You'd be the envy of every boy in town."

"Maybe I don't give a damn about that."

"And maybe you do," she whispered before kissing him again. This time he didn't resist. The arms that had held her at bay surrounded her, yanking her willing body close to his. He let out a low, deep growl that caused Cassidy's blood to tingle as he kissed Angie with an angry ferocity that was pure animal lust.

Cassidy had to bite back the little squeak of protest that rose in her throat as Angie wrapped a calf around his leg. Unable to watch another second, Cassidy turned too quickly. Her foot caught on a root and she stumbled, her injured shoulder slamming against a tree. Pain jolted up her arm, but she kept running, trying to ignore the dampness on her cheeks. Foolishly, she'd begun to cry.

Over Brig McKenzie.

Who thought of her as a pesky little kid.

Rage and impotence swept through her, and she knew what she had to do. Let Brig and Angie make out and do whatever they wanted; it didn't matter. But Cassidy was done waiting around and spying on her older sister. She raced through the shadows to the stable. Though her shoulder still ached a little, she was certain she could handle Remmington, and she was going to ride that colt so fast the images of Brig and Angie would be forced out of her mind.

From this minute on, she didn't care what they did. Yet as she opened the door to the stable, she wished that she was the woman in Brig's arms, that she was kissing him, that she was feeling the hard weight of his body pinning her to the ground. Because, unlike Angie, Cassidy, at sixteen, was certain she was in love with Brig McKenzie and she hated herself for it.

Eight

Felicity wiggled into her bra. It was no use trying to seduce Derrick when he was in one of his moods. He didn't seem to notice her anymore. Oh, sure, he'd drive her all the way to Portland on the pretext of taking her to a movie, then he'd pay for a room in this dump of a motel and he'd make love to her, but he wasn't really with her; not like he used to be. And he didn't even know the truth.

Black hair mussed, he was lying on the bed, and smoking a cigarette. A reporter was going on about the heat wave, how long it was going to last, how bad it was for the crops, how people shouldn't water their lawns.

Who cared?

Rolling off the bed, she walked to the window and peered through the blinds. Across the street a restaurant claiming to serve authentic Northern Chinese cuisine was bustling with activity. Under the streetlights, men and women flocked to the front doors, laughing and talking. Holding hands. Falling in love.

How long had it been since Derrick held her hand? Or took her out? She swallowed the lump forming in her throat. It didn't work to cry with him; it only served to make him angry, and Derrick's temper was worse than her own. Fingering the blinds, she tried to imagine what life would be without Derrick Buchanan. The thought was terrifying, and yet she felt a gnawing deep inside her, a fear that she was losing him.

Felicity's heart tore a little. Once upon a time she and Derrick had been in love. He would have walked through heaven and hell to be with her, but now . . . she glanced at the bed where he lay, his eyes at half-mast, a neglected cigarette growing ash between his fingers. Tall and lean, well-muscled and tanned, he was the firstborn son of Rex and Lucretia Buchanan, as strapping as his father, as good-looking as his mother.

He was arrogant and knew that as the son of the richest man in Prosperity, any number of girls would climb willingly into his bed. As she had. The daughter of a judge, no less. But she hadn't slept with him because he was rich; she'd made love to him that first time in the backseat of his Jaguar because she loved him with a passion that wouldn't die.

He hadn't even had to take her out.

She felt more than a little shame, because, before Derrick, she hadn't let a boy touch her. Several had tried to get their sweaty paws into her bra, but she'd been selective because of Derrick. She'd known she was in love with him when she was only eleven years old and had confided in Angie that someday she was going to marry him.

Angie had laughed. Who would want her brother, who, at sixteen, was gawky, all arms and legs with a bad complexion?

But Felicity had known. Even then. And she'd saved her virginity for him. She planned to marry him and the subject had come up more than once, usually at her suggestion, but lately, Derrick didn't have much time to give her.

Tonight, while the air-conditioning wheezed and the television was muted, they'd made love. Once. And it had been a lot of work. Almost a duty.

At first Derrick hadn't been all that interested—his mind was on other things—but eventually she'd teased him into putting aside his problems back home in Prosperity and he'd responded to her new black bra and garters. Now, though, as he stared at the television and it reflected in blue shadows across his face, she could have been bare-ass naked and he wouldn't have cared. Something was bothering him, and not for the first time, he was shutting her out.

She tried again. Moving sensuously and catlike to the bed, she crawled up the mussed covers, between his legs, letting her breasts, which he used to love, hang down into the tight little cups of her push-up bra. She licked her lips. "Maybe we should go out," she cooed, her voice low and sexy, her breath whispering across his abdomen.

He flicked a glance at her. "Later."

"Why not now?" She kissed his navel, but beneath his shorts she saw no erection springing to life.

"I just want to watch the news. Okay?" He didn't bother hiding his irritation as he jabbed out his cigarette.

"You can watch it tomorrow. Right now, we could have some fun . . ." She trailed her tongue up his sternum and teased at a nipple nestled in curling dark chest hair.

"Are you really that horny?"

"With you?" She lifted an eyebrow and tossed her elegant mane of thick red hair. "Always."

Derrick's lips moved slightly. "Then prove it."

"What?"

His eyes narrowed into wicked slits. "Prove it, Felicity," he said, lifting her up so that she had to straddle his chest. "Put on your best show."

"I—I don't understand."

"Sure you do. *Make* me want you. So that I never think of another woman. Show me what you've got that makes you so special." He snapped a garter against her thigh and she jumped. Then his finger hooked under the front clasp of her bra and he dragged her closer to him, so that his breath fanned her nipples beneath the black lace. "Show me how I make you feel; get down and dirty."

"I—I love you," she said, her voice quivering a little. He scared her when he got like this, when he seemed so desperate for something . . . something more than she could give him. And beneath the fear, she felt anger. Just a tiny spark, but anger nonetheless.

Oblivious to her warring emotions, he leaned back against the pillows, stacking his arms behind his head, staring up at her. "Good. Then prove it," he said with a cruel glance. "C'mon, baby. Do me."

With moonlight for her guide, Cassidy hunched low over Remmington's shoulders and dug her heels into his ribs. She hadn't bothered with a saddle and rode him bareback, clamping her legs firmly around his sleek sides. The game colt took the bit in his teeth and raced across the dry grass, his hooves thundering as he kicked up dust. Wind screamed against Cassidy's face, tangling her hair and bringing fresh tears to her eyes.

She knew running the horse flat out through the fields was dangerous, but she didn't care. All she wanted to do was erase the image of Angie and Brig kissing and making love, an image that seemed burned into her brain.

She rode through the connecting fields until she could feel the horse breathing hard, then pulled up and let him walk in the shadow of a copse of oak and maple trees. Away from the lights of the ranch, she gazed into the dark heavens to the millions of stars that winked against a sea of black.

Remmington yanked on the bit, shaking his head and rattling his bridle, trying to communicate to her that he was still the boss, but Cassidy was having none of it. The colt had become more docile since Brig had been working with him but he was still headstrong and Cassidy didn't let him get too close to the overhanging branches of the trees for fear that he would try and scrape her off. Her shoulder was still a little tender, and she didn't want to risk another injury.

"Come on," she said, clicking her tongue and riding along an overgrown trail where the scents of honeysuckle and skunkweed mingled with dust in the dry air. Cassidy spit to clear her throat and guided the horse up a small rise where remnants of an abandoned sawmill camp still stood. The buildings were weathered and rotting, windows broken long ago, roofs collapsing on the old sheds where men had once cut timber into peeled logs and two by fours. That was a long time ago, before loggers had chased the stands of old growth farther into the hills and before the old man-made pond had dried up. The empty pond, flat as a fritter and stretching for half a mile, was her destination. A horse could gallop across the smooth surface without fear of stumbling in a mole hole or tripping over a log hidden in the tall grass.

"Let's go," Cassidy said, once again digging her heels into Remmington's sides. The colt responded, lunging forward with enough speed to steal Cassidy's breath. Wind whistled past her ears as his long legs stretched and bunched, reaching farther, hooves thudding in sharp counterpoint to the rapid beating of her heart. "That's it," she said as the horse streaked across the old pond. At the far side a grass-covered dike kept the swift water of the river from leaking into the dry pond bed. She pulled on the reins and caught her breath as Remmington turned. Yelling at the top of her lungs, she urged him forward. The colt bolted, hurtling over the flat surface again.

Exhilaration swept through her blood as she squinted against the moonlight-drenched fields. Tears blurred her vision, and she forgot about everything except the powerful animal beneath her, feeling his muscles strain as he raced against the wind, faster and faster. "Run! Run, you devil!" she cried as the ground swept beneath them. Heart pounding, she felt his sweat lather against her legs and heard him breathing hard. Finally, she pulled up at the edge of the pond and, gasping, let him walk over the weed-covered dune to stop near the dilapidated old sheds of the sawmill.

"Good boy," she said, patting his wet hide. "You're the best." She slid to the ground. The stubble of thistle and grass tickled her legs, but she barely noticed. As soon as she was off his back, Remmington snorted and half-reared. The colt tossed his head, stripping the reins from her fingers, sending fire through her injured shoulder. "Hey, wait! Whoa—" she commanded, ignoring the pain screaming down her arm as she lunged to catch hold of the leather straps.

Remmington let out a triumphant neigh and twisted as

she reached for the damned reins. "Hey—Remmington—"
He bolted forward, his hooves pounding out a sharp tattoo
against the hard ground as he disappeared over the grassy
dike.

"Damn it all to hell!" Cassidy yelled in frustration, kicking at the ground with the toe of her worn Adidas running
shoe. Now she was in for it. But good. She couldn't possibly
track down the mule-headed horse in the middle of the night.
The ranch stretched for thousands of acres, and though each
portion was fenced off from the others, Remmington could
roam through the connecting fields or the foothills, some of
which were thick with scrub oak and brush. She'd have
enough trouble finding him in the full light of day.

At dawn, when Mac made his rounds, he would discover
Remmington missing and there would be hell to pay.
Cassidy cringed at the thought. As things stood now, if she
made it back to the house undetected and kept her mouth
shut, Brig would probably be blamed for the missing horse.
Brig attracted trouble as easily as a magnet drew iron filings.
And it would serve him right for letting Angie lead him
around by his . . . well, his nose.

She swore under her breath, already knowing that she
wouldn't let him take the fall. He'd lose his job for sure, and
it wouldn't be fair. Although it warmed a cold, vengeful part
of her heart to think that he and Angie would be thwarted
and wouldn't be able to see each other as easily as they could
while he worked for Rex Buchanan, she couldn't blame him
for her own idiotic mistake.

"Son of a—" She heard it then, the unlikely huff of air—
almost a snort. The warning hairs on the back of her neck
lifted one by one, and she squinted into the darkness, wondering what she could use for a weapon. Sometimes bums
wandered through the hills and spent a night or two in whatever shelter they could find at the old sawmill. Her throat
turned to sand.

"Lose something?"

Brig's voice was a dark whisper that sent her already-
pounding heart into a sharp double-time. Whipping around,

she found him leaning against a beam holding up the sagging porch of the old cook shed.

"What're you doing out here?"

"I think that's what I should ask you."

Shoving her hair from her face, she tried to hold on to some shred of her dignity. "I thought I'd go for a ride."

"Is that what you were doing?"

"Yes! Since no one will let me ride *my* horse—"

"Because you can't handle him."

"I can!"

"Didn't look like it to me," he drawled, his grin flashing white and infuriating her.

"You probably spooked him," she argued, though she knew in her heart that he was right. She'd lost control of the mean-spirited colt.

"Yeah, right." He barked out a laugh and she heard the jangle of a bridle. For a foolish second she thought Remmington had returned until she noticed the dun-colored gelding tethered to a post near the old pump house.

"How'd you know where I was?"

"Followed you."

"You what—?" she asked, her heart knocking painfully as he pushed himself away from the post and strode slowly over to her.

"Serves you right. You were spying, Cass," he said, his voice familiar as he said her name. He stopped just in front of her and she felt suddenly young and small.

Shaking her head, she said, "I don't spy—"

"Sure you do. And you saw me with Angie at the pool, and you jumped to all sorts of conclusions."

Good Lord, couldn't he hear her heart drumming wildly? She wanted to deny it, to tell him that he was mistaken, but the words seemed frozen on her tongue.

"I . . . don't—"

"Don't lie, Cass. It's not your style."

A breeze, blowing hot over the hills, stirred the grass and somewhere off in the thicket of trees an owl hooted softly, only to be answered by a horse's nicker. Remmington! She should go and try to catch him, but right now she was mesmerized by the moonlit fields, the dark shadows of the night and Brig McKenzie.

She let out a tremulous sigh. "Okay, so I saw you."

"And you got mad—"

"I did not—"

"Shh." He pressed a callused finger to her lips and shook his head. "You're doing it again," he warned in a voice so low she could barely hear his words.

"But how did you—?"

He stared at her long and hard. "That's the strange thing. I felt that someone was watching, which isn't something new. I've felt it before. I thought it might be Willie—you know how he sneaks around—or maybe your old man checking out his daughter, but there was something different in the air. Oh, hell, what do I know? But I heard you run off, trip and swear under your breath."

"I didn't say a word."

"Didn't you?" he asked and his finger moved slowly, tracing the edge of her lips in a slow motion that caused a swirling sensation in the pit of her stomach.

Involuntarily she licked her lips and touched the pad of his finger, tasting salt and tobacco. For a moment he didn't move, just stared down at her, his eyes narrowing to slits in the moonlight. "What do you care if I'm with your sister?"

The words balled up in her throat. "I don't—" He tilted back his head and she knew she was falling into the trap of lying again—to protect her dignity as well as her pride. "I— I guess I, um, don't like her manipulating you."

"You don't have to worry about that."

"You don't know her."

"Maybe not yet. But I will."

Cassidy's heart seemed to shatter. "She'll hurt you and use you and—"

"I don't think so." He dropped his hand, and his gaze seemed to soften a little. "I'm askin' again. What do you care?"

"I just don't like it when she tries to twist men around her fingers."

"She hasn't twisted me."

"Yet."

"She asked me to go to that big deal of a party thrown by Judge Caldwell."

"I heard. You said you'd go."

His smile turned brittle. "Me and The Judge. We go way back."

Cassidy had heard stories, of course, rumors about Brig's wild youth. How he'd nearly killed his brother once with a gun that neither boy thought was loaded. Chase still bore the scar of a bullet hole in his shoulder. The weapon, a small pistol that one of Sunny's men-friends had inadvertently left at her trailer, had been returned to the man. There had been other stories as well, but for some reason, no charges had ever been filed against Brig. "I don't think it's a good idea for you to go with Angie," she blurted suddenly.

"No?" Brig's fingers curled into a fist, which he used to lift her chin so that she would have to meet his eyes. "Why not? Won't I fit in?"

"That's not the reason," she said, barely able to breathe. The night seemed to close around them.

"Then what is?" He lowered his head, closer to hers, staring at her with such an intensity that she felt as if she was burning inside. "Maybe you're jealous."

"No," she whispered and he smiled.

"There you go lying again, Cass. Didn't I tell you it doesn't suit you?"

Cassidy knew he was going to kiss her, yet when his lips brushed gently over hers, she wasn't prepared for the quake that slid down her entire body or the feel of him so close— the smell of him so earthy and male.

With a groan, he grabbed her roughly, drawing her fast against the hard angles of his body. Lips that had been so gentle turned rough. Cassidy's blood began to pound in her temples. The tip of his tongue slid like a supple knife against the seam of her lips, and she opened her mouth to him. Groaning, he gathered her closer still, dragging her willing body against his, crushing her breasts to the unyielding wall of his chest.

Her heart was thundering, her blood pumping wildly. It seemed the most natural act in the world when his knees buckled and he pulled her onto the ground. His kisses turned anxious, his tongue flicking across the roof of her mouth, sending ripples of pleasure through her limbs.

"Cass," he murmured into her open mouth.

His hands moved easily over her sweatshirt and dipped beneath the hem. He touched one small nipple with his thumb and she gasped, her abdomen pressing against her spine.

"This is what you wanted, isn't it?" he said as his fingers joined his thumb and he gently kneaded one small mound. She couldn't answer, didn't dare breathe, and when he lifted her sweatshirt, dragging it over her head, exposing her breasts to the light of the pale moon, she closed her eyes.

Feeling the chain holding her St. Christopher's medal, he paused. "Still wearing this?"

"Always."

He picked up the silver disk; it winked in the moonlight.

He held the disk between her breasts, pushing the engraved metal against her skin. Closing his eyes, he shook his head, as if to regain his composure, as if he was going to stop, and she, heart beating, drew his head down and kissed him again, her inexperienced tongue pushing eagerly into his mouth. He groaned a protest. "Cassidy—"

Her fingers splayed over the soft fabric of his shirt, instinctively searching for his flat nipples.

"Don't—" he whispered.

"Please—"

"You don't know what you're asking."

"I know I'm with you." She kissed him hard and he responded, giving in to the demands of his body. Rough hands moved expertly over her skin, sending shivers down her spine, and stoking fires deep within her, dark sweet fires he stoked so well.

"Tell me no, Cass—" he said, still touching her and causing sweet sensations to spark through her blood. "For God's sake." His arms surrounded her and he drew her upward, forcing her spine to curve away from the ground as he touched a nipple with the tip of his tongue. A tremor ripped through her and he groaned, his breath hot against her wet skin. She arched upward and his lips surrounded her breast, drawing, tasting, sucking hungrily.

Her body ground against his, her fingers curling in the thick strands of his hair. A deep, moist need began to awaken and yawn between her legs.

The world seemed to blur as the hand at the base of her spine pulled her closer still and she felt a stiff bulge beneath his fly. Soft, worn denim couldn't hide his erection, and he rubbed it against her cutoffs.

One hand slid up the inseam of her shorts, touching the elastic of the leg of her panties. He shifted, so that he could slip his finger past the flimsy barrier of cloth.

Cassidy's mouth went dry, and she cried out as his fingers parted her, exploring and touching. She gripped his head, and his teeth pulled on her nipple as he touched a part of her she hadn't known existed. The world began to spin as he stroked her, and she moved with his rhythm, breathing hard and fast, holding him tight as a pressure, sweet and dark, built inside her, a pressure so blinding that she thought of nothing other than moving with him. She thought she might explode and still he worked, his finger dipping in and out, his tongue licking her skin.

"That's a girl," he whispered across her nipple as she began to gasp in sharp little breaths. "Let go."

"Brig—"

"Come on, darlin'. It's all right. I'm here."

Her body convulsed. The ground shifted beneath her, and her bones seemed to melt as the stars behind her eyes collided.

"Oh, God," she whispered, feeling his hand withdraw, leaving that which was once white hot instantly cold. "Oh, God. Oh, God." And all at once it was over. She let out a shaky breath. He rolled away from her with a curse and left her breathless and covered with a sheen of her own perspiration.

"Brig?" she whispered, once her heartbeat had slowed. She heard him strike a match and watched as the flame illuminated his face.

"You're a virgin." He drew hard on his cigarette; it glowed bright in the dark.

Why did it sound like an insult? "I'm only sixteen."

"Hell." He wiped a hand over his brow and shot out a stream of smoke.

"You knew how old I was."

He smoked in silence, and she was suddenly embarrassed, as if somehow she'd disappointed him. "Cover up, would you?"

She looked down at her breasts, small and white with nipples that were larger than usual, and she felt ashamed. Compared to Angie, her breasts were so small and . . . Angrily she threw her sweatshirt over her head. "What is it you want from me?"

"Nothin'!"

"Nothing? After what just happened?"

"Nothin' happened."

"How can you say that after . . ." Her voice cracked.

"So you came. Big deal."

She was shocked. Was that what had happened? She'd come—had an orgasm? "But you . . . you didn't." She knew enough about bulls and stallions, and what men did, to realize that he'd somehow denied himself. Or that he didn't want to go all the way with her.

"Look, Cass, if you're horny, you can do yourself. You don't need me."

"You mean—?" She drew away, disgusted.

"Happens all the time." Standing, he dusted off his hands on his jeans.

"I don't want to—"

"Then don't. It's none of my business." He stared at her, and disgust curved the corners of his mouth. "Are you ready to leave?" he said, dropping his cigarette onto a boulder and squashing it with the toe of his boot. "Maybe we should try to find your horse."

"And just forget that we nearly—?"

He reached down and hauled her to her feet. "As I said, *nothin'* happened. It was no big deal. I got a little carried away and thought you should at least experience what it's like to get your rocks off, that's all!"

"Bull! You felt it, too!" she said, stung.

"I *feel* it with a lot of girls."

"I don't believe you."

"Including your sister!" he said, and Cassidy felt as if the flick of a whip had cut through her heart.

She shrank away from him. "You couldn't!" she cried. "Not now. Now when you just—!"

"You saw us by the pool."

"But—"

"You should've stuck around for the real show." His mouth twisted into a grim, bitter line. "Maybe then you could've learned something. Your sister, she's a real hot pants!"

With a gasp, Cassidy hauled back and slapped him so hard that the sound ricocheted off the surrounding hills.

He grabbed her arms and held them high over her head. "Don't hit me," he warned, his face turning savage in the darkness. "And take tonight as a lesson. Don't be giving it away for free to just any boy."

"I wouldn't."

"You nearly did."

Angling her face up to him, she said, "I thought *nothing* happened."

He snorted. "Only because I'm so goddamned noble."

"I love you!"

He froze and silence prevailed over the night-washed land. She stared him straight in the eye.

"Cassidy," he said and his voice gentled. "You don't have to try and mix up lust and love. You . . . you wanted to experiment and see what it was like to get laid and that's not really all that bad, except when it becomes an obsession like with your sister, but shit, you don't have to tell a guy you love him just because he got into your pants."

"I wouldn't let anyone in I didn't love."

"Oh, hell—"

"I love you, Brig McKenzie, and I wish I didn't." She inched her chin up a notch, and he shook his head. Some of the hard edges left his features, but a trace of sadness touched his eyes.

"You don't love me and I don't love you. And we're never, *never* going to have this conversation again." Slowly he lowered her arms and released her. "What happened between us a few minutes ago is over. I made a mistake. I thought I was doing you a favor—"

"Like hell, you wanted me!"

"Just because a guy gets a hard-on—"

She threw her arms around his neck and kissed him with renewed passion borne of desperation. He was trying to break it off with her before it ever got started. "I love you, Brig," she said and his body tensed, but he didn't shove her away and his lips held hers. His arms surrounded her, pulling her close against him, muscle straining against muscle, heart pounding next to heart. His groan was one of tortured surrender, and she felt him dragging her down to the ground again only to stiffen his sagging knees.

"No!" he growled, throwing her away from him so that she stumbled backward and nearly fell. "Don't you get it, Cassidy? This isn't right. You're jailbait and I'm on probation with your father as it is!" He strode over to his horse, grabbed the reins and tossed a look over his shoulder. "Coming?"

Her cheeks were hot with embarrassment and tears threatened her throat and eyes, but she found some bit of dignity and nodded.

"Good." He slapped the reins in her hands. "Go home and go to bed. I'll take care of Remmington."

"No, I'll—"

"Don't be silly, Cass. This is the only way it'll work."

Her fingers curved over the soft leather straps, and humiliated beyond belief, she climbed into the saddle. Yanking on the reins, she eyed him from astride the gelding. "You know, Brig, you can say anything you want and believe whatever makes you feel better, but I love you and I probably always will."

He glared up at her but didn't move.

The horse twisted and reared as she added, "In the future, please, don't do me any more favors!"

Nine

The sun wasn't yet up, but the first rooster of morning crowed from a farm in the distance and the hills to the east began to silhouette against the coming dawn. The colt was dead tired, head low, ears pricked forward as he stood in a corner of the field. "You miserable son of a bitch," Brig muttered. Remmington's usually glossy coat was dusty, his eyes wild. "You're lucky I don't have a gun or I'd shoot you myself and sell you for dog food right here and now!"

Remmington snorted, challenging him.

"Run and I swear, I'll track you down and kill you." But the horse was beat and it took little coaxing to grab hold of the dangling reins and climb onto his back. "Maybe next time you'll think twice before running off.

"You're more trouble than you're worth." Clucking his tongue, Brig dug his heels into the colt's sides and decided they had a lot in common. They were both rebels, ready to buck authority at every turn. He let the horse walk or lope slowly through the connecting fields, but he wanted to get back before Mac and the rest of the hands showed up for work.

It was daybreak when Brig rode into the paddocks surrounding the stable. The first lights in the big house were already glowing. No doubt the cook and servants were scurrying around trying to get the day ready for the Buchanan royalty. Soon Mac would drive into the yard, and though Brig had worked a full day and been up all night, he would be expected to put in another eight or ten or twelve hours.

But that wasn't the hard part. Facing Cassidy would be the real test. He'd been a fool last night, letting his emotions off their usually taut rein. He hadn't planned on kissing her, or touching her, or nearly stripping her of her virginity, for Christ's sake, but he hadn't been able to put on the brakes. He'd damn near climbed onto her willing body and taken her regardless of the fact that she was only sixteen and the daughter of his boss.

It was sick how he was attracted to her—a little mite of a thing who didn't know up from sideways when it came to men or sex.

Unlike Angie. He gritted his teeth, damning himself for his weakness where the Buchanan women—make that *girls*—were concerned. Though Angie's blatant sexuality disgusted him, he couldn't help being a little turned on whenever she was around.

God, if Chase could see him now!

He never thought he'd have this kind of woman trouble, where the most sought-after female in Prosperity was chasing him down and he was attracted to her spitfire of a little sister. What was wrong with him?

Not bothering with the lights, he led the horse into the stable and felt, rather than saw, another person. Willie, no doubt. He had a room over the stable. "What're you doin' up so early?" he asked, as he reached for a pail to get the colt some water.

"You cock-sucking bastard!" A fist slammed into his face.

Brig's head snapped back. Pain exploded in his jaw. He spun against the wall and could barely breathe.

His fists clenched instinctively. "What the hell—?" Rounding on his heel, he hadn't recovered before his attacker threw another punch. The knuckles on the man's hand popped. Brig's jaw cracked again. He hit the floor with a thud and rolled instinctively toward the door.

"Stay away from her!"

As Brig's eyes adjusted to the darkness, he recognized Derrick, his face flushed and twisted in rage, his eyes bright with hate. The smell of used whiskey filled the air. "You hear me, McKenzie? You keep the fuck away from my sister!"

Cassidy's image seared through his mind. "I haven't—"

"I've seen you, you bastard. You're droolin' all over yourself." He kicked at Brig, but this time Brig was ready. His hands wrapped around Derrick's polished boot and twisted hard. "Wha—" Derrick lost his balance and landed on his back. Smack! His head bounced against the wall. "I'll kill you!" he roared. "I'll cut off your fuckin' balls."

Horses neighed and Brig backed up as Derrick scrambled to his feet and reached into his pocket. With a sharp click, his switchblade flashed deadly.

Brig's insides froze. "Go sober up, Buchanan," Brig advised, wiping at the blood that drizzled from his nostril, keeping his eyes trained on the knife, watching Derrick struggle to his feet. "Or else I might have to hurt you."

"You'd like that, wouldn't ya?" Derrick's smile was pure evil. "Well, try it, McKenzie. Just try it."

"Leave it alone, Derrick."

"You've been with her, haven't ya? Gettin' into her panties—"

"Shut up." Guilt burned through his brain.

"I know it. I've seen you and I'm not the only one; the half-wit, he's seen you, too. Been mouthin' off about it." Derrick wiggled his knife in the darkness. "You're a no-good bastard son of a bitch, McKenzie. White trash that needs to be taught a lesson." He lunged again, but Brig moved, rolling quickly onto the balls of his feet and reaching into his pocket for his jackknife. Crouched and ready, he wanted nothing more than to take Derrick down a peg or two.

Derrick's knife sliced the air, slashing in a wide arc. Brig ducked, but not before the blade carved an arch in his shirt, the fabric ripping, the point of the knife burning into his skin.

Brig pounced, leaping onto Derrick's back, holding his knife against Derrick's throat.

"What the fuck!" With a swift kick, Brig's heel smashed against Derrick's knee. "Christ!"

Shifting his weight, making the drunk fall down, Brig was on him in an instant, pinning him down, knife at his throat, nostrils quivering. "You rich bastard, don't you ever insinuate—"

"What the hell's going on here?" The door flew open and a switch clicked. The stable was suddenly awash with flickering fluorescent light. Tall and furious, Mac loomed in the doorway, his weathered face a mask of hatred. "Didn't I tell you I didn't want any trouble, McKenzie?"

"The bastard's trying to kill me!" Derrick yelled.

"Get off him!" Mac ordered.

Brig hesitated.

"Now, McKenzie! Move it!"

Snapping his knife closed, Brig crawled off Derrick and shoved the jackknife deep into his pocket. With the back of his hand, he wiped the blood that oozed from the corner of his mouth and stained the front of his shirt.

Derrick, smelling of liquor and smoke, climbed to his feet. "He jumped me when I came in to check on the horses."

"That so?" Mac's eyes thinned, as if he were weighing the truth in Derrick's words. "Since when're you interested in the stock?"

"Hey—I care about this place. Gonna own it someday."

"You smell like a brewery."

"I had a couple of drinks. So what? Anyway, this son of a bitch was waitin' for me. Jumped me from behind."

"That so, McKenzie?" Mac eyed Brig's shirt, pulled down the cut flap and frowned at the semicircle of blood where Derrick's blade had scratched Brig's chest.

Brig had been down this road too many times to care. "It happened just like he said except he got the names twisted around. He jumped me."

"You lying bastard. You know what happened."

"Shut up, Derrick. Let him tell his side of it." Mac wasn't taking any crap from either of them. His gaze bored into Brig. "So what were you doin' here this time of day?"

He could lie and say that he'd come to work early, but Derrick knew better, had seen him with the horse. His motorcycle wasn't parked in its usual spot, and he was wearing the same clothes he'd worked in the day before. But if he told the truth, he'd get Angie and Cassidy in trouble. "Cassidy's horse got loose last night. It took a while to find him."

The lines on Mac's face seemed to deepen. "Got loose where?"

"Out in the north pasture, by the old sawmill. Cassidy's been pesterin' me to ride him and I thought I'd give him a trial run first, make sure she could handle him. Trouble was he shied at a snake and threw me. I spent the next nine hours tryin' to track him down."

"You lost a fifty-thousand-dollar colt?" Mac demanded.

"Found him again. Unharmed."

"Jesus H. Christ!" Mac lifted his hat and shot stiff fingers through his hair.

"That's what happens when you hire fuckin' trash," Derrick snarled. "Can't even stay on the horse. What kind of a ranch hand do you think you are, McKenzie?"

"Enough!" Rex Buchanan's voice boomed through the stable, and Derrick's lips curved into a smirk. "What in the Sam Hill is goin' on? The noise you all are makin' is enough to raise the dead. Holy Mother of Mary, look at you!" he said upon seeing his son. Derrick's hair was mussed, filthy from rolling on the floor; cobwebs, dust and hay stuck to his head. A welt was forming under his eye. "What happened . . ." Then his gaze landed on Brig and his spine seemed to stiffen, vertebra by vertebra. "Derrick?"

"He jumped me when I came into the stable."

Rex's eyebrows inched up. "That so, McKenzie?"

"Other way around."

Mac glowered at the two younger men. "McKenzie, here, claims he got throwed off Cassidy's colt and spent the night trying to find him. When he got back, Derrick was waitin' for him."

"You believe him?" Rex asked Mac.

The foreman looked from Brig to Derrick and back again. "Someone's got to be lyin'." He rubbed the stubble on his jaw. "McKenzie here isn't a fool and I don't think he'd risk his ass by attacking your boy here. Derrick's been drinking and—"

"All right, so I took a swing at him," Derrick admitted angrily, "but he deserved it. I've seen him with Angie, Dad. Kissing her and touching her and—well, hell, for all I know he might've already—"

"Don't even think it," Rex growled, but his eyes had turned as dark as midnight, his lips white with rage. "What have you got to say for yourself, boy?" he said. "I gave you a job, trusted you with the most valuable horses on the place and what have you done—nearly lost a prize colt for beginners."

"That much is true."

"And my daughter?" he demanded.

Brig thought of Cassidy and how he'd been unable to fight temptation and nearly taken her—how close he'd come to giving in to his lust and how much restraint it had taken to keep from making love to her over and over again. So she'd been a virgin—that hadn't stopped him before. For the first time in his life he felt genuine remorse about his relationship with a woman.

"Have you been sleeping with Angie?" Rex's voice was a cold, harsh whisper.

"No." Brig stared him straight in the eye.

"Why should I believe you?"

"I guess you shouldn't," Brig answered, "but maybe you should have more faith in your daughter."

"That's not answering the question," Derrick said, and his face was pale with hate. "I should rip your lyin' tongue from behind your teeth, then slice off your nuts!"

"Enough!" Rex slammed his son up against the wall so hard a bucket that had been hung from a peg near the door clattered to the floor. "Clean up your language and go sleep it off," Rex said, shoving Derrick toward the open door. "And you, Mac, leave us alone. This is personal."

With a nod of his head, Mac walked out of the stable and Brig was left with the man who had hired him, the man who had been kind to his family when others in town would rather have looked the other way, the man who adored his daughters.

Fury dilated Rex's eyes and his nostrils quivered. He pointed a thick finger at Brig's chin and jabbed the air. "Don't you ever, *ever* go near her again. Y'hear? I gave you this job because I thought you needed a break, because you're good with the stock, but if you ever so much as lay a finger on Angie, I swear Derrick will be too late. I'll cut off your balls myself."

The air in the stables simmered, though night had just turned to day and the first rays of dawn were streaking through the open door, backlighting the most powerful man in the county, seeming to gild his white hair.

"Now, you've got work to do," Rex pointed out. "I suggest you get on with it. But remember. I'll be watching you. Even when your back is turned, and believe me, I'm not a man you want to cross." Jaw clenched, he strode out of the stable, and Brig was left with a bad taste in his mouth. From this point forward, no matter what kind of trouble occurred on the ranch, he was sure to be blamed.

Cassidy couldn't sleep. She thought of Brig and what he'd done to her; how he'd made her feel. The same exhilaration as riding Remmington flat-out, only different. She'd been as breathless as if she'd run for miles, her blood had seemed to spark as it had rushed through her veins and she'd tingled in the deepest parts of her.

She stood in front of the mirror naked, her body slim and athletic, her hips slender, her breasts small and high. Cocking her head, she eyed herself critically and wondered what he saw in her—a lanky tomboy without a feminine curve to her name. Her waist was small enough, she supposed, her abdomen flat, but still—if she shoved her hair into a baseball cap, wore men's jeans and a big flannel shirt, no one would suspect that she was female.

But Brig hadn't seemed to mind. Or had he? Was she just an easy substitute for Angie? Suddenly the image in the mirror seemed to mock her, and she felt foolish. She snatched up her clothes and tried not to think about the way her nipples puckered when she thought of Brig's kisses or how, deep inside her, there was a new warm moisture.

"Cassidy?" Angie's voice rang through the hall, and Cassidy dived into her underpants. She threw on a bra—what a joke—and slid into a faded pair of Wrangler jeans. "Hey, could you come here a minute?"

"Just a sec," she called out as she shoved her arms through the sleeves of her favorite T-shirt and yanked it over her head.

"I need some help."

"Great."

"Oh, come on—"

On bare feet she hurried to Angie's room, where her sister sat on the window ledge, hands outstretched, fingers separated by balls of cotton as a shiny shade of apricot polish dried on her nails.

She, too, was undressed, wearing only a lacy bra and bikini panties. Her skin was bronzed, her breasts nearly spilling out of the confines of silky red cups. Though her abdomen wasn't as flat as her younger sister's, she had the curves that made up for it.

"Good. I wouldn't ask, Cassidy, but I've got to get going and—well, Felicity's not here and your mother doesn't like me enough to do my hair."

"Of course she does—" But Angie's sharp, knowing glance cut off the lie.

"We both know that she resents me; it's no big deal. But I'm not going to ask her to do my hair." Careful with her fingernails, she climbed to her feet and crossed the room to her vanity, where she caught Cassidy's gaze in the mirror. "Now, I know it's not your thing, but would you mind braiding my hair—French braid. I'm supposed to go into town with Felicity and I did my nails first. Stupid, huh?"

"I'm not very good at this," Cassidy hedged.

"Please. You know I wouldn't ask, but . . . I need you." Angie's eyes were wide, and with a sigh, Cassidy crossed the room that was decorated in shades of pink and white. Lace curtains matched the canopy of an antique bed, and embroidered pillowcases were cast over a raw silk comforter in a shade of dusty rose that matched the blinds. One wall held a portrait of Angie with her mother, Lucretia. One-year-old Angie sat on her mother's lap in a matching dress. Angie, with curling black hair and blue eyes, had been a beguiling toddler. Lucretia, in her early twenties, was a gorgeous woman with the same shade of eyes and hair as her daughter. The portrait had been mounted for years in their father's study, but eventually Dena had redecorated and the portrait had been cast out. Angie had claimed it and, over her stepmother's protests, hung it in a prominent spot in her room.

Angie was right; Dena had never much cared for a step-daughter who was the spitting image of Rex's beloved first wife.

In a glass bookcase, Angie's collection of dolls was proudly displayed, everything from a Chatty Cathy and Betsy Wetsy to a series of Barbie Dolls—every Barbie that had ever been made. China dolls with hand-painted smiles, rag dolls with plastic faces and eyes that blinked, even dolls that cried or peed, depending upon the owner's mood. But the Barbies were Angie's favorites, and they stood prominently in the front of the case, wearing their ball gowns, bathing suits, shorts sets, cocktail dresses and ever-present high heels. Many of the voluptuous dolls were escorted by matching boyfriends, Kens in tuxedos, suits and casual slacks, all smiling, all seeming perfectly matched to their dream date.

Cassidy cast a glance at the dolls with their swelled busts, tiny waists and long legs. She'd always hated Barbie. Didn't think much more of Ken.

"Hurry up, we don't have much time," Angie said, tossing her hair over her shoulders.

"I don't like this."

"I know, but it's time you started paying attention to feminine things—"

"Like those?" Cassidy asked, casting a glance at the dolls.

"You could take a lesson from their wardrobes."

"I think I'll pass." She wound her fingers through a hank of Angie's thick hair. "I'm not sure I can do this the way you want—"

"Just pretend I'm a horse and you're braiding my tail or something." Angie's eyes flashed indignantly. "You know, Cassidy, there's really more to life than hanging around a stable. You're pretty enough if you'd just do something with yourself. If you want I'll help—with the lipstick and nail polish and hair."

"Thanks, but—"

"Don't you want boys to notice you?"

Only Brig. "It doesn't matter."

"Sure it does."

"Do you want your hair braided or not?"

"Well, of course," Angie said petulantly. "That's why I called you in here."

"Then get off my case, okay? I like the way I look." That was a little bit of a lie, but Cassidy wasn't interested in emulating her sister or some plastic creation from Mattel, for crying out loud!

"Fine," Angie huffed. She bit her lip, looked about to say something, and a shadow passed in front of her eyes—that secret desperate shadow that Cassidy didn't want to notice. "I was just trying to help, but if you don't want it, then just get on with the braid."

Gritting her teeth, Cassidy picked up the brush. Her fingers worked deftly and soon a shiny black plait fell neatly between Angie's shoulder blades. She twisted a rubber band over the end. "There. Now you owe me one."

"Two," Angie said absently as she turned her head to one side and touched up her blush with a brush. "I owe you two, if we're counting. You helped me out last night, remember?"

Cassidy had to bite her tongue. "Yeah, right," she said feeling a little jab of guilt.

"I'm not kidding. If Dad ever caught me with Brig, he'd skin us both alive."

"I suppose," Cassidy said, remembering the magic of Brig's hands on her body—the way his mouth seemed to mold possessively over hers. A knot of desire started to unwind deep in her abdomen, and for the first time she understood why girls got bad reputations, why they risked everything to be with a boy. That's how she felt with Brig, silly though it was. She started to turn when she saw the black and blue mark on Angie's body. Partially hidden by the red silk of her bra, the bruise was just visible and Cassidy couldn't help but stare. Her stomach seemed to drop as she recognized the hickey for what it was. A man had placed his lips on the tender skin of Angie's breast and sucked hard enough to discolor her skin.

Cassidy felt the blood drain from her face.

Angie didn't seem to notice as she leaned forward and blew across her nails, but another bluish mark showed on her inner thigh, maybe just a bruise, but the perfectly round shape could have been made by lips—Brig's lips as he sucked on Angie's skin in the height of passion.

Vomit threatened the back of Cassidy's throat.

"Hey, thanks a lot," Angie said as Cassidy, without a word, turned on her heel and hurried out of the room. She clutched her stomach and wished she'd never seen the telltale marks. So Angie had hickeys—so big deal. Didn't she date a million boys?

Yeah, but last night she'd been with Brig, and if she'd been covered with hickeys earlier, wouldn't Cassidy have seen them when Angie was swimming naked in the pool? True it had been dark, but . . . Oh, God, she didn't want to think about Brig making love to Angie, then turning his attention on her. It was perverted and sick and—she ran to the bathroom and threw up in the toilet.

Fool! That's what she was—a stupid, naïve fool. Brig must be laughing at her now, at her inexperience, how she'd nearly melted when he'd touched her, how she'd arched up, silently begging him to do to her what stallions did to mares. Like an animal in heat—that's what she'd been.

She flushed the toilet, then rinsed her mouth out in the sink and brushed her teeth so harshly she probably stripped off some of the enamel.

By the time she reached the stable, Brig wasn't around. Remmington was in a field grazing, and the night before seemed almost as if it had been a dream—a silly schoolgirl fantasy—and that's how she was going to think about it, as if her lovemaking with Brig had never really happened.

Ten

"Well, if you don't look like something the cat dragged in and then, on second thought, dragged back out again." Chase, stripped to a pair of faded jeans and tattered leather gloves, was spreading gravel on the drive, filling the potholes. A toothpick was wedged into the corner of his mouth and sweat gleamed on his skin.

Brig climbed off his motorcycle and his back popped. "About how I feel." Every muscle and joint in his body ached, and all he wanted was a cold bottle of beer and to fall face first into bed. He'd sleep around the clock if he had to. Maybe then he'd quit feeling so damned guilty about Cassidy. Maybe then he'd stop considering what it would feel like to lie naked with her and make love to her hour after hour, all night long. Shit, he was getting hard just thinking about her. A drop of sweat slid seductively down his spine.

And what about Angie? What the hell are you gonna do about her?

"Out tom-catting last night?" Chase asked.

Brig forced a smile. "Chasing runaway nags. That mule of Cassidy's took off on me." Wincing, he worked a knot out of his shoulder.

"Sure." Chase picked up the handles of the wheelbarrow and shook out a load of gravel before grabbing a rake and spreading the dusty pebbles.

"You need help?"

" 'Bout done."

"Guess my timing's just about right."

Chase leaned on the handle of his rake and rubbed his jaw. "You know, I saw Angie in town today."

"Did you?"

"Yep." Chase looked thoughtful and all his cockiness faded. "I hate to admit it, but I think she's the most beautiful woman I've ever seen."

"You like her because she's got money," Brig reminded him.

"That helps," Chase admitted, "but even if she was dirt poor, she'd still be something." He smiled ruefully, as if he were ashamed to admit he could look beyond the almighty dollar.

"Christ, I don't know what I'm saying. Just that she's gorgeous, I guess."

"If you like trouble."

Though his eyes didn't spark with their usual light, Chase's grin was wide, showing off even teeth. "Since when don't you?"

"There's trouble . . . then there's trouble," Brig said. "You know the kind I'm talkin' about, the kind that follows you to the grave. That's the Angie Buchanan kind."

"Yeah, but what I wouldn't do for a little piece of it." He pushed the wheelbarrow back to the pile of gravel and began shoveling. Pebbles rained on the rusted bottom of the metal cart.

Jamming his hands into the torn back pockets of his Levi's, Brig said, "She wants me to take her to the Caldwell barbecue."

"Jeeezuz." The muscles in Chase's back stiffened for a minute before he threw himself into his task again. "You goin'?"

"Don't know."

"You'd give up a chance like that?" Chase threw down the shovel. "You can't, Brig. You've got to go."

"Why?"

" 'Cause of the people you'd meet. Might be someone there who'll give you a way out of this hellhole."

"Is that any way to talk about our hometown?"

"This is no time for jokes. You go to that party, Brig. Hell, I'm trying to find a way to wangle an invitation myself. I'd go with Velma Henderson, if I could, and she's got to be eighty-five."

"Ninety, I think."

"Doesn't matter. I'd kill to get there. And now you have the chance to go with Angie Buchanan? Hell, Brig, what have you got for brains?"

"This is where we're different, college boy. See, to you getting ahead, getting out, making a whole pile of money, matters."

"And it doesn't to you?" Chase asked.

Brig reached into the pocket of his shirt and found his pack of Camels. He shook out a cigarette and squinted at the horizon. "I figure it's the same here as anywhere else. Oh, maybe there's more people, or less. Some good, some bad. But the rich ones still own the town, and the poor bastards just try to scratch out a livin'." He scraped a match against the book and lit up, blowing a cloud of smoke into the air.

"Yeah, well, I'd like to try being on the other side." Chase grabbed his rake and began moving the gravel again. "Sure beats breaking your back working for someone else." He frowned a little, then spit out his toothpick. "Besides, aren't you tired of being known as the son of a half-breed fortune-teller?"

"Doesn't bother me."

"Well, it should, Brig, 'cause she's getting worse. Just today, before she took off for town, she had one of her 'spells.' The headache didn't last long, but she had one of her 'visions' or whatever the hell you want to call 'em. Claims it was so vivid, she was sure it was real. Says that you and me are in some kind of danger."

"She always says that."

"I know." Chase's face became stern, and when he gazed up at Brig, his eyes were serious. "But it's worse now. She was nearly hysterical. Like she was on LSD or peyote or some such crap. I'm telling you, Brig, sometimes she's real spooky. She drove off into town to get something—hell if I know what—but she took off like a bat out of hell and I haven't seen her since."

"Leave her alone."

"I think she needs to be committed."

"You what?" Brig said, then sucked hard on his Camel. The old metal sign with its faded single eye creaked on its hinges in a gust of wind. PALM READING. TAROT CARDS. FORTUNE TELLING.

"She's got more than one screw loose, you and I both know it. Always been that way, but ever since she lost Buddy—"

"That was years ago—"

"Yeah, well, I remember it like it was yesterday—him falling into the creek and screaming and me not able to get to him." Chase's face turned chalky and his eyes centered on the middle distance as they always did when he thought about the brother Brig had never known, the boy who was only two years younger than Chase.

"You're still blamin' yourself."

"Can't help it," Chase said as he picked up the damned shovel and rammed it into the diminishing pile of gravel. For years Chase had tried to erase the memory, but still it haunted him—disturbed his dreams, sometimes crept up on him unaware in the middle of the day.

"You were only five, couldn't swim yourself."

"Let's not talk about it," Chase snapped and Brig, flicking his cigarette onto the freshly strewn gravel, seemed to agree. "I need a beer. Want one?"

"Later." Chase pushed the wheelbarrow farther down the road and heard Brig climb up the steps and go inside the house. *Don't blame yourself.* How many times had he heard that same tired phrase? From his mother, even his old man while he was still around. A school counselor somewhere along the way had mouthed the same empty words, but Chase knew the truth. Though it had happened nearly twenty years before, he could still remember that cool spring day as if it had been yesterday.

His mother had been in the trailer house recuperating from giving birth to Brig. Hers had been a difficult labor, an emergency cesarean, an expensive delivery and Sunny's last. She'd nearly died, though Chase didn't know it at the time. He only knew that he and Buddy had been left with their father, and while Frank McKenzie was working at the Buchanan sawmill, some starchy women from a church had watched him and his little brother. They'd been all smiles when he'd looked their way, but had clucked their tongues and gossiped on the phone when they'd thought he wasn't listening. They'd talked of Jesus being good and God being wrathful. Chase had been only five at the time, but the memory of that day was forever seared into his brain.

When Sunny had returned from the hospital, she was still weak, and, Chase learned years later, she'd been released too early because of trouble paying the medical bills. At home, Sunny wouldn't accept any help from the ladies. "Thanks much, but we'll get along just fine," she'd told Earlene Spears, the spindly, severe-faced woman who was married to the preacher. She wasn't as old as Mama, but the lines of strain around her face and her too-thin body aged her beyond her years.

"The boys will be too much for you." Earlene always smiled, though her grin somehow looked forced and grim, as if she were in pain.

"They're my boys. We'll make out," Sunny had insisted, but she hadn't counted on the fact that she would start hemorrhaging or that while she was nursing her infant son, she would fall asleep and both Chase and Buddy would escape out the front door of the trailer.

It had been an early spring, the weather in the surrounding hills warmer than usual, the water runoff from the snowpack filling the creeks and rivers to the tops of their banks. Chase had met Andy Wilkes down at the bend in Lost Dog Creek, which was normally little more than a brook that cut through the southeast corner of the property. Andy was a year older, and they'd decided to build a dam at a narrow point and catch crawdads and salamanders.

Chase hadn't only forgotten his jacket; he hadn't realized that the door to the trailer hadn't latched, that he'd left the gate to the fenced yard open and Buddy had followed him, wandering past the old stumps and clumps of berry vines in the field.

"Why'd ya bring him?" Andy asked. He was knee-deep in the stream, piling rocks from one bank. His hands were red, his nose running.

Chase turned and saw his brother for the first time. "Go home," he said, angry that Buddy had puppy-dogged him. Ever since Mama had come home with the baby, Chase had been expected to look after Buddy.

"No." Buddy clambered after Chase, even when he waded into the stream in his tennis shoes. Mama would kill him when he got home because he hadn't bothered with his boots, but he didn't care. Andy was his best friend, and Mrs. Spears, from the church, hadn't let him play outside while she'd watched them.

"Get outta here," Chase said. "We don't wanna play with you. You're just a baby." Buddy's little face folded in on itself and tears threatened his eyes. If he ran back to the house now and tattled, Chase would be in big trouble. "Okay. You can stay. But don't come near the water." He turned back to Andy. "Don't pay any attention to him; he's just a kid."

Andy laughed, wiped his nose with the back of his jacket sleeve and began working again. Chase waded across where the creek wasn't so swift and he began building from the far bank, forgetting about Buddy as the water started funneling swiftly through the narrowing channel. Spurred by their progress, he and Andy piled rocks as fast as they could.

Andy began telling dirty jokes—the kind Chase didn't understand, but he laughed anyway, trying to impress the older boy. From the corner of his eye he saw Buddy step into the swift water just downstream of the dam. "Hey—don't—"

But it was too late. Buddy took another wobbling step and was in over his knees.

"Buddy, go home!" But the stupid kid started plunging through the water. "Mama's gonna tan your hide, and if she don't, I will!" Chase yelled, using his father's favorite threat to impress Andy.

"I help, too!" Buddy said as he stepped on a slippery rock and lost his balance. With a scream he fell into the water.

Chase felt instant terror. He scrambled over his dam, knocking off the top layer of rocks and splashing through the icy current.

Buddy surfaced, screamed again, then his head submerged as he was carried downstream.

"No!" Chase ran through the water, slogging through the ripples, and Andy, too, plunged through the current trying to catch the flailing boy. "Buddy! Hang on! Buddy!"

"Chase!" He heard his name over the wind and from the corner of his eye saw his mother, carrying the baby as she stood in the open doorway. "Is Buddy with—"

"Mama! Help!"

"Oh, God!" Her scream was filled with anguish. She ran, still clutching the infant, her black hair streaming behind her. "Catch him, oh, please catch him!" The baby started to wail.

Buddy was facedown in the stream. Chase slipped, fell and gulped water, but kept plowing forward. Andy climbed onto the bank and ran, trying to get ahead of the drowning boy.

But they were too late. Buddy didn't stop until he hit the fence line, where a cattle guard spanned the creek. Buddy's little body caught against the metal grate and Andy, crying, yanked him out of the tangle of weeds and leaves and branches that had been blocked from being carried farther downstream.

"Buddy, Buddy, oh baby!" Mama cried. Her bathrobe billowing in the wind, she plunged into the water. Still cradling baby Brig, she managed to get an arm around Buddy. "Go home," she yelled at Andy. "Tell your mom to call an ambulance! Get help! Now!"

White-faced and scared spitless, Andy scrambled over the sagging wire fence and took off like a shot.

Chase was crying, sobbing wretchedly as Mama worked her way up the bank. "Go into the house and get dry. Take the baby and put him in his bassinet," she ordered, placing a howling Brig into Chase's sodden arms.

"But Mama, I'm sorry, so sorry!"

"Go!"

"Buddy—"

"I'll take care of Buddy!" she'd said, looking fierce. For the first time Chase noticed the stains of red running down her legs—the way her nightgown was plastered to her body, that her lips were a strange, scary shade of purple.

"You're bleeding," he said, his chin trembling, tears rolling out of his eyes.

"Just go!" she said sternly as she lay Buddy on the ground, face up. Buddy's skin was blue; his eyes were open and didn't move. His chest didn't rise or fall. *I've killed him. I've killed my brother!* Chase was more scared than he'd ever been in his life. Mama leaned over as if to kiss Buddy on the lips, then blew hard for a few seconds before pressing with both her hands on his little chest. She lifted her eyes to his and there was an unusual tranquillity in her eyes. "Go on, Chase, be Mama's helper. Take care of the baby and call the sawmill—tell the secretary to send your dad home. It's an emergency. And . . . and tell the secretary to tell Rex Buchanan that there's trouble at the McKenzie place."

"W-who?"

"Daddy's boss. Now go!"

Again she leaned over Buddy to blow into his small mouth and Chase took off, running, nearly tripping, holding the baby next to his sodden chest.

He'd murdered Buddy. He knew it. As sure as if he'd shot him with Daddy's hunting rifle. Chase glanced up at the gray skies and realized that God was punishing him for being careless. Hadn't Mrs. Spears preached to him every day for a week that God punished evil little boys who didn't obey, and today, because Chase had gone against his mother's orders, he'd made God mad. Real mad.

Chase had never seen Buddy again after the ambulance took him away. His mother had explained that Buddy was in the hospital, that he would come home someday, but he never had. Nor had he died, at least not that Chase knew of. He'd never gone to a funeral; never had his mother taken him to a cemetery. When he'd asked about Buddy, Sunny had always seemed distant and only replied that his brother was fine—being taken care of.

When he'd gotten older, Chase had gleaned that Buddy was probably alive, but paralyzed or severely retarded or unable to take care of himself, a ward of the state in some institution somewhere.

And the guilt had never left him. Maybe that's why at twenty-four, Chase hadn't moved away. He felt as if he owed his mother something. Buddy's accident had changed the climate of the little family, and Frank McKenzie, unable to deal with the loss of his son and his wife's depression after another hospital stay for a hysterectomy, had gone off to work one day and never come home.

He'd left his family the small scrap of land he'd inherited from his father, and a beat-up old Chevy and a pile of hospital debts that Sunny couldn't possibly pay. For years there had been talk in town of taking Brig and Chase away from a mother who couldn't afford them. The welfare people and social workers had made monthly visits.

Chase and Brig had grown up with the knowledge that at any minute they might be stripped away from their mother. They'd heard the talk in town. Not only had Sunny proved herself unfit and already lost a healthy son by her own neglect, but her husband had left her because of rumors of infidelity. Worse yet, she couldn't support herself and the boys properly. Chase had taken a paper route at age seven and his mother had started reading palms.

He and Brig had gone to school in hand-me-downs and torn jackets—shoes with holes in them and bare heads. "It's no shame to be poor," his mother had always said. "But there's no excuse for being dirty." So his ragged jackets were always clean and pressed, his patched jeans crisp, his too-small shoes polished.

Sunny had done her best, and Chase, probably because of the guilt he still felt about Buddy, had stuck around. As much to protect Sunny from the sting of sharp tongues as anything else.

But he couldn't protect her from herself and the craziness that seemed to grow with each passing day.

Now, yanking off his gloves, Chase swiped at the sweat on his forehead and swatted at a wasp hovering nearby. He hated thinking back. All it did was depress him.

He heard the rattling clunk of her old Cadillac's engine and shoved his wheelbarrow aside to allow his mother to drive down the freshly graveled lane. As he waved, she smiled and braked under the lean-to he and Brig had built for her car. The Cadillac was long and silver, with a furry fake cat lying on the ledge near the back window. Its eyes blinked in tandem to the turn signals and Sunny adored it. Chase cringed a little as he glanced at the cat. His mother— the town nutcase.

And Brig wondered why he envied the Buchanans.

Eleven

Rex Buchanan believed in God. He believed in heaven and hell and that a man would be punished if he didn't try to do good while here on earth. He'd been raised a Catholic, and even though in this community, Catholics were a minority among the Methodists, Lutherans, Baptists and every other sect of the Protestant religion, he'd held fast to the faith that had been with him since he was a boy boarding at an elite Jesuit school back East.

In his lifetime, he'd tried to do what was right for the most part. Though he was as guilty of being tempted as the next man, he'd atoned whenever possible, confessed his sins to the priests, given a lot of money to the Church and felt more guilt than most men.

He never questioned the word of God. Never doubted his faith. Never wondered why he was being tested. It was just the way it was. Rex Buchanan tried to do everything humanly possible here on earth to pass by Saint Peter and make it through the glorious gates of heaven when his time came.

But he was, after all, only a man and sometimes not a very strong one. This was his curse.

He poured himself a stiff shot of brandy and tossed back the drink. His philanthropy was important, not only in the eyes of God but for the community. It was good for the local people who worked for him to see that he cared for those less fortunate, but sometimes his interest in the poor was a damned pain in the butt.

As was the case with Brig McKenzie. The kid wasn't

much good, but in Rex's estimation the boy had never been given two cents' worth of a chance. The week he was born his brother got himself caught in the swift waters of Lost Dog Creek and then Brig's father, Frank, the coward, had taken off. Sunny McKenzie had nearly collapsed. Beautiful, nonbelieving Sunny. Rex wondered how she had survived. She seemed to have no faith in God, no fear of the Almighty's wrath, no concern for the devil as she laid her tarot cards on the table or traced the lines of a man's palm with her sensual fingers.

For years people in town had tried to get her to leave Prosperity. There had been shots fired at the old trailer, and the palm-reading sign that hung over the front door had been peppered with buckshot more than once. Someone had even left a dead cat draped over her mailbox. The boys had been ridiculed at school, but Sunny was a proud woman and wouldn't pull up stakes.

Not even when Reverend Spears had personally gone to her home and tried to show her the evil of her ways. Then again, Spears knew all about evil. He, too, was just a man, though the way his congregation flocked around him, Rex thought the preacher considered himself some sort of deity. Spears even claimed to talk to God.

And people believed him.

Rex snorted. Pouring another shot of brandy, he considered the reasons that Sunny stayed in Prosperity. He alone knew the answer. It weighed on his mind as heavily as a load of bricks, but he was used to the burden; he'd carried it for years.

Swallowing the musky liquor, Rex felt the warm familiar burn of the brandy against his throat. Soon it would seep into his bloodstream. He liked the feeling, the little buzz that caused a flush to color his skin. He refused to think of liquor as another one of the devil's temptations. No, as he sipped his second drink—slowly, not to rush things—he didn't want to get drunk, because when he'd had too many he lost his power to think rationally—weigh all the consequences—

and then his demons, that devil that was constantly sitting on his shoulder, took control. Evil things happened when he drank too much, so he was careful, regulating his intake of alcohol, dancing warily with Satan, inviting him to come close, only to slam the door on his hideous face when he capped the bottle.

Dena had driven into town, the ranch hands were busy and Rex thought he was alone. Topping off his glass, he walked to the main hallway and took the stairs to Angie's room, one of his favorites in this huge monstrosity of a house—the house he'd built for Lucretia. His old heart ached as he paused at the door, then pushed it open.

Feeling guilty—like a peeping Tom—he stood in the hallway and looked inside. A thick cloud of perfume drew him closer. The clutter of bottles on her vanity reminded him of her mother. Almost everything Angie did reminded him of Lucretia—beautiful, spoiled, weak Lucretia. He stepped into the bedroom and eyed the portrait—his portrait—of Lucretia and Angie. His throat closed in on itself as he studied the lines, the gorgeous lines, of his wife's face. He'd fallen in love with her the first time he'd seen her, a shy debutante at a Christmas party at Waverley Country Club. She'd been sixteen, and he'd been pushing thirty. He'd pursued her with a relentless and hot passion that bordered on the unholy and married her two days after she turned eighteen. Her parents had been pleased—he'd offered a considerable marriage settlement, though they didn't call it such these days—and Lucretia, the virgin, had lain in his bed.

Closing his eyes, his lips trembling slightly, he remembered their honeymoon at the Hotel Danvers in Portland, where they planned to spend one night before flying out to Hawaii the next morning. Rex hadn't wanted her to change into a nightgown that she'd bought for her wedding night, but had insisted instead that she wear her wedding dress. They'd drunk nearly a bottle of champagne at the wedding and another in the hotel, and then when he could stand it no longer, he'd slowly taken the pins from her hair, allowing her black curls to fall free to rest on the snowy gown. He knew that he was as close to heaven as he would ever come in this life.

Drunker than he should have been, he carried her to the bed. The beads on her dress caught the light of the fire crackling in the marble fireplace. Her eyes, wide with fascination and innocence, watched him as he pulled the dress down to her waist, and he, still in his tux, played with her gorgeous breasts, kissing them, nipping at huge dark nipples that beckoned him, feeling as if he would explode at any second. She tried to respond, but was clumsy—he'd never touched her this way before. Desire pounded through his blood, making him crazy and blind to her fear. After nearly two years of celibacy and jacking off at night while fantasizing about the sweetness of entering her, he couldn't wait a second longer.

"Rex," she cried, as he got a little rougher than he'd intended. "Rex, no. W—what're you doing—"

Dizzy from the champagne, he bunched up the huge lacy skirts of her gown and quickly unzipped his fly. His member, swollen and anxious, was hard as stone. "Making you my wife," he'd said.

She took one look at his erection and drew back in revulsion. "Oh, no. Rex, please, wait—"

"I've waited too long already, Lucretia." The champagne talking. With a grunt of pure pleasure, he forced himself into her. She was tight and dry, but then she was a virgin and he couldn't stop. He'd held off so long and his blood was on fire, pounding in his brain.

"Rex, oh, God, don't—" She was panicked now, trying to scoot away from him, but he had her pinned with his body weight. He placed a sloppy kiss on her lips and forced his tongue past her teeth and down her throat.

He pushed harder, felt her give way, heard her scream somewhere in the back of his alcohol-soaked consciousness and ruptured her maidenhead. She'd get over it. Virgins were always dry and tight at first.

"Nooo—" she cried, but he was out of control as he started moving, penetrating, fusing her wriggling body to his. He'd been with virgins before and knew that she would soon loosen up, her juices would flow and she would be panting, begging for it, arching up to meet him, her pink-tipped nails digging into his buttocks. She'd throw herself at him, kissing and tasting and even taking him into her mouth, letting him come. Oh, this was heaven! A hundred wild horses galloped through his brain, and though he tried to stop his glorious release, he plunged deep into her dry, tight well and spilled himself into her.

Sweating, breathing with difficulty, he fell against her, nearly unconscious from the ecstasy, smashing her breasts with his weight, believing that he would do this over and over again like a stallion trying to impregnate a mare in heat. He'd take her from the front, the back, in the shower, on the floor, every way and everywhere he could imagine. She'd drive all other women from his mind—sexy, hot, wanting to make love to him every hour of the day.

When his breathing finally slowed and his heart stopped pounding with love for her, he felt his tux sticking to him where his sweat had congealed. Lifting his head to kiss her, she turned away and tears shimmered in her eyes. "You bastard," she hissed. "You clumsy, ugly oaf!" She kicked him off her and rolled from the bed. Her huge, beautiful breasts rose and fell in her fury, and she tried to hold the bodice of the dress over them, covering up, ashamed of her nakedness. Blood stained the wedding gown and a look of sheer hatred twisted her young features. "Don't you ever touch me again," she said, lifting her chin high. Eyes bright with condemnation, she fought tears. "Don't you *dare* act like a filthy, disgusting animal with me!"

He couldn't believe his ears and reached for her. "Lucretia, no. I love you."

Stepping backward, toward the fire crackling in the grate, she trembled in revulsion. "Leave me alone, Rex. I won't be your whore."

He was confused and more than a little drunk. "No, of course not, I'm your husband. You're my wife—"

"Then treat me with some respect. What just happened

was"—her beautiful lips were curled in disgust—"was vulgar and cheap. Sick! Like two animals grunting and rutting. Mother said this would happen, she told me that I'd have to put up with you heaving and panting on top of me, that it was my duty, but I thought you . . . that you respected me, that you wouldn't treat me like some filthy little slut!"

"No, oh, Lucretia, no. God, I'm sorry—" What was happening? Why was she acting this way? Didn't she feel the joy in making love with him?

"You *used* me! Used my body as some kind of dirty jar!" Great sobs racked her body, and she glared at him with a malice so deep it cut into his soul.

"You knew this would happen," he said, confused. What was going on here? Was she frigid? If only she'd give him the chance, he'd be more gentle—making sure that she came, too.

"I thought we would make love—like two people who cared for each other . . . not just . . . screw—" She said the word as if it tasted as ugly as it sounded. Her eyes were round, her voice high with near rage. "There's a difference."

"Oh, honey—" He climbed off the bed, his tuxedo askew, his fly gaping open, his mind cloudy with champagne. Zipping up, he nearly stumbled. "I'm sorry, I should have been more careful. Come back to bed, I promise, I'll make you feel good."

"Don't ever touch me again, Rex Buchanan!" She was in full-blown hysteria now and reached behind her for the poker, her fingers desperate until she found a weapon and held him at bay. "You try to rape me again, and I swear to God, I'll kill you."

"Oh, Jesus, Lucretia, I didn't—"

She waved the poker in front of his nose. "And don't take the Lord's name in vain, or even say it in this horrid place! I'll be your wife, Rex, I just promised I would. I took my vows and I'll honor them. But I don't remember anything in the wedding vows about being a cheap whore for your sick perversions."

"Sick? No. Lucretia, you don't understand—"

"Oh yes I do. You married me just so you could throw me on my back and shove open my legs and grunt on top of me like . . . one of your expensive stallions mounting a mare that's held in place for him. Well, it won't happen again!"

This was crazy. He had to talk some sense into her and tell her he'd made a mistake; that he wouldn't be such an oafish boor again; that he'd pleasure her. But as he closed the distance between them, she seemed to shrink into herself, stepping backward until her shoulders hit the mantel and the hem of her long bridal gown brushed against red coals. With a sickening hiss, the fire ignited, crawling up the back of her gown like a rapid thief, flames racing eagerly up the fabric.

In an instant, as if she were truly an angel with an aura, her body was silhouetted by the flames. She seemed like a vision from heaven in her burning white dress, though Lucretia shrieked as if she were in hell.

Rex flung himself at her, throwing her onto the floor, rolling with her, over and over as he slapped at the flames and quickly extinguished the fire. Terrorized, she clung to him, wailing in sheer panic. He worked quickly, carrying her into the bathroom, stripping her of the smoldering gown and setting her into a tub that he filled with cold water. The burns on her legs and his hands were minimal, but as she shivered naked in the heart-shaped tub and stared up at him with dark, hate-filled eyes, he realized his touch of heaven had been brief and was over. Forever. Her gaze, still panic-stricken, dropped to the charred, bloodstained gown.

"I'll call the doctor," Rex said.

"No." She covered her breasts and her crotch with her hands. God, she was beautiful. So perfect. He wanted her again. Despite what they'd just gone through.

"But you're injured—" Not only burned, but probably psychologically seared as well.

"No one is to ever know of this, Rex. Promise me this, for as long as I live, we will pretend that we are the happiest couple ever to walk this earth."

Pounding erupted on the door to their suite.

"Hey—are you all right in there?" a hefty male voice yelled.

He swallowed hard. "I don't know—"

"Promise me!" She grabbed at his arm, her breasts left naked for a second, rosy-hued nipples seeming to float in the water.

He could deny her nothing, and he felt an incredible guilt weigh heavy on his shoulders. It was his fault she was wounded, his fault for thinking only of himself, his fault that she would probably never sleep with him again. "Lucretia, please, I think—"

"Promise me, you bastard, that as long as I'm alive, no one will ever know what you did to me!"

"Hey—are you okay?" the man yelled through the door again. His voice was muffffled. "Maybe we should break it down or call the manager—"

Rex swallowed hard. "Everything's okay!" he yelled, lying through his teeth. "Leave us alone!"

"You sure?" The voice wasn't convinced. "I heard screaming."

"We're fine, really," Lucretia called out, her voice amazingly calm. "On our honeymoon."

"Jesus!" the voice said in awe and wonder.

"Don't worry," Rex added.

"Sorry to bother you. Jesus."

Then the room was silent.

"Promise me," she repeated, her eyes as hard as diamonds.

Rex Buchanan hadn't cried since he was a child, but tears suddenly blurred his vision of her cringing and cowering away from him in the molded pink tub. "All right, Lucretia. I promise," he'd said, but the words were hollow. Though Derrick had been conceived on their wedding night, and Rex had stayed away from his young wife during her pregnancy, later, he'd insisted on his marital rights and she'd given in, lying as cold as stone beneath him, not touching him with her hands, never kissing him, doing her duty as her mother had warned her she would have to. He'd felt like a fool straddling her, trying to turn her on, watching as her expression had changed from cold indifference to disgust when he'd kissed her breasts, rimmed her navel with his tongue, even, one time sloppy drunk, when he'd tried to get her to touch his erection, to maybe even take him in her mouth.

"C'mon," he'd said, twining his fingers in the fragrant rope of her hair, trying to get her to pleasure him. "It's not so bad."

"It's the most disgusting thing I've ever heard."

"I'm your husband!"

"Well, I'm not your whore. Go find someone else."

"You don't mean it."

"Don't I?" She'd looked up at him with seductive blue eyes, scooted down on the bed and seemed ready to suckle. Instead, she'd spat on him, spraying him with her contempt. "I'm pregnant, you sick bastard."

Awash in embarrassment, he'd somehow felt a sense of joy. Another baby might change things. He'd forgotten his anger. Tears glimmered in his eyes. "Good, Lucretia," he said. "That's good."

"I want an abortion."

"What? No, you can't mean—"

"I do mean it, Rex. I don't want another baby. You've got your son. You don't need another."

"But it's a sin—"

That alone had stopped her. Her eyes had glazed in misery and she'd rolled off the bed. She, too, had been brought up in the Church, believed its teachings, knew that taking a life, even a life so frail it couldn't live on its own, was a sin so dark she could never be absolved. "All right," she said, snatching her robe from the corner of the bed and covering herself quickly. "But this is the last."

"Baby, listen—"

"Don't," she said, her back stiff and unbending as she cinched her belt around her tiny, perfect waist. "I'll have this one, but there will be no others."

"I can't promise—"

She whirled, facing him in all her wrath. "Sure you can. You can move to another room and leave me alone. Forever."

He felt as if he'd been kicked in the gut. "That's unnatural."

"Not to me."

"Lucretia—"

"I've already talked to Dr. Williams, so it's your decision. If you want the baby, fine, then promise to leave me alone. If not, I keep my appointment."

"How could you?" It was his turn to be repulsed.

"This baby is for you, Rex. If you want it."

"But you could miscarry."

She lifted a shoulder.

His faith grappled with his lust and in the end his faith won. He moved into another suite at the far end of the hall. Lucretia paid a locksmith for a new dead bolt on her bedroom door and, true to her word, had given birth to Angie nearly seven months later. From the day the baby had come into the world, Rex had never regretted his decision, nor had he ever knocked on, listened through, or broken down his wife's door.

He'd found other women, just as he had before he'd met her, hated himself for his weakness, and made larger offerings to the Church, hoping that through his tithing and philanthropic causes, he could absolve some of his guilt.

It hadn't worked. The more money he gave, the more he felt compelled to give. The more foundations he headed, the more charities he funded, the more he needed to.

And all the while during his marriage he'd been unfaithful. He hadn't wanted to, but he'd been a healthy red-blooded American male and he'd needed sex—pure, raw, animal sex. The kind his wife wouldn't give him. The kind his mistresses would—especially the one he'd had for over twenty years.

The one he still visited.

Now, as he stared up at Lucretia's portrait, he blinked hard. God, he missed her. She was the one woman who wouldn't bend to him, the one woman who'd been his greatest challenge, the one woman who hadn't wanted him. And Angie looked so much like her. It was a curse he'd bear the rest of his life.

"Brig didn't lose Remmington," Cassidy said, facing her father in the hallway just below the stairs. Rex was holding his briefcase in one hand, his jacket was slung over his other arm.

"If he didn't lose the horse, then who did? You?" He lifted a skeptical brow.

"Yeah," she said on a sigh. Fidgeting, she added, "I, um, was mad because no one was letting me ride my horse and so the other night I snuck him out of his stall, rode out by the old mill pond, got thrown again and lost Remmington. Brig found me, sent me home on another horse—the buckskin he'd ridden—and started looking for Remmington." She'd spoken quickly, trying to get the story out, afraid that her father, in his fury, would fire Brig and she couldn't let that happen. He couldn't take the fall for her mistake. "I know it was stupid to go behind your back," she said, sincerely repentant, "but jeez, Dad, I was tired of waiting around."

"You wouldn't be trying to protect him, would you?" he asked, frowning slightly, and Cassidy wished she could wipe her sweaty palms on her back pockets.

"Why would I do that?" Her heart was pounding with the truth, that she loved Brig McKenzie, and though she wasn't lying this time, she would lie for him. Somehow, she managed to keep her face impassive.

"I don't know. Your mother seems to think you have some kind of fascination with the boy."

"He's just the hired help, isn't he?" Cassidy replied, knowing that she had to keep her secret safe and hating the superior tone in her voice. Brig was more than the hired help. Much, much more.

"Hired help you don't mind hanging around." Angie, who seemed to have heard the conversation on the landing, breezed down the stairs in a short white skirt, wide belt and scooped-neck top. Cocking her head to one side, she fastened her second gold hoop earring.

"He takes care of my horse," Cassidy said nervously.

"Mmmm, right." Angie sent her sister a knowing smile. She reached into her purse for a pair of sunglasses, and Cassidy tried not to notice how her father seemed to light up whenever Angie was near, how his face relaxed the same way it did whenever he knelt before statues of the Virgin in church.

Standing on her tiptoes, Angie brushed his cheek with her lips.

"Where're you going?" he asked.

"Felicity and I are driving to Portland. Shopping for something to wear to the barbecue," Angie replied, flashing a grin. "Have credit cards, will travel."

Rex laughed, a deep comfortable laugh.

"Want to come along, Cass? You could use something new."

"No, thanks."

Angie's eyes skated down her sister's cutoffs and T-shirt. "You can't go to the barbecue looking like a country bumpkin."

"Why not?"

"Because it's a *formal* barbecue and I know that's weird, but Judge Caldwell, he's a little strange. He likes to do things his way and we all know that his party isn't a place to go in your jeans and sweatshirt."

"Which is stupid."

"Maybe, but that's the way it is."

"Look, I'm not interested anyway," Cassidy said, wishing she could avoid going altogether.

Angie's lips puckered in disdain. "Okay. Whatever. You can't say I didn't try." Then she was off, her white sandals slapping the cool floor, a cloud of Chanel No. 5 wafting in her wake.

Cassidy didn't want to think about the Caldwells' barbecue because it would be torture, sheer torture, watching Brig hold Angie in his arms.

Twelve

The fire was straight from hell.

Flames crackled.

Fire raged, burning and breathing, a living thing fed by a dark, malevolent wind.

Evil existed just behind the ring of fire, an unseen force that watched with cruel, hungry eyes.

Sunny's heart pounded painfully. She felt the blast of heat, blistering against her skin, as she watched the flames burn ever upward, consuming whatever they came in contact with and separating her from her sons.

"Chase," she yelled in a voice that was muted by the raging firestorm.

"Brig!" she tried again, but to no avail. Her vocal chords were stilled, seared to the point that no words would pass her lips.

Panicked, she knew her boys were trapped inside the wall of flame that they could not escape.

And it was all because of the evil presence that was forever creeping after them. She watched the wall of fire grow ever upward, a flaming, immense mountain that roared and breathed, and she knew in her heart that her sons were doomed.

This was their funeral pyre.

Fire and water.

Just as she'd seen the water rushing over her young son the day that Buddy had been caught in the stream, she now saw the ghastly inferno that would destroy Brig and Chase.

In her mind's eye, she saw pain and death. Black smoke

that reeked of burning flesh billowed to the heavens, and she began to cough.

"No, no, no . . . please no," she whispered aloud.

Fire and water.

"Ma, what is it?"

Chase was beside her suddenly, shaking her awake, his blue eyes bright with concern. She'd nearly fallen asleep on the couch when the vision had slammed through her brain. Startled, she blinked herself awake but couldn't erase the image of death that lingered, like the foul breath of a demon.

"You can't go to this party," she said solemnly.

Chase's concern gave way to anger. All the muscles in his face turned hard. "We've already been over this. I'm going—"

"And I'm serious. You and Brig, you must not go." She shook her head violently. "No way. There's too much danger. I won't hear any more of it." But her forbidding tone didn't seem to make any difference, and Chase's chin only tightened in stubborn defiance. So like his father. The resemblance was frightening.

"Don't start pulling any of this crap, Ma. I've wanted to go to this for years and finally someone asked me. So I'm not letting Mary Beth Spears off the hook." He offered her the hint of a smile—the grin that always broke her heart. "Besides, Ma, I'm too old for you to boss around."

"You're going with the *reverend's* daughter?" Sunny's insides dissolved.

"Just because she's related to old Bartholomew—"

"Oh, Lord, Chase. Even Angie Buchanan is a better choice than the Spears girl."

"But I didn't have a pick now, did I?" he said impatiently. "And don't give me any garbage about Angie. I know how you feel about her. You don't want Brig to have anything to do with her."

"Of course I don't. But Mary Beth is the reverend's daughter, and no matter how much he pretends to be a man of God, Chase, he's evil, do you hear me? Evil."

"I'm going, Ma. It's important. I needed an invitation and Mary Beth was charitable to offer one." His voice was sarcastic, like acid. "Besides, I can meet a few people who might help my career; senior partners of law firms who might be looking for a law student or an intern to work in their offices. Believe it or not, I'm not going to spend my life working for old man Buchanan and kissing his ass like everyone else in this town."

She decided against wringing her hands but shook her head. Trouble. Big trouble. Mary Beth Spears and Angie Buchanan. Again the mountain of fire flashed through her mind. "I can't believe that Earlene would allow her to go with you."

"The woman's a dishrag. Does whatever her husband says."

"Okay. So why is he allowing his daughter to date you?"

"For crying out loud, Ma. Am I so bad?" He chuckled.

"Of course not," she said proudly. "You're the best."

"Then there shouldn't be a problem."

"I can only hope." But her voice belied her confidence.

"Hey, don't be such a prophet of gloom and doom. This might just prove to be the best night of my life. Look—" He walked to the room he shared with Brig and brought a tuxedo wrapped in plastic back to the couch. "This is the big time, Ma. So quit pouting and wish me good luck."

"I do, son," she said. "But the vision . . ."

His eyes clouded, but Sunny would have none of his disdain for her predictions. Curling her fingers around his forearms, she held on as tightly as possible, her fingernails biting into his skin like snake fangs, the tuxedo quivering in its plastic sheath as he held onto the hanger. "Listen to me, Chase. Do not mock me. Did I not see the water, just before Buddy—"

"I don't want to hear any of this mumbo jumbo, Ma." He jerked away from her then, straightening and pinning her with his vicious glare. "You're starting to sound crazy again."

"I speak only the truth."

"Oh, for Christ's sake. You make predictions, Ma. Half the time you're wrong. Most people think you're a nutcase."

"Do you?"

"I don't know," he said, honesty evident in his features. "I don't want to."

"Then trust me, Chase. This tragedy will happen."

"Unless I give up the opportunity of a lifetime."

"Yes."

"God, help us!" He hung the tuxedo on the drapery rod and raked his fingers through his hair in frustration. Sunny understood his feelings. He'd been taunted for years, called the son of a crazy woman who couldn't keep her husband, or accused of being a mama's boy to a woman who was considered at the very least mentally incompetent, at the worst a sayer of evil. Chase had found the dead cat hung over the mailbox and he'd buried it himself, hiding his tears as he kicked the shovel into the ground. No doubt he wondered how he'd been so unlucky to have been born to such a strange woman.

Sighing loudly, she pushed herself onto her feet. She understood why he envied the people with money, those who didn't have to struggle as he had for years, helping put food on the table. He'd had a paper route when he was only seven, graduated to a busboy when he wasn't legally old enough to work but was willing to lie about his age just to make a little more cash. Eventually he'd started working in the same mill his father had worked, but that wasn't enough for Chase. He seemed to survive on less than three hours sleep while putting in eight- or ten-hour shifts. He managed to get straight A's, earn himself a couple of scholarships and now was nearly finished with his undergraduate studies. He planned to go to law school winter term.

She was proud of him, her firstborn, and she understood that he'd sacrificed everything, his pride, his social life, and his dignity, just to better himself. It had taken him extra years to graduate because of his devotion to her, and she felt a little jab of guilt at that.

It was time he settled down with a nice girl, started his own family, lived his own life.

He sat glumly at the table and even she, with her knowledge of the future, couldn't deny him a little bit of happiness. "Just be careful tomorrow night," she said as she stopped at the sink, turned on the faucet and let the small stream of water fill a glass.

"Is the bogeyman gonna get me?" he mocked.

"I hope not." She stared out the small window and bit her lower lip. "I hope to God that I'm wrong."

"What about Brig? Him, too?" He didn't bother hiding the sarcasm in his voice.

"One of you or both. I can't tell which."

Chase swore under his breath. "Ma—"

Knowing his argument before he uttered the hideous words, she held up a hand to silence him. "I'm not going to any psychologist. They cost a lot of money and usually have more problems than their patients."

"They're trained professionals."

She rested a hip against the sink and took a sip of the water from her glass. "They should be coming to me for advice," she said.

"Anyone ever tell you that you're stubborn?"

"Just a sassy, know-it-all son who thinks he's gonna be some hotshot lawyer."

One side of Chase's mouth lifted. Lord, he was a handsome man when he smiled. "I don't think, Ma. I know."

"So do I, son," she replied, pride welling up inside her. "So do I."

Brig put his Harley through its paces, listening to the engine whine long and loud before he switched gears. The wind tore at his hair, screamed past his ears, and he hunched low, leaning into each corner, watching the countryside flashing past in a blur.

He'd managed to dodge Derrick ever since their fight, but it wouldn't last. No doubt he'd run into him at the damned barbecue and Brig would be with Angie. That should set her older brother off as well as her old man. Bobby and Jed, too, would see red. Come Monday he wouldn't have a job and there was a good chance he'd be sporting a broken nose.

However, the thought of Jed Baker and Bobby Alonzo trying to beat the piss out of him made him smile. Let 'em try.

But what about Cassidy?

He gritted his teeth. She was a problem. A kid. Jailbait. Didn't even have much of a chest. But she got to him. In the worst way. Not only was she slim and athletic, her small butt round, her waist tiny, but she was smart, too, and had an irreverent wild streak that appealed to him. Squinting against the wind, he wished he'd never touched her, never kissed her, 'cause now he wanted her. Bad. And he respected her enough to keep his hands to himself. She deserved better than he had to offer.

As for Angie, well, she was a different story . . . she was begging for it. Why, he didn't know. He didn't trust her, she was one of those manipulative women who could turn a man's thinking around, and he wasn't going to fall for it. But it was damned hard not to take what she so willingly offered. She, too, was beautiful. Drop-dead gorgeous with a body that wouldn't quit. Trouble was, she knew it.

Well, he wasn't one for planning the future—he left all that worry to his brother. He'd just go to the damned party for a little while, then he'd leave.

But not before having one dance with Cassidy Buchanan. Screw the fact that she was just a kid. He was going to hold her in his arms one time and the devil could take care of the rest of the night.

In the hallway near Angie's room, Cassidy heard the soft sobs, muffffled by a quilt and a door. She knocked softly.

"Go 'way!" Angie said, sniffing loudly.

"What's wrong?" Cassidy couldn't imagine why her older sister, the girl with everything, would cry.

"Just leave me alone."

Cassidy hesitated, took a calming breath of air and twisted on Angie's doorknob. It didn't budge. "Come on, Angie, let me in," Cassidy said.

"Would you just go away! Oh, God, why me? Wait a

minute, will ya?" A minute later the door opened and Angie stood barefoot in her bathrobe, one hip thrown out, her face drawn in irritation. "What d'ya want?" Her eyes were rimmed in red, her face flushed.

"What's wrong?"

"Nothing."

"But you've been crying—"

"Oh, for the love of God!" She opened the door a crack, pulled on Cassidy's arm and shut the door firmly behind her. "I have *not* been crying."

"I heard you."

"Just allergies—" Angie grabbed a Kleenex from her vanity and dabbed at her eyes.

"No way."

Sighing, Angie walked to the window, arms crossed over her waist. "It's nothing."

"Sure."

"Just my time of the month, you know how that is. And tomorrow's the barbecue and all. I'm just nervous."

"Why?"

"Because the shit hit the fan, okay?" She sniffed defiantly. "Dena and Dad found out that I asked Brig to take me to the Caldwells and they both hit the roof—told me I couldn't go with him. So much for Dad championing the little people. As far as I'm concerned, his philanthropy is all for show. Big talk; no action. A crock of shit."

"Oh." Cassidy, despite her sister's misery, felt her heart leap in joy that Brig wouldn't be able to escort Angie. "That's—that's too bad."

"Is it?" Angie turned and her eyes filled with tears again. "I've seen you around him, Cass. You're half in love with him yourself."

Cassidy gasped. "No, I'm—"

"Save it for someone who'll believe it." Sniffing loudly she blinked back her tears and thrust her chin forward defiantly. "Doesn't matter," she said, squaring her shoulders. "It doesn't matter how you feel or what Dena and Dad think, because I'm going to the barbecue with Brig."

"They'll kill you."

"I don't think so." A darkness slid across her eyes and Cassidy felt a premonition of doom. Angie swallowed hard and fresh tears sprang to her eyes. "You see, Cassidy, I really don't have much of a choice." She sounded bitter—so bitter. "Brig and I—" She lifted trembling fingers to her temple and rubbed, as if trying to ease a headache out of her skull.

"Brig and you what?" Cassidy asked, her voice sounding far away, her heart beating in desperation as the seconds ticked by, and Angie fought a losing battle with her tears.

Clearing her throat, she managed a weak smile as she stared straight into her sister's eyes. "Brig and I are going to get married."

Thirteen

Cassidy's feet hurt, her head pounded, and ever since Angie's announcement about marrying Brig yesterday, she'd had stomach cramps.

Brig and Angie married? No! No! No! She wouldn't believe it. This was just some fantasy Angie had conjured in her mind.

So why then, had she been crying?

"You're going to have a wonderful time," Dena said from the front seat of the Lincoln. She turned her head and offered Cassidy an encouraging smile. "There'll be lots of boys and girls your age—now, come on, quit pouting."

"I'm not—"

Dena's perfectly penciled brows slammed together in frustration. "Yes, you have been. Now, listen, Cassidy, you go in and have yourself a fantastic time tonight and you make sure that The Judge and Geraldine know it!"

Rex pulled up to the front of the huge house and dropped the keys into a valet's waiting hands. With dread in her heart, Cassidy climbed out of her father's Lincoln and wished she were anywhere else on earth other than the Caldwells' mansion. Stark white, two stories, the house looked like it belonged on the set of *Gone With the Wind,* because it was as close a replica to Tara as any home Cassidy had ever seen. Long green shutters graced the windows, and a wide front porch topped by a veranda ran the length of the building. Ivy climbed several of the red brick chimneys and gardens of rhododendron, azaleas and roses bordered the wide expanse of lawn. Music filled the night, old songs and new melodies floating on the fragrant breeze.

"Come on, come on," Dena said, hurrying her daughter. Angie was supposedly with Felicity, but Cassidy suspected that her half sister was riding Brig's motorcycle, her arms wrapped around his chest, her cheek pressed against his back as the wind screamed by.

They're not getting married. It was just another of Angie's lies! Have a little faith.

Squaring her shoulders, Cassidy followed her parents into the foyer, where a black man with a starched white collar, black suit, gleaming teeth and eyes that didn't quite smile led them to the back of the house, where a bank of French doors had been thrown open to the backyard.

"Rex!" The Judge greeted his old buddy. Ira Caldwell was a big man whose wide girth, when not hidden by judicial robes, stretched his belt to the final hole. With thin hair and eyes set deep in the folds of his face, he grinned. "I was wondering when you'd show up. And Dena"—he grabbed Cassidy's mother's hand and pumped it furiously between his palms—"you look lovely as always."

"You're gushing as always," she teased as she reached into her purse then slid a cigarette into her fingers. The Judge was quick to offer her a light.

He chuckled and snapped his gold lighter shut. "Hey, who's this? Well, Cassidy-girl, I never would have recognized you in a dress! Look at you. My, you're as pretty as your sister."

"Prettier," Dena said, blowing smoke coyly to the ceiling.

Cassidy wanted to die. She hated the comparisons to Angie that always occurred whenever she was around her folks' friends. If only she could drop through the inlaid marble floor. Maybe she could plead a stomachache, or maybe she could just take off walking through the connecting fields and call her folks when she was back at the house. What would they do then? Come home and drag her back to the party? She doubted they would dare make a scene. *No one,* not even Jesus Christ Himself if He'd been invited, would dare cause a spectacle at Judge Caldwell's social event of the year. Ruining The Judge's party would be tantamount to social death.

She fidgeted while her father and mother made small talk. Mom was sporting a new shade of red hair, a creamy lace suit and the new ruby ring Dad had given her. She wasn't afraid to flash it under the lights as she smoked and laughed and flirted outrageously.

"Where're the girls?" Dena asked and Geraldine lifted her shoulder.

The lines of strain around Geraldine's face deepened. "Felicity said something about coming later with Derrick."

"He left the house hours ago," Rex said, his smile fading a little. "Angie, too."

"Well, I haven't seen hide nor hair of her." Geraldine looked genuinely perplexed, but Cassidy sensed a little gleam of triumph as Felicity's mother shook her head. The two girls, though best friends, had always been rivals. It would please Geraldine if Angie were in some kind of trouble.

"Let me get you a drink!" The Judge clapped Rex on the back. "Cassidy, there's a bunch of kids out by the pool—all the girls eyein' the boys." He gave her an exaggerated wink.

Cassidy had begged her mother to let her stay home, but Dena had been adamant, insisting that Cassidy start socializing with kids her age; she was to start tonight at this damned party. Dena had even gone so far as to buy Cassidy a ridiculous white dress that fell over her shoulders.

Now, in the stupid dress, Cassidy felt like she was trying to imitate one of Angie's silly Barbie dolls. It was ridiculous. She found a way to extricate herself from her parents and headed outside where the crisp country air was clogged with smoke from the barbecue. Ribs and chicken, steaks and lobster all sizzled over the coals attended by hired chefs. Drinks were available at the portable bar set near the steps.

Clusters of women sat at umbrella tables smoking and gossiping while their husbands stood near a portable bar stocked with expensive liquor. A tent, adorned with miniature lights, shaded tables laden with salads, desserts and hors d'oeuvres.

From the corner of her eye she spied Bobby and Jed, partially hidden in the shadows near the back of a tent as they glanced over their shoulders, fished in their pockets and nipped from hidden flasks. Ties already askew, eyes narrowed, they were looking for a fight. "Tonight," Jed said, his voice barely audible. "Just you wait. McKenzie'll get his."

Cassidy's heart slammed.

"The bastard has it coming to him," Bobby agreed before he shut up, as if suddenly aware that they could be overheard. She took a step closer.

"Cassidy?" The male voice was nearly familiar, and she turned, half expecting Brig to appear. Instead she stared at Chase McKenzie, dressed in a tuxedo, a smile firmly in place as he approached. "You're Cassidy Buchanan, aren't you? I'm—"

"Brig's brother."

His lips tightened a fraction. "Chase."

"I—I know," she said, a little tongue-tied when she realized he didn't like being recognized because of his brother, just as she resented always being compared to her sister.

"Having a good time?" he asked, and his concentration was solely on her, his eyes the same startling blue as Brig's, his build and height the same. But he was more refined than his rough-edged brother or so everyone, including her mother, said.

"Isn't everybody?"

One side of his mouth lifted. "You didn't answer my question."

"Well, this *is* the event of the season." She wasn't interested in small talk. She was waiting. For Brig.

"Still didn't give me a yes or no." He leaned forward and whispered, "You may as well know that I'm going to be the best damned lawyer this state has ever seen in a few years and I won't let anyone duck a question. Not even a pretty girl."

"But I'm not on the witness stand, am I?"

"And I'm not that lawyer yet." His eyes twinkled. "How about a dance?"

She was suddenly tongue-tied. Dance? With Chase McKenzie? In front of God and everybody? She was already sweating and her mind was elsewhere. "I don't know how . . . I mean I don't think I can—"

"Come on," he insisted. "It'll be fun."

"But aren't you here with someone—?" she asked, then bit her tongue for insinuating that he hadn't received a gold-embossed invitation himself. A spark of anger flickered in his eyes and he looked suddenly like Brig. Her throat turned to dust. She couldn't imagine Brig's brother's arms around her. Chase was so much older, probably somewhere around twenty-five.

Rubbing his chin thoughtfully, he stared at her as if she were an intricate puzzle that he was determined to figure out. "My date doesn't dance."

"Why not?"

"I came with the Reverend Spears's daughter and he thinks dancing is some kind of weird sexual ritual or something. Anyway, according to him, a waltz is at least a class C sin. As for disco dancers—I swear he'd like to lock 'em up and throw away the key." He slanted her an evil grin that made her laugh.

"Then why's he here?" Cassidy asked, looking over the sea of faces to find the preacher, his clerical collar in place, seated at one of the tables and eating from a plate of barbecued ribs and corn on the cob. Drops of sweat rolled down his sideburns as he feasted hungrily, as if he hadn't eaten in days. His wife Earlene sat next to him and eyed the crowd. Her lips were pursed in disgust, her face devoid of makeup, her hair scraped back into a severe knot at the base of her skull. Her brown suit and blouse with its stiff white collar seemed to cluck its tongue at all the ostentatious and sparkling gowns of the other women.

Chase followed her gaze. "You know, I've given it a lot of thought, and I think the good reverend comes just so he can watch everyone in his congregation. He keeps tabs on them— how much they drink, who dances with anyone other than his spouse, who pats whose fanny and who sneaks away from the crowd for a quick feel. I bet he goes home and writes down his notes. Then he'll get up tomorrow morning, have his divine toast, pure coffee and blessed oatmeal, stroll over to the church, pick a rosebud for his lapel, climb up to the pulpit and belt out a sermon about hellfire and damnation and the wages of sin."

"That doesn't make a lot of sense," she said but smiled. "Why bother?"

"It's guaranteed to fill the church's coffers. All those guilty consciences. And maybe, just maybe, he'll manage to line his pockets in the meantime."

"You sound like Brig."

"Do I?" One side of his mouth lifted. "I'll have to fix that. So, tell me, Cassidy Buchanan, why're you here?"

To find Brig! To talk to him. "My mother made me come."

"That doesn't make much more sense than ol' Bartholomew Spears's reasons. On the other hand, I came because this is the place to be in Prosperity. Being here is the right social move."

"And that's important?" She couldn't hide the hint of mockery in her voice.

"Yeah," he said, seeming suddenly uncomfortable. "It is when you want something so badly you can taste it. But you don't have that problem, do you? You don't want for anything."

Only your brother, she thought, biting her lip. Her deodorant was already failing and the night was turning muggy. Thick, threatening clouds rolled across the pale face of the moon.

"Maybe to you this is just another boring party, but to me, it's a golden opportunity. One I intend to enjoy, so come on, Cassidy. Let's have some fun. Dance with me." His smile was gentle and she let herself be led down the brick steps to a flat area by the swimming pool where a polished wooden dance floor had been assembled. Japanese lanterns, suspended from wires strung through the surrounding trees, floated on the breeze and reflected red, yellow and green on the surface of the pool. Torches were lit to keep the insects at bay, and a gleaming grand piano was positioned on a knoll above the dance floor. Music floated down the hillside, and the pianist, dressed in long tails and a bow tie, was playing requests. A few couples danced while others gathered in clusters, nursing drinks, talking and laughing.

"I don't know about this," Cassidy whispered as they joined the few other brave souls moving easily across the floor.

"I do." Gathering her in his arms, he pulled her close and she didn't resist. He was so like Brig, yet different. Older. Rock-steady. He smelled of aftershave and soap, and his hair was combed neatly in place. His breath was warm and tickled her hair as they began to dance. But he was Brig's brother. Not the boy she loved.

Somewhere over the mountains, thunder rolled.

She felt clumsy, but Chase wouldn't let her embarrassment force her off the floor. "You're doing fine," he insisted when she muttered her sixth apology for nearly tripping over her own two feet.

"Yeah, sure. So where's Arthur Murray when you need him?"

He chuckled, a deep rumble in the back of his throat, and she relaxed a little. He wasn't Brig, but he was safe. By the way he held her, carefully, as if he was aware that she was about to bolt off the floor at any minute, she knew that she could trust him.

But still she searched for Brig, and Jed's words, spoken with such hatred, ran through her mind. *McKenzie'll get his.* Oh, God, she had to warn him. Considering confiding in Chase, she bit her lip and caught Mary Beth Spears's gaze. Instantly she went rigid all over again, for the preacher's daughter was glaring at her with undisguised malice.

Great, one more enemy, she thought sarcastically. There seemed to be a lot of hatred going around tonight.

"Looks like part of the family has arrived," Chase whispered, and Cassidy's heart leaped at the thought of seeing Brig. She looked anxiously over Chase's shoulder to see Felicity, her arm looped possessively through Derrick's, sweep through the French doors. Her dress was green silk, and diamonds glimmered at her throat.

"Felicity!" Geraldine's voice was breathy. "And Derrick."

" 'Bout time you two showed up," The Judge boomed.

Felicity didn't let go of Derrick's arm as she hugged her mother and father. Her cheeks were high with color, her eyes bright, and she had the same look about her that Cassidy's father did every time he negotiated a good deal on a new, expensive horse. Derrick, on the other hand, was slightly drunk, though he was fighting to appear sober. His gaze raked over the crowd before it landed unerringly on Cassidy. Shaking loose of Felicity's arm, he weaved over to the dance floor.

"Where is she?" he asked, ignoring Chase.

"Who?"

"Angie—where is she?"

"Not here yet."

"I think she's with my brother," Chase said, his arms clamped firmly around Cassidy.

Derrick's eyes darkened. "That bastard! I'll wring his neck and—"

Chase reacted quickly, grabbing Derrick by the lapels. "Leave Brig alone," he warned, his voice low as he uncurled his fists and took hold of Cassidy again. "He has every right to come here. He was invited. By your sister. So you can quit worrying about him and bothering us. I think your date is waiting. If I were you, I wouldn't embarrass her tonight."

Derrick's gaze skated around the yard. Only a few couples dancing nearby had noticed the altercation.

"You're white trash, McKenzie—well, white trash with a little Indian blood thrown in."

Chase's smile was deadly. "Don't push it, Buchanan," he cautioned. Chase, for all the rumors about him being the easygoing brother, could only be pushed so far.

"I just want to know where my sister is."

"Leave it alone, Buchanan. Angie's a big girl. She can take care of herself."

"The fuck she can!"

Felicity, closing in, gasped. Her face turned as red as her hair, but Derrick didn't notice her. He glared at Chase and bit out, "She's out of her mind, that's what she is. When he shows up, I swear, I'll kick his ass out of here."

"Maybe he'll do the kicking," Chase observed.

"You're next, man." Again his gaze raked up and down Chase, almost daring him to throw the first punch. Chase's muscles bunched, his teeth clenched and an angry tic developed under his eye but he held on to his temper as Felicity practically dragged Derrick off the dance floor. He flung off her arm.

"He's got a problem," Chase observed as Derrick demanded another drink.

"Not just one," Cassidy replied.

Chase's gaze followed Derrick's every move. "He's looking for a fight."

"Always," Cassidy admitted, embarrassed.

"Why does he hate Brig?"

"I have no idea. He's just—angry all the time." She really couldn't explain her brother or how he'd changed in the past few years.

"Nice guy," Chase mocked.

"He used to be," Cassidy said, *but that was a long time ago, when we were little kids.*

Threatening clouds blocked the moon and stars. A breath of wind stirred the warm air, and the atmosphere seemed to change. The roar of a motorcycle thrummed through the night, drowning out the music before dying suddenly.

Cassidy tensed.

Brig had arrived.

Within minutes Cassidy saw him walking through the French doors with Angie in tow. Angie's hair was windblown, her cheeks flushed, her eyes bright. Her dress, designed in pink gauze, was strapless and hugged her body before flaring into a skirt that swirled around her knees. Diamonds and pearls circled her throat and wrist. She was, as always, breathtaking.

Every eye on the patio turned in her direction, noting Rex Buchanan's adored daughter and the rebel boy in his black jeans, suit jacket, and open-throated white shirt.

Cassidy's steps faltered.

Chase's smile faded. "Wouldn't you know," he muttered under his breath. "Couldn't even buy himself a suit. Didn't bother with a tie."

Brig's gaze scanned the crowd and landed on Cassidy. For a second she could barely breathe—it was as if a vise had surrounded her lungs and was tightening with every tick of the clock. For a long, heart-thudding instant their gazes collided and the world seemed to stop. The party faded away. A vein throbbed at Brig's temple. Cassidy's pulse skyrocketed and she was vaguely aware that she was supposed to be dancing.

Angie whispered something into Brig's ear, and a slow, treacherous smile slid across his jaw. Lacing his fingers through hers, he tugged her onto the dance floor. Her laughter trailed after them, and Cassidy felt suddenly hot and young and stupid—a naïve little girl. Everything came back into sharp, hard focus. "I need to talk to your brother," she said.

"Why?"

She looked up and found Chase staring down at her, his eyebrows slammed together in concentration, his eyes snapping with fury, and she wondered if he understood her fascination with Brig. "Because I overheard a couple of guys who were planning to beat him up."

Chase laughed without a trace of humor. "Sounds like a typical Saturday night."

"I think they meant it."

"Only two of them?" Chase remarked, his gaze returning to Angie and Brig as he twirled her near the piano. "He can handle them."

Why didn't he understand? "But they don't fight clean."

"Neither does Brig. Don't worry about it." Then he looked at her again, and his fury gave way to dark concern. Lines of worry etched his forehead. "Don't tell me you have a thing for him?"

A thing? Like what she felt was just a schoolgirl fantasy. "I—I just don't want to see him get hurt."

"He can take care of himself."

"Bobby Alonzo and Jed Baker are—"

"A lot of hot wind, that's all." He sighed against her hair, and his arms surrounded her body as if to protect her from the world. "Don't worry about them." Then, seeming to read her mind, he added, "And don't get hung up on Brig. It's not healthy."

She lifted her head and started to protest, but the censure in his gaze kept her from saying a word.

He hesitated, as if weighing his words, then swore under his breath. "You're too young for him, Cassidy. And you're too young for me. The difference is, he'll break your heart and I won't. I respect you, your age and who you are. I have honor; Brig doesn't know the meaning of the word—or maybe he has his own skewed interpretation of what honor really is because of the size of the chip he hauls around on his shoulder." Chase stared down at her, brushed a chaste kiss across her temple, and as the song ended he said, "I think I'd better pay attention to my date." With that he left her and she felt a mixture of relief and disappointment. She knew instinctively that Chase Buchanan was solid as a rock whereas Brig was like quicksand—ever moving, never dependable, always a danger—but she couldn't just turn off her emotions like water in a spigot, could she?

But she might have to, if Brig and Angie got married.

Fourteen

Chase made his way to the bar and tried to tamp down the jealousy that burned through his blood. Not only was Angie Buchanan interested in his wayward brother, but, it seemed, the younger girl was as well. "I'll take a bourbon and water, a double, and a Shirley Temple." He waited for the drinks and watched Brig and Angie. She seemed to be pleading with him to dance again, but he walked back to the patio, leaned against the railing, shook a cigarette from the pack in his jacket pocket and lit up. He was angry about something already and that spelled trouble.

Chase couldn't believe the way Angie cuddled up to Brig, wrapping an arm around his waist, brushing her breasts against his jacket as Brig smoked, and then it hit him. Like the proverbial ton of bricks. Angie and Brig were lovers. A mixture of envy, awe and raw jealousy spurted through his blood. Then he felt fear—bloodcurdling, mind-numbing fear. If Brig was sleeping with Angie Buchanan, his days were numbered. Her old man would kill him.

But Chase understood his brother.

Hell, the thought of making love to Angie was seductive, and he knew it was impossible not to want her. Worth the risk.

Chase tore his eyes away and ignored the heat in his loins. Just looking at Angie, at the cleavage from breasts packed tightly into a strapless bra and bulging slightly over the dipped neckline of that pink dress, made him hard. God, what he would give for a taste of Angie Buchanan. He was as bad as his randy brother. The difference was that Chase was responsible and would have given up part of his life to make love to her.

"Your drinks, sir?" The bartender's voice brought him out of his fantasies, and he swallowed the bourbon and water in one gulp, then ordered another, hoping to quench the thirst that suddenly parched his throat.

He carried the drinks to the table where Mary Beth was seated with her parents.

"Why, thank you." Mary Beth's brown eyes filled with gratitude that he'd deigned to return, though he sensed a deeper emotion that she quickly hid. He felt like a heel for ditching her earlier.

"Dancing," Mary Beth's mother said, her lips drawn so tight it was as if they were pulled by a purse string. "The devil's doing."

Chase smiled. "I wouldn't say that too loudly if I were you, Mrs. Spears. Seems a lot of people here like it. They might not take kindly to being told they're doing some kind of devil worship."

"I hate to admit it, but you're right," the reverend admitted to Chase. He patted his wife on the crook of her arm, as it she were a dog that needed reassurance. "This is not the time nor the place. We've accepted Judge Caldwell's hospitality and we won't condemn certain aspects of it."

Earlene Spears, effectively rebuked, looked down at her clasped hands. She was whispering to herself, as if praying, and Chase was reminded of physical education class when he'd said the coach was a jerk and had been overheard. He'd been forced to drop and do fifty push-ups in front of the class. If he failed with any one of the push-ups, he'd be forced to do fifty more. He ended up doing nearly three hundred and feeling as if he were dying—his penance for mouthing off. He wondered if Earlene's prayer, muttered under her breath so quickly after her husband's reprimand, was her atonement for speaking out of line. Suddenly, he felt sorry for the woman. "Would you like a drink?" he asked, interrupting the movement of her lips. She glanced up quickly, swallowed hard, then shot a look at her husband—as if she were asking to be granted permission.

Bartholomew's smile drizzled away. Chase didn't give a damn. "How about a glass of wine—or a ginger ale?"

"That . . . that would be nice. The soda," she said nervously.

"You got it." Flashing her a wide grin, he grabbed Mary Beth's arm and said, "Come on. You can help me."

Mary Beth's face turned the color of roses, and the blush helped give depth to her features. She was a plain-looking girl with a tiny nose and small eyes that continually blinked, probably from the contacts that had replaced her thick glasses. Her cheekbones were high, and Chase suspected that with a touch of makeup she'd be pretty. She was twenty-two now and had just graduated from some Bible college, but she still acted as if she was a shy seventeen-year-old coed.

He'd been surprised to run into her at the drugstore in town where he'd picked up a couple of bottles of aspirin and a tube of Ben-Gay for his mother. He'd said hello as a matter of courtesy, and she struck up a conversation, then stunning him, had asked him in her tongue-tied, desperate-virgin manner to the barbecue. He'd agreed for solely selfish reasons—to meet the powers that be in Prosperity, Portland and Oregon City— and now he felt like a jerk. Already, he'd left her twice, once to talk to Jake Berticelli, a downtown corporate lawyer with a major firm, and then to dance with Cassidy.

Now, he told himself, it was only right that he plant himself firmly at her side, smile and give her the attention which she deserved . . . at least for a while. His eyes strayed to Angie again. God, she was beautiful—such a princess.

At the bar he ordered the ginger ale as well as another bourbon and water for himself, then tried not to notice Cassidy standing alone, looking out of place when she should have been having the time of her life. She was interesting in a different way. Pretty enough, but pale in comparison with her half sister, Cassidy seemed quick, a lot smarter than Angie, even though she was still a skinny kid wobbling in her first pair of high heels. She'd probably age well, become more interesting and beautiful with the passing of time. Trouble was right now she seemed hung up on Brig. Just like Angie. Chase's jaw tightened so hard it hurt.

". . . around here, you know, in the Portland area?" Mary Beth asked, blinking up at him, and he realized he'd been ignoring her again. She followed his gaze and stiffened when she recognized Cassidy.

"Pardon me?"

"I asked if you planned to practice law somewhere around here."

"Depends." He lifted a shoulder and grabbed the two drinks.

"On?"

"What I'm offered, I guess."

"I thought you might stick around, you know, because of your mom."

Something in her tone caught his attention—the same self-righteous inflection that he'd heard from the women of the church who'd tried to help out when his brother Buddy had nearly drowned a long time ago. All at once the time faded and he remembered years back, riding home on his bike, seeing the dead cat draped over the mailbox, glazed eyes staring blindly at the road, flies already gathering at the stench. Bile roiled up the back of his throat, and he wondered, as he had a thousand times over the years, if the well-meaning reverend or a zealot from his congregation had been responsible for the carnage. "Ma can take care of herself," he said, his voice clipped. No reason to get defensive. Not here. Not now.

"Good." Mary Beth's smile appeared genuine but he still felt that little prick at the back of his scalp, the one that warned him things weren't exactly as they seemed. "My father, he worries about everyone in the community, you know, whether they're a Christian or not."

"And Mom's not?"

"I don't know." She sipped her drink. "Is she?"

He considered his crazy mother and his own plans about having her see a psychiatrist. "Mom's just unconventional," he said and heard the thread of steel in his voice, felt a trickle of perspiration at the base of his spine. Though he'd grown up ashamed and embarassed of his mother's eccentricities, he wouldn't let anyone else put her down. "But she's the fairest, most decent human being I know."

Mary Beth's eyebrows quirked in surprise. "Then why did your father—" She stopped short, blushed again and shook her head. "Never mind."

"No. What were you going to ask?" he demanded, vaguely aware that the music had changed and the notes of an Elton John song drifted over the crowd.

"It was nothing."

"Go ahead. Tell me."

"Really, Chase, it was just a silly thought."

He felt a tense tic in his jaw. "What about my old man?"

Licking her lips nervously, she looked down at the ground for a second before angling her chin upward and meeting his gaze. Curiosity and something else, something murkier and deadlier, lingered in those innocent brown eyes. She swallowed. "Then why did your father leave?"

A question that had haunted Chase all his life. *Why? Why? Why?* Guilt settled over his shoulders. Was it something he'd done? Was it because he hadn't been able to save his younger brother? "I don't know," he admitted, feeling like that impotent five-year-old boy he'd been so long ago. "But I think it had a lot to do with Buddy—my younger brother—"

"Yes, I know—"

"When Buddy nearly drowned, Dad snapped. Just left for work one day and didn't bother coming back."

"Don't you ever hear from him? He is your father."

Chase felt a familiar pain and dealt with it the only way he knew how. Tossing his drink back, he refused to answer, to think of all the reasons Frank McKenzie had bailed out on his family. Chase had wondered about it often, just as he'd wondered about what had become of Buddy, but he'd never

asked; the subjects were taboo in the house and anytime anyone dared mention either Frank or Buddy to Sunny, she
would clam up for days, get lost in herself somewhere dark
and far away. "Come on, your mother's drink is getting
warm." With a smile he'd practiced for years, Chase ushered
Mary Beth over to the tent where the Spearses were still
seated and handed Mrs. Spears the ginger ale.

"Thank you," she said, grateful for a little kindness cast in
her direction.

"No problem," he replied and told himself not to push it,
to hang on to his poise, to ignore the rise of temper that his
brother always gave in to. This was the worst place in the
world to get into it, but the spark of interest in Mary Beth's
eyes when she talked about his family and the memory of
the dead cat and the way the ladies of Reverend Spears's
church had tried to force Mom to give up her little family,
whispering that she wasn't a fit mother, welled up in his
mind. He wondered, as he had off and on for years, if the
Spearses had been behind the bullets shot at the palm-reading sign or the gutted cat . . . All his self-imposed control
went to hell as he favored Mrs. Spears with a smile. "Now, if
you don't mind, I'd like to dance with Mary Beth."

"Out of the question!" the reverend said, wiping the barbecue sauce from his lips with the corner of his napkin.

"She's over eighteen, old enough to make up her own
mind, don't you think?" Again he flashed his wear-ever grin.

"She'll not be partaking in any of that hedonistic ritual,"
he replied, lips beginning to whiten. "It's the work of Satan,
boy."

"Mary Beth, sit down," Earlene commanded softly.

Mary Beth tried to wiggle her fingers free from Chase's,
but he held on tight, clenching her hand in a death grip.
"What do you say, Mary Beth—we shouldn't be discussing
you behind your back. Will you dance with me?"

She squirmed. "Please, Chase, don't—"

"You don't want to dance with me?"

"It's not that, but—"

"That's enough!" the preacher hissed. His hands splayed

on the table, he shoved himself upright and rose to his full six-feet-three-inches. With hawkish features, huge hands and a voice that could boom and whisper at the same time, he was an imposing man. He glared down at Chase. Hatred shimmered in the air. "You heard her, boy. She doesn't want to dance with you."

"I think she can speak for herself."

A hush came over the crowd, conversation ended, ice cubes stopped rattling in their glasses. Dancers paused and even the strains of an old Beatles tune faded away as the piano player, too, let his fingers drift from the keys.

Chase sensed every eye on him, and the gazes on his back nearly burned through the fabric of his rented tuxedo. Rex Buchanan, his boss, the richest man in Prosperity, Judge Caldwell, his host, and whom he might appear before should he pass the bar exam, Jake Berticelli and Elliot Barnes, both prominent local attorneys—they all were here. Watching him. The governor and a fledgling senator were supposed to be in attendance. *Be careful,* his mind warned, *don't blow it! You've worked too hard to get here. Don't piss anyone off just because this lying jackass thinks he's better than you and your mother.*

"Mary Beth, get your things," Reverend Spears ordered quietly. He glanced at the crowd, obviously noting that he had everyone's attention. "Earlene, I think we should leave."

"Not until I get my dance." Chase's fingers dug into Mary Beth's hand.

"No way, son. If you think my daughter's going to dance with the son of a woman who practices witchcraft and Satanism—" He caught himself then and cleared his throat. His anger was quickly disguised beneath a mask of benign contemplation. "Look, boy, I don't think we should make a scene. This is, after all, a celebration for The Judge and his lovely wife."

"You insulted my family," Chase reminded him.

"A mistake, you know, that's all. I pray for your mother and those lost souls who come to her for guidance instead of seeking out the truth of our Lord, Jesus Christ. Every night I kneel at the altar of our beloved Father and pray that she'll give up her deal with Satan, that she'll no longer pay tribute to Lucifer."

"You don't know a thing about it."

"She's a troubled woman, son."

"Go to hell!"

Brig had heard enough. He'd seen Chase with Mary Beth and noticed the fire in his brother's eyes. His brother, damn him, was in way over his head. These people would love to have a reason to blackball Chase McKenzie forever, and if he caused a scene at The Judge's party, he could kiss his law career in Prosperity, and probably Portland, good-bye. Idiot. Brig vaulted over a chair to stand next to his brother. "Ease up," he advised.

"This isn't your fight."

Brig's smile widened. "Sure it is; they all are."

"Hey, now, folks, let's not get into this." The Judge intervened, spreading his hands in gentle supplication while his hard little eyes glittered furiously. His wife Geraldine strode quickly to the piano player, issued a terse directive, and soon the notes of "In the Mood" filtered through the sticky night air.

"You'll pay for this, both of you," Reverend Spears predicted as he shepherded his little family through the crowd. "Judgment Day isn't that far off."

Brig snorted. "See ya there." He plucked a grape from a nearby table and tossed it into his mouth, then turned his gaze on his brother. "Boy, do you know how to make an impression."

"Don't remind me." Impatiently, Chase plowed his fingers through his hair. "I probably just cut my own throat." He glanced over to the cluster of attorneys who all worked for Jake Berticelli, but their gazes slid away. Well, screw 'em.

"Maybe not," Brig argued. "Some guys might like a lawyer with balls enough to stand up to that pompous ass."

"Some guys don't." Chase, now that people were turning back to their conversations and their drinks, relaxed a little.

"Looks like I lost my date." Mary Beth glanced nervously over her shoulder but, at a sharp word from her mother, hurried away.

"Her loss."

"What about you—where's the Angel?"

Brig's mouth quirked a little. "Angie? She's in the ladies' room."

"I thought maybe I could have a dance."

"You'll have to stand in line." Brig reached into his pocket for his cigarettes. As he'd suspected, he shouldn't have come here.

"That bother you?"

Brig shook out a Camel. "Everything bothers me." As he cupped the flame to the tip of his cigarette, he noticed a movement in white near the rose garden and his stomach seemed to shove up against his diaphragm when he recognized Cassidy and some boy—Rusty Something-or-Other. Rusty seemed intent on talking to her, though Cassidy, from the looks of her, didn't want to be bothered.

"Interested in the younger one?" Chase asked as Brig blew out a stream of smoke in disgust.

"The younger what?"

"Don't insult me by playing dumb. You know who I'm talking about. Cassidy Buchanan. You were looking for her the minute you walked in the door. Even though you had her sister hanging on your arm. When you saw her dancing with me, I thought you might start throwing punches."

"You're too old for her," Brig observed.

"So are you."

"I'm not interested."

"Like hell." Chase rubbed his jaw. "You'd better be careful, Brig. Sisters don't appreciate it when a man can't make up his mind. But by the way, she's worried about you. Claims that Jed and Bobby are out for your blood."

"So what else is new?" Brig wasn't concerned.

"Cassidy Buchanan cares about you."

"I told you I'm not interested in either of the Buchanan girls."

"Yeah," Chase replied with more than a modicum of sarcasm. "And I'm next on Reverend Spears's list for canonization."

Angie wanted to die.

Her stomach was queasy as it was and then the McKenzie boys nearly came to blows with Reverend Spears, of all people.

She dashed upstairs and down a darkened hallway to be sick in Felicity's private bathroom, where, after throwing up and rinsing out her mouth, she brushed her teeth with Felicity's toothbrush, touched up her lipstick, took one look at her wild hair from the motorcycle ride and groaned. Her tangled locks were a lost cause. Instead of trying to comb the knots free, she tossed her head around and decided to go with the untamed look. She may as well get used to it. With Brig.

She felt better now and some of her color had returned. So she had to face The Judge's illustrious guests, deal with old men with a few drinks in them trying to flirt with her, face her father and Lord knew what else.

Give me strength.

Of course she'd expected Brig would make a scene. It had been inevitable, she'd told herself, but what the hell was wrong with Chase McKenzie, picking a fight with Reverend Spears? The entire party had nearly stopped. This wasn't going well, not at all.

And then there was the situation with Derrick and Felicity. What a joke. Why didn't she just dump him? They were always fighting. Always. Couldn't she figure it out that he didn't care about her? That he just used her?

Lately Felicity seemed so desperate, so determined to have Derrick all to herself.

As if that would ever happen.

Satisfied that she'd done everything she could to look her best, Angie slipped into the shadowy hallway and felt, as she had the other night, someone watching her.

Get over it!

No one was lurking in the darkened rooms and alcoves of The Judge's huge Southern-looking mansion. For God's sake, she was leaping at shadows.

Lately she'd been a jangle of nerves . . . well, she had her reasons.

Thud!

She nearly jumped out of her skin. *Some*one was up here. She glanced over her shoulder and her breath caught as she felt, rather than saw, a bedroom door—one of the guest rooms—quietly shut.

Her heart dropped and her skin crawled.

You're imagining things! You're at a party with hundreds of people. It's safe here. Nothing out of the ordinary. Even if someone is up here, it's no big deal. Just someone looking for a bathroom, or snooping.

And yet there was something that just felt wrong about it. Her curiosity got the better of her and she knew she had to face whoever was in that room. Quickly she strode down the hallway and, without knocking, threw open the door. She flipped the light switch, and two matching table lamps glowed to life on either side of a queen-sized bed with a floral coverlet.

The room was empty aside from the bed, writing desk, bureau and a few plants near the French doors. Angie crossed to the doors but they were shut.

She noticed a scratch on the edge of one of the nightstands, a smear of green, and she touched the scrape. Wax. As if a candle had fallen . . . but there was nothing on the floor. Again her skin prickled, but she ignored it. The room looked and smelled empty. She thought about looking under the bed, in the closet and adjoining bath, but told herself she was being ridiculous. Besides, she couldn't leave Brig to his own devices for too long. Either he'd get into another fight or find some other woman. And what would she say if Judge Caldwell or his wife or Felicity found her snooping around?

Get a grip, she told herself as she walked to the door. *You're not Nancy Drew, so give it up.* Angry with herself, she snapped off the light and hurried down the hallway to the sounds of the party—music, laughter and the buzz of conversation that wafted up the wide, split staircase. She had to find Brig.

She didn't have time for her own paranoia.

Clutching the damned candle, I watched her leave.

Stupid, beautiful bitch.

My back teeth ground together and I let out my breath. I'd gotten lucky. She hadn't stepped out onto the small balcony where, if she'd confronted me, I'd have had to make up an excuse for being upstairs, an excuse that she would buy.

Fortunately, it hadn't come to that.

And everything was still going according to plan. I shouldn't have followed her to the bathroom, but I'd seen how upset she'd been, wondered why she fled to the second story, and expected her to meet her lover in a darkened upstairs room.

Instead, she'd gone into the bathroom and, from the sounds of it, puked her guts out. The sounds of retching and the stale smell of vomit had slipped through the bathroom door.

Served her right.

No matter how sick she was, it wasn't bad enough.

Quietly I slipped back into the guest room, replaced the candle that I'd knocked over inadvertently in my haste and hurried to the door. I cracked it open, half expecting to see her waiting in the dim hallway, but the corridor was empty and I could make good my escape.

Which was perfect.

I had a lot to do and little time.

I licked my lips in anticipation.

The stage was set . . . it was just time for the final act.

I smiled at that, imagining what was to come.

Tsk, tsk. Poor Angie. Beautiful, smart and soon to be, oh, so dead.

* * *

Cassidy felt a warm hand on her arm, and she closed her eyes.

"How about a dance?" Brig asked, and his fingers left hot impressions on her skin.

"No," she said quickly. "You'd better leave. Jed and Bobby are on the warpath."

"I heard."

She turned pleading eyes up to him. "They're dangerous."

"They're all big talk. Snot-nosed kids."

"Don't tell them that," she said.

"Now, the dance—?"

Her heart leaped before she remembered that Angie planned to marry him. Her dreams scattered. "I don't think so."

"You danced with Chase."

"He twisted my arm."

Brig smiled. "Is that what it takes?" His grip tightened.

Her heart was knocking wildly. He wanted to be with her. "What—what about Angie?" she asked, turning to face him. There was something different in his gaze, a tortured ghost that seemed to pass behind his eyes.

"Her dance card's filled."

"I think she wants to be with you." *For the rest of her life.*

"She'll wait," he said, and then instead of drawing her toward the dance floor, he led her behind a thicket of fir trees to a small garden, where he pulled her into his arms. Tipping up her chin with one finger, he cursed himself, then his lips claimed hers. He tasted of tobacco and liquor, and he held her close enough that she could feel the angles of his body, hard and wanting. Closing her eyes she melted against him, kissing him until her heart was racing so wildly she couldn't breathe, couldn't hear, couldn't think, and the beast of desire was awaking deep inside her, stretching and yawning.

The music faded and the shadows surrounding them seemed to deepen as he held her fiercely, kissing her hungrily, his hands moving against her back, skimming her bare skin.

He wrenched his lips from hers and that same dark angel

she'd witnessed before appeared in his eyes. Resting his forehead against hers, he let out his breath in an agonized sigh. "No, no, no."

"What—?" She felt dazed and elated that he'd found her, drawn her to this private little garden and held her as if he never intended to let go. Now he was arguing with himself.

"I just wanted you to know that it's over."

"Over—what?"

With a shuddering sigh, he stared into her eyes and she felt a tremor of despair. "Everything. This—you and me—it can't be. We both know it. You want things I can't begin to promise and you make me want to promise them. Hell, Cass, I'm all wrong for you and we shouldn't even be having this conversation." She tried to protest, but he shook his head before a word crossed her tongue. "I'm quitting working for your old man."

No! "But why—?"

"There are things . . ." His voice failed him and he glowered at the sky where clouds roiled noiselessly, blotting out the stars. "Things you don't know about me. Things you don't want to know. Things that—"

"I don't care."

"You would," he said, his voice low as the wind rushing through the branches overhead. In the darkness he appeared older than his nineteen years, world-weary.

"Why don't you tell me and let me be the judge?" But she didn't want to know, not really, didn't want to hear his horrid confession that he'd been making it with Angie, that they had been lovers for weeks, that toying with Cassidy had been a big mistake, that he was going to marry her half sister. With a sickening jolt of her heart, she realized that he'd fallen for Angie, not just been seduced by her but fallen in love with her as well. Just like all the others.

"You're too young, Cass."

"And you're afraid." She pushed away from him, her humiliation and mortification complete, tears hot in her eyes before they splashed down her cheeks.

"Afraid of what?"

"Me!" She jerked her thumb at her pitiful little chest.

He snatched her wrist in his big hands. His smile twisted sardonically, but he didn't argue. "I just thought I should say good-bye."

Bereft, her silly little-girl dreams dashed, she yanked her arm away from him. "Go to hell," she whispered, surprised at the vehemence behind her words as she spun away and headed into the darkness.

"Believe me, I'm already there." His words trailed after her, but she didn't pause, didn't listen, just tried to run through the gardens in the damned high heels and wished for all she was worth that she'd never met Brig McKenzie, never kissed him, never been stupid enough to give him her heart.

Fifteen

Crack!

Pain exploded in the back of Brig's head. His head snapped. He fell off his motorcycle. His face slammed against sharp gravel. The Harley, engine still thrumming, skidded across the drive to land against a fence. He tasted blood and he couldn't see.

"Where is she?" Jed Baker's voice registered somewhere beyond the pain throbbing through his brain.

Brig fought the urge to pass out. Groggily, he looked up. Jed stood above Brig, silhouetted by the feeble light shining from the trailer's windows. Breathing hard, his face a mask of loathing, he snarled down at Brig. His teeth gleamed in the poor light, and he gripped a baseball bat in one meaty hand. "Angie. Where is she?"

"What's it to ya?"

"You half-breed cocksucker, tell me. Where is she?"

Brig tried to get his feet under him, but he was still woozy. "None of your business."

"You mean none of yours. You leave her alone. Y'hear me, boy?" Jed swung the bat hard. Brig rolled onto his side. The weapon grazed his shoulder, then smashed into the ground. "You just don't get it, do you? She's mine!"

"Maybe you'd better tell her." Brig rocked into a crouch, but the bat hit him full in the back, popping against his spine. Pain ricocheted up his backbone, erupting in his brain. He fell to his knees. Gravel cut through his jeans.

Jed laughed and sucked a breath through his teeth. "You just stay away, you bastard."

On his feet in a heartbeat, Brig saw red. He spun quickly, wrapping steely fingers around the bat's handle, kicking out with his feet and nailing Jed in his groin.

With a wail Jed dropped to the ground. Brig wrenched the bat from him and started swinging. "Hey—watch out!"

Thud! The bat shuddered in Brig's hands as he smashed it hard against Jed's shoulder. Jed screamed like a cat hit by buckshot, then staggered backward. Crack! The bat found Jed's ribs, splintering a couple. Another hideous wail. "Shit, McKenzie. I'll have you up on charges!" Brig didn't care. Crunch! Jed's nose flattened. With a yowl he sank to the ground, hands splayed over his mouth and nose, crying like a baby, begging Brig to stop as blood spurted through the beefy fingers trying to hold his nose in place.

"You deserve this, you arrogant son of a bitch!" Breathing hard, sweat running down his face, Brig swung the bat over his head, intent on shutting Jed up forever.

"Stop!" Sunny's voice rang through the darkness. "Brig," she commanded. "Stop it, now!"

The first drops of rain fell from the sky.

Brig's fingers tightened over the slick wood.

Jed cowered and babbled, "You can't do this, you can't." He was crying, sobbing hysterically. He'd wet his pants and blood ran from his nose and mouth. "You fuckin' bastard. Fuckin' Injun bastard."

Brig let the bat slide from his hands. "Get out of here."

"I'll get you for this."

"Get the hell out!"

Sunny hurried down the steps and glared at both boys. Her long hair, black shot with gray, fell past her shoulders, and her long robe billowed around her in the wind. "I'll call an ambulance."

"No!" Jed staggered to his feet, nearly fell, but somehow managed to stay upright.

"You're hurt. You're both hurt."

"I don't need your kind of help—none of that witch doctor bullshit. It's all fake anyway," he sneered, tears trailing from eyes that were already turning black. "I'm gonna talk to the sheriff and I'll have you up on charges, McKenzie. You can't go around assaulting people."

"Try it," Brig suggested.

"Yes, do," Sunny said and before Jed could react, she grabbed his hand and held on fiercely.

"Let me go—" Jed tried to wrench free.

A strange light came into her eyes. "Yes, go and tell the authorities and they will find out the truth. About Brig. About you. About Angie Buchanan . . . This blood"—she wiped a drop from his chin—"will prove that you're a liar." Her voice faltered a bit, then took on a high pitch and she started chanting in a language that Brig suspected was Cherokee, but he wasn't certain as her eyes closed and she began to sway to the repetitious litany.

Jed shuddered and his eyes rolled back in fear.

The chanting continued and he seemed to snap to attention.

"Let go of me, you witch!" Jed screamed, his eyes nearly bulging from his head. "What's she doin' to me?"

"Don't know, but it sounds like a curse," Brig answered, enjoying the game. Ma was playing with Jed, and the boy deserved it.

"Leave me alone!"

The chanting continued, keening high over the rising wind that blew the first dry leaves around their feet and whistled over the rumble of the motorcycle's engine as it lay, wheel spinning on the gravel.

Jed tore himself free, fell into a pothole Chase had missed while filling the driveway. He scrambled to his feet. "Go to hell," he yelled in a voice strangled by terror. "You all go to hell!"

A cat howled in the darkness and Jed took off running. A few seconds later the sound of a huge engine—that of Jed's Corvette—gave forth a mighty roar and tires spun on loose gravel. The noise of the engine faded and gears ground, whining and disappearing in the night.

"And good riddance," Sunny said.

"What was all that about?" Brig asked his mother. She reached up, touched him on the forehead, and he winced.

"You have to learn to beat your enemies with your head, Brig, not with your fists."

"You're a fake, Ma."

"Only when I have to be." Her eyes were calm and dark. "But I do see danger for you, Brig. More danger than this unimportant boy."

"Watch out, Ma. You're starting to believe your own press."

"I do believe."

"Bull," he said as rain peppered the ground.

"Just because I put on a show for the Baker boy doesn't mean I don't believe. Jed needed the pee scared out of him. But what I see for you. For Chase. It's real."

"I think you scared more than the pee out of him."

"I intended to." She glanced down the lane and her smooth brow wrinkled. "He won't bully anyone again."

"Look, I'm not worried about Chase and me," Brig lied, as he wiped the sweat from his forehead and felt a dozen raindrops hit his scalp.

"You should be."

"I gotta go—"

"Not yet." She glanced at the sky and frowned at the clouds moving restlessly over the moon. "You have to tell me about the Caldwells' party. You're back early."

"It was a bore."

"And there was some altercation."

"You guessin' or you have one of your visions?"

She crossed her arms under her breasts and frowned. "Next time I'll curse you," she teased but there wasn't any laughter in her voice, and she rolled her bottom lip over her teeth as she stared at the bloodied bat.

"Okay, there was a little trouble, but nothing serious," he lied. "No one even bothered calling the police." He dusted off his jacket and reached for his Harley. There was trouble, all right, big trouble, and it went far beyond a few insults whispered about Sunny or a couple of knocks with a damned baseball bat. He thought of Cassidy and felt a sweeping sense of guilt. Hell, that girl had somehow managed to get under his skin. Then there was her sister. Angie. She'd acted strange tonight. Instead of seductive most of the evening, she'd almost seemed morose, alternately clinging to him sadly, or flirting and dancing with the boys that seemed to follow after her in a pack. Then, when Brig had had enough of the lavish party and small-minded guests, he'd tried to get her to leave. She'd agreed and they'd walked up a path between the trees at the side of the house. Suddenly she'd started to cry and drawn him into a private little spot behind the greenhouse away from the party.

"What's wrong?" he'd asked warily, not trusting her.

"Everything."

He didn't believe her. Angie Buchanan had the world by its tail. But tears tracked down her pretty face, and in the darkness he'd sensed that she was in some kind of trouble. Trouble he didn't need.

"Help me, Brig."

"How?"

"Just hold me."

"Angie—I think it's time to go home."

"Not yet." Seeming almost desperate, she'd lowered the front of her frothy pink dress, baring one of her beautiful breasts, and offered herself to him.

"For Christ's sake, put that back on—"

"Please, Brig," she'd said, taking his hand and laying it on the firm flesh of her body, letting him watch as her nipple stiffened in anticipation, allowing him to touch the heat and fire burning under her skin. He was nineteen and it had been a while and she was so tempting. "Let me make you feel good," she whispered. "I have before . . . remember?"

Desire pounded at his temples. Her skin felt like smooth silk beneath his rough fingers and it had taken all his will power to draw his hand away, but she'd been insistent, brought his fingers back to the other side of the dress, helping him tug the fabric downward so that both of those glorious globes swung free in the feeble moonlight. "You like me. I know you like me. I remember . . ."

Shame burned through his brain, and yet his heart knocked in anxious anticipation. His manhood betrayed him and sprang to attention as she moved closer and kissed him full on the lips, her naked breasts brushing against his shirt, teasing, enticing. Heat fired his blood and he was blind to everything save losing himself in her. He'd already been valiant and noble, telling Cassidy that he'd never see her again, so why not take what Angie so willingly offered? It wasn't as if he hadn't been tempted before . . . as if he hadn't touched her intimately the first time she'd been foolish enough to let him see her naked.

Oh God, he'd acted like a randy stallion that time. But that was before he knew that Cassidy was hung up on him. Since then he'd thought of Cassidy, and his sick fantasies had been with a girl barely sixteen. She was too young for him, too naïve, deserved better, no matter how he felt about her—and Angie . . . oh, hell, she felt so damned good. Gritting his teeth, he shoved Angie backward—away from him. "I don't think this is a good idea."

"Sure it is."

"Get dressed. I'll take you home." He closed his eyes, trying to think, forcing his mind from the lust burning through his blood. He heard the welcome hiss of a zipper sliding on its track. "Don't—" A few seconds later when he opened his eyes he saw that her dress had fallen to the grass in a pool of rosy chiffon and she was standing before him wearing only silky panties that rode low on her hips, exposing her tan line. A single lacy rose barely covered curling hair at the apex of her legs. "Get dressed," he repeated, but his voice was rough and lacked conviction.

She came to him then, her wet mouth full and open. Standing on tiptoes, she wound her arms around his neck, and stretching, letting her breasts rub up against him, she kissed him.

"Marry me, Brig," she'd whispered into his open mouth as she'd rubbed her chest against his shirt and snuggled against him, the front of her panties sliding seductively over the bulge in his jeans. She wrapped one leg around his and moved slowly up and down his thigh, leaving a moist, hot trail on the denim—a trail he could still smell. "Marry me and I'll be yours forever."

Now, as he walked away from his mother and righted the still-idling motorcycle, he knew what he had to do.

"Brig! Don't—"

"Later, Ma." Ignoring the raindrops splashing on the ground, he climbed astride the Harley and headed back to the road leading into town. He had a couple of scores to settle.

"I swear I'll kill him with my bare hands!" Derrick, drunker than Cassidy had ever seen him, staggered through the den and into a private room where glass-faced gun cases lined the walls.

"Who?" she asked, her heart fluttering wildly as she followed him through the house. He'd roared into the driveway a few minutes before and made so much noise that she'd hurried downstairs, only to discover him in the foyer, swearing and ranting, in a blind fury.

"McKenzie, that's who." He tried to open a case but it was locked. "Son of a bitch," he growled, then walked back to the den where he yanked open a drawer and threw out pens and papers until he found a ring of keys. He stalked back to the gun room.

Cassidy was frantic. No one else was home. She'd pleaded a headache and had gotten a ride home with Mr. and Mrs. Taylor. She'd just changed her clothes when she'd heard Derrick storm into the house, stumbling and cursing and swearing about revenge.

Against Brig. Or Chase.

He shoved a key into the lock. It wouldn't turn. "Fuck!"

"I'll call Dad," she warned.

"Go ahead. When he finds out that Brig McKenzie's been screwing Angie, he'll want a piece of him, too."

Cassidy's stomach turned over and she nearly retched. She steadied herself on the doorframe. "You don't know that—"

"Don't I?" He jammed another key into the lock and nothing happened. "God damn it!" The third and fourth key wouldn't even slide through the keyhole. "You know what, Angie told me herself. She and Brig have been carrying on ever since he first set foot here, maybe even earlier, I don't know. That's probably why he applied for the job anyway, to get close to her."

"No—"

"Christ, Cassidy, grow up! You know what a big man it would make him feel like to be getting it on with Rex Buchanan's daughter? McKenzie would love it. After years of groveling at the old man's feet, he'd get one up on him. Well, it backfired 'cause Angie thinks she's going to marry him." Teeth bared, a vein throbbing furiously near his hairline, he kicked at the door. Glass shattered. Reaching past the dangerous shards, he yanked out his shotgun.

Terror gripped her throat. "Don't—"

"He's not marrying her. He's never going to touch her again and I'm going to make sure of it." His eyes glittered with hate. "This time he fucked the wrong woman!"

Cassidy grabbed his arm, throwing herself on him. Her weight pulled his hand down and she managed to loosen his fingers. The shotgun clattered to the floor.

Quick as a rattler striking, Cassidy snatched up the huge gun and pointed both barrels at her brother's chest. Her knees were shaking, but she managed to hoist the stock of the shotgun upward, steady against her shoulder. "Go upstairs, Derrick. You're drunk and you're ranting and raving and not making any sense. Sleep it off."

"What? Now *you're* going to shoot *me* when all I'm trying to do is save our sister's honor. Give me a break!"

"Let Angie save herself."

"Jesus, Cassidy, you cry when I shoot a squirrel or a raccoon or even a damned bird. You're not going to put a bullet through me."

"I will! I swear it, Derrick." Her heart drummed in her chest. Sweat soaked her palms. Her fingers tightened over the trigger. "I will if you think you're going to take after Brig with this shotgun and—ooh!"

He grabbed the barrel of the gun and wrenched it from her unwilling fingers. "You're as bad as she is," he growled. "Always sticking up for that low-life half-breed bastard. Now, just leave me alone."

"You can't—"

"Watch me!" He stalked out of the room and down the hall, but Cassidy was right on his heels. "The way I figure it, getting rid of McKenzie should make me some kind of hero around here. I'm doing you, me, Angie and the whole damned town a favor!"

"I'll call Mom and Dad."

"Go ahead."

"And the police. If anything happens to Brig, I swear I'll turn you in and—"

He whirled around and glared down at her with furious, red-rimmed eyes. His breath was a sour mixture of stale liquor and smoke. "You don't seem to understand, do you? Brig Buchanan raped Angie."

"Raped?" she said.

"You bet. You think she would want it with him?" Derrick's face twisted in disgust.

"But she—"

"She flirted with him. She flirts with everybody. But she didn't want to make it with Brig. He forced the issue."

"I—I think it was the other way around," Cassidy said. "I heard her and Felicity talking, and Angie told Felicity she planned on seducing Brig."

"You're lying," he snarled, towering over her in all his fury.

"No, I'm not. If you don't believe me ask Felicity."

Derrick's eyes thinned to angry slits. "She's the last person I'd ask."

"Then talk to Angie! She'd tell you."

His nostrils trembled in rage. "She'd lie to protect him, too. But it's too late. It's time Brig McKenzie paid his dues!" He hitched the shotgun upward and unlocked the door.

Leaving Cassidy sagging against the wall, he strode into the night. Her legs threatened to crumple. Her threats were useless; neither her parents nor the police would take her seriously. Brig had a history of being in trouble with the law, and Derrick was just considered a boy who hadn't quite grown up. So he drank a little. So he wrecked a few cars. So he was in a brawl or two. So he slept with everyone he could—nobody had ever been hurt except Felicity Caldwell, who had made the mistake of loving him forever. And there was never any real damage because Rex Buchanan had willingly paid off anyone who made claims against his son.

But Brig McKenzie drew trouble like a lightning rod enticed jagged streaks of electricity. The authorities would take Brig's story and turn it around.

She heard the roar of Derrick's truck. "Oh, God," she whispered and silently prayed that her brother didn't find Brig and Angie together.

Cassidy's stomach knotted painfully. She'd witnessed Derrick's cruel streak all too often, and it seemed that in the past few years, it had grown worse. He'd whipped horses until they'd bled, shot squirrels and stray cats for target practice and burned Willie with cigarettes in some kind of sick game. Willie had never said a word, but Cassidy had guessed the truth and had confronted her brother, claiming that if he ever did it again, she'd tell their father.

Derrick had laughed.

"Are you kiddin'?" he'd thrown back at her when she'd threatened him. "It'll be your word against mine. Even the idiot won't back you up."

"Of course he will. He knows what you've done to him."

Derrick's slow-spreading grin had been positively evil. "He knows, but he won't say."

"Why not?"

" 'Cause he's a pervert, that's why. And if he rats on me,

I'll rat on him and he doesn't want our sweet, trusting daddy to know how sick he really is. Otherwise he might end up in a mental institution weaving baskets where he belongs."

"You're disgusting."

"One of my finer qualities."

"Willie's not a pervert!"

"No?" Derrick had asked, his eyebrows rising. "Well, if I were you, little sister, I'd keep my blinds closed and my windows shut. You never know when Willie might quit staring and start acting. He watches, you know. Sees everything that goes on here. He's seen you wearing nothin' but your birthday suit and that St. Christopher's medal, and he's seen Angie, too. I think he likes that red bra she parades around in. I've caught him watching."

Cassidy had recoiled. The thought of anyone, including Derrick, observing her made her skin crawl.

"So Willie won't be divulging any secrets anytime soon unless he wants to end up in the loony bin."

"You threatened him, didn't you?" she said, seeing the depths of her brother's perfidy for the first time.

"Just pointed out a few facts to him. But he's not as dumb as he looks. He figured out right away that he has to keep his mouth shut to keep livin' here, and believe you me, he wants to stay, seems to think that a mental hospital is some kind of twentieth-century torture chamber. He believes he might end up with a lobotomy or electric shock treatments with a cattle prod. It could be painful. Real painful. Scares the piss right out of him."

"That's what you told him," she guessed.

"Just pointed his options out to the boy."

"But that's all a lie! They don't do lobotomies or any of that stuff anymore! So help me, Derrick, if you ever do anything to Willie again . . . If you tease him, taunt him or hurt him in any way, I'll let Dad know about it and he'll believe me."

"Dad doesn't even know you're alive, Cassidy. I hate to hurt your feelings, but Dad only really cares about Angie—

because she reminds him of Mom. Talk about sick. You know, sometimes the way he looks at her worries me. You don't think he wants to get it on with his own daughter, do you?"

"No!" Cassidy cried, covering her ears.

"I hope not, because the idea's pretty damned ugly." Beneath Derrick's cocky need to shock, there was another emotion, something murky and dangerous and evil. "But if he touches her, I swear to God, I'll kill him."

And now he was after Brig. For the love of God, she couldn't let him get away with it. She ran to the phone in the den and dialed Brig's number. The telephone rang and rang. Ten times. Twelve. Fifteen. Twenty. In desperation she slammed the receiver into the cradle and started searching through the drawers for an extra set of keys. There were trucks parked near the stable, and if she found the right key . . . she didn't have her license yet, but she knew how to drive . . . *come on, come on.* Her fingers slid over pencils, pens, staples and rubber bands. No keys. Then she remembered. Derrick still had the key ring.

Desperate, she ran outside, felt the rising wind, searched in each truck but found no extra key, no way to start the damned rigs. She couldn't let Brig down; she had to warn him. Where the hell was he?

With Angie.

Her heart settled like lead, but she couldn't let her own feelings stop her from trying to alert him. But how? She couldn't get very far on foot. Teeth sinking into her lip, she scanned the parking lot and garages before landing on the stable and the answer to her prayers. *Remmington.* She could get anywhere on the colt. But how could she possibly find Brig?

With no answers, she started running, her legs moving swiftly, her heart drumming in fear. She had no idea where she was going, but she knew that she had to get there fast.

She didn't bother with the lights, just yanked a bridle from the peg near Remmington's stall. No one, not even Willie, could know that she'd left. Several horses snorted and rustled the straw of their boxes. "It's all right," she whispered.

A hand from out of the darkness shot over her mouth.

A scream died in her throat and she knew in that instant she was doomed.

Sixteen

"Shh. Cass. It's me." Brig's voice only caused her racing heart to beat more wildly, in counterpoint to the rain pounding on the roof of the stable.

"Brig?" she whispered as he lowered his hand and let it rest against her shoulder. She tried to ignore the feel of his fingers, warm pads that burned through her shirt. "What—What are you doing here?"

"I was supposed to meet Angie."

Cassidy's heart dropped like a stone. "But she was with you—at the party."

"I dropped her off a couple of hours ago. Downtown where she'd parked her car. She and I met earlier—I don't think she wanted me rollin' in here on the Harley to pick her up or bring her home."

"Why not?"

"She said she got in a fight with Derrick. Seems as if your brother has some bone to pick with me. Threatened Angie and even your old man agreed that she shouldn't be with me."

"But she went anyway."

"Yep. Snuck out of the house with some flimsy excuse about going over to the Caldwells' early, then met me downtown."

"And you went along with it." She noticed a muscle work in the corner of his jaw.

"Your sister . . . she can be pretty convincing."

"So you're not immune after all."

"I just like to get the best of the rich boy."

Cassidy felt as if a ball of lead had settled deep in her stomach. She tried to pull away from him, but his fingers, still holding fast to her shoulder, only dug in deeper.

She tried to hide the pain in her voice. "Angie's not home yet and Derrick's on the warpath."

"Against me?"

She heard the smile in his voice.

"It's no joke, Brig. He's got a gun and he's convinced himself that he's doing everyone, including Angie and the rest of the town, a favor by . . . by—"

"What?"

"By killing you."

"Spoiled-boy theatrics," Brig predicted. "Don't worry about him."

"He was serious," she said, her heart hammering in fear. "Believe me, he'll kill you."

"Just let him try." He sighed. "So where's Angie?"

"You need her for something?"

"Hell, no," he said, then caught himself short. "She told me to meet her here."

"In the stable?"

"That's what she said. Trouble is I'm a little late 'cause Jed Baker wanted a piece of my hide. Seems like I'm a popular guy tonight."

"Derrick means business."

"So did Jed."

He didn't seem to understand. From what little she could see of him, the contours of his face illuminated by the pale light filtering through the windows, he wasn't too concerned about her brother, though there were still traces of blood on his forehead from his fight with Jed. "Look, Brig," she said, still aware that he was touching her. "Derrick's been drinking and he can be real mean when he's drunk. You should stay away from him."

"Maybe someone needs to teach him a lesson."

"No. It won't work. Other people have tried." She shook her head violently and wished there was some way to convince him that he was in danger. "Derrick is more than mean. Sometimes . . . sometimes I think he *likes* to hurt other people. He gets off on it."

"Time to change that."

"No. Not you. Not tonight." Desperate, she grabbed him by both arms. "Go home—or no, go somewhere safe, somewhere far away. Let Derrick sober up."

"So that he can nail me the next time he has a few too many?"

"Until he finds someone else to pick on."

"Like who? You?" he asked, and her head jerked up.

"I can handle myself."

"But I can't?" Mockery invaded his words and she felt foolish and young, a girl caught up in adult emotions.

"Derrick . . . he cares about me. He wouldn't hurt me. Even if he didn't like me, he's afraid of Dad, of what he would do if he found out that Derrick was bothering me."

"Or Angie?" Brig asked, his voice low.

"Or Angie. Dad . . . he would protect us." It hurt the way he talked about Angie. "Why did you agree to meet her here?"

"I shouldn't have," he said on a sigh. "But she was . . ." His voice faded. ". . . scared."

"Of what?"

"I don't know."

"Maybe she was faking it," Cassidy said. She knew her older sister pretty well, and though she didn't completely understand what made Angie tick these days, Cassidy was certain that Angela Marie Buchanan hadn't been really frightened of anything in her life.

"Maybe." Brig didn't sound convinced, and the silence stretched between them with the rain pattering on the roof and the warm smell of horses filling the air. "What're you doing out here?"

"I—I thought I'd go for a ride."

"In the middle of the night? In the rain?" He didn't bother hiding his skepticism. "That's crazy. Even for you."

"I—"

"You what?" he asked, and his face was so close that his breath, smoky and hot, caressed her face.

"I was going to go looking for you," she admitted, realizing that she was still touching him, her hands were still around his arms, and he'd stepped closer, bridging the small distance between them.

"For me?"

"To warn you. About Derrick."

"I can handle Derrick."

"I told you—he's . . . he's got a gun." His hand moved closer to her neck, and her bare skin tingled where the tips of his fingers grazed her throat.

"So you were going to try and protect me." His voice was low. Sexy.

"He's dangerous." He was so close, she could barely breathe. Her heartbeat thundered in her ears.

"So am I." Tilting up her chin with one long finger, he kissed her, and in that second's time she seemed to melt inside. His tongue invaded her mouth, and she willingly opened to him, like a flower to the sun. His arms surrounded her and her knees buckled; her bones turned liquid. His mouth was hard and hungry and eager.

She was hot, so hot, and his hands only fueled the fire that burned beneath her skin. *Love me,* she silently cried, *please Brig, love me.* She pressed hard against him, wanting more, knowing that only his touch would salve the desire that brought sweat to her spine. Anxiously he peeled away her shirt, and she fumbled with the buttons of his. The tops of her breasts bulged over her bra, to rub against the springy hairs on his chest.

"Cassidy," he whispered, his voice strangled, as if he wanted to stop but couldn't find the strength. He unlatched her bra and her breasts spilled into his waiting, callused hands. "Cassidy, sweet, sweet Cassidy."

His thumbs caressed her nipples, and they swelled for him, puckering as liquid heat raced through her blood. Lowering himself to his knees, he pressed wet kisses against her skin and buried his face between her breasts, pushing the supple flesh against his cheeks.

Deep inside, she began to ache.

A moan sprang from her lips. She tangled her hands through his hair and held him close to her. His breath fanned her nipple before he took her into his mouth and her legs turned to water. He kissed her, touched her, and his fingers cupped her buttocks.

The ache became a dusky want that throbbed between her legs.

She felt the button on her cutoffs give way and heard the series of pops as her fly opened willingly in his hands. The ragged shorts dropped to the floor, and Brig buried his face in her abdomen, his breath searing her skin, his hands curling around the backs of her thighs to tickle and tease. "God, I want you," he said, his voice throaty, his lips wet and filled with promise as they brushed so intimately against her skin, against the silk. His hot breath invaded the frail barrier of her panties and she quivered inside.

Her heart soared. "I—I want you, Brig."

"No!" he rasped. "You don't even know what you want; you're . . . you're . . . God, you're only sixteen!"

"Just love me."

"I . . . I . . . can't." He dropped his hands and threw back his head, squeezing his eyes shut. Shuddering, he took deep gulps of air, as if in so doing he could tamp down the desire thundering through his blood.

"Because of Angie," she said.

"What? Angie?" His eyes flew open. "No—" Then he caught himself.

"No?" she asked, hardly daring to believe that he would deny her. She was offering herself, her virginity, her love, and Angie stood in the way. Tears of shame threatened her eyes.

"She has nothing to do with this."

"But you said you and she—"

"I lied," he admitted, shoving his hair away from his face impatiently. "I lied. So that you'd leave me alone."

"But I saw you together, by the pool—"

"You saw what you wanted to see."

Desperately she yearned to believe him. With all her heart, she needed to trust those words. She slid to her knees, and taking his face between her hands, she kissed him, long and hard.

"Don't do this, Cass," he warned.

But she didn't stop. Her fingers ran down the sinewy muscles in his arms, pushing off his shirt before exploring the taut washboard of his ribs. He groaned, swore under his breath and then he gathered her into his arms and kissed her as if his life depended upon it. They tumbled to the hay-strewn floor. No more holding back, no more tremors of denial. He took what she so willingly offered. His hands were on her breasts, touching, kneading, making silent promises as his mouth skimmed her skin. He traced her navel with his tongue, pushing her onto her back. She quivered, liquid heat swirling inside her. Her skin was on fire, and she couldn't think of anything save the urgent need of his body melding with hers.

He ripped off her panties and tossed them into the corner, then kicked off his boots and jeans. His mouth kissed her thighs, her buttocks, then moved upward, breath hot, tongue wet, lips persistent. Closing her eyes she felt the earth begin to move as he kissed her in the most forbidden of places. Warm, moist need yawned between her legs. Her blood pumped wild as he moved and she writhed, anxious for more, wanting something she couldn't name, breathing his name in short quick gasps.

Suddenly he was above her, naked, hot, hard and sweating.

She looked straight into his night-darkened eyes.

"Tell me no," he begged, his breath uneven, his lips drawn back against his teeth in frustration.

"I can't."

"For God's sake, Cassidy—"

"Brig, I love you."

"Don't—"

"I'll always love you."

His face twisted in torment. "Cass . . . I can't make any promises. Oh, hell. I should be shot for this." And then, sweeping her legs apart with his knees, he gave in to the desire she saw in the bulge of veins in his neck. "No—" he ground out as his body reacted and he delved deep into her, breaking past the barriers of her childhood, making her a woman. "No! No! No!"

Her breath caught in a split second of pain and she felt a rending, not of flesh, but of the adolescence she so willingly gave up. She clung to him as he moved, slowly at first, making her dizzy, causing her breath to catch at the back of her throat, creating a kaleidoscope of colors whirling through her mind. She felt her hips leave the floor as she caught his rhythm. Perspiration fused their bodies, moans of pleasure passed her lips. Faster and faster the world seemed to spin, and suddenly the moon and sun and the stars above the stable shattered in a flash of light that electrified the night.

She convulsed and he caught her. "Brig! Oh, Brig!" she cried, clutching him and whispering in a voice she didn't recognize as her own before falling damp and spent against the floor.

"Cass—" he cried as he shuddered and fell against her. He lay there, breathing deeply, his sweat mingling with hers, his arms protectively around her. His heart was still knocking wildly, his breathing not yet slowed when he rose up on his elbows and stared down at her with tortured eyes. Swallowing hard, he brushed a strand of hair from her cheek.

For a few seconds all she heard was the sigh of the wind, the rapid drumming of her heart and the rain pelting against the roof and walls. She snuggled against him, resting her head on his shoulder.

His muscles flexed. "Oh, Jesus, what have I done?" His voice was harsh with self-loathing and he sighed bitterly.

As if seeing her for the first time, he squeezed his eyes shut. "Damn, damn, damn!" He pounded the floor with his free fist.

"Brig—?" He acted as if something was wrong, as if he was disgusted with himself. With her.

Rolling to his feet, he grabbed his jeans and glared down at her so harshly that she wanted to shrink away. "Nope," he said, disgust tainting his words as he yanked on his clothes. "I was wrong. Shooting's too good for me. I should be hung up by my balls." He kicked furiously at a split bale of hay. "Shit, what was I thinking?"

"Brig—"

"You were a virgin," he accused, as if it were a sin.

"I—of course—I never. You knew—"

"Yes, but I didn't care. Sweet Jesus! A sixteen-year-old virgin!" Throwing back his head, he stared at the rafters. "I'm just a fool, Cass. A damned fool!" Again he kicked, this time at an empty water pail, and it went reeling, noisily bouncing off the walls. Horses neighed nervously. "Hell, what a mistake!"

"Mistake?" she said, reeling, afterglow fading and humiliation burning through her brain. She found her shirt and covered herself. She needn't have bothered, because he wasn't paying her any attention. Instead he was scowling out the window, frowning fiercely at the storm outside. "You know, Cass, I didn't want this."

"You could have fooled me."

"I mean—I mean I did and I didn't."

"That makes it clear," she snapped, wounded.

"It was a mistake."

"You keep saying that," she said, anger and shame surging through her veins.

"That's because I know."

"Know what?"

His smile was cold as he whipped his shirt from the hay and stuffed his arms through the sleeves. "What kind of a mess sex can lead to."

"It was more than sex."

"That's exactly what I'm talking about. It wasn't—"

She dropped her clothes and walked up to him stark

naked. Placing a finger over his lips, she said, "Don't lie to me, Brig. I don't care whatever else you do, but don't lie."

"I'm not—"

"Bull!" She jerked her thumb toward her breastbone. "I was there, damn it. I *know* what I felt, what *you* felt." To her mortification, her voice broke.

"You have no idea. This was your first time, but it wasn't mine."

"Meaning?" She hardly dared to breathe, not sure she wanted to hear.

His voice was harsh. Relentless. "You'll have other orgasms, but I won't be the one giving them to you. This was just sex, Cass, nothing more. It'll happen with a dozen other guys—"

Her reaction was instantaneous. She drew back and slapped him. The smack ricocheted through the stable. "Never!"

"Like hell." He rubbed his cheek and she saw the pain in his eyes, believed with all her naïve heart that he was trying to be noble.

"Brig, I'm sorry. I didn't mean—"

"Of course you meant it. Just as you did before. Grow up, Cassidy," he said, striding toward the door. "But don't count on me to help you."

"It's because you love Angie, isn't it?" She felt so stupid and young—so naive.

Every muscle in his body flexed, and his spine was suddenly rigid. When he turned to face her, the lines on his face made him look ten years older. "I don't love Angie," he said through clenched teeth. "And I don't love you. I don't love anyone, and that's the way I like it."

She felt as if she was the one who'd been slapped. Her throat worked and tears burned in her eyes.

"You'll get over this," he said, though his words lacked conviction.

"I won't."

"Sure you will. And someday when you're older, you'll marry someone with the same dreams you've got—someone your parents will approve of, someone who deserves you."

"Brig—"

"I don't love you, Cassidy. So don't make me a part of your silly little fantasies. It won't work."

She watched as he walked through the door and out of her life. A part of her—that foolish little girl part—seemed to wither and die as rain splashed and gurgled in the dusty gutters and horses pawed nervously in their stalls. Cassidy felt tears burn behind her eyes and she gathered up her clothes. What had she expected? Claims of undying love? From Brig McKenzie? She was a dreamer. Remember, he was here waiting for Angie.

She heard the engine of his Harley rev loudly. Gravel spun and the gears whined to an ear-shattering pitch before he shifted and the sound disappeared in the rain.

"Good riddance," she said, though she didn't mean a word of it. If he drove back this very minute, she'd end up kissing him and making love to him again.

Making love. She'd done it. Instead of her sister, she'd seduced Brig McKenzie. That thought made her stomach turn sour. She stepped into her panties and thought about Angie. Where was she? Why had she wanted to meet with Brig? As she snapped up her cutoffs, she knew the answer. Angie had planned to seduce him again. Instead, her little sister had done the honors.

She blinked hard, buttoned her blouse and decided she couldn't think about it anymore. She loved Brig with all of her heart, but he would never love her.

However, Derrick was still on the loose. With a gun. Her insides froze.

She pulled on her shoes, grabbed Remmington's bridle and, with the colt in tow, ran out of the stable. There was a movement in the shadows near the door, and she nearly screamed just as a car's engine rumbled closer and the beams of headlights bore down on her from the drive. Like a doe caught in the glare of a pickup's headlights, she froze. A car she didn't recognize jolted to a stop and her mother, half-stumbling, climbed out of the car. "Thanks for the ride." She opened her umbrella as the car tore away, leaving her standing face-to-face with her daughter in the downpour.

"What do you think you're doing?"

She had to lie. "Just checking on Remmington."

"Hmm. 'Stha' so?" Dena was tipsy. "He looks fine to me and you're not s'pose to ride him. 'Specially not at night in the rain."

"I know, but—" She was frantic. She had to save Brig. From Jed. From Derrick. From Angie. From himself.

"Don't argue with me." Dena wagged a finger in front of Cassidy's nose. "Put that beast 'way and come on out of the rain—" She plucked a piece of straw from Cassidy's hair and her lips pursed suspiciously.

Cassidy had no choice but to do as she was bid. But her heart was jackhammering as they headed toward the house.

"Is your father home?"

"No—just Derrick, but he left." *To shoot Brig. Please, God, keep him safe.*

"Rex hasn't shown up?"

"No." Who cared about her father at a time like this? Brig was in danger!

"That lying son of a gun. You know what he did, don't you? Left me stranded at the Caldwells' party. Claimed he was going for a smoke and then took off in the car. I've never been so mortified in all my life." She shook the umbrella on the porch, walked into the foyer and nearly tripped on the bottom step. "Well, I know where he is, and believe me, he'll catch hell in the morning. And you"—she turned to look over her shoulder—"run up to bed and go to sleep. It's late."

Right. And even now Derrick could be hunting Brig down, taking aim and—

Dena's eyes slitted. "Is som'thin' wrong?" She clicked open her purse and fumbled for her keys.

Everything! Cassidy's palms were slick with sweat. "No—"

"Then go to bed." Dena dropped the keys then scooped them up. "I'll be back soon."

"Mom, you can't go now, you've had a lot to drink and—"

"And don't argue with me." Dena stiffened her back and tried to look sober.

"Where are you going?"

"To find your father."

"Why don't you just wait for him?" If Dena would just go upstairs and fall into an alcohol-deep sleep, Cassidy could sneak out of the house and take after Brig.

Dena's face was suddenly drawn. "Because I'm tired of waiting," she said with a sad smile. "I've waited for your father to do the right thing by me for a long time. I think it's time he knew it." Squaring her shoulders, she reached for the handle of the door. The keys jangled in her fingers. "Don't wait up, sweetie," she said. "I don't know when I'll be back."

"Mom, don't! You can't drive like this—"

"Get out of my way, Cassidy. You hurry upstairs and go to bed." She sidestepped her daughter as Cassidy reached for the keys. In a few seconds she was gone.

Cassidy didn't waste any time. She knew what she had to do. No matter what the consequences.

Angie walked through the open door of the old mill and smiled to herself. She'd seen his car; knew that he was waiting. So maybe the night wasn't completely lost. So things hadn't worked out with Brig . . . there was always her backup plan, though it was certainly not as solid.

"Helloooo . . ." she called, walking through the doorway, her voice echoing back at her. God, this place was creepy with its gaping, creaking roof and cobwebs and . . . and . . . the mess on the floor that looked like a bunch of feathers and crap from birds that had been nesting in the rafters.

She should have brought a flashlight. Or something.

Goose bumps rose on her flesh even though she was sweating; the temperature in this old mill was probably still well over eighty degrees.

"Hey . . . it's me. Are you here?" she said and then she saw him, lounging against the back wall, a dark figure in a dusky, cavernous room. She felt a second's relief before he moved toward her.

BAM!!

An explosion ripped through the old timbers.

Screaming, Angie flew backward and was thrown face-down on the floor.

Crack! The back of her head collided with ancient, dusty floorboards. For a second the world spun and went black. She blinked hard, roused herself. She couldn't pass out. Not in the middle of this . . . this . . . Oh, God, what was this? She struggled to her feet when she smelled the smoke and turned to find eager, hungry flames climbing up the walls, already blocking the main door and charring the old tinder-dry rafters.

"No!" she cried, scrambling backward, away from the black, lung-clogging smoke and wall of fire. She lost a shoe. Didn't care. She had to get out. *Now!* There were doors in the back of the building; she was sure of it.

Then she remembered. She wasn't alone. He could help. He'd save them. Whimpering, tears of fear streaming down her face, she ran to the spot where she'd seen him and found him lying crumpled on the floor.

"Come on, we have to get out of here," she cried, her voice shaking, panic gripping her in a stranglehold. "Hurry!"

He lay as he had been, not looking up at her.

"Please . . . ooohhh . . ." she whimpered, biting her lip. "You have to be all right. We have to get out of here. There isn't much time." She looked over her shoulder and saw the terrifying spectacle. Crackling, cruel flames devouring everything in sight.

Bending on one knee, smoke curling around her, she reached for him. "Hey!" she cried, but still he didn't move. She touched his shoulder, rolled him over, and fell backward screaming as she saw his face, a mangled, bloody mess, as if he'd been beaten to a pulp. Blood pooled on the floor, and she saw spatters against the wall where the blast had thrown him. Sightless open eyes stared blankly.

Gasping, coughing, she knew she had to leave him. She had no choice but to save herself. To save the baby.

Her lungs were on fire as she made her way toward the back rooms, where the trapped smoke had collected. She ripped off part of her dress, held it over her nose and mouth, remembered prayers she'd thought she'd long forgotten as she eased through the blackness, bumping into poles, her eyes burning, blinded by the smoke.

There had to be another way out of here. Had to! Oh, God, why had she agreed to meet him here? Why? It was foolish.

Think, Angie, think . . . you don't have time for this.

Frantically she rushed to the back room and tried to ignore the heat that radiated as if from a blast furnace. Coughing, gasping, stumbling, she moved deeper into the building, through smaller rooms that had once been offices . . . Where were the damned windows!

She saw none and she was panting now, terrified beyond belief. Surely she would get out. She *had* to. For herself. For the baby.

She smelled a new odor . . . burning flesh . . . and she threw up as she flashed back to the crumpled man on the floor. Sweet Jesus, the flames had reached him. He was being cremated in this burning hell.

Where was the damned door!

Then she saw it. Through the smoke . . . a change in the wall. Thank God! She threw herself at the old panels, found the knob. Her fingers burned as she turned the brass fixture and she yanked with all her might.

Nothing happened.

She tried again, threw all her weight into pulling the damned thing open.

It didn't budge.

Oh, no!

"Help!" she cried, coughing, banging on the door, hearing the first sounds of sirens in the air. "Help me! Now!" Her voice was pitiful against the roar of the flames, a scratchy, raw whimper.

She was coughing now, hacking and fighting to drag in air. She couldn't be dying. Not now. She was so young. Crying, screaming, pounding on the door, she prayed that someone would hear her . . . someone would save her . . .

Her knees buckled.

She had no air.

The heat was so intense she had to fight to keep from blacking out . . . she lifted a fist. Pounded again and noticed the flames, licking across the floor, creeping around her, circling that little spot where she stood.

"No!" she screamed, clutching her abdomen as she struggled for a last, searing breath and realized with horrifying certainty that she was going to die.

Seventeen

I pulled my gloves off with my teeth, rammed the truck into gear and tromped on the accelerator. The tires chirped and I eased off.

Don't speed. Whatever you do, you can't risk a ticket, can't be caught anywhere near the old gristmill.

I checked my watch and swallowed hard. Any second now, I thought, adrenaline shooting through my veins. I wanted to drive by the mill, to check and see if Angie had arrived or if only her lover would die tonight.

Don't do it. You'll ruin everything you've worked for!

I caught my reflection in the rearview mirror and saw the flush of excitement on my features. What a rush!

My hands sweated over the wheel and my heartbeat thundered in my head. I eased into the traffic heading out of town and checked my mirrors for any signs of the police or people I knew . . . so far nothing. All I had to do was drive to an out-of-the-way spot by the river, change my clothes and . . .

Boom!

An explosion shook the ground.

I glanced in the mirror again, saw nothing for a second and then a spray of fire that lit up the night sky like a torch.

Yes!

A thrill swept through me . . . the man who'd shown up at the mill deserved to die. What a fool! And Angie, if she didn't get it tonight . . . it would only be a matter of time.

I heard the sound of a siren . . . and then another . . . all heading away from me.

Just as I'd planned.

Blinking against the rain, Rex laid a single white rose on Lucretia's grave. Tears stung his eyes and he realized belatedly that he'd had too much to drink. He'd have to be careful. There were always problems when he drank too much.

Staring at the headstone, he bit his trembling lower lip. *I love you,* he thought, though he didn't say the words. *I've always loved you.* But he hadn't been faithful to her; not even when she was still alive, and he knew deep in the darkest recesses of his heart that she killed herself because of his infidelities. Lucretia had a code of honor, and though she hadn't wanted him in her bed, she had hated it when he'd turned to other women, most of whom didn't mean anything to him.

Except one.

And now this . . . this torment of seeing Angie every day, watching her blossom into a woman so like her mother physically that it was uncanny. Sometimes when she walked into the room, his breath got lost in his throat and he was certain he was seeing his wife, or the ghost of his dead wife in their daughter. It was those painful times when the years rolled backward and he forgot that she was his own flesh-and-blood, when truth and fantasy blurred, and he wanted—damn it he wanted—her to be his beloved wife.

"Forgive me," he whispered, as he always did when he laid the rose on Lucretia's grave. "I did you a great dishonor and I swear I'll never let it happen again."

Clearing his throat, he headed back to his car. He'd left Dena at the party, though she thought he'd only gone out to walk and to smoke one of his cigars. No doubt she'd lose track of time. He checked his watch, climbed into the Lincoln and eased through the open gates of the cemetery.

* * *

Bang!

An explosion rocked the earth. Sunny felt it beneath her bare feet and fear caused her insides to congeal. Rain pooled in the driveway, stirring the dust when she saw the first sparks. In the dark cloud-covered sky over Prosperity, embers shot like missiles into the night, bright fingers of light clawing ever upward, reaching to the heavens.

Rain and flames. *Fire and water.* She collapsed against the side of the trailer. Brig. Chase. Buddy. They were all going to die . . . she knew it. Her heart pounded and she began to shake. Oh, God, no! Quivering, she knew without a doubt that the horrifying visions that had disturbed her sleep for the past few months had arrived. The end of her world was upon her.

She didn't bother with slippers or a coat, just ran through the rain to her car and climbed inside. Maybe it wasn't too late! Maybe she could save at least one of her boys.

"Help me," she prayed, slamming the old Cadillac into reverse. "Help me, God."

But she knew he wouldn't hear. He'd turned a deaf ear to her pleas all her life. As she backed the car from its lean-to the beams of her headlights cut through a curtain of rain and washed the old trailer in stark illumination. She saw the sign over the door swinging in the wind, mocking her with its faded letters: PALM READING. TAROT CARDS. FORTUNE TELLING. Deep in her mind, she heard laughter and screams and wished that she could give up her own life to save her boys.

"Take me," she prayed desperately as she turned the ancient Caddy around. "Take me or someone else, but please, God, spare my sons!"

Boom!

Cassidy was on her way to the stable when she heard the distant explosion, loud enough to cause her heart to kick, but she couldn't worry about it now; not when she had to find

Brig. She'd given Dena a twenty-minutes head start and was almost to the stable when she heard the first distant wail of emergency vehicles. Far away, the sirens screamed mournfully, alarms shrieking and bleating through the night.

Cassidy's heart stood still.

Brig!

Derrick had caught up with him!

Even now, Brig could be lying, bleeding, *dying* because of her brother. Because she hadn't made him listen to her, because she hadn't saved him. "Please, God, no," she whispered, yanking on Remmington's bridle and leading him from his stall. The sirens were still shrieking when she entered the paddock, and the colt, already pulling on the reins, sidestepped.

"I don't have time for this," she warned, running to the fence where she could climb onto his bare back. Rain ran down her face as she yanked on the reins and threw herself astride his broad back. He bucked, tossing her off as easily as a limp rag. The bare earth rushed up at her. She shoved out her arms to break her fall. *Snap!* Pain exploded up her arm. Her head and shoulder slammed against the hard ground.

With a groan, she tried to move, to clear her head, but the fire in her wrist made her immobile for a second. Sucking in her breath, she forced herself to a sitting position.

Remmington galloped to the far end of the paddock, snorting and kicking and whinnying nervously. That's when she smelled it, just a little hint at first, but a scent so strong and deadly it caused her to panic. The acrid odor of smoke tinged the fresh scent of rain. She closed her eyes for a second. No one was smoking, it was the middle of the night and—

Fire!

Head throbbing, she wrenched her neck to stare at the house, but no one was home, no one would have started a fire in the grate in these last hot days of summer. But the smoke lingered in the air, like mirthless laughter. Staggering to her feet, she checked each of the outbuildings, searching for any hint of sparks or smoke or flames. None.

Pain shot up the back of her hand as she leaned against the fence. Her breath whistled through her teeth and the taste of charred wood touched her tongue.

Somewhere—somewhere nearby—something was burning. Fear began to coil in her gut. She couldn't climb on Remmington without first binding her wrist, so she made her way out of the paddock and, holding the pained arm carefully, trudged up the hill. The house had never seemed so far from the stable. But she couldn't give up. Somewhere Brig was out there and he had to be warned . . .

At the porch she stopped, turning back to survey the vast acres owned by her father. From her vantage point on the hill, she looked over the tops of fir trees to the orange glow of the town. Her heart kicked as she saw flames, a great wall of flames spewing sparks high into the air.

Brig! No. Oh, please, God, no!

Though her mind screamed to deny it, she knew that he was in danger—more danger than she'd first imagined. Maybe hurt. There could have been an accident near a gas station, or a blast from Derrick's shotgun might have hit something flammable—like Brig's motorcycle or a parked car or . . . *oh God, oh God, oh God!*

Without realizing what she was doing, she ran back to the paddock. The pain in her arm seemed to disappear as fear—horrible, gut-jelling fear—numbed her mind and body. Racing to the stable, she tried to erase all images of Brig from her mind. She wouldn't think of him lying injured, unconscious, flames crackling near his face . . . oh, Lord. She sent up prayer after prayer as she dashed, stumbling, crying, always moving toward the stable.

Run! Run! Run!

Inside, horses snorted and stamped nervously. She scooped up a handful of oats with her good hand and ran outside, blinking against the rain, forcing the gate open and shutting it with her rump. "I don't have time for any of your crap," she said, stalking the colt who seemed determined to escape her.

"Not now," she warned him. "For God's sake, Remmington, not now!" She held out her treat—oats slipping through her fingers washed by the rain. "Come on, Remmington. For God's sake, just calm down. I won't hurt you. I need you!" The wayward horse, after a worried flick of his ears, stepped timidly forward. Cassidy was ready. The colt reached for the oats, his soft lips brushing her palm, and she didn't wait. As fast as lightning striking, she grabbed the reins, kicked open the gate, climbed onto his rain-slickened back and wound her fingers in his mane.

"Let's go!" she shouted, giving him his head. He tore off down the lane, slinging mud, splashing through puddles and racing as if the very devil himself were on his tail.

"Stand back! Jesus Christ, what do you think you're doing here? People, stand the hell back!"

The fire chief was way beyond irritated. He yelled loudly, over the crackle of hideous flames, over the rush of gallons of water being pumped through huge hoses to arc over the blackened shell of the old gristmill. Black smoke rose in huge, billowing clouds and heat seared through the crowd.

Cassidy stared at the terrible conflagration in disbelief. She prayed no one was inside because no one would survive.

People coughed, men yelled, news reporters pushed closer and the fire raged despite efforts of the volunteer fire department. Choking smoke clogged the air, and flames rose hellishly from the charred beams and crumpled tin roof. Like the mouth of hell, the fire grew before the wind finally turned. Only then did the wall of water being pumped from huge hoses overcome the flaming beast that roared and crackled.

Standing next to people she didn't know, Cassidy watched in impotent horror as the firemen relentlessly sent the fire into its hissing death throes.

Brig! Please do not let Brig be trapped inside!

She'd tied Remmington to a post that supported the upper balcony of an apartment building owned by her father, then had run through the throng of people pushing toward the terrifying inferno. Her heart thumped wildly, fear constricting her chest. But it was only the old gristmill—it wasn't Brig's motorcycle or her mother's car, or Derrick's gun or anyone she knew. Just an empty shell of an old mill. Yes, her father owned the historic building that had been scheduled for renovation, yet Cassidy was relieved that it was a vacant structure that had burned. She stood in a crowd of onlookers—townspeople who, in hastily donned jeans or bathrobes, had come from their houses to help or just watch the incredible inferno.

Reporters and television crews shouldered their way to the front of the barricade, braving the downpour while blue, red and white lights of emergency vehicles strobed in the night.

"Chief Lents—what do you think started the fire?" a reporter yelled above the noise of the firemen and crowd.

"Too early to tell." His face was smudged and dirty, his yellow rubber coat slick from the rain.

"Arson?" another reporter asked.

"I just told you it's too early to tell. Now back off." He turned, yelling at one of his men. "Garrison, move that pickup out of the way. Get the number four truck closer—"

"Anyone in the building?" A female reporter asked.

"Not that we know. We couldn't get in before. Hell, that old tinderbox went up like a book of matches. But we're checking now."

"What caused the explosion?"

The chief's attention wasn't on the reporter. "I said move that damned pickup!" he barked. "Holy Christ, this ain't a picnic!"

Another fireman talked to the owner of the truck blocking an alley, and slowly the pickup backed up through the crowd.

"Does Rex Buchanan know that his building went up in flames?"

"We've gotten word to him."

Someone near Cassidy snorted an envious little laugh. "I

bet they found him three sheets to the wind at Judge Caldwell's place."

Cassidy took a step backward, so that the two men couldn't see her face.

"One building more or less isn't going to matter to him," a shorter man said.

"What does he care anyway? He owns half the town already, and this old building is probably worth more in insurance money."

Someone near the first man, a woman in a faded chenille bathrobe with curlers lodged in her hair, nodded sagely. "If there's a way to turn a buck on this, Rex Buchanan will find it."

Cassidy inched her way from the gossips, shouldering her way between people, but she continued to stare at the building, now reduced to smoldering rubble that steamed angrily in the rain.

Three monstrous hoses still sprayed the black remains and ashes.

One reporter pushed forward, nearly tripping over Cassidy. "Say, Chief, you mind if we get a little closer—"

"Listen, if you'd just back up, I'll have a full statement for you in a couple of hours. But now, just let us get our job done here, okay?"

Two firefighters kicked in the charred door and stepped into what was left of the blackened interior.

"God, what a mess," the chief said, tossing his cigarette into a puddle. "We're lucky it started raining and the wind turned."

A reporter scribbled and said something into his tape recorder. Onlookers shifted, but didn't leave, still talking to neighbors and fascinated by the now-dead inferno.

"Hey!" One of the firemen was yelling from inside the blackened building. His voice was harsh. Studded with disbelief. "Hey—we're gonna need some help in here!"

"Oh, hell—" The chief headed toward the door. "Blackman and Peters, you two go find out what's going on—"

"Christ, did I ask for some help? Pronto! Get the EMTs and an ambulance!"

No!

All eyes turned to him, and Cassidy nearly screamed as the fireman appeared carrying a blackened body. Her stomach turned over and she had to fight the bile that rose in her throat.

"Holy shit—" someone whispered. "Get the paramedics. Now!"

Cassidy trembled all over. An ambulance and all the paramedics in the world wouldn't help. "No!" she cried, a cacophony of noise roaring in her ears. "God, no!" The woman was dead, unrecognizable, her skin burned to the color of coal, and yet Cassidy knew, without a second's doubt, that she was staring into the sightless, dead eyes of her half sister. *Angie! Oh, no!*

"Hey, we got another one!"

Cassidy's knees buckled and she turned away, refusing to look.

"It's a man!"

Her throat swollen, tears burning her eyes, she ran, faster and faster, her feet slipping on the wet pavement, her vision blurred. Choking sobs burned her throat and people stopped to stare at her, but she didn't care, couldn't think, wouldn't believe that she'd not only lost her sister, but Brig as well.

"Please, God, no! Don't let him be dead, too. And Angie . . . Oh, Angie!" She wanted to fling herself down on the wet street and pound her fist on the ground and rail at God for this horror. She wanted to roll into a ball and cry and cry until she had no more tears. She wanted to scream and rant, to hit anything and everything, and still she ran, rounding the corner to spy Remmington, still tied to the post, his eyes wide with fear as he tossed his head and snorted, pawing at the street and pulling back against his tether. "Shhh . . . it's okay," she said, then heard her own lies. "Oh . . . no . . . no . . ." she whispered, untying the reins, her fingers fumbling, her mind whirling in painful circles—memories of growing up with Angie, how she'd looked up to her sister and been jealous of her.

And Brig . . . she could still feel his skin against hers, the taste of his mouth on her lips, the way he'd felt as he'd come to her.

And then he'd been with Angie. She was sobbing now, throwing herself upon Remmington's powerful back, letting the rain wash the tears down her face. She had to get away. From the town. From the fire. From the truth.

In furious agony, tears running from her eyes, she dug her heels into the colt's sweaty sides, held on for all she was worth and sent the horse racing blindly through the night.

Eighteen

"Where've you been?" Dena's voice was filled with accusations when Cassidy, filthy and wet, made her way into the house.

"Out riding," she said, then noticed the pasty pallor of her mother's face. Instead of the lecture she'd been expecting, Dena grabbed her daughter and began to sob. Mindless of the fact that she was ruining her silk dress, she held Cassidy's grimy body close.

"Thank God you're safe. There was a fire—"

"I know."

Dena clung to her. "Two bodies were discovered."

Cassidy closed her eyes, refused to think of the charred remains that the fireman had carried from the gristmill. *Angie and Brig. Please, don't let it be.*

"They haven't identified them yet—a man and a woman, but Angie's missing and Derrick, and oh, my God, Cassidy, if they're dead, I don't know what we'll do, what Rex will do."

"Angie?" she repeated, her heart icy with dread though she knew the truth. How she'd gotten back to the house she didn't remember. She'd given the horse his head and he'd turned homeward, but the ride passed without her knowing where she was, what she was doing. All at once she'd ended up in the lane . . . She didn't even remember dismounting . . . Oh, God, please, please, no . . .

"Angie's car was parked just two blocks away," Dena said brokenly.

"No." Cassidy shook her head and started stepping backward, trying to shake the horrid image from her mind, denying what her own eyes had seen. "It's not Angie. It's not." She was shaking, her teeth chattering, fear clutching her heart in its terrifying grip. If she said it over and over again, if she could convince herself that Angie was alive, then maybe she'd wake up from this agonizing nightmare and—

"I hope you're right." Dena shoved trembling fingers through her hair. "Your father, he's with the police right now and . . . Derrick—" Dena's voice cracked and she blinked against tears. Mascara ran down her face, trailing black lines across the hills of her cheeks.

Cassidy remembered her brother's face, twisted in rage, hatred gleaming in his eyes, a deadly weapon in his hands. Out for blood. "I can't . . ." Cassidy's voice barely worked. "I won't believe it. Derrick and Angie. They'll come home. They have to." *And Brig. He has to be alive. They all have to be alive.*

Dena let out a pitiful little moan. "Oh, baby, I wish."

"They're all right!" Cassidy nearly screamed, refusing to believe the horror she'd witnessed with her very own eyes. But Brig's words haunted her. He'd been looking for Angie tonight; she'd wanted to meet with him even though they'd been together at the Caldwells' barbecue.

"Just pray it isn't true." Dena sniffed, her shattered composure slowly disappearing. "I'm just thankful you're alive. So thankful. Now, come on in and . . . clean up. I'll make some tea and coffee and cocoa, or maybe you should just go to bed . . . Oh, God, where's Rex? He's been gone for over an hour, and it really shouldn't take that long with the police." She began crying again, muttering something about this being her fault. Cassidy, fear congealing her insides, led her mother to the stairs. "I need a cigarette." Dena searched the hallway for her purse.

At that moment beams from headlights splashed through the windows and Cassidy saw cars, three of them, rolling down the lane—looking for all the world like a funeral procession. This was it. Cassidy's throat burned, the stench of smoke still clung to her and she began to shake violently. A police car was first, followed by Rex Buchanan's Lincoln and Judge Caldwell's Mercedes.

Stomach churning, Cassidy opened the door and walked on numb legs to the front porch. Dena clutched her arm. "Oh, God, no. Please, no," Dena whispered.

Cassidy watched in despair as her father climbed unsteadily from the passenger side of his car. His face was ashen, his hair matted by the rain, and the stoop of his broad shoulders foretold the pain in his heart.

Dena let out a mewl of protest.

Bile rose in Cassidy's throat, and she barely felt pain when her mother gripped her injured wrist fiercely.

With The Judge and Sheriff Dodds as support, Rex walked slowly to the front door. Before he could say a word, Derrick's truck screamed down the lane, squealing to a stop in the yard. Derrick hurled himself from the cab. Nostrils flared in outrage, wet hair plastered to his head, he strode toward the house.

"I'll break his fuckin' neck!" He was still carrying his shotgun and his shirt was ripped, his hands and arms black with soot, his eyes slitted in pure hatred. "I swear to God I'll kill him!"

"What—?" Dena asked her husband. "Not Angie—"

Rex's eyes squeezed together so tightly that he swayed and Cassidy was certain he would pass out.

"No, Dad, it can't be," she said, not wanting to hear, refusing to believe the death she saw in her father's eyes, unable to accept what she, herself had witnessed. "No—"

"Go upstairs, Cassidy," he said.

"But Angie—"

Tears pooled in her father's eyes. "She's with her mother now."

Derrick let out an agonized howl of disbelief. In his pain, he aimed his shotgun at the cloud-blotted moon. *Crack!* The gun went off. Buckshot sprayed the yard.

"Drop it, son," The Judge insisted, crossing the lawn swiftly, his hand extended toward the weapon.

"Leave me alone!"

"Derrick," his father reprimanded, his voice barely audible over the wind. "Come inside."

"Like hell! She's dead, Dad, *dead* and that McKenzie bastard killed her!"

"Stop it, son. Do as your father says," The Judge insisted.

Again the shotgun blasted, firing buckshot to the heavens. Derrick dropped to his knees and began to sob brokenly.

Cassidy couldn't move, couldn't speak.

Dena wrapped her arms around her husband, holding him close, as if afraid he might disintegrate. "It's all right," she whispered aimlessly. "Somehow it'll be all right and we'll get through this."

Rex Buchanan staggered and his wife helped him up. The Judge managed to convince Derrick to come into the house, and the sheriff, a big man with red hair and a bulbous nose, looked stern.

"Can't you come back later?" The Judge asked as they all settled into the den.

"Sorry. This has got to be taken care of."

"But Doc Williams is coming by and he'll probably give Rex a sedative . . ."

"Then we'd best get this over with. Look, Judge, I know you're just trying to be kind, but I got a job to do. Three people are dead, if you count the baby and—"

"Baby?" Dena's head snapped up.

"That's right, Mrs. Buchanan. The coroner's report is preliminary, of course, but it looks like your stepdaughter was a couple of months pregnant."

"No—"

Rex fell into his favorite recliner and buried his face in his hands. "Angie," he whispered, over and over again. "Angie, Angie. My baby."

Cassidy leaned heavily against the doorjamb. Her knees felt like water, and she had the urge to throw up at the thought of Angie being dead, never laughing again, never flirting outrageously, never commenting on Cassidy's sorry taste in clothing, never pleading with her to braid her hair . . . Tears tracked silently down her cheeks. Angie had been pregnant; no wonder she'd seemed so depressed at times. Nausea roiled up from Cassidy's stomach. No one needed to tell her who the baby's father was. It had to be Brig, just as he had to be the man with her at the time of the fire.

No! her mind screamed, and she bit her tongue not to let out the sound.

"We're not certain who the man with her was, but we've got a couple of leads. Bobby Alonzo and Jed Baker are missing, as is Brig McKenzie."

Cassidy's heart jolted.

"McKenzie?" Dena repeated.

"Yeah, his bike's down there, parked near to Angie's car."

"No!" Cassidy shouted, and every eye in the room turned on her.

"Why not?" the sheriff asked.

"Because . . . because . . . he was here earlier and he couldn't have had time to get to the mill and . . ."

"What the fuck was he doing here?" Derrick yelled. He stormed across the room to tower over Cassidy. "What?"

"He—he was looking for Angie."

"That goddamned prick."

"Stop it!" the sheriff commanded. "Then he couldn't have got to the mill in time."

"I don't think so," she said, hardly daring to breathe, hoping beyond hope that she was right, that he wasn't dead, that he and Angie hadn't been in that horrid inferno.

"It's all crap—a pile of smelly, disgusting crap!" Derrick said, striding to the bar and wiping his eyes with the back of his hand. Grime and soot covered him from head to foot. "I shoulda killed him when I had the chance."

"Derrick!" Rex's raspy voice commanded everyone's attention. "I don't want to hear any nonsense."

"Chances are he's dead already," Sheriff Dodds said. "His mother was down there chanting and crying and carrying on, claiming that she saw this fire in some sort of vision. You know how it is with her—half the time I'm not certain that she shouldn't be locked up. Anyways, I had someone take her to see Doc Ramsby. He opened the clinic and will probably give her a tranquilizer or something. Her other boy—Chase—he's with her. The Alonzos and the Bakers are out of their minds with worry."

Derrick swore loudly at the sheriff, "Listen, you stupid bastard! You don't understand. He killed her! He had to have! I saw Jed earlier and he was out for blood. McKenzie had already beat him senseless with a baseball bat. He's your man, Sheriff, and if you let him slip through your fingers, everyone in town will know it."

"Sunny's boy wouldn't hurt Angie—" Rex's voice was broken and lacked any ounce of conviction.

"He won't slip through," the sheriff said, but he didn't look pleased as Derrick's words settled into his mind. "I've already sent a car to the McKenzie place and I've got men posted on all the roads leading out of town."

"So you do suspect him?"

"I don't know what to think, that's all. Until this is all straightened out, everyone's a suspect. Even you." His eyes narrowed on Derrick.

"Fine. 'Cause the truth will come out, and when it does, I hope McKenzie hangs by his fuckin' balls."

Dena cringed at the foul language.

Cassidy couldn't stand it anymore. The house seemed to close in on her. She eased away from the hallway, where no one was paying any attention to her anyway, and staggered out the back door. At the bottom of the steps, she couldn't help herself. She leaned over, retching over and over again, pain throbbing at her temples, denial screaming through her mind.

She wiped her arm over her mouth and ran to the stable, where she always sought refuge. She'd climb on Remmington's back and ride and ride and ride until she could go no farther, until all the pain in her heart would somehow drain away.

Inside the barn, she stumbled, tears blurring her vision, her legs too weak to support her. Her arm had begun to ache, but she didn't care, the pain in her heart far greater than her wrist. Yanking down the bridle, she reached for the gate.

"Cassidy?"

"Brig?" Had she imagined his voice, conjured it up from her disbelieving subconscious. Was she going crazy? "Brig?"

"Shh. I'm here." Suddenly he was beside her, his strong arms drawing her close, his face, smelling of ashes and smoke, pressed against hers.

"You're alive," she said, the words barely audible. Tears fell from her eyes. He was safe. *Safe!* "But how—" It didn't matter. She clung to him, her fingers digging deep into his flesh, her lips moving urgently over his rain-soaked face. "I thought. Oh, God, I thought . . ." Then she was sobbing. Deep soul-jarring sobs tore through her.

Folding her into his arms, he buried his face against her neck. His sinewy muscles surrounded her, and for a second she thought that everything would be all right. Then the weight, the horrible weight of the truth, fell down on her again. "You . . . you have to leave," she said. "Angie's dead."

He stiffened. "I know."

"And someone died with her."

"Baker."

"How—?" She swallowed hard and drew away from him. Soot smudged his bruised face, smoke clung to him. "How do you know?"

"I was there. I saw their cars. But I was too late to save them."

She gave a strangled sound of protest.

"It was like being in hell," he said, his voice distant.

"They'll try to say you did it—" She touched the scrape above his eye, tried to ignore the doubts swirling through her mind.

"I didn't."

Fear pounded an alarm through her brain. As soon as they found out that Jed was the boy with Angie, as soon as the sheriff checked out Derrick's story that Jed and Brig had al-

ready had a fight . . . her mind raced to the inevitable con-
clusion.

"Did anyone see you there?"

He stared into the darkness, and his hands flexed in the
folds of her blouse. She felt her body respond and knew that
she would believe anything he told her.

"I didn't see anyone."

"You've got to leave." She forced the words over her
tongue and felt as if she was dying inside because she knew
if he left he would never return. She'd never see him again—
the love she felt for him would slowly die.

"I'm not running from—"

"You have to," she cried, desperate to save him. "But
don't take your bike—they've already found it." Her mind
was galloping ahead with the only plan feasible. "Take
Remmington. I'll say that I was out riding and he threw me
again and took off. By the time they have it figured that he's
missing, you'll be gone—"

A muscle worked in his jaw. "Don't lie for me."

Tears clogged her throat. This really was good-bye.
"I'll—I'll have to. Otherwise you'll go to jail—"

"You don't know that." But the defeat in his eyes told her
she'd already guessed the truth. Unless . . . unless . . .

"I didn't set that fire, Cassidy. I don't care what the whole
damned town believes, but I have to know that you trust me."

"I—I do," she swore, staring up at him with naïve, believing eyes. "Don't you know that? I'll always believe in you."

A groan ripped from his throat, and he yanked her closer
still. "I don't deserve you." His lips claimed hers in a kiss
that was as desperate as it was brutal.

"I can't do this," he admitted, his voice rough. "The sheriff's here. I'll talk to him. Tell him the truth—"

"No! Brig, you don't understand. They've already nailed
you to the cross. I was there; I heard him. Derrick's told
them about your fight with Jed, and they know you were
there. The sheriff needs to hang this on someone . . ." Tears
slid down her cheeks, his or hers she couldn't tell, and she

felt his long, smudged fingers tangle in her hair. "Please, do this. Save yourself. What good would it do to stick around for the rest of your life in jail?"

"You don't believe in justice?"

"In Prosperity? When Rex Buchanan's daughter and the Bakers' son was killed? What do you think?"

"I've never believed in the system."

"Then go." She wrenched herself away. Her heart was pounding in dread, and she couldn't lift the saddle over Remmington's back. But Brig helped her, and within seconds she was handing Brig the wet reins. His fingers twined over hers for a heartbeat, and she fought a losing battle with hot tears.

"Take me with you," she whispered, and she felt him stiffen. "Just to the south edge of the property, then head east through the mountains. I—I'll make it look like I fell there."

"Forget it."

"Brig, please—do this. For me."

His jaw clamped tight, but he helped her onto the horse and swung up behind her. In silence, through the sheeting rain, they rode through the fields where the air was still thick with the smell of smoke and dawn would appear within the hour. With each stride of the colt's long legs, Cassidy knew she was closer to never seeing Brig again. She felt his arms around her and wished he'd never let go. Finally they had reached the far end of a field.

"Stop here," she said. Brig pulled Remmington to a halt. "This is it . . . Here," she said, twisting in the saddle and slipping her chain over her head before placing it around Brig's neck. "For luck."

He hesitated, then swept her into his arms one last time, his head bent to the crook of her neck, his hard body trembling. "This is wrong."

"It's all we can do." She kissed him, ignoring the painful tug on her heart. She slid to the ground to stare up at him astride the horse he'd tried to tame. Then she reached down, picked up a rock and flung it at Remmington's rump. The colt squealed and took off at a dead run into the mist-shrouded hills.

"I love you," she whispered, realizing that she'd never see him again, never hear his laugh, never look into his eyes, but her words were drowned by the steady drip of the rain and the echo of fading hoofbeats.

Nineteen

Seated on the window ledge of her father's den, Cassidy wanted to scream that Sheriff Dodds's theory was lies—all lies, concocted by people who wanted to see someone, *anyone,* convicted of the crimes. Especially if his name was McKenzie. It had been only a few days since the fire, but Brig McKenzie, the missing town hellion, had been all but tried and convicted.

Dodds filled an overstuffed chair, alternately studying Rex's silent daughter and looking through the door to the gun room at the rifle cabinet with the smashed glass front. He smoothed his big hands over knees of pants that were already shiny.

Her father sat listlessly behind his desk, a cigar burning forgotten in the ashtray.

"The way I got it figured, McKenzie wouldn't have run unless he was guilty as sin. Looks as though it's just like your boy Derrick said. Jed Baker and McKenzie were at blows over Angie; they'd already had a knock-down, drag-out fight at the McKenzie trailer in front of Sunny. My guess is the Baker boy prob'ly whopped the tar out of McKenzie with his bat; that boy never did play fair. Anyway, he left McKenzie hurtin', and once that boy got on his feet again, he tore out after Jed."

"Cassidy said Brig was here looking for Angie," her father said without much interest. Nothing interested him much the past few days, and he'd been walking around as if in a fog, a haze of medication keeping him sane.

"Maybe he did and maybe he didn't."

"Cassidy doesn't lie." Her father cast her a quick glance as she sat at the window, staring outside to the sun-bleached hills that shimmered with the afternoon heat.

"I know, but young girls, sometimes they take a notion, make things a little better than they were. The way I hear it, Cassidy might have been sweet on the McKenzie boy, too."

"That's ridiculous." But her father's voice didn't have any of his old fight in it.

Cassidy sensed the sheriff's suspicious gaze boring into her back.

"They danced at the Caldwell barbecue."

Cassidy didn't say anything, afraid that if she began to speak, her lies would quickly unravel. If the truth ever came out, the law might find Brig and convict him. The gossip spreading like wildfire was that Brig was guilty of arson and double murder. As to the father of Angie's baby, everyone seemed to have their own suspicions but Brig McKenzie was at the top of the list.

Rex sighed. "I danced with Geraldine Caldwell. That doesn't make me—how did you phrase its—*sweet* on her."

Cassidy cast a look over her shoulder.

The sheriff had the decency to blush. "You're not a teenage girl all full of romantic notions now, are ya?" He motioned with his hands, as if frantically pushing all of Rex's arguments aside. "Doesn't matter anyway. Whether McKenzie stopped by here or not, he ended up in town lookin' for Angie or Jed or both of 'em. He probably found Jed's Corvette and tracked him to the mill, where Jed had planned to meet Angie. We all know how crazy he was about her. McKenzie must've jumped Baker, broke a couple of his ribs then knocked him out before setting fire to the building."

"He wouldn't have killed Angie," Rex said dully. "And Sunny said the fight took place at her house—that Jed had a baseball bat and used it."

Dodds nodded. "Well maybe, but the way I figure it, McKenzie probably didn't know she was there. Or"—the sheriff's eyes slitted—"maybe he did know. Maybe he heard some discussion about the baby. He'd been seen with Angie himself and the thought that she was sleeping around on him—"

Rex's fist thumped against the arm of his chair. "She did not sleep around!" His voice was strained with the same quiet authority few dared to cross. "Whoever's baby she was carrying, she loved him very much!"

"Coulda been McKenzie's."

From the corner of her eye, Cassidy watched her father's face contort in rage. Blind, dark rage. "Watch your step," he warned. "We're talking about my daughter."

"Who happened to be pregnant."

Cassidy's stomach cramped painfully. The baby. Angie's baby. *Brig's* baby. Her hands began to shake, and she laced her fingers together. She wanted to run from the room, away from the discussion, but she couldn't—she had to find out anything she could about Brig.

Dodds backed off a little. "Okay, okay. Anyway, let's just say McKenzie didn't even mean to do it. He smokes and could have carelessly dropped a match and that old mill— criminey, it had to have been a hundred years old—"

"A hundred and twenty."

"Yeah, well, it was a damned tinderbox and caught fire quick as a spark to gasoline. But the fire department has found a device and it looks like gas or kerosene was used. We're still figuring it out. Maybe McKenzie planned to torch the place. Didn't know Angie would show up."

"I don't know—"

"Well, Rex, he didn't much like you, did he? Didn't you nearly fire him here a few weeks ago?"

Picking up his cigar, Rex admitted, "He'd been fighting with Derrick."

"There ya go. Probably didn't mind that he was burning down a historic sight, because he had a bone to pick with you."

"I think maybe the fight was Derrick's fault."

"But you can't fire your own son now, can you? And

come on, Rex, be truthful, you didn't like the way McKenzie was hangin' around your daughter."

Her father just drew on his cigar, blew smoke to the ceiling and watched the ash turn white.

"My guess is that he took off on foot or stole that horse of yours—the one that's missing—to avoid the roadblocks."

"It's my daughter's horse," Rex said, lifting his eyes to Cassidy. Blushing slightly, she turned away from him to stare out the window again. It was hot outside—the storm drying up the day after the fire. Flies collected in the windows and all the puddles from the cloudburst had disappeared, leaving hornets to hover over the drying mud.

Angie and Jed, after autopsies, had been buried in separate ceremonies for different faiths. In Angie's case, St. John's had been packed, people flowing down the steps, citizens lining up to show their sympathy and offer their condolences. The house was still filled with flowers despite Rex's plea that money be given in Angie's name to St. Therese's Girls' School in Portland. Fragrant floral arrangements filled every nook and corner of the big house. People continued to show up each day bringing food and cards and teary eyes. Everyone in town was welcomed into the grieving Buchanan home.

Everyone but Sunny McKenzie. Dressed in some kind of Native American garb and speaking incoherently, she had been turned away at the door and told politely but firmly that her company wasn't wanted. Ever. Cassidy had seen her from an upstairs window and had raced outside only to watch the wide rear end of her Cadillac roll away.

Heartsick, Cassidy had walked back into the house and tried not to notice that in the foyer of the great house, between the sprays of roses, carnations, lilies and chrysanthemums, was a long polished table, topped with nearly a hundred votive candles, their flames burning bright beneath a huge picture of Angie, her smile in place, her eyes gleaming innocently. A basket for cards and donations to St. Therese's had been placed discreetly near the shrine.

Father James visited daily, as did Dr. Williams; one dispensed blessings and God's knowledge, offering comfort to the soul, while the other prescribed pills and rest, relief for a weary body, all of which was supposed to help Rex scale the mountain of his grief.

"Cassidy said she rode the horse that night," Rex said, still obstinately defending Brig to the sheriff.

"I did," she replied, holding up her arm with the cast around her wrist and forearm. "Got this to prove it."

"She was thrown off the colt again," her father said, his eyes seeming suddenly ancient. He tapped the ash from his cigar. "That useless colt—"

"But McKenzie, he could have found the horse and taken off on him, or . . ." His suspicious eyes regarded Cassidy in a new light.

"Or what?" Rex asked.

"Or he could've gotten himself some help."

Cassidy's heart nearly stopped. Her throat constricted and sweat trickled down her scalp. Sheriff Dodds was smarter than he looked.

"Who would have helped him? Cassidy?" Rex snorted in disgust.

Dodds pushed himself to his feet. "We'll find out. I've got the best men and dogs in the state taking off over them hills. We'll find him." He came up to stand behind Cassidy and stare at the eastern mountains. "He won't get far."

"It's been almost a week," Rex reminded him.

"But he don't have much money and only his two feet— the horse can only go so far if he's got it. We'll get him," he said, hitching his pants over the roll that was his belly. "It'll just take a little time."

Shivering, Cassidy attempted to appear calm though her stomach revolted each time she thought about what would happen to Brig if they caught him.

"You still can't be certain it's McKenzie."

"Maybe not yet, but we found someone who seems to be an eye witness."

"What?" Rex was suddenly interested. "Who?"

Cassidy's breath was instantly trapped in her lungs.

Rolling proudly on the soles of his worn shoes, Dodds kept his eyes on Cassidy. "Willie Ventura. Found him down by the river, just staring into the water. Seems he was at the gristmill that night. Got himself a pair of singed eyebrows to prove it."

"Sweet Jesus," Rex whispered. "Willie?"

Oh, God, no. Please, no— But she remembered seeing Willie skulking through the red and gold shadows of the fire, in the alley.

"You think he could be involved?"

"Interrogated him every way up from sideways. His story doesn't change. He saw Brig and Angie and Jed there that night and he keeps sayin' the same thing over and over again. 'She burned! She burned!' " The sheriff's big nose wrinkled in disgust. "He carries on somethin' awful."

"Why wasn't I told?" Rex demanded, his eyes brightening with interest. "He lives here, you know. Over the stable. Works for me."

"I told you now. We just found him this afternoon, for crying out loud. The way I see it, Willie was lucky he didn't die, too. Prob'ly got the piss scared out of him and hid in the woods. The dogs found him while we were lookin' for McKenzie."

"Where is he now?"

"Down at the county office, gettin' cleaned up and feedin' his face. He's . . . well, I was gonna say he's all right, but he's always been a little off."

"Oh, God," Rex whispered and buried his face in his hands.

"So Willie, half-wit that he is, saw Brig at the scene." Dodds seemed to figure Willie's testimony was the final nail in Brig's coffin.

"Willie tells stories," Cassidy said, unable to stand the deceit any longer. Though she suspected that the sheriff was trying to get a rise out of her, in his own way questioning her, she couldn't help but come to Brig's defense. "I like Willie and all, but I don't think you can take his word as testimony."

"Why not?"

She had to think fast, keep her lies straight even as she wove them into the truth. "Because Brig wouldn't have hurt Angie, ever, and he was looking for her that night. He came here; he told me he'd had a fight with Jed and hit him with his own bat, probably broke some of his bones." Frantic, she faced her father. "You have to believe that Brig wouldn't have killed her."

"Why not?" Dodds asked, running his tongue around his teeth.

"Because . . . because I think he loved her," Cassidy said, the admission tearing her apart. "I think he was going to marry her." Her voice was ragged, the words torn from her throat. "The baby—it was probably his."

"No!" Rex was on his feet. "I won't believe it—"

"Well, I'll be damned." The sheriff stared at her and rubbed his jaw. "Why didn't you say this all earlier?"

"No one asked and it's . . . it's only what I think."

"Well, if you think right, then he'd better come back and turn himself in and tell us exactly what happened. Otherwise we've got no recourse but to believe Willie and the corroborating evidence."

"Brig McKenzie is *not* the baby's father!" Rex shook his head as if in denying the truth, it would change.

"Dad—"

"She wasn't interested in him, not really."

"Oh, God, what does it matter now? Angie's dead," Cassidy cried. The walls of the room seemed to close in on her. Running as fast as her legs would carry her, she made her way out of the den, raced past the hundreds of flickering candles and slipped upstairs to Angie's room. The door was closed, but she pushed it open and nearly stepped back at the rush of perfume—Angie's scent—that wafted over the threshold. The huge portrait of Angie as a baby with her mother glared down at her and the dolls—Barbies, Kens, Chatty Cathy, and all the rest stood in perfect attention in their cases.

Grief tore at Cassidy's soul, and she shut the door quickly.

Leaning against the upper hallway wall, she fought tears and her knees gave way. Where was he—she wondered as she slid to the floor. *Where?* She buried her face in her hands but not before she saw Sheriff Dodds, eyes narrowed, reaching into his back pocket for his can of chew, looking up past Angie's shrine and the railing to the place in the hallway where Cassidy had crumpled.

Cassidy glanced at the calendar. Over a week had passed since the fire, and the house was still in a state of mourning.

Deciding to escape her room, she stopped midway down the stairs as two of her mother's best friends, Geraldine Caldwell and Ada Alonzo, were waiting in the foyer, believing themselves to be alone. "Losing Angie will kill Rex," Geraldine predicted in a hushed whisper. From the looks of the open boxes they were carrying, they'd dropped by with homemade casseroles and a whole sliced ham, enough to feed the entire Third World, though no one in the house had any appetite. "He doted on that girl."

"Don't I know?" Ada, Bobby's mother, made a swift sign of the cross and bowed her head, giving Cassidy a bird's-eye view of the gray roots she tried so vainly to conceal with hair dye. If only all the do-gooders would just go away and quit circling like vultures, showing up at any hour day or night, offering condolences and advice, wearing grief-weary faces, patting Cassidy's shoulder whenever she was near. As far as she was concerned, they were all fakes. Even Earlene Spears, wife of the minister. Though Rex Buchanan had been a devout Catholic all his life, Earlene seemed to consider it her duty to represent her husband's church and express her condolences. She'd come by, yesterday, stiff as starch, her lips drawn into a permanent frown as she noticed the flickering candles in the foyer.

"A shame . . . such a shame," she'd said, her eyes pitying, her bony hands fingering the cross suspended from a chain around her neck. "Such a lovely girl. I just hope they find that McKenzie boy. He's nothing but trouble—always has

been even from the time he was a baby. I should know, I tried
to take care of his older brothers when he was born . . . oh,
my, I'm rattling on and I just wanted to extend my most sincere condolences from myself and the reverend as well as
the congregation . . ."

Cassidy hadn't been able to breathe while she was in the
house and now, with Ada and Geraldine whispering in the
foyer, she retreated from the banister and moved back into
the shadows of the hallway toward her room, where she'd
taken refuge ever since the fire. A few of her friends had
stopped by, but they'd each beaten a hasty retreat once they'd
said they were sorry about Angie and discovered that Cassidy
was still shell-shocked and wasn't good company.

"Dena," the two women said in unison as Cassidy's
mother approached from the family room. Mary had probably answered the door—she'd taken over the role of butler as
well as cook and housekeeper these days.

"We've been sick with worry." Ada's voice. Sincere.
Nasal.

"Yes, is there anything I—we can do? The Judge is beside
himself and swears that whoever did this, if he comes before
him, will get his. Believe me."

"I hope he roasts in hell," her mother said, and Cassidy
felt sick inside. "He's a bad seed. Always was and Angie—
well, God rest her soul."

"Felicity can barely function," Geraldine admitted. "She
was so close to Angie and now she's lost her best friend."
She let out a breathy sigh. "Besides her own grief, she's got
to deal with Derrick."

"The poor boy." Ada again.

"He's beside himself these days," Dena said, obviously
not afraid to sound uncharitable about her stepson. "He
wants us to hire a private detective, hunt Brig McKenzie
down like a dog and string him up. I swear this entire family
is falling apart."

"How's Cassidy holding up?" Ada asked.

"Oh, she'll be fine. Always—bounces back. She's torn up
about Angie, of course, but just between you and me, it's a

good thing that McKenzie boy is out of our lives. He was starting to show Cassidy some attention—you know how his kind is, always looking for a way to be with decent girls."

"His brother, too," Geraldine agreed.

"Yes, but Chase is different," Dena hedged. "He knows his place and works hard. Rex lent that boy money to go to school, and he's working off the loan. Somehow he managed to get some sense. It's a pity he's related to Brig. It'll always stand in his way."

"Will Rex be all right?" Geraldine asked kindly.

"Who knows? He adored Angie. To tell you the truth, she was his favorite, over his son and other daughter. I just hope that now he realizes how lucky he is to have Cassidy."

Ada agreed. "A lovely girl. Maybe I should suggest that Bobby ask her out."

"She'd love it," Dena said and Cassidy shuddered at the thought.

"They could help each other through this."

No way!

"Yes," Geraldine said. "Just like Felicity and Derrick."

Cassidy imagined her mother smiling. "Now, if I could just convince Rex to fire that half-wit, Willie. He was there at the fire, you know. Saw the whole thing. But who knows? He and Brig were friendly. I wouldn't be surprised if Brig put him up to it."

"He should be in an institution," Geraldine agreed.

Ada added, "With others who are mentally handicapped."

"Rex won't hear of it. Thinks he owes that boy something. Won't admit that the retardation is as bad as it is. I tell you, there's no reasoning with that man sometimes. Well, come in and have some iced tea. We don't have to stand out here in the hall."

Insides churning, Cassidy closed the door behind her. A date with Bobby Alonzo? Prearranged by his mother? Fat chance. She kicked off her shoes and flipped on the radio. An old Rolling Stones song warbled through the speakers. Cassidy closed her eyes and listened to Mick Jagger complain about painting something black. She knew how he felt.

There wasn't a knock at the door, but she felt the change in atmosphere, the movement of air as the door opened and the curtains billowed at the windows. Turning, she found Derrick in the doorway. "Can I come in?" he whispered. He looked gaunt and strained, as if he'd lost twenty pounds as well as part of his soul.

Lifting a shoulder, she watched him close the door behind him. "God, I feel awful," he said, and tears shimmered in his near-dead eyes. "Angie didn't deserve this."

She didn't answer, afraid her voice would fail her.

"I loved her, y'know. She was a pain in the butt, but I loved her."

"Yeah, I know."

Derrick blinked rapidly. "I—I'm sorry about the other night, with the shotgun. I wouldn't have hurt you."

"I wasn't worried about myself."

He wandered over to the dresser, where he saw a photograph of Cassidy astride Remmington. Picking the snapshot up, he frowned, then glanced at the mirror and met Cassidy's gaze. "Dad should never have hired McKenzie." Derrick's mouth flattened at the mention of Brig. "If he hadn't, this wouldn't have happened."

"You don't know that."

His hands clenched suddenly, crushing the photograph. "I can't believe she's gone!" He looked up at the ceiling as if searching for answers.

"Neither can I."

He drew in a ragged breath and pinned Cassidy with his watery eyes. "I'll kill him, you know. If that bastard ever sets foot near Prosperity, I swear I'll kill him with my bare hands."

"Even if he's innocent?"

"He's not, Cassidy," Derrick said, sniffing loudly. "The bastard's guilty as hell and someday he's gonna pay."

Twenty

She felt like a criminal, tying the old mare to a tree in the woods surrounding the sawmill, waiting in the shadows during the shift change. Men, covered in sawdust and dust, were taking off hard hats, lighting cigarettes, laughing and joking as they walked through the chain-linked gates and into the parking lot.

On the other side of the fence stood a huge sign. It indicated that AUTHORIZED EMPLOYEES ONLY were allowed inside and suggested that A SAFE WORKPLACE IS A HAPPY WORKPLACE. Rigs of every shape and size were scattered across the pockmarked asphalt—Jeeps and trucks and station wagons and sedans. Saws screeched and forklifts with heavy loads of lumber rolled through the huge stacks of raw lumber, milled and planed, ready to be shipped.

Cassidy watched as the men left, younger ones tearing out of the parking lot in flashy cars, older men with families in dusty, dented trucks.

The new shift was arriving, and Cassidy spied the pickup she was looking for, an old Dodge that had once been turquoise but now had splotches of gray primer on the fenders and tailgate. Chase McKenzie's truck.

He unfolded himself from the cab and stretched the kinks from his back. Her heart began to pound triple-time at the sight of him, so much like Brig and yet so different. Telling herself it was now or never, she waited until most of the men had passed through the gate before she called to him.

"Chase!"

Squinting against the lowering sun, he turned. "Yeah?"

"It's me—"

A smile grew against his square jaw. "Cassidy. What're you doin' down here—no, don't tell me, your father wants everyone in your family to know firsthand how to work the green chain."

She shook her head and he must've noticed the worry in her eyes because his grin slowly faded. "This is about Angie, isn't it? And Brig."

"I—I wondered if you'd heard from him."

His eyes darkened to a dusky shade of blue. "Not me, and if Ma has, she's kept it to herself."

"Oh." She couldn't hide the defeat in her voice and kicked at the gravel with the toe of her boot.

"I, um, I know that you were . . . well, interested in him."

She glanced up sharply, wondering if he was teasing, but he was serious.

He hesitated, looked off in the distance, then as if weighing all the options, added, "If I hear anything, I'll let you know."

"And your mother?"

"You'll have to ask her yourself." He shook his head and looked suddenly world-weary. "But no tellin' what she'll say; she's, uh, she's not taking this well."

"Oh. I'm sorry."

"So am I," he said softly. "So am I."

She started to turn away, but he grabbed her and strong, work-roughened hands circled her good wrist. The tips of his fingers seemed to press against her pulse.

"Look, I know this is hard and . . . and it's probably not my place to say this, but I'll do what I can for you and . . . well, if you ever need anything—I know that sounds silly considering your station and mine, but I'm serious—if you ever need anything, you can count on me."

She swallowed hard and gazed into his troubled eyes. "Thanks . . . I—I won't. I just want to know about Brig."

A shadow passed over his face, and his jaw tightened just a bit. "You got it," he said, before he released her and jogged across the parking lot, forcing his hardhat onto his head as he passed through the open gate.

The trailer, having seen better days, was beginning to rust. Cassidy felt an overriding sense of guilt for having grown up in the mansion her father had built for Lucretia while Brig and Chase had lived here, in this run-down old single-wide for all of their lives.

Heart in her throat, she drove her mother's sedan along the gravel lane and stopped behind Sunny's car. The fake cat eyed her with glassy disinterest, and Cassidy tucked the keys in her purse. She'd taken the car without permission, while Dena and Rex were in Portland, because she couldn't stand the not-knowing any longer. She'd prayed all the way that she wouldn't be stopped by the police, as she still didn't have a driver's license. She'd gotten lucky. So far.

Nervous sweat collected at the base of her neck, and she waited for a second, until the dust had settled on the windshield. She felt a breath of wind against her back, though the windows were rolled up. Nerves. Just nerves. Gritting her teeth, she knew she couldn't put off her mission forever and she didn't have much time; even now her folks might be returning. She forced herself from the car.

The front step of the McKenzie home was a dusty crate and the rusting metal sign swinging over the door was faded and pockmarked from bullet holes.

"It's now or never," she told herself, raising her fist to pound on the door.

Before she could knock, Sunny opened the door, her eyes dark and haunted, deep lines of worry guarding her mouth. Her hair seemed to have grayed in the past few weeks.

"You're the Buchanan girl." It was a statement, not a question.

"Yes, and I wanted to talk to you, to apologize for the way you were treated at my house. I—I'm sorry."

The door opened wide. "Your father blames Brig for the fire. For your sister's death."

"No, it's the sheriff and my brother—" What was the point? She leveled clear eyes at the older woman. "I don't."

A smile flickered on Sunny's lips. "But your father, he favored your sister and he feels as if a part of him has been ripped from his soul. He needs to blame someone."

"I—suppose." Cassidy felt a chill of premonition as she stared into Sunny's intense brown eyes. Sunny McKenzie was interesting but a little scary.

"Come in. Please."

Inside, the trailer was as faded as the outside—the linoleum had a path worn through it; the shag carpeting was dull and thin. Cassidy had trouble seeing Brig—so wild and free, a rebellious soul—living here in such cramped quarters. A radio near the sink was playing gospel music. Sunny snapped it off.

"You want to know about him," Sunny said, motioning to a plastic chair near the table. "About Brig."

"Yes."

Sunny's eyes glistened. "Don't we all? He hasn't called, he hasn't written, and he's far away. Perhaps dead already. I can't tell." Sadness stooped her shoulders.

"He's not dead." Cassidy would never believe that Brig wasn't alive.

"I hope you're right." Again the sad smile. "But I see great pain for him and"—she shook her head—"and death. Fire and water."

"Look, I don't know about your visions or whatever they are. I just came here because I want to talk to Brig to find out if he's okay, so if you hear from him—hey!"

Suddenly Sunny reached forward, grabbing Cassidy's good hand, clasping it between her callused fingers and closing her eyes. Cassidy wanted to draw away, to pull her arm away, but she didn't dare move as the dark-eyed woman stared past her shoulder to the middle distance, seeing her own vision.

Skin crawling, Cassidy bit her lip. This woman was so unlike her sons—so creepy. Outside, the wind began to pick up and the palm-reading sign groaned loudly.

Cassidy's heart nearly stopped.

Sunny sighed.

"I—I will always believe that Brig is alive," Cassidy said, finally wrenching her arm away. "He's alive and fine and will come back to Prosperity and prove that he's innocent."

Tired brown eyes stared up at her. "There is only pain in the future," Sunny said, seeming suddenly weary. "Pain and death and you, Cassidy Buchanan, you will cause it."

"No—" Cassidy said, already reaching for the door. It had been a mistake to come here. For once the sheriff was right; Sunny should be locked up, put away in a mental institution to blabber about her visions to other patients. "Just tell Brig I care about him, that I'd like to know he's all right, that—"

"It's already written. You'll marry my son."

"Marry him?" she repeated, sweating anxiously, her heart pounding. "But he's gone—you even said you thought he might be dead." She found the doorknob and yanked hard. A gust of wind shoved the door from her hand and it banged against the wall with a thud.

"Not Brig."

"Wh—what? Not Brig?" The woman was certifiable. Cassidy stumbled down the sorry step and sprinted to her mother's car, but Sunny's voice followed after her, like a shadow she couldn't outrun.

"Cassidy Buchanan," it warned above the rising wind, "the man you will marry will be my other son."

Oh, God, no! Get me out of here! She fumbled for her keys.

"Someday, daughter, you will become Chase's wife."

Part II

1994

Twenty-one

The woman was lying. And she was good at it. Damn good.

Detective T. John Wilson had put in too many years with the Sheriff's Department not to smell a liar. He'd seen the best the county had to offer—two-bit con men, thugs, snitches and killers—and he recognized a rat when he was facing one.

This beautiful woman—this beautiful *rich* woman—was hiding something. Something important. Lying through her gorgeous, white teeth.

The smell of stale smoke hung heavy in the interrogation room. Pale green walls had turned a grimy shade of gray since the last paint job before all the budget cuts, but T. John felt comfortable here. At home in the beat-up old chair. He reached into his breast pocket for a pack of cigarettes, remembered he'd quit smoking two months before and reluctantly settled for a piece of Dentyne that he unwrapped slowly, wadded and shoved onto his tongue. The gum wasn't the same as a good drag on a Camel straight, but it would have to do. For now. Until he gave up his continual battle with his addiction to nicotine and took up the habit again.

"Let's go over it one more time," he suggested as he leaned backward in his chair and crossed a booted leg over his knee. His partner, Steve Gonzales, was propped up against the door frame by one shoulder, his arms folded over his skinny chest, his dark eyes glued to the woman who was at the center of this mess—murder, arson and probably much,

much more. Casually, T. John picked up the file and began leafing through it until he came to her statement, the one she'd made without an attorney present just a few hours before. "Your name is—?"

Her amber eyes blazed in outrage, but he didn't feel one iota of guilt for putting her through it all again. After all, she'd do it to him if the situation was reversed, and she wouldn't give an inch—just set her teeth in and hang on. Reporters never let up. Always on the case of the law or the D.A.; it felt good to get a little of his own back.

"My name is Cassidy McKenzie. But you already know who I am."

"Cassidy *Buchanan* McKenzie."

She didn't bother responding. He shook his head, dropped the file and sighed. Tapping the tips of his fingers together, he glanced at the soundproof tiles in the ceiling, as if wishing God Himself was lurking in the joists and would intervene. "You know, I was hoping you were going to be straight with me."

"I am! Going over it again isn't going to change anything. You know what happened—"

"I don't know shit, lady, so cut the crap!" His boots hit the floor with a thud. "Look, I don't know who you think you're talking to, but I've seen better liars than you and busted them, like that." He snapped his fingers so loudly the sound seemed to ricochet around the cinder-block walls. "Whether you realize it or not, you're in deep trouble here; deeper than you want to be. Now, let's get down to it, okay? No more bullshit. I hate bullshit. Don't you, Gonzales?"

"Hate it," Gonzales replied, barely moving his lips.

Wilson grabbed the file again. He felt as if he were losing control. He didn't like it when he lost charge of any situation. Especially one in which he thought his career was on the line. If he solved this case, hell, he'd be able to run for sheriff himself and oust Floyd Dodds, who needed to retire anyway. Floyd was becoming a real pain in the ass. But if T. John didn't solve the case . . . oh, hell, *that* wasn't even a possibility. T. John believed in thinking positively. Even more, he believed in himself.

He glanced at the clock mounted over the door. The seconds just kept ticking by. Through the window, the last rays of sunlight settled into the room, causing shadows to creep along the walls despite the harsh light from the overhead fluorescent bulbs. They'd been at this for three hours and everyone was growing tired. Especially the woman. She was pale, her skin stretched tight over high cheekbones and sunken gold eyes. Her hair was a fiery red brown that was pulled off her face by a leather thong. Tiny lines of worry pinched the corners of what might have been a pouty, sexy mouth.

He tried again. "Your name is Cassidy Buchanan McKenzie, you're a reporter with the *Times* and you know a helluva lot more than you're telling me about the fire at your daddy's sawmill."

She had the decency to blanch. Her mouth opened and closed again as she sat stiffly, her denim jacket wrapped around her slim body, her makeup long faded.

"Now that we've got that straight, you might want to tell me what you know about it. One man's near-dead at Northwest General in CCU, the other in a private room unable to talk. The doctors don't think the guy in Critical Care is gonna make it."

Her lips quivered for a second. "I heard," she whispered. She blinked, but didn't break down. He hadn't supposed she would. She was a Buchanan, for Christ's sake. They were known to be tougher than rawhide.

"This isn't the first fire to occur on your daddy's property, is it? It seems to me there was another fire in another mill years back." He climbed to his feet and began to pace, his gum popping in noisy tandem to the heels of his boots clicking against the yellowed linoleum floor. "And if I remember right, after the last one, you up and left town. Said you'd never come back. Guess you changed your mind—oh, hell, everyone has that right, don't they?" He flashed a good-old-boy smile. His best.

She didn't even flinch.

"But now listen to this. It's what bothers me. You gave up a job most men and women would kill for, came back home married to one of the McKenzie boys and guess what? Lo and behold, we have another hot-damn fire the likes of which we haven't seen in—what—nearly seventeen years! One guy nearly killed in the explosion, the other guy hanging by a thread." He threw up his hands. "Go figure."

Gonzales shoved himself away from the door, exited for a few minutes and returned with cups of coffee.

Wilson turned his chair backward and straddled it. Leaning forward, he glowered at her. She held his gaze. "We're still trying to figure out exactly what happened and who was there. Fortunately your husband was carrying a wallet, otherwise we wouldn't have recognized him. He's a mess. His face is swollen and cut, his hair singed, his jaw broken and one leg's in a cast. But they managed to save the injured eye, and if he works at it, he may even walk again." He watched as the woman shuddered. So she did care about her husband . . . if only just a little. "The other guy we don't know. No ID. His face is busted up pretty bad, too. Swollen and black and blue. He lost a few teeth and his hands are burned. Hair nearly singed clean off. We're havin' a helluva time figuring out who he is and thought you might be able to help us." Leaning back in his chair again, he picked up his cup of coffee.

"What—what about fingerprints?"

"That's the hell of it. John Doe's hands are burned; no prints. At least not yet. With all those broken teeth and messed-up jaw, dental impressions are gonna take some time . . ." Wilson narrowed his eyes on the woman, and he scratched thoughtfully against the stubble of two days' growth of beard. "If I didn't know better, I'd think the bastard burned his hands on purpose; you know, to throw us off."

She grimaced. "You think he started the fire?"

"It's possible." Wilson picked up his mug, took a long swallow and scowled.

"I told you I don't know who he is."

"He was meetin' your husband at the mill."

She hesitated. "So you said, but I . . . I don't keep up with my husband's business. I have no idea whom he met or why."

T. John's eyebrows quirked. "You got one of them marriages—you know, he does his own thing, you do yours?"

"We were thinking about separating," she admitted with a trace of remorse.

"Is that so?" Wilson swallowed a smile. He'd finally hit pay dirt. Now he had a motive—or the start of one. And that's all he needed. "The fire chief thinks the fire was caused by arson."

"I know."

"The incendiary device, well, hell, it could be the spittin' image of the one used seventeen years ago when the old gristmill was torched. You remember that, don't you?" She winced a little, her lips losing some color. "Yeah, I guess you couldn't very well forget."

She looked away, and her hands trembled around the thin Styrofoam. Of course she remembered the fire. Everyone in Prosperity did. The Buchanan family—all of them—had suffered a horrible, tragic loss, one from which most of them had never recovered. The old man—Cassidy's father—had never been the same; lost control of his life, his company and his willful daughter.

"Maybe you'd like to come to the hospital, see the damage for yourself. But I'm warning you, it's not a pretty sight."

She leveled steady whiskey-colored eyes at him, and he was reminded again that she was a reporter as well as a Buchanan. "I've been demanding to see my husband ever since he was injured. The doctors told me I couldn't see him until the sheriff agreed—that there was some question about him being a suspect."

"Well, hell, let's go!" Wilson said, but as she started to climb to her feet, he changed his mind. "Just a couple more things to clear up first." Her spine stiffened, and she slowly settled back in the worn plastic chair. She was a cool one;

he'd give her that. But she was still lying. Hiding something. T. John reached into his pocket and pulled out a plastic bag. Within the clear plastic was a charred chain with a burned St. Christopher's medal attached to it. The image of the saint was barely recognizable, twisted and blackened from the heat and flames.

Cassidy's mouth rounded, but she didn't gasp. Instead she stared at the bag as T. John dropped it onto the battered old table in front of her. Her hands gripped her cup more tightly, and she drew in a quick little breath. "Where'd you get this?"

"Funny thing. The John Doe was holding it in his fist, wouldn't let it go, even with as much pain as he was in. We had to pry it from his fingers, and when we did, guess what he said?" Wilson asked.

She glanced from one detective to the other. "What?"

"We think he yelled your name, but it's just a guess because his voice wasn't working right. He was screaming his lungs out, but not making a sound."

Cassidy swallowed though she hadn't taken a sip of coffee. Her eyes seemed to glisten ever so slightly. He was definitely making headway. Maybe with the right amount of pressure she'd crack. "I guess maybe he thought he needed to see you . . . or maybe he did see you there, at the mill that night."

T. John's dark gaze fixed on the woman.

She licked her lips nervously and avoided his gaze. "I already told you I wasn't anywhere near the place."

"That's right, you were alone in the house. No alibi." Wilson turned to his partner, and picked up the plastic bag. "Has this been printed?"

Gonzales nodded slightly.

"Funny," Wilson said, staring at the woman as he pulled out the darkened silver chain. "Wonder why a guy who was being half-burned to death, would hang on to this damned thing—you know, like it was real important?"

She didn't answer as Wilson let the plastic bag fall softly back to the table and allowed the St. Christopher's medal to swing, like a watch in a hypnotist's hands, in front of her nose. "Wonder what it means?" he asked, and he saw the tiny spark of fury in those round eyes again. But she didn't say a word as he dropped the blackened links onto the table and they slithered together.

She stared at the charred metal for a minute, frowning, her throat working. "Are we finished? Can I go now?"

Wilson was pissed. This woman knew something and she was holding back, and here he was sitting on the biggest murder and arson case in his nine years with the department—his ticket to ousting Floyd Dodds. "You're not changing your story?"

"No."

"Even though you don't have an alibi?"

"I was home."

"Alone."

"Yes."

"Packing? You *were* planning to leave your husband."

"I was working on the computer at home. There are time logs, you can see for yourself—"

"That *someone* was there. Or that someone took enough computer courses and knows how to get into the guts of the machine—the memory—and change the entry times. Let me tell you, you're pushing your luck." He snapped up the chain and dropped it into the plastic bag. "You know, whatever you've done, it will go easier on you if you 'fess up. And if you're protecting someone . . . hell, there's no reason for you to take the rap for something you didn't do."

Her eyes shifted away.

"You're not . . . protecting your husband, are you? Nah, that's silly. You were gonna split anyway."

"Am I being charged?" she demanded. Two spots of color caressed her high cheekbones and beneath her jacket she straightened her thin body, a body that must've dropped five pounds in the twenty-four hours since the fire.

"Well, not yet, but it's still early."

She didn't smile. "As I said, I'd like to see my husband."

Wilson sent his partner a look. "You know, I think, Mrs. McKenzie—you don't mind if I call you that since you're still legally married—I think that's a damned good idea. Maybe you should see the other guy, too; there's a chance you can tell me who he is, though in the shape he's in I doubt if his own mother would recognize him."

Gonzales shifted against the door. "Dodds won't like it—not without him there."

"Let me handle the sheriff."

"It's your funeral, man."

"I'll give old Floyd a call. Make it official, okay?" Wilson stretched out of his chair. " 'Sides, he don't like much that I do."

Gonzales still wasn't convinced. "The doctors gave strict orders that the patients weren't to be disturbed."

"Hell, I know that!" Wilson reached for his hat. "But how can they be disturbed? One guy's so far gone he's nearly in a coma and the other . . . well, he's probably not long for the world. This here's the wife of one of the men, for God's sake. She needs to see her man. And maybe she can help us out. Come on, Mrs. McKenzie, you wouldn't mind, would you?"

Cassidy tried to control her ragged emotions though a thousand questions ran in long endless paths through her mind. She hadn't slept in nearly two days, and when she had managed to doze, horrifying nightmares of the inferno at the sawmill blended into another terrifying fire, that hellish hot beast that had destroyed so much of her life and her family seventeen years ago. A shudder ripped through her body and her knees nearly gave way as she remembered . . . oh, God, how she remembered. The black sky, the red blaze, the white-hot sparks that shot into the heavens as if Satan himself were mocking and spitting at God. And the devastation and deaths . . . *please help me.*

She noticed the detective staring at her, waiting—and she remembered he'd asked her a question—something about going to the hospital. "Can we go now?" she asked, steeling herself. *Oh, God, please, don't let him be in agony!* Tears threatened her eyes, riding like drops of dew on her lashes, but she wouldn't give Detective T. John Wilson the satisfaction of seeing her break down.

She should have asked to have her attorney present, but that was impossible as her attorney was her husband and he was clinging tenaciously to his life. Though she hadn't been able to visit him, the doctors had told her of his injuries, the broken ribs and jaw, punctured lung, cracked femur, and burned cornea of his right eye. He was lucky to be alive. Lucky.

Pushing herself to her feet, she slid a final glance at the tarnished silver chain still coiled, like a dead rattler in the clear plastic bag. Her heart seemed to rip a little bit, and she reminded herself it was only a piece of jewelry—not expensive jewelry at that—and it meant nothing to her. Nothing.

The hospital noises were muted. Rattling carts and gurneys, the sound of doctors being paged, quiet footsteps, all seemed to melt away as Wilson held the door open for her and she stepped into the hospital room where her husband lay unmoving beneath a sterile white sheet. Bandages covered half his face including his right eye as well as the top and back of his head. The flesh that was exposed was bruised and lacerated. Stitches tracked beside his swollen nose and yellow antiseptic sliced across the scratches on his skin. Dark beard stubble was beginning to shade that part of his jaw that was visible and all the while an IV dripped fluid into his veins.

Cassidy's stomach lurched and she gritted her teeth. So this is what it had come to. *Why was he at the mill that night? Who was he meeting—the man who lay dying somewhere in the labyrinthine rooms of this hospital? And why, oh, God, why, had someone tried to kill him?*

"I'm here," she said quietly, walking into the room and wishing she could turn back time, somehow save him from this agony. Though they'd stopped loving each other a long while ago, perhaps never really had been in love, she still cared for him. "Can you hear me?" she asked, but didn't touch the clean sheets covering his body, didn't want even the slightest movement to add to his discomfort.

His good eye was open, staring sightlessly toward the ceiling. Its white had turned a nasty shade of red, and the blue—that clear sky blue—seemed to have dissolved into the surrounding tissue.

"I'm here for you," she said, conscious of the detective standing near the door. "Can you hear—?"

Suddenly the eye moved, focusing on her with such clarity and hatred that she nearly jumped back. Her husband stared at her for a long, chilling minute, then looked away as if in disgust, his gaze trained on the ceiling once more.

"Please—" she said.

He didn't move.

The detective stepped forward. "McKenzie?"

Nothing.

She said softly, "I want you to know that I care." Her throat clogged painfully on the words as she remembered their last argument, the cruel words they'd hurled at each other. The eye blinked, but she knew it was useless. He couldn't hear her. Wouldn't. He didn't want her love now any more than he ever had, and she was just as incapable of giving it. "I'll be here for you." She remembered her marriage vows and felt a deep rending in her heart, an ache that seemed to grow as she stared at the broken man who had once been so strong.

She'd known from the start that their marriage had been doomed, and yet she'd let herself believe that they would find a way to love each other.

But she'd been wrong. So wrong.

She waited and eventually the eye closed, though she didn't know if he was sleeping, unconscious, or pretending that she wasn't in the hospital, that she didn't exist, as he had so many times in the past.

Cassidy walked out of the room on wooden legs. Memories washed over her, memories of love gained and lost, of hopes and dreams that had died long before the fire.

The detective was in step with her. "You want to tell me about the chain and the St. Christopher's medal?"

Her heart jolted. "I . . . I can't."

"Why not?"

She wrapped her arms around herself and despite the soaring temperature felt a chill as cold as November. "It didn't belong to my husband."

"You're sure?"

She hedged because she wasn't certain. "To my knowledge, he never owned anything like that. It . . . it probably belonged to the other guy—the one who was holding it."

"And who do you think he is?" Wilson asked.

"I wish I knew," she said fervently, not allowing her mind to wander to another time and place, another love and a shining silver chain with a St. Christopher's medal dangling from its links. "I wish to God that I knew."

They walked the length of one corridor and took the elevator down a floor to CCU. Wilson couldn't convince the nurse on duty or the doctor in charge to let them see the man who had been with her husband, so they passed through the exterior doors to the outside of the hospital, and there, in the simmering afternoon heat, Wilson handed her a photo of a charred man, his face blistered, his hair burned off. She closed her eyes and fought the urge to retch. "I already told you. I—I don't know him. Even if I did, I don't think, I mean I can't imagine—"

"It's all right." For once Wilson's voice was kind, as if he did have some human emotions after all. "I said it was a long shot." He took the crook of her elbow and helped her walk across the parking lot to the cruiser to which he'd been assigned. Glancing back over his shoulder to the whitewashed hospital, and the wing in which CCU was housed, he shook his head. "Poor bastard. I wonder who the hell he is."

Twenty-two

The dying man had to be Brig.

There was no other explanation.

Feeling as if she'd been kicked in the gut, Cassidy dropped her earrings onto the dresser and told herself that, no matter what else was true, Brig McKenzie was lying in the Critical Care Unit of Northwest General Hospital, his life seeping out of him. Why else the St. Christopher's medal? True, they weren't that uncommon, probably dozens of people in Prosperity wore one, but it seemed too much of a coincidence that the man charred in the fire at the sawmill, meeting Chase, clutching the medal, silently screaming her name, could be anyone but Brig.

Brig. Over the years, she'd forced herself to stop thinking about him, to stop believing that he would return, to stop loving him. It had been difficult at first, but as the years had passed with no word from him, the reality had finally sunken in that whether he was living or dead, he wouldn't be a part of her life. As she'd grown up and become her own person, she'd slowly let go, dismissing her feelings for him as little more than a schoolgirl crush: puppy love complicated by fate, underage emotions and sex. Sex in a time when her personal morals told her that she couldn't sleep with a man if she didn't love him and wasn't committed to him for the rest of her life.

She'd been such a child. A silly, willful child. Brig was best off without her.

But now he was back. Nearly dead. Meeting with her

husband, who had probably known all along how to contact him, who had lied to her when he'd said that neither he nor his mother had received any word about Brig and had assumed that he was dead.

"Even if he is alive," Chase had told her years ago before they had married, "he's dead to us. He knows how to reach Ma—she's never moved, never changed her telephone number always hoping he'd call—and I'm in the phone book. It would be a simple enough matter to pick up the telephone; so he's dead or decided to let us think that he is—either way, it's all the same, isn't it?"

Except that Chase had lied. Why? To save their marriage? She frowned at her reflection. She felt betrayed and dead tired. The past two days had been exhausting. Even before the fire there had been problems. Serious problems. Between her and her husband. She glanced at her wedding ring—a simple gold band with a solitary diamond. It winked at her, as if sharing a private secret, the knowledge that her marriage had never become the loving, caring union that she'd hoped for; nor had it been what Chase had wanted.

They'd married for all the wrong reasons and they'd both known it—even then. With a sigh, she ran her fingers through her hair. The marriage had been for better or worse, and it wasn't going to get much better for a long, long while. She couldn't sit around moping and worrying. She had to do something; she'd be faithful to Chase, help him recover, then they could reexamine their marriage. But first she had to talk to Brig. Before he died.

Despite the fact that a part of her wanted to throw herself onto her bed, fall asleep and eventually wake up from this nightmare, she strode to the walk-in closet—lined in cedar, only the best for Chase McKenzie's wife—and grabbed her jacket again. It was time she pulled herself together—someone had to. With Chase lying injured in the hospital, her father with a bad heart, Dena wringing her hands and Derrick as volatile as ever, it was up to her to get to the bottom of this mess.

After all, she'd been a pretty damned good investigative

reporter before she'd given up her pocket recorder for a wedding ring and settled for a comfortable, but dull job at the local paper.

Frowning at the changes in her life, she walked quickly down the tile floors of the glass and redwood house Chase had built for her the year after they'd said their "I do's." Complete with brass bath fixtures, marble from an Italian quarry, crystal lamps and furniture handcrafted to Chase's expectations, the house was a showcase—more museum than home. Persian rugs sprawled over hardwood floors; porcelain sinks from England caught water that didn't dare drip from gold or brass spigots; designer window coverings added color; railings that had taken a European craftsman nearly a year to fashion and install, curved on three separate staircases from the basement to the second floor.

This ostentatious monstrosity of a house. Chase had wanted it—hungered for it—and Cassidy had agreed that they should build it, thinking the furnishings and new house would make him happy.

Of course they hadn't. Nothing had made Chase happy. Nothing had satisfied him.

The phone rang and Cassidy paused near the French doors of her den, listening as the recorder picked up. There had been nearly fifteen calls since she'd come home from the hospital: some friends who were concerned, some workmen at the mill, and reporters—her peers, anxious for a story, smelling a scandal. She hadn't bothered calling anyone back. Not yet.

"Cassidy? Are you there? Would *you please* answer?" Felicity's voice, filled with worry and a trace of agitation. A pause. "Look, I know you're there, so you'd better pick up the phone. Derrick and I are worried sick, for crying out loud. I've got calls from two news stations as well as the local paper and the *Oregonian.* They're all expecting some kind of statement and . . . well, Derrick's not up to it. You . . . probably know how to handle those people better than any of us." She hesitated and Cassidy could picture her worrying her lower lip. "Cassidy? Oh, for the love of God, I don't need this. If you're there, pick up the goddamned phone!"

Telling herself she was making a big mistake, Cassidy lifted the receiver. "Okay, so I'm here." She leaned a hip against the corner of the desk. "Don't worry about the reporters. If any more call, tell them I'll talk to them within the day—"

"Thank God. I've been going out of my mind. These people are vultures! No offense," she added hurriedly, as if Cassidy was concerned about the sanctity of her chosen career. "But I've heard that they're staked out at the hospital and that Dena and Rex have even been bothered in Palm Springs! Can you imagine?"

Oh, she could imagine all right. Hadn't she once been part of the throng anxious for a story, spending days on courthouse steps, all-night vigils at prisons, sleepless hours driving in the worst of conditions for that all-important interview? That part of her life seemed so distant now.

"Bad news travels fast, I guess," Cassidy said dryly. Even to Palm Springs.

"Well, you know how we feel about Chase," Felicity barreled on. "Derrick and I are so sorry about everything . . ."

Lies. Felicity and Derrick had eloped to Lake Tahoe not long after the ashes from the fire that killed Angie had cooled. Felicity's concern right now rang false. She was a parrot for her husband, and Derrick had always hated everyone associated with the McKenzies. He and Felicity had been stupefied when Cassidy had married Chase; the whole family had been in shock and her half brother and sister-in-law had never hidden how disgusted they were in her choice of a husband. Maybe that was one of the reasons Cassidy had decided to tie the knot. In the first few months, when they'd been happy, Chase had jokingly referred to himself as the new outlaw rather than in-law. But that was all so long ago now. "Don't worry," Cassidy heard herself saying. "He'll be better soon."

"Will he? I mean, I know he's in bad shape—"

Cassidy snapped back to the present. "Dr. Okano thinks he'll be fine."

"You talked with the doctor? I thought you were with that detective."

Cassidy didn't have time for the third-degree from Felicity. "I was but I went to the hospital with Detective Wilson, then later, once he was done interrogating me, I drove back, stayed with Chase awhile until I could speak with the doctor." She wound the telephone cord around her fingers. "Dr. Okano's very encouraged. He'll be released by the end of the week."

"Is he coming home?"

The question was one she'd asked herself a dozen times. "Where else would he go?"

Felicity sighed loudly. "Don't get defensive. It's just that we all know that you were having some problems."

The muscles in the back of Cassidy's neck grew rigid. No matter how bad her marriage was, she never confided in anyone, not her mother, her brother or his wife. Her relationship with her husband was private. "Look, Felicity, Chase is getting better and he's coming home. Period."

Felicity didn't press the issue. "What about the other man?"

Cassidy's throat caught. *Brig.* "I'm not sure," she admitted, the cord twining over her fingers. "No one's allowed to see him, but I don't think it looks good."

"Who the devil is he?"

Was that her heart pounding so loudly? "I don't know. The police are still trying to figure it out."

"I hope they find out, and soon," Felicity said vehemently. "I won't feel safe until we know who he is and why he tried to burn down the sawmill."

"You think he was behind it?" *Brig? Why would he come back here to burn the sawmill?*

"Who else?"

"Anyone."

"Oh, come on, Cassidy. Your husband's fighting for his life—near dead from the fire—and you're defending some drifter that the police can't identify? Of course he's behind it!"

"We don't know that. We don't know anything right now." She tried not to sound defensive; it was better if Felicity didn't guess that Brig was back. "Besides, if you believe he's behind the fire at the mill, you won't have to worry." Beads of sweat dotted her brow, and nausea rolled up the back of her throat again. "It . . . it looks like he won't make it."

"Good. It'll save the criminal justice system and the state thousands of dollars." Felicity seemed relieved. "I know you're a bleeding-heart liberal, Cassidy, but you would change your mind if you had children and worried day in and day out about their safety."

Cassidy felt that old empty place in her heart again, the one she'd reserved for children of her own. The one that would never be filled. "Look, I've got to go—"

"I won't keep you. But remember, we're not safe. Who knows what that guy was trying to do? He could have an accomplice, couldn't he? Some nutcase still out running around? That's what worries me. It could be some idiot who holds a grudge against the family. And if you ask me, I'll bet Willie Ventura's involved. He's been missing, hasn't he?"

"Willie wouldn't—"

"He's not right, Cassidy. I know you've stood up for him all your life, but he's a half-wit; a boy in a man's body. Who knows what goes on in his mind? I won't let my girls around him, believe you me, and I don't trust him. He's a pervert—always hanging around, staring."

Cassidy remembered the day by the pool years ago when Felicity had dared to pull off her T-shirt and flaunt her breasts just to see Willie's reaction.

"I just hope they solve this soon. It's got to be hard on your dad. He called here, talked to Derrick. He and Dena will be flying in tomorrow."

"Good." Cassidy wasn't ready to face her parents, but she couldn't put off the inevitable. Rex Buchanan had aged so much in the years since the original fire; it was almost as if the life had been stripped from him. Dena had become a fussbudget, flitting around her husband, seeing to his every need, enjoying semiretirement, complaining that she didn't have any grandchildren of her own—not that Angela and Linnie, Felicity and Derrick's girls, weren't charming, gorgeous little things, but not really her blood. Dena was content to let Derrick, Chase and Cassidy run the family business.

Cassidy made some excuse to hang up. She and Felicity had never gotten along and were just civil to each other, but usually it didn't matter. Slinging the strap of her purse over her shoulder, she headed through the door. She had to stop at the newspaper office where she worked, then she'd head to the hospital.

Outside the wind was hot, late August refusing to give up its sweltering grip on the weather. Cassidy climbed into her Jeep and headed toward Portland.

Her head was throbbing, pain building behind her eyes as she thought of Brig. How many years had she prayed that she could see him again? *But he's going to die. Before you can ask him one question, before you can touch him, before you can even be certain it's really Brig, he's going to die.*

Twenty-three

"So how does it feel to be the focus of a story for a change?" Selma Rickert asked as she leaned against the partition that separated her work space from Cassidy's. Gold bracelets jangled around her wrists, and her eyes were tinted a vibrant green, courtesy of new contact lenses. She appeared nervous, as she usually did since the paper had been declared a smoke-free workplace and she and a few others were forced to go outside for a cigarette every now and again rather than leaving one forever burning in the ashtray that still sat buried somewhere on her desk.

"To tell you the truth, I'd rather be the one asking the questions."

"Yeah, I know what you mean." Scratching a bare forearm with the painted nails of her opposite hand, Selma added, "You'd better watch out for Mike. He's on the warpath—arguing with the powers-that-be again over the 'direction and attitude' of the *Times* or some such crap." The powers-that-be were Elmira Milbert, owner of the *Valley Times* after inheriting it from her husband just this past year. "Besides, he's hell-bent to get the inside scoop on the fire from you-know-who."

"Me? Like I have it?" Cassidy rubbed her temples and prayed for an aspirin.

Selma nodded and glanced at the door to the editor-in-chief's glassed-in office. "You're the wife of one of the injured parties."

"I don't know anything."

"More than we do, honey. That's all that matters."

A weight settled in Cassidy's stomach. "What's he want?"

"What do you mean, what's he want? A story, natch. From someone close to the fire." Selma shrugged. "You know Mike. He's always looking for a different angle—after all, that's what this paper is all about: the alternative viewpoint."

"But he wouldn't mind a little sensationalism."

Selma grinned, showing off her slight overbite. "Not if it sold a few papers." She winked and settled back at her desk while Cassidy stared at the chaos that was hers. She'd only missed a few days of work, and yet it seemed that the whole world had collapsed since then.

She sorted through her mail and messages, finished a story she'd started a few days before about a new theater troupe, then put a call into the hospital to check on Chase. Ignoring another assignment that wasn't due until next week, she scanned all the news stories on the fire as well as a copy of the police report that someone had managed to pry out of the Sheriff's Department's hands.

An hour passed before Mike Gillespie stopped at her desk and glanced at her copy of the report. "Sorry to hear about Chase," he said, his eyes, behind thick glasses, looked concerned. A big man with the start of a sagging stomach, he smelled of cigar smoke and coffee.

"It looks like he'll be okay. It'll just take time."

"Helluva thing, though."

She'd never felt nervous around Mike before, but that's because they were always playing on the same team. This time, because of the fire, they were on opposite sides—or at least that's the way it felt.

"If you need more time off . . ." He let the sentence trail, giving her the opportunity to reply before he'd even finished his thought.

"I might want to work more at home, once Chase is released from the hospital. I'll fax things to the office."

He lifted a shoulder and rolled up his shirtsleeves. "Just

let me know. We've got other people willing to fill in for you."

"I appreciate it," she said, though she felt her stomach clench and knew she was bracing herself for something. *Here it comes,* her mind warned, *don't let him blindside you.*

"Bill has been working on the story about the fire."

Bill Laszlo was one of the best reporters on the paper. She didn't respond, just waited until Mike got to the point.

"He might want to ask you a few questions, you know, since your father owns the mill and your husband and brother run it . . ."

"And my husband was nearly killed."

His face was suddenly world-weary. "It's news, Cassidy. Big news around here. That's what we report. You wouldn't expect us to ignore it, would you?"

" 'Course not. I just don't like being a primary source, okay? This has been rough on my family as it is; I'm not going to be the one spilling her guts to the media."

"The shoe pinches a little when it's on the other foot, doesn't it?"

"Just tell Bill that I don't know anything more than he does. The police aren't confiding in me."

He hesitated a little and pulled on his lower lip. "The way I hear it, they might suspect you."

She stared at him as if he'd sprouted horns and a tail. "They told you that?"

"No, but you were called in for questioning."

"Because my husband was hurt. That's all!" she nearly shouted, instantly indignant. What was Mike pulling? "They talked to lots of people."

"All the talk in Prosperity is that the mill was losing money and insured to the hilt."

She wouldn't rise to that one. "So that's the talk, is it? Sounds like pure speculation to me. I thought this paper only printed facts."

"We were hoping to get them from you."

"I don't have any."

"What about the John Doe?"

Her heart nearly stopped, and she tried to keep from snapping. "All I know is that he's in CCU and it doesn't look good."

"You think he's the arsonist?"

She shook her head vehemently. *I think he might be my husband's brother—the boy with whom I lost my heart and my virginity.* "I don't *know* anything about him."

"But if you find out, I'll be the first to know, right?" His eyebrows rose behind his glasses.

"Sure. Right after I call the tabloid shows."

"Funny, Cassidy," he said sarcastically as he rapped his knuckles on her desk and turned away. "Very funny."

"Chase . . . can you hear me?" Cassidy sat in a straight-backed chair in the hospital room next to her husband, as she had off and on for two days, knowing that there was supposedly nothing wrong with his hearing, believing that he was purposely tuning her out. Though the nurses said he hadn't uttered a word and the police hadn't been able to wrest so much as one syllable from his lips, he did finally respond, managed to eat a little food, drink from a bent straw in a cup, and glare at the world through one ugly eye. He was still swathed in bandages and didn't so much as turn that blood-shot eye in her direction. The drugs he was given for pain might prevent him from connecting with her, but Cassidy suspected he was just being stubborn, playing out the same scene he always did whenever they argued.

She wondered if she'd ever loved him. Certainly, right after the fire that had taken Angie's life, when she'd visited Sunny McKenzie, she'd had no intention of ever getting involved with Brig's brother.

Sunny's prediction that night, that she would marry Chase, had pursued her all the way home, but she'd shoved the silly thought aside. After all, she loved Brig. Not his older, more sophisticated brother. She and Chase had barely seen each other the next couple of years. He'd gone to law school in Salem, she'd finished high school in Prosperity, wondering about Brig, telling herself to get over him, barely having a social life at all. She'd worried her mother, but her father had barely noticed any change in his second daughter.

When Angie had left this earth, a part of Rex Buchanan had followed after her. His love for life had withered. His visits to the cemetery became more frequent, and he was forever locked in his den, drinking brandy and staring morosely into the fire. Cassidy was certain that if she'd curled up and died, Rex wouldn't have noticed.

Her horse had never been found. Nor was there ever any sign of Brig. Cassidy had gone to college, grateful to get away from Prosperity and the charred ghosts that still haunted her. She'd given up her interest in horses and shoved her cowboy boots to the back corner of her closet. She'd studied journalism voraciously, dated a little, made a few friends and finally, after graduation, had landed a job with a small television studio in Denver. From Denver, she'd moved to San Francisco and finally to Seattle, where she had through years of hard work become a reporter with a decent reputation. Chase, a corporate lawyer, had seen her on the news, called and asked her out.

She'd only agreed to see Chase to find out about Brig. She'd met him in an Irish bar in Pioneer Place. They'd laughed and caught up, and Chase's smile, softer than Brig's, but heart-stopping nonetheless, had gotten to her. That had been the beginning. They'd taken it slow, neither one wanting to commit, and yet, as the months had passed, she'd finally accepted the fact that her schoolgirl crush on Brig was just a lingering shadow that she had to banish from her heart and from her mind.

Chase had helped her in that first year or so, she thought now as she stared at the hospital bed where he lay. Helped her forget the man who had left her.

For that she'd be eternally grateful. She cleared her throat and tried to communicate with the silent man lying under the stiff bedsheets. She owed him this much—to help him get back on his feet again. She was, after all, still his wife. She reached for the fingers of his good hand and took them gently in her own. "Chase? Can you hear me? I've been thinking . . ."

He didn't move, hardly breathed, gave no indication that he'd heard her though he wasn't in a coma, or so Dr. Okano told her.

She didn't blame him for not responding. Blinking against tears, she remembered the night of the fire and the horrid fight they'd had, the worst ever, insults and pain ringing through the house by wounded, unhappy people. He'd accused her of never loving him, not as she had Brig, and she'd flung back that he'd married her because she was a Buchanan, and he'd always wanted to sidle up to the Buchanan money. In the fight she'd ended up suggesting divorce. It had seemed the only solution, even though she'd witnessed the wounded look in his eyes that night. Pain beneath his anger.

Oh, God, how she regretted those words. Chase had always been good to her. Fair. And as much as she'd tried, she never had loved him with the careless, wild abandon which she'd so naively thrown at his brother.

Who was now dying.

How had it come to this? She buried her face in her hands and refused to cry. She wouldn't show her feelings to the hospital staff or, worse yet, to the reporters who had collected in the lobby and had tried to come up with ways of getting a word with her, the doctor or even one of the victims.

Even now, in this private room, she felt as if someone were watching; that the monitors attached to Chase by all sorts of tubes and wires somehow were attached to cameras, or that someone was looking through the clear window to the nurses' station even though the flimsy curtain was drawn.

You're imagining things.

Exhausted.

Jumpy.

Give it a rest.

But then she heard it . . . the soft creak of a footstep.

So what? Probably a nurse or an orderly or other employee. She looked up quickly, squinted through the curtain and saw no one, not even a nurse with a clipboard at the nurses' station.

Cassidy climbed to her feet and walked to the door that she'd left just slightly ajar and expected to see someone about to enter the room and check on Chase . . . but the hallway was empty, the light lowered for the evening. She heard soft voices coming from a room down the corridor, but that was it aside from the steady whirr of the air-conditioning and soft little beeps of the monitor.

You're letting this get to you, Cass . . . cool it. Find a way to calm down and get through it.

Chase let out a quiet moan and she was instantly at his side, linking her fingers through his. "I'm here for you," she said, biting her lower lip and staring at his swollen face. "I promise we'll find a way to make this work."

I thought I might be sick.
Seeing Cassidy playing the role of dutiful wife.
What a joke.
As if she'd ever loved Chase McKenzie.
As if she knew the meaning of the word.
She was as big a slut as her sister. When she couldn't have one of the McKenzie brothers because he'd run off like the coward he was, she'd married the other. And she hadn't even traded up. Chase McKenzie was a snake . . . but he was nearly a dead snake. I smiled at that and slipped through a back door to a service staircase.

Two floors down, I ducked into the unisex restroom without being seen and changed quickly from my lab coat and scrubs to dark jeans, black T-shirt, jacket, and baseball cap. I tossed the used surgical gloves into my small athletic bag with my disguise, then slipped a pair of tinted glasses over the bridge of my nose. Quickly, seeing that no one was lingering around this part of the first floor, I crossed the hallway and took the stairs to the parking garage. From there I sprinted three blocks to the alley where I'd parked the truck and stashed the bag behind the seat. As I slid behind the wheel and slammed the rig into gear, I berated myself for failing.

Both men were supposed to be dead.

The blast should have killed them instantly.

Instead they were here, lingering on, holding on to life with tenacious, burned fingers. *Shit!*

I thought maybe I'd have a chance to help Chase into the grave tonight but not with his wife sitting at his side, holding vigil, for Chrissakes!

Damn it all to hell.

Patience . . . you've done this before. You still have time.

I glanced again at my reflection. Saw the determination in my eyes. Knew that it was only a matter of time. My hands curled over the steering wheel in a death grip, and as I came to a stoplight in the middle of town, I convinced myself that I would try again.

And next time I wouldn't fail.

Twenty-four

Cassidy convinced Detective Wilson that she had to visit the man in CCU. If Brig was still alive, she was determined to see him. T. John was only too happy to pull a few strings, talk to the doctor and escort her through double doors to a nurses' station that was hub to several rooms with three walls. From a desk that looked like the controls of the starship *Enterprise,* the nurses could read screens as well as see the patients in their beds, unless a curtain was drawn for privacy.

Stay calm, she warned herself as she glanced at the filled beds. Three men and two women lay in bed, sleeping or drugged, tubes, wires and catheters hooked up to their bodies.

"This way," T. John said softly and led her to the third cubicle.

The marrow of her bones seemed to turn to ice. This— this broken man was Brig? Little hair, face battered, swollen and discolored beyond recognition, barely breathing. Wires held his jaw together; bandages covered parts of his head and arms and legs. She bit her lip as images of him as a young man—a healthy, vigorous, irreverent man—flitted through her mind. Brig with his head tossed back as he laughed, Brig's body tense, muscles straining and gleaming in the sun as he fought Remmington, Brig's eyes flashing dangerously as he lit a cigarette and Brig kissing her in the rain.

She held back a little sound of protest and wanted to turn away, to run as fast and as far as she could go. Forcing herself, she approached him slowly. A sick feeling grew in the pit of her stomach. Tears burned her eyes.

"He regained consciousness?" T. John asked a nurse who was changing IV bags.

"No."

"What's the prognosis?"

"You'll have to ask the doctor."

T. John frowned at the dying man as Cassidy fought to keep her composure. He couldn't be Brig!

"You know him?"

She shook her head. "It would be impossible to tell . . ."

"Any educated guesses?"

"No," she said, deciding that even if this man turned out to be Brig, she would keep his secret, at least for a little while. He'd been running for so long; she'd helped him escape all those years ago, and the truth of the matter was, she couldn't be certain. Just because he was with Chase and he'd been found with a half-burned St. Christopher's medal wasn't enough. If only he would open his eyes and look at her. Maybe then she'd see a little of the man she'd known so long ago.

"I'm sorry, but if you're going to stay longer, I'll have to clear it with Dr. Maloy."

T. John glanced at Cassidy, but she shook her head.

"All right, then," he said, taking her by the elbow and propelling her past the nurses' station and through the door to the outer hallway. Her feet were leaden, her insides shaking.

The detective reached into his pocket for a pack of gum. "Want a stick?" he offered, extending a pack of Dentyne, but she mutely refused, barely hearing him over the rush in her ears. "Not a pretty sight, was it?"

"No."

He unwrapped the gum, formed the stick into a ball, then plopped it into his mouth. "The doctors are surprised he's lasted this long, you know. His heart was supposed to give out before this, but it seems to still be beatin'. He's one tough son of a bitch, I'll grant him that. Still hangin' in here. He wasn't so much burned as all busted up inside, you know; lost a helluva lot of blood when one of the beams fell and pinned him. I'd say he was lucky to have made it this far, but—"

"He didn't look lucky to me." Finally she could talk, though her voice sounded foreign and strange, as if she were trying to speak through glass.

T. John glanced at her. "Maybe you'd better sit down."

Rather than argue, she fell into a chair in a small waiting area where some other worried people—presumably friends or relatives of patients in the Critical Care Unit—sat or paced. White-faced, lines of worry etched across their faces, hands wringing shredded bits of tissue, they waited for news of a loved one fighting for his or her life. *Like Brig—but that man can't be Brig!*

"I can get you some water—maybe coffee?"

"No." She waved away any kindness and reminded herself that she couldn't trust him. Law or not, T. John Wilson was the enemy. At least for a while. "I—I'll be fine."

"You're sure?"

"Yes."

He waited, leaning on a post, arms folded over his chest, booted ankles crossed, while she struggled to pull herself together, while she tried to keep her wild imagination from galloping away with her. If the man was Brig—what was he doing at the sawmill? Why had he been with Chase? How long had Chase known that Brig was alive—just recently, or had he been lying to her for months, maybe even years? Maybe ever since the first fire, the blaze that felt as if it had occurred a lifetime ago.

The world seemed to crumble beneath her feet. Had Chase known his brother was alive when he'd first started dating her and then just neglected to mention the fact? Nausea washed over her and she thought she might be sick. She swallowed twice and finally stood on unsteady legs.

"You're sure you're all right?"

No! I'll never be the same again! Oh, God . . .

"Yes," she lied with more conviction than she felt. "I—I think I'll visit my husband."

T. John stared at her so hard she wanted to shrink away. "I thought you two were separated. Didn't you have some kind of big fight that night?"

"I already explained—"

He held up a hand. "I'm just pointing out that on the night he was nearly killed, you argued, told him you wanted a divorce—isn't that right?"

With a sigh, Cassidy nodded. She'd tried to be as truthful with the detective as possible.

"And then he left all angry and in a huff. And you—what did you do—stayed at home and worked on some story?"

"That's right," she said.

He obviously didn't believe her. "I hope you're not lying to me, Mrs. McKenzie, 'cause I don't take kindly to bein' lied to."

"Neither do I, Detective. Nor do I like being treated as if I'm obstructing your investigation. I didn't follow my husband to the mill that night, if that's what you're insinuating."

"He's insured for a lot of money."

Cassidy glared at him. "I don't care about money."

"Oh, that's right. You're one of the few women in the world who have enough. And even though you wanted a divorce—"

"I didn't want it. I felt that . . . that there was no choice."

"But now you feel duty-bound to sit at his bedside and hold his hand?" Wilson didn't bother hiding his disbelief.

"I want to."

Lower lip protruding slightly, the detective's eyes narrowed as he chewed thoughtfully on his wad of Dentyne. Nothing seemed to escape him, and despite his laid-back, I-don't-really-give-a-damn manner, he seemed restless. No, she couldn't trust him.

"I'm still married to Chase."

"Yeah, I know."

"He needs me right now."

"The way I heard it, your husband never needed anyone."

The barb stung, but she didn't let her temper get the better of her. "You don't know him."

"But I will, darlin'," he assured her as she turned toward the elevator. "Before this is all over, I'm planning to know your husband backward, forward and inside out."

Don't bet on it. No one really knows Chase McKenzie. Believe me, I've tried.

There were more flowers in the room. Huge baskets of roses, carnations, bachelor buttons and seemingly every other bloom known to man had found their way inside to crowd around the IV drip, plastic furniture, sink and bed. Balloons, tethered by ribbons, floated near the ceiling. But despite the splashes of bright colors and good wishes from friends and employees of Buchanan Enterprises, Chase looked just the same—unmoving on the bed. Cassidy took her seat beside him, reached for his hand through the metal slats of the bed and tried to get his attention.

"They say you're not cooperating," she said softly.

No response.

"They think you're awake, but you won't say anything."

The single eye continued to fixate on the ceiling.

He was shutting her out. Again. Just as he had for years.

"I was hoping that you'd be getting well enough to come home."

Nothing.

Cassidy wouldn't give up. She tried another tack. "Mom and Dad are supposed to be here this afternoon. They're anxious to see you and tomorrow your mother is coming over. I—I arranged it with her nurse—"

The eye blinked then refocused.

"Brenda, you remember her, she's your mother's new private nurse. She was hired by the hospital a couple of months ago. Anyway, Brenda says that your mother's been very upset since your accident . . ."

More than upset; Brenda had admitted that Sunny, upon hearing the news of the fire at the mill and her son's injuries, had been hysterical. She'd ranted and raved, thrown things and insisted on being set free, then wept openly for her boy.

Worse yet, she'd predicted the fire. Her psychiatrist, Dr. Kemp, a balding man who still wore his thinning hair in a ponytail and kept three days' growth of gray beard forever on his chin, was concerned, and had been forced to sedate Sunny. He'd been studying her for years, trying to separate her psychosis from her supposed E.S.P., and appeared to be getting nowhere.

"Sunny's visions are becoming more frequent, I guess, and she keeps saying that this was bound to happen." Cassidy removed her hands from the bedsheets and twisted the handle of her purse, uncomfortable when speaking about her mother-in-law, a woman she respected, yet didn't completely trust. "I'll bring her over tomorrow afternoon and—"

"No!" His voice was raw, barely audible, but vehement in its passion.

Cassidy jumped, dropping her purse. Her keys and wallet slid through the open zipper compartment and onto the tile floor. So he could hear her after all. He'd been pretending. Relief and a tinge of anger surged through her as she scooped up the contents of her handbag, then reached through the rail of the hospital bed again to touch the fingers protruding from one bandaged hand. "You can hear me!"

Silence. Stubborn, stony silence.

"Sunny's anxious to see you, to touch you, and rest her mind that you're all right—"

"I said no!" The voice was a rough croak, slurred as he fought to speak through his wired jaw.

"For God's sake, Chase, she's your mother! She's worried sick, and even though she can't sometimes distinguish between what's real and what's not, she needs to see you with her own eyes, to see for herself that you're going to make it."

"Not like this!"

So this was about pride. His damned pride. But Cassidy suspected there was more to it. Chase had never been comfortable around his mother ever since he'd had to force her from the old trailer by the creek, the home she'd loved. For her own good. Or so he'd said.

He'd found her one night, not long after he and Cassidy

had married, unconscious in her small bathtub. Blood had seeped from the wounds in her wrists, clouding the already rust-stained water in thin red streaks. Chase had dialed 911. Sunny, unconscious, had barely been alive when the paramedics had arrived.

Now Sunny McKenzie resided in a private hospital that had once been a rambling brick mansion. The hospital was run by an efficient medical staff who reported weekly that Sunny's condition, not particularly stable to begin with, would probably never improve. Though she'd stopped inflicting pain upon herself, there would always be a chance that she could become violent again. To herself. To others. Chase had reluctantly agreed to have her committed. His eyes had glistened as he'd signed the papers, then hurried down the wide steps of the hospital. He'd grabbed hold of Cassidy's hand and stalked blindly past landscaped gardens and serene pools, never saying another word until they reached the parking lot. "She'll hate it here," he'd predicted in frustration. Swiftly, he slid behind the steering wheel of his Porsche and jabbed his key into the ignition.

"Why not let her go home?" Cassidy suggested. She'd been scared to death the night she'd first visited Sunny after Angie had died and she'd run from Sunny's prophesy, but over time she had learned to respect Sunny McKenzie.

"And have her slit her wrists all over again? Or hang herself? Or turn on the gas? God, Cassidy, is that what you want?" He pumped the accelerator, twisted the ignition, and the powerful engine roared to life.

"Of course not, but she needs her freedom."

"Maybe later." A determined edge had developed around his features, and the bone in his jawline showed white. "She'll be safe here. She'll hate it, but she'll be safe."

And that was that. Cassidy had offered other ideas over the years, even suggested that Sunny come to live with them. Chase hadn't heard a word of it. Sometimes Cassidy thought he was embarrassed because of his mother the palm reader; other times she thought that he believed Sunny finally resided in the best place for her, that he really was concerned about his mother's safety and mental health. Hadn't he lived with her long after most sons would have moved out, even after Brig had taken off? Hadn't Chase been the ever-dutiful son?

Her husband, she thought sadly, was a complex man; difficult to understand. Sometimes impossible to love.

"Chase," she whispered softly, willing him to respond. But he seemed to have tuned her out again. "Detective Wilson from the Sheriff's Department is going to ask you questions. Lots of them. About the fire and about the man you were with."

He didn't so much as flinch, and she wanted to shake some sense into him. Didn't he hear her? Didn't he care?

She tried again. "I suppose you've overheard us talking and know that he probably won't survive. He's lost too much blood, I think, and he's got internal injuries." She didn't really know the extent of the other man's wounds, just understood that most likely he wouldn't pull through. Her mouth seemed to turn to dust. "Who was he?"

The eye closed.

"Chase, please. I think I should know." She reached for his hand and he flinched. "Chase—"

His eye flew open. "Don't!" he nearly yelled in his harsh, unrecognizable voice. "Don't touch me." Finally he turned his horrid gaze at her—startling blue against angry red. "Don't ever touch me again."

The words were harsh and thick with his inability to use his jaw, but they cut as deeply as the slice of a bullwhip. "Just tell me about the man you were with," she insisted, refusing to back down though her heart was drumming so fast she could barely breathe. His gaze bored into hers, and she couldn't help blurting what she knew had to be true. "It's Brig, isn't it? I know you told me a long time ago to forget him, that he was dead, at least to you and me, but . . . but I never really believed it and now . . ." Her voice cracked with emotion. ". . . and now I think, oh, God, I don't know what to think, but you met with Brig for some reason and—"

"Brig's dead."

"Not yet! He's in a hospital bed in CCU fighting and losing his life—"

"I thought we already talked about this. I thought you understood." His voice was low and gravelly, his hands, despite his cast, curled into fists.

"I, um, I think you deliberately let me think that Brig was dead and that he was really alive somewhere."

"For the love of God, Cassidy, give it up! He's gone. Been gone for seventeen years. Accept it."

She stood on trembling legs and grabbed the top rail of the bed so hard her knuckles bleached white. Glaring down at him, she tried to remember why she'd wanted to marry him, why she'd given up her fantasies, her dreams, her career, for him. "Then who was he?"

"I don't know."

"Like hell, Chase. You're stonewalling me again. And if the guy isn't Brig, then I'd like to know who he is—why you're covering for him. You know the insurance company is already making noise that you might have wanted the sawmill burned. They can already prove that it was arson. Now all they need is a culprit."

"Why would I want to burn the mill?"

"So that you could collect and not have to look like the bad guy for throwing people out of work—people you actually worked with a long time ago, people in town who look up to you, people who depend on their jobs to support their families. There's only so much timber left on Buchanan property, and with all the restrictions on federal land, the investigators have begun to think that it might have been more profitable to torch the mill."

"And nearly kill myself?" he asked, sweat beading his black and blue brow as he tried to speak.

"Maybe that was a mistake; or you took a chance to throw suspicion away from yourself."

"You're unbelievable."

"And it seems to have worked. Detective Wilson suggested that maybe I set the fire."

"Wilson's an idiot."

"I just want answers," she said.

"I know. Always the reporter."

Her fingers uncurled and she fought a sudden thickness in her throat. What was she doing? Chase was still recovering. His flesh was still discolored and swollen, one eye patched, his legs and a wrist in casts, and she was badgering, hammering at him for the truth. She'd have to be patient. It was only fair.

God help me. Help both of us.

On unsteady legs, she walked to the window and stared outside to the parking lot, where the sun glinted brightly on the hoods and roofs of cars parked in even rows. "I'm sorry, Chase," she said after silently counting to ten. "I didn't mean to come apart . . . I've just been worried. About you. About everything. Wilson is relentless. Determined." She motioned uselessly with her fingers. "He'll want to ask you questions. You should be prepared."

"You really think I started that fire?" he asked thickly.

Cassidy rubbed her arms. "No—I'm sorry, I was just angry and frustrated. It seems like there's a lot you know—some things that you hide from me." Her chin wobbled a little. "I don't think you'd torch the sawmill and risk killing yourself, but the police won't be so charitable and the insurance investigators will probably be ruthless. So be careful, Chase." Slinging the strap of her purse over her shoulder, she paused at his bed again, forcing herself to stare at his immobile form. A pang of loneliness cut through her heart. They had once been happy—if only briefly. "If you need an attorney, I'll call—"

"I didn't do it," he repeated. "As my wife, I expect you to believe me."

"And as my husband, I expect you to be honest with me." She paused near the door. "The authorities think this fire might have some connection to the one that killed Angie and Jed. I just thought you should know. Good-bye, Chase. I'll— I'll be back later."

"Cass—"

At the sound of her name, her steps faltered. "Yes."

"Call the doctor. Tell him I want out of here."

"But you can't come home yet." She almost laughed except the situation was so tragic. "You're—"

"I know what I am, Cassidy, but I've got to be released."

"In time—"

"Now!"

"For God's sake, Chase, relax. They'll let you out when you're well enough."

"That may not be soon enough."

"For what?"

He stared at her so hard she nearly flinched. His throat worked, and for a breathless second she remembered that she'd cared for him once. "I need to be out of here," he stated. "The sooner the better."

Twenty-five

The sawmill was barricaded. Slick yellow crime-scene tape roped off the debris of charred saws, twisted black beams and rippled, heat-destroyed aluminum that had been the siding of several of the sheds. The office was a shell of broken windows and scorched walls, the roof gone; file cabinets, computers, desks and chairs reduced to black rubble. Some of the raw timber had been saved, but stacks of cut lumber, graded and planed and ready to ship, had been ruined by the blaze and the thousands of gallons of water pumped onto the inferno. Caused by arson. Just like before.

Fire and water.

As Sunny had predicted.

Though the temperature was over eighty degrees, Cassidy shivered. She didn't get out of her Jeep, just let the engine idle in the pockmarked lot, listened to the radio with half an ear and stared at the remains of the heart of her father's business.

Chase wouldn't have burned it down. Despite the depression in the timber industry, Buchanan Logging and Sawmill was breaking even while other parts of the conglomeration that was Buchanan Industries were reporting record profits. Who in his right mind would burn down one of the few mills in the state that was working at full production and ruin thousands, maybe millions, of board feet that were worth more each day as lumber prices continued to soar? Chase was no fool. He understood money. Growing up poor had taught him early lessons in finance.

Through the dusty windshield, she spied several people clustered around the remains of the mill, peering through the twisted chain-link fence and past the old safety sign with the letters that had peeled off under the heat. They talked and joked between themselves, pointing at a forklift that had endured the blaze, the tires flat and melted, the tines of the fork black as coal, the padded seat burned away and the engine useless.

She didn't hear her brother until he rapped on the glass with his knuckles. She rolled down the window.

"It's a bitch, isn't it?" he said, nodding toward the ruined mill as she rolled down the window. Warm, muggy air drifted into the Jeep. Hazy clouds blocked the sun, and Elvis's voice crooned through the speakers.

Derrick motioned to the radio. "Turn it off."

"Why?"

"I hate Elvis. You know that." It was true—ever since they were kids, Derrick had ranted and raved, been nearly out of his mind, whenever Angie or Cassidy had played any of the records they'd found stashed in the attic along with Lucretia's clothes and books.

She snapped off the radio. "What're you doing here?"

"Gawking, just like everyone else." Derrick rubbed his jaw thoughtfully. A sprinkle of gray shot through his hair. When he was sober, he was a handsome man who looked more and more like their father with the passing of the years. "Christ, what a mess."

"Amen," she agreed.

"Felicity says Chase is gonna make it."

"Yes." She sounded positive. Around her brother she always put up a good front. He'd been against her marriage to Chase from the start, and Cassidy was determined never to give Derrick the satisfaction of knowing he'd been right about her happiness. Even if she and Chase divorced, she hoped that all Derrick would find out was that they didn't get along, that they had just drifted apart, that there was no guilt, no lie, no suspicion, and certainly no hatred.

"He comin' home?" Derrick scrounged in his pocket for a pack of cigarettes.

"Yeah. If he had his way, he'd be out today."

"And then what're you going to do?" He found a Marlboro and jammed it between his teeth.

"Take care of him, I suppose. Until he's on his feet again. It'll be a while. Physical therapy five times a week for six months to a year."

"He won't like it." Derrick shook his head and squinted his eyes against the lowering sun. "You're only asking for trouble again by sticking with him, you know."

"He'll need help."

"And you'll give it to him. Over and over again. You know, Cassidy, I never figured you for being a—what's the current fashionable term? An enabler, that's it." He clicked his lighter and drew hard on his cigarette. Smoke drifted from his nostrils. "I think that's just a fancy name for a doormat of a woman. You know the kind. A woman who will do anything to keep her man. Even let him walk all over her, stomp all over her emotions and her heart, then keep doing what he wants to because the woman lets him."

He sounded like he was describing his wife. Felicity had been in love with Derrick for as long as Cassidy could remember; she'd chased after him in high school, become best friends with Angie so that she could be closer to Derrick and had finally trapped him with a baby. Now, despite Derrick's affinity for Jack Daniels and his rumored passion for other women, she stuck by him, the ever-dutiful martyred wife.

Cassidy decided to ignore the attack on her character. "Is there something you wanted?"

"Not really," he said, surveying the mess as the wind kicked up and the scents of burned wood and exhaust from the idling Jeep wafted through the interior. "I was just coming from the house—Dad and Dena finally showed up. I gave Dad an update on what's been going on around here, then was heading into town when I saw your rig. Thought I should stop by, offer my condolences or whatever the hell they are and tell you that Dena's looking for you."

Cassidy sighed. She wasn't ready to face her mother—not yet.

He frowned. "You don't have to stick by Chase just because he's your husband."

"Of course I do."

"He doesn't deserve it, Cassidy."

She rammed the Jeep into first. "I think I'll be the best judge of that."

"You know, him being laid up puts me in kind of a bind."

"Puts *you* in a bind?" she repeated incredulously. "Chase is lying in a hospital bed—battered and burned—and it puts *you* in a bind?"

"Of course it does. I've got to hire people to fill in for him while he's gone. A couple of lawyers to start with and then some troubleshooters . . ."

"I wouldn't start filling Chase's shoes too quickly."

Derrick drew hard on his cigarette. "The man's a cripple, Cassidy. He can't talk, can't walk, and for all we know, he could be brain-dead."

She couldn't help laughing, but the sound was bitter. "You wish. He's far from brain-dead and talking already. Be walking sooner than you know."

"Think about it. He won't be able to come back to work and I can't hold up the entire operation because of it. But I could buy him out. Hell, with the amount of shares he owns, you'd both be set for life."

"What about my shares?" she asked knowing that Derrick had always resented that Cassidy owned a portion of the company. Not much, but enough to remind him that he wasn't the only heir to their father's fortune.

"I'd buy them, too."

"Over my dead body." Cassidy stepped on the gas, and the tires chirped as she cranked on the wheel and headed out of the parking lot. She didn't know why she suddenly felt so possessive of a few stock certificates, but she wasn't going to let Derrick bully her. The entire idea of him offering to buy both Chase and her out so soon after the fire smelled bad, as if he wanted to profit from the blaze.

She glanced into the rearview mirror and was surprised at the determination she saw reflected in her eyes. What was it about her brother that could make her protective of a husband she hadn't loved in a long, long while and possessive of stock she once would have given away?

"You're losing it," she confided to the gold eyes staring back at her. "Definitely losing it."

"We've been worried sick!" Dena's voice cracked through the foyer of the home where Cassidy had grown up. She pushed the door open a little farther and threw her arms around her daughter. "We took the first flight we could get. Oh, dear, let me look at you." Holding Cassidy at arm's length under the chandelier, she studied her daughter. Little lines of worry pursed a mouth still tinged with traces of peach lipstick. "How's Chase?"

"He'll be okay. Right now, he doesn't look too great, but the doctors are optimistic."

"Cassidy!" Her father walked stiffly into the foyer and a smile pulled at the corners of his mouth. "It's good to see you."

"You, too, Dad." She meant it. She'd been dreading facing her parents, but now that they were here, she was glad they were home.

He grabbed her hand. "How're you holding up?"

"Pretty good, I think."

"Need a drink?"

Cassidy shook her head. Her nerves were jangled already, her emotions snarled, her imagination running wild. What she needed was a clear head. "I'm fine."

"Well, I need one."

Dena's gaze was reproachful, her tone slightly scolding. "Rex, I don't think you should—"

Rex didn't hear his wife, or if he did he chose to ignore her advice and strode purposefully to the den.

"This is killing him, you know," Dena confided as they

walked into the kitchen. "Those horrid old memories"—her fingers fluttered at her sides—"all back again." Her face looked suddenly pale and old as if she'd been forever fighting a no-win battle with age. "I thought it was behind us, but oh, no. He even insisted that on our way over here we stop at the cemetery, for God's sake. After the flight, we couldn't even come home and take off our shoes or unpack. No way. He had Derrick pull off at the cemetery and he spent about twenty minutes praying at Lucretia and Angie's graves." Her chin wobbled a little, and she took a seat in one of the kitchen chairs near the window. The sadness that her husband would never love her as much as he'd loved his first wife made her shoulders slump. "He'll never forget her, you know," she admitted, wiping at a spot on the tile inlay of the wooden table with a long finger.

"Angie?"

"Lucretia." Dena reached into her purse for a breath mint. "And Angie, too. They looked so much alike. He . . . well, you know how he felt about her." She gave a little shudder and looked as if she might break down. "He always treated her as if she were some kind of princess—a replica of her mother. Sometimes I wondered if . . ." She swallowed hard, then shook her head, as if in denial to herself.

"You wondered if what?" Cassidy asked, feeling a needle of dread prick her heart.

"Nothing . . . nothing . . ." Dena said quickly, forcing a smile. "I thought he'd change," she admitted. "Forget Lucretia." She wrapped an arm protectively over her waist. "But losing Angie. It only made it worse."

Their gazes touched briefly, and her mother's eyes were dark with a private torment. Cassidy's insides seemed to congeal.

"Sometimes I wonder why I married him."

"I think your mother's had a long day," Rex Buchanan's voice whispered through the room, and the temperature in the kitchen seemed to sink five degrees. "You're tired, Dena."

Dena's shoulders stiffened.

Rex, swirling a short glass of some amber-colored liquor, smiled sadly. "Your mother's been having these spells—"

"I have not!"

"She's mixing up fantasy and reality."

"Oh, for God's sake, Rex, don't try to confuse Cassidy. She won't buy it. She's a smart girl and she remembers how it was. How you treated her."

"Stop it!" Cassidy hissed. "What's wrong with you two?" Then, to calm everyone, she held up her hands. "Let's not get into all that, okay? Angie and I were different. Dad treated us differently and it was fine with me, really." Her father stared down at his feet. "Dad, really, I never wanted you to treat me like you did Angie. I was afraid that after . . . after she died you might . . . well, change and look at me like you did her. When you didn't, I was relieved."

"It wasn't fair!" Dena put in. "He should have adored you the same way he—"

"He loves me, Mom. I know it. He knows it. I'm not Angie, and thank God for that!"

"You left after Angie died because of the way he treated you," Dena charged.

"I left because it was time to go. To find out who I really was. To get away from all this . . . this fighting. Now, come on, let's just put this all behind us. For now."

"Dena didn't like me stopping at the cemetery." Rex took a long swallow of his drink. "She's making more of it than there is."

"I don't like you moping around for a dead woman and a dead daughter. It's been too long. Just because there's been another fire doesn't give you the right to start acting melancholy all over again. You grieved over Lucretia forever, then you grieved for Angie and I understood it, but it's been too long, Rex, too damned long. I won't put up with it anymore." She blinked rapidly.

"The problem is you're jealous."

"Damned right, I'm jealous. I never measured up, did I? Never as good as Lucretia. I played along with it, thought you'd eventually forget her, but you didn't, and I'm tired of being understanding, pretending I don't hurt every time you look at her portrait, that I didn't notice how you ignored Cassidy whenever Angie was around—"

"Mom!" She couldn't hear this now, not while Chase was fighting for his life and Brig . . . dear Lord, she couldn't shake the image of his broken body from her mind. "This isn't the time."

"Cassidy's right. We've got other problems."

"Do we? Sometimes I wouldn't know." Shooting a scathing look over her shoulder, Dena glared at her husband before walking stiffly out of the room.

Rex finished his drink and dropped the glass into the sink. "She exaggerates." He turned and managed a well-practiced smile. "Now, tell me about Chase and how he's doing. The prognosis."

She filled him in as much as she could, suggesting that Rex and Dena visit him as well as talk to T. John. They discussed the arson, but stayed away from the obvious fact that the two fires were similar.

Rex finished his drink. "They have any idea who the other man is—the John Doe?"

"No."

"Chase doesn't know?"

"He says not."

"Ah, well. Another mystery." He rubbed his temples, sadness slid across his eyes. "Willie's been missing, hasn't he?"

"Unfortunately, yes. He hasn't been at the house, or at work."

"Damn." He twisted his glass in his fingers and stared through the windows. "I hope he's okay."

"Willie's tough."

"But innocent. Naïve. And it looks like a storm's brewing." He studied the darkening clouds, his face reflective. "Nothing like a summer storm." Rubbing the back of his neck, he asked, "Do you believe in curses, Cassidy?"

"What? No." What was he talking about? Why the sudden shift in conversation? She felt a sudden sense of foreboding. It was odd, she thought, but then she and her father weren't particularly close. She couldn't remember the last time they'd had a conversation, just the two of them.

"Good. That's good." He spoke softly as he stared out the window, past the pool, to a distance that only he could see.

"Do you, Dad?" Where was *this* leading?

"Of course," he said without even a second's hesitation. "And I think I've been cursed for a long, long time. I only wish it didn't involve you or your brother or your mother. It was bad enough that it destroyed Angie and Lucretia."

"What—what are you talking about?" she asked, and wondered if she really wanted to know. There were secrets in the Buchanan house. They all had them, and she sensed her father was about to share his.

"I think it's time you knew a few things about me."

Oh, God, she was right! Rex wanted to make a confession. A dull roar seemed to build in her ears.

"Oh, God," he whispered, almost as if it were a prayer. "I don't really know how to say this, but . . ." His fingers gripped his empty glass so hard his hand shook. "It's my fault they died, you know. All my fault." He blinked rapidly, fighting the urge to break down.

"You didn't kill them," she said, hardly daring to breathe. Surely he wasn't saying . . .

"Not intentionally, no. But I destroyed them; as surely as if I'd turned the ignition in Lucretia's car or struck a match to the old gristmill." Tears glistened in his eyes.

"But how? Dad, this is crazy talk."

"By not being faithful. A man should always be faithful."

The grandfather clock in the den began to chime. Rex glanced at his watch and seemed to pull himself together. "Jesus, look at the time. I guess we'd better go visit Chase."

"Wait a minute," she said. "What do you mean that you weren't faithful? You can't make a statement like that and just leave, Dad." She was angry, afraid of what she was about to hear.

"I suppose not." His features grim, he closed his eyes. "It's simple, Cassidy. I cheated on Lucretia. There were other women. One who I really cared about—not like Lucretia, you understand; I didn't love the women, but I did care about this one."

"You mean Mom?" Cassidy's stomach quivered.

He closed his eyes, and his lips moved silently as if he were sending up a prayer. "No," he admitted, his jaw sliding to one side.

Cassidy's fingers clenched around the edge of the counter. "Then who?"

"It's ironic, really," Rex admitted, dropping his empty glass onto the table. "The woman I cared about—the one I went to when I was lonely—was Sunny McKenzie."

Twenty-six

The sky was the color of slate—thick clouds covered the sun, the sultry heat oppressive. Cassidy drove as if her life depended upon it; as if putting distance between herself and her father would keep her from believing anything she'd heard.

The inside of the Jeep was warm, the summer air muggy with the threat of rain. Humidity made her sweat; disgust and disbelief kept her heart thumping wildly. Her mind was racing a million miles a minute to dark, suppressed corners she didn't dare peer into too closely.

The first splat of raindrops drizzled down the windshield, causing winding rivulets on the dusty glass. She didn't bother with the wipers, barely noticed the thin stream of traffic on the winding county road.

Her father had an affair with Sunny? Chase and Brig's mother—a woman whose husband left her because he questioned the paternity of her children. *It's only rumors. Just gossip. Just because Rex Buchanan slept with Sunny didn't mean that he fathered . . . oh God!* Her mouth went dry, the taste of stomach acid rising in the back of her throat.

For years she'd trained herself to be unemotional, to look at each news report, no matter how sordid, no matter how violent, no matter how depressing, with professional and uninvolved eyes. Though she'd had sympathy for the victims of crimes or accidents, she'd been able to report each story objectively. Afterward, late at night at home, she could confide in Chase, let her emotions pour out, but while she was on camera or writing her story, she kept her outrage or sorrow at bay.

But when it came to her own family, she couldn't find that inner thread of steel that kept her emotions under wraps. She'd been speechless when her father had admitted his affair with Sunny, and though she'd tried to question him further, he'd clammed up, as if he instantly regretted confessing to her. He'd made an excuse to go upstairs and look in on her mother. As if he cared!

Maybe it was just the booze talking. For years she'd suspected her father relied on alcohol to numb him; to help him cope with problems he'd rather not face. He'd used Scotch or brandy to soak his brain as he'd relied upon the confessional to assuage whatever guilt he bore for his sins.

Other dark thoughts coiled through her mind—ideas that slithered like poisonous snakes she couldn't outrun.

If Rex had engaged in a long-term affair with Sunny during his first marriage, wasn't it possible that he could have fathered Chase? Or Brig? The thought made the contents of her stomach turn sour. Her fingers gripped the wheel and she eased up on the accelerator as she approached a curve in the road. Surely if he'd sired Chase, Rex would have confided in his daughter—insisted she stop seeing a man who could be her half brother.

For the love of God. Her half brother!

Maybe Rex didn't know. Maybe he really believed Frank McKenzie was Chase's father.

Her mouth filled with saliva. She cranked on the wheel and pulled over. The belly of the Jeep was brushed by long, dry grass. Wheels squealed in the gravel of the shoulder, and the Jeep jolted to a stop. Throwing open the door, Cassidy jumped to the ground and ran to the ditch, where she retched violently, the contents of her stomach splattering in the weeds and litter of the dry gutter. "Please, God, don't let it be true," she whispered and wiped her mouth with the back of her hand.

Dropping to her knees, she felt fat drops of rain plop against the back of her neck and shoulders.

Maybe not Chase. Maybe, if Rex fathered any of the McKenzie boys, it had been Brig. Hadn't Frank McKenzie left Sunny only days after Brig had been born? Hadn't there been rumors of Sunny's lover siring her infant son? And hadn't Rex bent over backward giving Brig every chance possible, hiring him when other men wouldn't give the black sheep of the McKenzie brood the time of day?

Saliva formed in her mouth and she spat before vomiting again. *Not Brig! Please, please, not Brig!* But if he had fathered Brig, didn't Rex deserve to know that his son was lying near death in the hospital? Didn't Sunny have the right to visit him one last time?

Leaning forward, she dry-heaved until tears ran down her face. Her entire life had shattered. Even if neither Brig nor Chase was Rex's son, she'd never feel the same. Still kneeling, she leaned backward so that her rump hit her heels and the rain fell on her upturned face. Her father and Angie? Her father and Sunny? The world began to spin and she shook. The corners of her eyes were shadowed as if she would faint before her stomach revolted again and she hung her head over the dry grass and weeds. No! No! No!

Tears burned her eyes and she ran the back of her hand under her nose when the retching ended. Slowly, she rose to her feet. "Get a grip," she told herself as she wiped her hand over her lips and spat into the ground. "This isn't the end of the world." But of course, it was.

It was cold—so cold. Impossible to get warm. Sunny shivered. Because of the boys. Her boys. Images of them as toddlers, youths and young men danced in her head. Handsome. Strapping. Full of promise.

It had been years since she'd seen Brig, even longer since she'd reluctantly given Buddy away, and Chase—how long had it been since he'd come to visit? She'd counted on Chase, knowing deep in her heart that one day he would turn his back on her. Long ago, she'd seen into his soul. She tried not to be bitter. It was only right for a son to leave his mother and take a wife.

She rubbed her hands over the thin cotton of her sleeves, hoping to infuse some heat in her body. She'd been a foolish woman, she knew, trusting some of the wrong people. Even when she'd looked into their eyes and seen their true spirits.

Rex Buchanan had been a mistake. She'd been young and dazzled, the wife of Frank McKenzie, a good, decent man who wanted nothing more than his meal on the table when he got off work, and peace and quiet so that he could watch television. His eyes had been clear and blue; honest mirrors. He didn't make excessive demands upon her, never raised his fist to her, never so much as yelled at her, but he'd had a violent streak, one he'd kept dutifully under wraps. Until he drank. Then Frank transformed from an easygoing mill-wright to a hostile being with a chip stuck solidly on one brawny shoulder.

He'd gamble then. Find a cockfight or a dogfight and wager part of his pay on the bloody outcome. That was the only time when they would argue; when Frank would come back from the pits, smelling of smoke and sawdust and blood, a gleam in his eye when he won, disappointment bitterly etched into the lines around his mouth when he lost. Those few-and-far-between times were the worst, for then Frank seemed to become the embodiment of evil, the same hateful kind of man her father had been.

Sunny despised Frank's weakness. She believed in the sanctity of life for all creatures and refused to be silent after his drinking, wagering, and watching animals trained to kill and disembowel each other. The only time she raised her voice to her husband was when he'd been to the pits. The animal fights were not only inhumane but illegal, and Sunny had called the authorities more than once; each time the pits had been closed, but within weeks a new location was found in the wooded hollows and old barns that dotted the foothills of the Cascade Mountains.

She'd never meant to be unfaithful. Though she was not a

religious woman, her wedding vows were sacred to her and meant to be revered. She hadn't planned on falling in love with Rex Buchanan, nor he with her. But it had happened. Violently. Passionately. Sinfully. In lust she'd borne him a son. Because of that lust, her marriage had ended.

She'd always considered it fate that they'd found each other, their destiny. He never would have known her, never crossed that forbidden line, if not for circumstance.

As a joke for his thirty-fifth birthday, some of Rex's employees had given him a gift certificate to have his palm read and his fortune told by Sunny McKenzie. Sunny had known the certificate, which she'd made out of posterboard and colored markers, had only been for sport, that she was being made fun of, that Rex Buchanan, lord of all that was Prosperity, Oregon, would never deign to show his face in her little trailer rusting on the shores of Lost Dog Creek. But she needed the business, and she'd gone along with the group of five or six blowhards from the mill and placed the certificate in an envelope sealed with purple wax. When Rex had sheepishly knocked on her door two months later, she'd been surprised and pleased, welcoming him inside and taking his strong hand in hers.

Immediately, she'd seen his spirit. Sometimes a spirit would hide beneath layers of well-developed personality, but not so Rex's. His hand had been warm, his grip strong, his fingers capable of violence or tenderness. As she'd stared into his mesmerizing blue eyes, she'd looked into his soul and witnessed his sorrow, known instantly that his wife was cold and unloving. "You are not happy," she'd said.

"I don't believe in this."

"I know."

He'd tried to ease his hand away from hers, but she'd held on fiercely, full of wonder about this powerful man. "But you're not happy."

"Of course I'm happy. Why wouldn't I be?"

She released his fingers. "You love your wife and son, but you're not happy." She saw his eyes narrow and color climb angrily up his neck. "You haven't been happy in a long, long while."

"You don't know a thing about me."

"I feel sorrow and suspicion."

"Who set this up? Roy? No, Harold. I bet it was Harold, wasn't it?" he demanded, then when she didn't respond, he grabbed her by the shoulders and pushed her backward, shaking her a little. "It was Harold Curtain, wasn't it? That idiot! God damn that pompous bastard. I should have him fired—"

"He has nothing to do with the words I speak. I only tell the truth, from my heart."

"Then you're crazy."

"You came to me," she said simply, and his fingers, digging deep into the flesh of her shoulders, loosened. "You came here because you are unhappy. Because you want to find a way to fix things with your wife, so that she will love you and trust you and sleep with you."

He sucked in his breath, and his fists clenched. For over a minute he said nothing and the air in the trailer seemed charged. "You don't know—"

"I know of your guilt. For the wedding night and . . . and the fire . . . the burned dress."

"God in heaven," he whispered, his face suddenly white as death. "But no one knows—" He glanced nervously around the small room as if afraid they could be overheard. The blood pounded in the pulse at his neck, and his lips barely moved as he spoke. "Lucretia's been here," he said. "My God, she's been confiding in you."

"I've never spoken with your wife."

"But she promised, made me swear I'd never say a word—"

"I see your pain in your eyes, Rex Buchanan. I feel it in your hands."

"For Christ's sake, what is this?" He stumbled backward, knocking over a chair, his faith in God shaken.

"Do you want to know the future?"

He'd hesitated. "I told you. I don't believe in any of this hocus-pocus. It's all . . . all just a pile of crap. I go to mass every week," he said, his voice rising in near hysteria, his face suffusing with color again. He hooked a thumb at his chest. "I believe in God."

"I know you do. I see in your eyes that you're a faithful man. What I do has nothing to do with God, nor with Satan. The dark one, he's who you really fear, and Lucifer is not here. I'm not a witch."

"I should hope not!"

"I can't even explain what I see," she said with a shrug. "If you want your money back—"

"No, keep it. It wasn't mine anyway. This was just a couple of guys' idea of a joke. A bad one."

"So you've paid. Why not glimpse into the future?" She managed a reassuring smile for this wealthy man with his superstitions and guilt woven so tightly around his neck they were choking the life from him. "It might ease your mind."

She saw the sweat forming above his brow and felt his fear—for that was what it was. "If you don't believe, certainly it won't hurt to listen to me. After all, it's only a joke, right? Innocent enough."

His gaze locked with hers, and she saw his hesitation, watched as he challenged whatever demons had a stranglehold on his heart. He straightened, then righted the chair. Again he was in control, a wealthy man who knew his own power. With a confident grin, he said, "Sure. Why not? Should be a kick." He sat down again, stuck out his hand defiantly and Sunny wrapped her fingers around his palm. She felt his heat even then, the restless energy that pulsed through his blood, fed by his guilt and the temptation to cross the line between good and evil.

His pain was all-consuming. She saw through it as clearly as if it had been mere ripples on water and she felt his sadness. "Your wife doesn't love you," she said simply, hurting for him.

He started to pull away, but didn't. "That's a lie."

"She cared for you once, but something happened on

your wedding night." Sunny saw the stark images—fire and white satin, flowers and blood, a rumpled bed and heart-shaped bathtub. And she witnessed his guilt, a dark ugly veil surrounding the past, as surely as if she'd been in the hotel with him on his wedding night. "You did something—"

His throat worked. "Never. She—"

"You think she turned you away, because of . . ." She cringed as she saw it then, the violent, one-sided coupling, Rex drunk, Lucretia young and frightened. And then, in the intervening years, the cold shell Lucretia had built around her heart.

"Oh, you've tried to atone," Sunny whispered, wishing she could ease his agony and knowing even then that no one could, "but she won't let you; she enjoys having power over you."

"It's not like that!"

Sunny didn't argue, didn't tell him that she saw the private torture in his soul, the bruises on his heart because his wife had rejected him, refused to love him. And beneath the hard muscles, fierce pride, rapier tongue, she glimpsed another man, a gentler man, a man who only wanted love. A wounded, misunderstood soul, not unlike herself. Sunny lifted her eyes to his, and their gazes mingled in the stillness of the hot trailer. She felt him tremble, felt her own suddenly frantic heartbeat.

"She will never love you, but she will give you another child."

His eyebrows drew together. "Just one?"

"Only one from this woman, though there will be others."

"No!" Rex stripped his hand from hers as if her fingers were suddenly white-hot and deadly. He jumped to his feet and backed to the door. "I *love* my wife," he insisted, visibly shaken. "Do you hear me, I love her! I always will."

"I know," she said kindly.

"All this"—he motioned wildly at the table—"is nothing, just some kind of trick. You were probably told to say it, just to get me going. That's it, isn't it? Harold and the boys in investments, they put you up to it."

She didn't bother to argue, just looked up at him with eyes that pierced into his soul and saw everything.

"And my wife, she loves me. She does."

"If you say so."

"Oh, hell, I don't know what I'm doing here!" He reached for the doorknob.

"Examining your life," she said.

"It's just a joke, okay? A goddamned joke. Now everybody's had their laughs and it's over." He yanked hard on the door and stormed out of the trailer, leaving the door to catch in the wind and bang against the already scratched pink and white aluminum siding.

He would be back. He was intrigued. As surely as water ran downhill, Rex Buchanan would return. Sunny knew it and wouldn't try to prevent it. She couldn't.

He'd shown up less than a month later. They talked, drank coffee, listened to music, and she always told him his fortune. He scoffed at her predictions, of course, but he began to smile, his visits becoming more frequent. Sunny saw herself in his future; knew that if she didn't refuse him, she would be emotionally tangled with him for life.

But she couldn't. She looked forward to his visits. He came only when he was certain they would be alone. They talked for hours. She never tired of hearing about his world of wealth and power or of discussing what was happening outside of Prosperity, in the rest of the state and in the world. His views were so much broader than her husband's; his interests more varied. And though she knew she was wading in dangerous emotional waters, she couldn't restrain herself. Wouldn't.

Though she fought her attraction to Rex, Sunny couldn't stop the course of their destiny. She spent long hours of the night with Frank softly snoring on the double bed beside her, while she was awake and longing, her dreams focused on a man forbidden to her. Restlessly she stared out the small window of the trailer and silently cursed the desire she couldn't seem to control.

Frank was a good man, a steady worker, a person who, as long as he stayed away from liquor, didn't raise his voice. He thought Rocky Marciano was a god, Marilyn Monroe the sexiest woman alive, and he looked forward to the day when he could afford a color television.

Rex, too, was a good man, a thoughtful employer, a person who would never stop adoring his cold wife. He and Sunny could never be together; she was married to a man who didn't believe in divorce, and he was married to a woman he idolized. He looked forward to the day that Lucretia would forgive him, though it would never happen.

At first Sunny ignored her wanton thoughts. She refused to dwell on her shameful lust. But as the weeks and months wore on, she began to listen for the smooth purr of his car in the lane, looked for him in a crowd in town, felt her heartbeat quicken at the familiar rap of his knuckles on her door.

Unable to explain her fascination with him, she let her emotions run free and wild. In her dreams, she saw Rex's face, and while making love to Frank, she imagined it was Rex claiming her body with his. Shame ate at her thoughts, but she couldn't help herself and she believed in destiny; knew that the course of fate, once set in motion, was nearly impossible to alter.

So when he first kissed her, in her shabby little trailer, she didn't resist, and when he shoved her gently onto the couch, she let her knees give way. From that point on, his lovemaking was fierce, without tenderness. Like a starved man given his first meal, he made love to her, panting wildly, touching her everywhere, forcing himself deep into her.

She knew it was a mistake, knew she was risking everything she owned to become a rich man's mistress; but her marriage to Frank was little more than convenient, the trailer, though her home, certainly nothing she couldn't give up.

Rex's visits became more frequent and he tried to buy her

gifts—a gold bracelet, a turquoise ring, a new dress of silk—
which she wouldn't accept. Even the flowers he brought,
though beautiful, could not stay. So she wore his baubles
only while he was with her; she let his flowers scent the air
while they were together, let him slip the pearl buttons
through the fastenings of the beautiful dress that no one else
would see, for when he left, he took everything he had
brought with him. She wouldn't accept payment—even a
small token of his feelings—for making love to him.

Because she knew that he didn't love her. When she
touched him, she sensed his hunger, even his gratitude for
her; but he didn't care for her the way he adored his wife.
And Sunny would not reduce herself to the level of a paid
whore. She would love him from a distance, content in their
affair, until he tired of her; then, she promised herself, she
would let him go.

Sunny's pain, after Lucretia had died and Rex had married Dena Miller, had nearly killed her. Though still legally
married at the time, Sunny was alone—Frank had already
left her. Yet Rex had turned to another woman. She'd never
felt more betrayed.

Now, years later, she stared at the walls of her tiny room
in the hospital where Chase had seen fit to imprison her.
Neat and clean, painted a soft, soothing green with built-in
bookshelves, a twin bed, table and color television, it was, in
many ways, much nicer than her old trailer parked close to a
well on a scrap of property near Prosperity. But it wasn't
home. Would never be.

The window was open, a breeze scented by roses whispered past the curved steel bars that were supposed to look
like artwork but were lashed across the window for confine-
ment.

Each morning for the past week, as she'd stared through
her window and looked beyond manicured lawns, trimmed
rhododendrons and rows of oak trees to the tall mesh fence,
she'd sensed trouble. Watching as the sun rose over the ridge
of mountains to the east, she saw the first rays reflect gold on
the morning dew and felt a chill as cold as death sneak up

her spine. She'd known her boys were in danger, had, in her mind, glimpsed the fire that had destroyed the sawmill, but the images of flames and death were distorted, as if shimmering heat waves and black smoke had deliberately clouded her mind.

Again she shuddered and wished she could escape. She wasn't as far gone as they told her she was; true, her visions had become more frequent and violent, but when she was lucid she knew who she was and why she was here.

Chase's treachery still seeped into her soul like poison into a well. She'd always trusted him, believed in him, thought he had her—as well as his—best interests at heart. But he hadn't. She'd become an embarrassment for him as he'd become more involved in the Buchanans' business. He'd stopped visiting so often and couldn't look her in the eye because he was plotting to have her committed, to get rid of her so that he wouldn't have to explain that the crazy woman in the trailer by the creek was his mother, so he wouldn't feel compelled to have her come and live with him in his fancy house. Rex, too, had turned his back on her, and without her children and her lover, she'd decided it was time to leave this earth.

Glancing down at the inside of her wrists and the crisscrossing of scars fading against her dark skin, she grimaced. She'd worn those scars like medals from a war, a war she would wage until the day she died.

But she couldn't fight her battles from here; she had to find a way out of this place. She'd dreamed of escape often. Just last night she'd had a premonition, a peek through a window leading to the future, and in her mind's eye she saw herself running through familiar fields and facing the devils of her past, those who had deceived her.

She smiled though she felt no trace of humor. She would confront them all. And soon. It was only a matter of time.

Twenty-seven

"I thought you might be interested in this." Gonzales dropped a charred wallet onto T. John's desk. "Don't worry, it's been printed. So have the contents."

T. John set down his cup of coffee and picked up the burned leather. He didn't have to ask. "The John Doe's?"

"Won't be John Doe much longer." Gonzales flashed a quick hard-as-nails grin then crossed to the window, staring out of the one-story office building and into the parking lot, where cars, trucks and motorcycles baked in the sun.

"How about this?" Wilson opened what was left of the wallet and flipped through burned bills—hundreds, for the most part. Over three thousand dollars' worth, and what had once been a driver's license but was now barely a corner of the document. "What state's this from? Alaska?"

"Looks like it. We're checking."

The picture—if there had been one—was burned off and some of the numbers were missing, but there were enough that, with some time and the cooperation of the Department of Motor Vehicles in the forty-ninth state, the identity of the man dying at Northwest General Hospital would soon be known. "Contact the state police, see if they've found any abandoned vehicles with Alaska plates—or for that matter, any cars. He could've rented one down here or bought a junker with the kind of cash he was carrying—and check the rental agencies, see if any cars are overdue, from Portland and"—he squinted at the license but the address had burned off—"all the major cities in Alaska."

"Already done," Gonzales said. "And we're sending this to the crime lab in Portland, see what they can reconstruct."

Good. They'd finally caught a break. Nearly everyone in town seemed to have an alibi for the night of the fire, especially the people who were at the top of his list of suspects— Rex Buchanan, Dena Buchanan, Felicity and Derrick Buchanan, Sunny McKenzie, Bobby Alonzo, even the parents of Jed Baker. He'd checked. The only person who didn't have one was Cassidy herself and the two men in the fire. Finding people who had the time to set the blaze had been a son of a bitch.

"Where the hell did you find this? I thought the boys had finished digging around down there at the mill," he said, frowning at the charred wallet.

Gonzales stretched his arms over his head and his back cracked. "That's the strange part. We got it off a local."

Wilson's head snapped up, and he pinned Gonzales with his hard glare. His pulse jumped a little. Gonzales was holding out on him. The shithead. He loved this little game of one-upmanship. "Someone around here?"

"Yep. And we lucked out, too."

"How?" T. John leaned back in his chair until it creaked in protest and stacked his hands behind his head, waiting.

"Our man here drank a little too much down at Burley's. Someone had the nerve to call him a moron and he took offense, landing a right cross to the name-caller's jaw."

"Who—who the hell is 'our man'?" T. John asked, his patience wearing thin.

"That's the interesting part," Gonzales drawled. "John Doe's wallet was found in Willie Ventura's back pocket." Gonzales grinned widely, showing off more white teeth than any single human had the right to own. "Yes sir, it looks like the village idiot has a helluva lot of explaining to do, don't it?"

Cassidy switched off the monitor of her computer and rotated the kinks from her neck as she sat at her desk at the newspaper offices.

After driving through the rain for nearly an hour yesterday, she'd gone home, taken a long bath and even drank a glass of wine before going to bed.

But sleep had evaded her. She'd been restless and worried, her mind spinning with images of Brig, Chase, Rex, Sunny and Dena. Even Angie and Lucretia had wormed their way into her thoughts, and after tossing and turning for hours, she'd given up on sleep at three-thirty, gotten up and outlined a story on her desktop computer at home and then driven to the office.

She'd been here alone before, but in these early hours, the connecting rooms seemed eerie. Or was it her imagination? Her body was tired, her mind restless, hyped up, and it probably didn't help that she'd made her way upstairs to the employee kitchen and brewed a pot of coffee, listening to the hot water drip through the filter as she walked to the wide bank of windows and stared out at the small town where street lamps shimmered a ghostly blue and the stoplights in town, two that she could see from here, blinked brilliant red.

Only a few cars drove past the storefronts of First Street, and the sidewalks were empty aside from a stray dog sniffing along the curb. The scent of coffee was strong, the pot chimed that it was through brewing and Cassidy poured herself a mug, then returned to the window where, as she lifted her cup to her lips, she spied a movement in the night's shadows, a dark figure slipping around the corner.

Probably someone getting to work early, she thought, but there was something furtive in the way the person had moved from the lamplight. As if he'd been looking up at Cassidy and quickly scurried away.

"Don't be ridiculous," she warned herself. Lately her nerves were stretched thin, her anxiety level at a fever pitch, that was all. *No one* was sneaking around peering at her, for God's sake!

With a snort of disgust, she turned and headed downstairs to her desk. She flipped on the entire main bank of lights, illuminating the shared office space and telling herself to get a grip.

Back at her desk, she started checking through old files and printing out everything that was available on disk about the fire in the gristmill that had killed Angie and Jed years ago. She closed her mind to the terror her sister and Jed must have felt, to the fact that Brig had said he'd been there, to the mystery of Angie's pregnancy—Cassidy couldn't go there if she was to be objective and professional. She had to push her emotions aside and think clearly, use all of her training and reporter instincts.

She, like the police, couldn't help thinking that the fire seventeen years earlier and the recent blaze at Buchanan Sawmill were related. The police said the incendiary devices were similar and both properties had been owned by her father . . . in one fire three lives, counting the baby's, had been taken; in the other, two men had barely escaped with their lives and one might not make it.

So if the fires had been intentionally set—for what purpose? She clicked her pen as she thought.

Chase had refused to give her any information. Why? Was he guilty of something? Covering for someone? Or just didn't know?

Having been married to her for so long, he had to realize she wouldn't just let the matter die. And she hadn't. She'd decided to do some investigating on her own. She already had detailed records of the first fire; she'd assembled her own personal file shortly after moving back to Prosperity, and now she'd keep a personal record of every shred of evidence, every suspicion, every rumor, every theory that was posed about the blaze at the sawmill.

She unlocked her file cabinet and pulled out her file on the original fire. It was a thick sheaf of papers, a collection of articles and references to television news stories and her own set of notes . . . but as she flipped through the yellowed pages, she had the sensation that they weren't as she'd left them . . . the pages were out of place. She glanced at the notes she'd clipped to the front flap of the file—the list of all her information—then checked them against the articles in the file. Several were missing.

"Damn it!" she muttered under her breath. No one else had a key to the cabinet. So why were articles, three of them, missing? Who had taken them? *No one, Cassidy. You just misplaced them. Who would want them?*

Was that it? Had she been careless?

She drummed her fingers on the desk and told herself it didn't matter. She'd catalogued the stories, could get copies.

But why were they missing?

She felt a change in the atmosphere in the office, as if someone had opened a window and let in a rush of cold air. But she was alone. She looked around, saw no one and told herself she was being paranoid, when she heard footsteps in the hallway.

"Someone there?" she yelled, looking at her watch. It wasn't even 6 A.M. "Hello?"

Her pulse was pounding as she pushed back her chair and walked to the hallway, flipping on lights as she did. "Hey? Who's there?" she said, but heard no response. No more footsteps. No heavy breathing. No fiendish laughter. "Oh, for God's sake!" she muttered. She was tired and nervous, seeing figures lurking on the street, hearing footsteps, thinking someone had stolen from her files.

"Get a grip," she told herself, but she couldn't shake the feeling that she was being watched somehow—the same uneasy sensation she'd experienced at the hospital. Sitting down at her desk again, she told herself that her case of nerves was because of Chase. She knew that he was worried and since whoever had intentionally set the fire was still at large . . .

Her skin crawled at the thought. She checked over her shoulder and wished some other reporter would come in early, so that she could have some company and chase away this ludicrous case of the creeps.

Forcing herself, she turned her attention to the most recent fire. What did she know about it?

Only that Chase had been working late; which wasn't unusual, especially lately. He was known for his long hours; Derrick had always chided him for not paying enough attention to Cassidy, for "kissing up" to the old man, for being a workaholic.

Cassidy had always assumed Chase had been alone when he'd been at the office. The mill wasn't currently running a graveyard shift, and there wasn't even a night watchman or guard dog on duty. Chase had often told her that he did his best work late at night, alone, when everyone, including his secretary, had left for the day, when the phones didn't ring and people didn't stop by his office and interrupt him.

But this time he'd lied.

Just as he may have lied in the past.

She felt betrayed, but tried to keep her objectivity.

Obviously the other man had been with him. She doodled on a new page of a legal pad she always kept handy and made a big question mark on the lined paper.

Brig?

She'd convinced herself that Chase was with his brother, but she had to consider the fire with less emotion and tunnel vision. He could have met with someone else. But who?

Was the injured man the culprit, or had Chase decided to set fire to the mill? Or was it another, as yet unidentified, person—an employee who had been fired and held a grudge against Buchanan Sawmill, or someone with a personal vendetta? Someone who hated Chase? Or Rex? Or anyone with the last name of Buchanan?

Tapping the eraser end of her pencil against her notepad, she tried to imagine what had gone on that night. Was the fire arson, or was it attempted murder? That ugly thought ran like an electric current through her mind. Was someone deliberately trying to kill Chase?

Goose bumps crawled up her arm.

The door opened and she nearly shot out of her chair before realizing that, for the reporters and secretaries who liked to get to the job a few minutes early, it was time to arrive. She waved to the photographer as he and the receptionist entered together.

"Come on," she muttered to herself. This was no time to freak out. She searched through the files, found the newspaper's copy of the police report, then made a copy for her personal file.

By the time she returned to her desk, Bill Laszlo was waiting for her. Tall and lean, he looked like he ran the forty miles a week he was so proud of. Lately he'd become an exercise and fat-intake expert, and the twenty-five pounds he'd lost in the last two years were testament to his philosophy.

"You've been avoiding me," he accused.

"No way. I've just been busy."

"If you say so." He didn't look convinced in his stiff white shirt, black slacks, suspenders and matching tie. "I've been assigned to report on the fire and its aftermath."

"I know. Saw your byline on the last piece."

"I'd like to talk to you," he said, resting a hip against her desk.

"I don't know anything about the fire."

He grinned, showing off teeth that were stained by tobacco, though he'd given up smoking at the beginning of his health kick several years ago. "Is that the same as 'no comment'?"

"Really, you probably know more than I do."

He glanced to the top of her desk, where her notes were visible. "But you've been thinking about it."

"My husband was nearly killed."

"I know. Bummer." He scratched his jaw, still studying her doodles, and she followed his gaze, noting the question mark as well as Brig's name. Without an excuse, she shoved the legal pad into a file folder. "You know, I'd like to talk to Chase."

"You and every other reporter in this state."

"How about I stop by the hospital this afternoon—"

"No." He gave her a wounded look that she wasn't buying for a second. "Look, Bill, I appreciate that you have a job to do—I probably understand it better than most people—but Chase is still recovering. He can only see members of the immediate family."

"And the police?"

"That goes without saying." She looked up at him. "So . . . what do you know about someone getting into my file cabinet."

"What do you mean?" Was it her imagination or did a guilty look pass behind his eyes?

"I mean someone's been snooping in my files, taking some articles and notes."

"You're the only one who has a key, right?"

"In theory," she said, glaring up at him.

"What?" His hands flew to his chest. "You think *I* would stoop so low as to break into another reporter's desk?"

"I'm just asking."

"Cassidy . . ." he cajoled. "Are you sure?"

"Dead certain."

His wounded look disappeared. "Seriously? Then we've got a problem."

"At least one."

"Sorry, I can't help you with that. I have no idea who could have gotten into your things."

"Humph."

"But I'd still like a word with your husband."

She managed an icy smile. "And the answer is still 'no.' "

Bill picked up a pencil from her desk and rolled it between his fingers. "You know, Mrs. McKenzie, if I didn't know you better, I'd think you might be hiding something."

"Like what?"

His grin was wicked. "I'm still working on it."

"Don't work too hard. It's a waste of time."

"Just give me some background on Chase, okay?" he insisted.

"I think the paper already has a file on him."

"I know, but I'm not talking about his résumé, for Christ's sake. Him being a lawyer and coming to work for Buchanan Industries after you were married—that's just boring junk that everybody knows. I need something a little deeper."

"There is nothing more."

His lips twitched and he worked the pencil a little more feverishly. "No? What about the John Doe?"

The knife-edged tone of his voice caught her by surprise. "What about him?"

"Looks like the police are gonna ID him soon."

Her heart nearly stopped. "How?"

"Seems as if they're finally getting a break. They found a wallet this morning, though they're not saying much about it. But my source—"

"Just who is your source?"

"Can't say," he said, shaking his head. "You know better than to ask." He gave her a wink that set her already frayed nerves on edge. "But the word is that the man in CCU is going to have a name soon. It's going to be interesting as hell to find out who he is, don't you think?" He dropped the pencil on her desk and stood. "Hell, it'll probably break this case wide open."

Why the hell didn't they die?

I drove through the dark streets of the town and cursed myself for underestimating them.

Both men, languishing in the hospital, *recovering* for Christ's sake. Rumor had it that Chase was about to be released to his wife and the other guy just kept hanging on, by the proverbial thread.

I hated it.

This was *not* how things were supposed to go.

But then, I realized, taking a corner and spying a police cruiser hidden behind a laurel hedge, nothing was going as I'd planned.

They should both be dead by now.

Buried and forgotten.

My jaw clenched so hard it ached, and I glanced in the rearview mirror. The police car had pulled up behind me. Crap! My hands tightened over the wheel. If I was pulled over, how would I explain the hospital garb? The surgical gloves on my hands?

In a panic, I pulled the gloves off with my teeth, first my left hand, then the right, one eye on the speedometer to make certain I didn't crawl over the speed limit, the other on the cop behind me.

Should I pull off, pretend that I needed an early cup of coffee at the local coffee shop? But then I'd have to get out of my car and I'd have the scrubs on . . . no, that wouldn't work. I could drive to the hospital as planned, but then, if there were any questions later, the cop might remember my truck, maybe even run the plates . . .

I began to sweat and I drove toward the county road, hoping this city bastard would get off my ass. Slow . . . it's only twenty-five.

My heart was hammering. He was following me. Laying back, but always there, his overhead lights visible as he passed under the streetlights, his silhouette black and foreboding in the wash of headlights from the car behind him.

At the sign post near the outskirts of town that upped the speed to forty, I pushed on the gas and the truck accelerated, seeming to leap forward. I checked the mirror. The cop turned off.

Hallelujah.

I couldn't risk another mess-up.

After a few minutes, I turned onto the county road and pulled a quick U-turn. I'd planned another visit to the hospital and, knowing that Cassidy was busy, figured I wouldn't be disturbed. I knew the hospital routine and when the shift change occurred.

I had just enough time.

Twenty-eight

Willie didn't like jail. He'd been in one before—a long time ago—and he hated it. A little afraid of the man in the cell next to him—a big, hulking prisoner with tattoos and whiskers and mean pig-eyes—Willie lay on his bunk, away from the guy and away from the urinal that smelled like pee. He wished Rex would come for him like he always did, and he listened for the tread of shoes on the cement floor, the jangle of keys in a lock, the sound of men's voices. Why weren't the officers returning, their expressions regretful as they explained that they were sorry they'd made a mistake in picking up a poor unfortunate like the half-wit. He didn't even mind the bad names—if he could just get out. Scratching his arm, he tried to fill his mind with images of good things so that he wouldn't go crazy. He was afraid of going crazy. Crazy people were put in institutions, and institutions were like jail. Like this.

Where was Rex? He bit his lip and tasted salt. His skin felt dirty and sweaty and he'd do anything to get out of here. Anything. He'd even tell lies. Just to be free. But Rex had told him not to lie or make up stories or say anything to the police. He was supposed to wait and keep his mouth shut. Above all else, he wasn't supposed to say a word.

With a clang, a door was unlocked at the far end of the hall. Voices drifted over the sound of footsteps. Willie was on his feet in an instant, standing at the gate, hoping that Rex had come for him. He knew what was expected of him. Rex would scold him like a little boy and Willie would promise that he'd be good again. Then they'd leave. He thought Rex had to pay some money to someone but he didn't really understand why, and he didn't care. He just wanted out.

His fingers curled over the metal bars, and he pressed his face against the grate, feeling the steel press into his cheeks as two men came into view.

"Well, well, well, looks like someone's anxious to be let go." The voice belonged to à man in a leather jacket and jeans—no uniform—but Willie didn't trust him. He was the same man who had been at the big house asking questions about the fire. Though Willie had been hiding in the shadows of the barn, he'd seen the man as he'd climbed out of his car with the flashing lights. The officer gave him a smile and popped his gum at the same time. No, he couldn't be trusted.

The other guy with him was the same skinny man with the hot black eyes and long hair. He'd already been in to see Willie, already tried to pretend that he was Willie's friend.

"Heard you took a swing at Marty Fiskus," the first guy said.

Willie didn't answer, was confused. *Don't lie. Don't lie. They'll keep you in here if you lie!*

"Marty Fiskus is an asshole." This, from the prisoner with the tattoos and stringy hair in the next cell.

"Stay out of this, Ben," the skinny officer warned.

Ben rolled off his grimy mattress, and instinctively Willie shrunk away. He didn't like fighting, but sometimes when he'd been at Burley's too long, he got into fights. Ben swaggered to the bars separating his cell from Willie's. "I want to see my lawyer."

"Yeah, well, I want to see the pope and it ain't happening."

"I got rights, Wilson."

"Not many, Ben."

"When I get out of here—"

"If, Ben. *If.*"

"Call my fuckin' lawyer." Ben's face was suddenly red, his lips curled into a snarl.

"Pipe down. He's been called. Isn't anxious to come and

visit with you again. Somethin' about an unpaid bill. Don't say as I blame him." The officer turned his attention back to Willie. "Sorry about that. I'm Detective Wilson, remember me? And this is my partner, Detective Gonzales. We visited you at the Buchanan place, just the day after the fire down at the mill."

"I said I want to make a phone call." Ben wasn't through. "You pigs have no right to hold me here. When I get hold of my lawyer, you'll be sorry you fucked with me."

"Believe me," Wilson said, "we're already sorry."

"Bastard!"

Wilson sighed. "Now, Ben, is that any way to talk to an officer of the law?" He reached into his pocket and pulled out a pack of gum. Slowly unwrapping a stick, he added, "You'd better be careful or someone around here might take offense."

"Fuck off, Wilson."

"Come on, Willie, let's go somewhere where we don't have to listen to this filth." Keys rattled in the lock and the gate swung open. Willie felt as if the metal belts that had been binding his chest were finally loosened. He could almost breathe. But he was still careful. Rex had warned him. *Don't lie. Don't lie.*

He followed the man who had introduced himself as Detective Wilson to a windowless room with a table and chairs. On the dark wooden table was a file folder filled with papers. Willie began to sweat and fidget. This wasn't good. He was supposed to be let go. Where was Rex?

"Have a seat," the detective said, motioning to one of the metal chairs. "And tell me everything you know about this." He dropped the wallet on the table, and Willie averted his eyes. He didn't want to look at the burned leather. It reminded him of the fires. Both of them. He licked his lips.

"Were you at the mill the night of the fire?"

Willie bit his lip. *Don't lie.*

"Do you know who owns this?" Wilson pushed the wallet closer and Willie recoiled. He heard his heart pounding in his head.

"It's not yours, is it?"

Don't lie.

"Where'd you get it? Did you find it somewhere? Or take it off some guy or—"

"I didn't steal it! I don't steal!" he suddenly blurted and the hard lines of Detective Wilson's face softened into a smile.

"I believe you, Willie. So how did you get it?"

"All the money's in there! I didn't take it." Willie sniffed and wiped the back of his hand under his nose. His whole hand was shaking.

"No one's saying that you did, boy. But the wallet's not yours, is it?"

Frowning, so scared he wanted to cry, Willie shook his head. "No."

"Well, then, I'm just asking if you know the man who it belongs to."

Willie's voice worked, but he didn't say anything. Sweat dripped down the sides of his face. It was so hot. So close. And Detective Wilson didn't believe him. He'd put him back in jail. For a long time. Willie's heart was pumping so hard he breathed in short little gasps.

"He's hyperventilating," Gonzales warned.

"Just calm down, Willie." Wilson picked up the file and opened it.

Willie didn't know why, but he felt an overwhelming sense of dread, the same way he felt whenever he was alone with Derrick. Nervously, he rubbed his arm, the one Derrick had burned with a cigarette years ago.

"Now, Willie, this here's your file," Wilson said. "Notice how thick it is. You got yourself quite a few little misdemeanors in here, son. Good thing Rex Buchanan and his team of lawyers always found a way to bail you out. Let's see what have we got? Drunk and disorderly. Driving without a license. Uh-oh, now I don't like the looks of this—some little girl complained that you were following her and looking into her windows, but the charges were dropped. You remember that? Her name was Tammi Nichols? You remember her?" The smile again. "What were you doin', Willie? Tryin' to get a free peek up her skirt?"

"No." Willie shook his head frantically.

"You like to see girls naked?"

A dull roar filled his head. His Adam's apple bobbed nervously. This was no good. *Don't lie. Don't lie.*

"Well, hell, Willie, we all do. It ain't a crime. Unless you're peekin' where you're not s'posed to be." He settled back in his chair, rocking it back on its hind legs as he popped his gum. "I think you like to see naked girls. Don't really blame you but . . ." He flipped the page and Willie's stomach twisted in fear. "Uh-oh again. Lookie here. Another girl. Mary Beth Spears. She thought you were starin' through her window while she was just dressed in her bra and panties." He clucked his tongue. "That bothered her a lot, you see, her bein' the reverend's daughter and all." Wilson's eyebrows arched. "You look at her tits, Willie?"

The edges of Willie's vision grew dark, and he had to hold onto the table to keep from sliding down in his chair.

"That ain't nice. The reverend, I bet he wanted to skin you alive."

The room spun.

"Now these charges, all dropped or taken care of one way or another, don't really mean much." The detective closed the file and shoved it aside. "But if there were more charges filed, say something more serious like withholding evidence in a crime, or obstructing justice, or maybe even participating in the crime itself, well, all of Rex Buchanan's money won't buy you out of it. No siree. His entire team of lawyers won't be able to keep you out of jail."

Sweat slid down Willie's nose and dripped onto the table. He was so scared his insides felt all jumbled together, like he might pee his pants. He didn't move, just clung to the table so he wouldn't pass out.

"But on the other hand, if you were to cooperate with us, you know, fill us in on what you know, well, I'd say the chances of you going free were pretty high. Wouldn't you say so, Gonzales?"

"Real high," the skinny man agreed.

"Do you understand?"

Willie didn't move.

"Okay, here's the deal." The front legs of his chair hit the floor, and Wilson leaned forward on his elbows. "You tell us the truth, and you get to walk out of here. You bullshit me or keep your mouth shut, and we'll have to put you back in your cell next to Ben. I hate bullshit, Willie. Don't you hate bullshit, Gonzales?"

"Hate it."

"So we can't have none. You got to be straight with us, Willie. Honest as hell and you can probably get yourself out of this mess."

Willie swallowed hard. Spit collected in his mouth. *Where was Rex? Why was he letting these men shoot ugly questions at him?*

The detective picked up the wallet and wagged it under Willie's nose. "Come on, boy. It'll be all right. All you got to do is just tell me how you ended up with this tucked in your back pocket."

"Cassidy Buchanan's here to see you."

T. John Wilson let the words echo through his little office, savoring each and every one. He knew she'd be back; in fact, he'd expected her a couple of hours ago. She was with the press, and already word on the street was that the John Doe was about to be identified. Wilson wished he knew how the hell the damned reporters knew things before he did, but so far, he hadn't been able to find or plug the leak in his department.

The door opened and Cassidy marched in. She'd pulled herself together since he'd last talked with her and now, with her auburn hair framing her flushed face, her brandy-colored eyes snapping with fury, she was downright gorgeous. Everyone in town had called her the plain sister—a girl who couldn't hold a candle to Angie Buchanan. T. John couldn't imagine it. He climbed to his feet—a polite habit he'd learned from his Virginia-bred mother.

"You know who the man in the hospital is?" she demanded.

"And 'good afternoon' to you, too." Waving her into a chair on the opposite side of the desk, he took a seat again. "Not yet, but we will soon."

"And you didn't tell me?"

"Why would I?"

"Because I'm—I'm involved; Chase's wife."

"But you're not related to the John Doe. You didn't recognize him."

"My father's mill burned down!"

"So?" He set the heel of his boot on the edge of his desk and leaned back in his chair. "Look, Mrs. Mckenzie. I brought you in for questioning. I went to the hospital with you. I hoped you would help our investigation—that you would cooperate—but I don't see that I have any reason to tell you anything else. Besides, you're a reporter. I make statements to the press every day—"

"I'm not interested in a press release, Detective. This isn't about a story. I just want to find out who burned down the sawmill and nearly killed my husband."

"That's what we're trying to determine."

"Who is he?"

"We're not sure," he said. "Just calm down, sit in that chair over there and I'll get you a cup of coffee."

"Don't bother; just tell me the ID of the John Doe." She looked desperate, more desperate than she should, given the circumstances.

"As I said, we don't know yet, but I'll tell you this, we found key information and it looks like ol' John will be identified. It might take a while, but we'll find out." He smiled, content with himself. Things were going better than he'd hoped. Whereas a few days ago he was faced with dead ends, today he had the wallet, information about the dying man and a whole new perspective on the case. Yep, things were looking up, and if Floyd Dodds didn't watch out, T. John was going to steal the election from him and become the next sheriff.

"Why don't you tell me what happened," Cassidy said, calming a little and settling back in her chair. She crossed one leg over the other, and T. John tried not to notice the length of calf.

"Once we ID the guy, check him out and contact his relatives, I'll release his name. Until then, he's just John Doe."

Cassidy tented her hands thoughtfully, her gaze centering squarely on T. John's face. "Have you spoken to my husband?"

"Last I heard, he's not talking."

"He talked to me."

The muscles in the back of T. John's neck tightened. "When?"

"The other day."

"And you didn't tell me?"

"I'm telling you now. He only spoke to me once."

His eyes narrowed. "What'd he have to say?"

"Not much except that he wants out of the hospital."

"In his condition?" T. John nearly laughed. Chase McKenzie had a reputation for being bullheaded. "Did you ask him about the identity of the man?"

"He denies knowing of or talking with him."

"You think he's telling the truth?"

"I don't know, but I trust Chase. Since I stopped by, he hasn't spoken a word, not to my parents who visited him, not to the doctors or nurses who have been caring for him. I'm not sure they believe he can talk."

He was ahead of her—way ahead. "So you think that if we gave you information and you took it to him, he might respond; but that he won't speak to us."

"Could be."

His boot clattered to the floor. "I might point out that you're not an officer of the law."

"I don't think he'll talk to one."

"Then he'll be charged with hindering an investigation."

"Do you really think he'll care? He's stuck in a hospital bed, his leg and arm broken, his face wired together, maybe blind in one eye. I don't think he's afraid of jail at this point."

"He might be smarter than you think."

"No, he might be smarter than *you* think." Her lips pursed together in fury. "You try and accuse him of a crime and he'll hire a team of lawyers who will find physicians who swear he can't talk, that his throat and voice were affected by the smoke or trauma or something; then they'll point out that he was sedated and on painkillers, that even if he did speak, he wouldn't be lucid. They'll parade a dozen experts in who'll cite instances where a patient was too traumatized to speak, too out of it to talk rationally. Since he's only spoken to me, it'll be my word against his, and I won't have to testify against him because he's my husband."

T. John forced a smile he didn't feel. "You're trying to tell me that if I want to question your husband, I'll have to go through you, is that it?"

"I don't even know if he'll speak to me again."

Frustration seared a hole in his gut. He could push the issue if he wanted to. He was certain he could convince Chase to talk to him without her help, but it might work to his advantage to follow her lead and watch how she and her husband got along. He still didn't understand their relationship, but something wasn't right.

"I'm taking his mother to visit him this afternoon," she said, seeming nervous.

"You won't mind if I tag along?"

"Of course I'd mind. You can't come in while he's with Sunny. But afterward would be okay."

"You know, Mrs. McKenzie, no matter what you may think, you're not calling the shots on this investigation."

"You don't get it, do you?" she said, her lips barely moving, anger burning bright in the patches of color on her cheeks. "I'm not interested in some power play. I'm just giving you the facts, and I'm hoping that for my efforts, you'll be honest with me." She leaned forward, planting her palms firmly on the edge of the desk as she stood. "I'd like to know who the man in CCU is, and I give you my word that I won't take his name to my paper."

He didn't trust her, but he couldn't help asking, "Why is it so important?"

Something flickered in her eyes, a private pain he didn't understand, before she said, "Isn't it obvious? He could be the man who tried to kill my husband." Swinging her purse over her shoulder, she left. As quickly as she'd burst into his office, she was gone, the door slamming shut behind her.

"Son of a bitch." T. John opened the top drawer of his desk and reached for his bottle of antacid pills. Some of the confidence he'd felt earlier seeped away.

Cassidy McKenzie wasn't just an attractive irritation, he thought as he poured four white tablets into his hand and tossed them into his mouth. She was going to try and road-block him every step of the way.

Why?

He crushed the tablets in his teeth and washed them down with a swallow of cold, stale coffee. Climbing to his feet, he walked to the window and stared out at the parking lot, where Cassidy, hair turning to fire in the sun, unlocked her Jeep and settled behind the wheel. She knew something, he guessed, but he couldn't figure what. Maybe she did know the ID of the John Doe, or maybe her husband had told her what he was doing at the sawmill that night. If the guy was talking. Just because she said so didn't make it a fact. He swirled the dregs in his cup. She definitely knew more than she was telling, and he didn't think it was because she hoped to scoop the other papers. No, this was personal to her. Real personal.

He wondered if she'd hired the man herself in hopes of burning the mill, killing her husband and collecting a little insurance to boot. According to everyone he'd talked to who'd known the McKenzies as a couple, their marriage was on the skids—only a step away from divorce.

Wilson polished his teeth with his tongue as he thought. Was it just coincidence that the arson device was similar to the one used in the fire that killed Angie Buchanan and Jed Baker? Or was this man the culprit both times? Or . . . was the man an innocent victim, someone who had either been meeting with Chase McKenzie or prowling around the sawmill for other reasons? One of the workers? A disgruntled employee? Someone who wanted papers in the office where the bookkeeper worked along with Chase, Derrick or his wife Felicity occasionally? Or a drifter—the same arsonist that sauntered through town seventeen years before?

T. John squinted and bit at his lower lip, watching as the Jeep roared out of the parking lot. Maybe Chase McKenzie had set the blaze to try and hide something or to collect the insurance or to kill the other guy. Maybe he was interrupted and caught in his own fiery trap. Or maybe the missus was involved; she could have wanted Chase dead rather than divorce him. It would cost her less money. Or hell, the whole damned fire could be an accident and the two poor bastards caught in the blaze just two stupid-ass guys whose luck had run out. T. John didn't believe it for a minute.

Too bad Rex Buchanan had picked up Willie Ventura before he'd cracked. Willie knew more than he was saying and he'd been at the first fire as well. Another coincidence? Or was Willie a firebug?

He'd have to question Willie again—that much was certain—and as for Mrs. McKenzie, well, it might not hurt to have her tailed. Willie couldn't remember where he'd been during the fire.

Sure.

And Cassidy McKenzie had been home. Alone.

Right. And I'm one stupid son of a bitch.

He set his empty cup on a battered old file cabinet and returned to his desk. Lowering himself into his squeaking chair, he opened a bottom drawer and pulled out two files, one so thick it had to be held together with a rubber band, the other barely started. The first was filled with yellowed papers and notes, reports that had been kept in the archives for years, the unsolved murder cases of Angie Buchanan, her baby and Jed Baker. The second was a new file, with crisp white paper, notes and computer printouts on the fire at Buchanan Sawmill.

His instincts told him the fires were related and there were a lot of people in town now who were potential suspects in the first investigation. He tugged on his lower lip. Too bad the first case was never solved and the bad-ass McKenzie boy had taken off before he could be questioned. From all accounts Brig was one helluva bad seed, always in trouble. It would have helped to know how he was involved in the first fire.

But he wasn't around. Probably dead or in prison somewhere far away.

Squinting at the file again, his heartbeat nudged up a notch when he considered the John Doe's driver's license. Alaska. Pretty damned far away. Still a frontier in the seventies. A man could get lost in that wilderness . . . Could all just be a damned coincidence. Or was it?

He reached for the intercom button and barked out a request. Within minutes Gonzales sauntered through the door. "Any luck with the McKenzie woman?" he asked.

T. John shook his head. "Not yet, but I want her followed."

Gonzales's dark eyes flared. "You got something?"

"Probably not, but Chase McKenzie is talking. At least she says he's talking, but get this, only to her."

Gonzales snorted in disgust.

"Yeah, I think it's bullshit. But we'll check it out. Then I want to talk to Willie Ventura again, and he can bring in a whole army of lawyers for all I care. They can try to block me up one side and down the other, but I want to talk to him."

Gonzales shrugged. "I'll round him up."

"Then—this is a long shot—but check with the Alaska DMV, see if they've got anyone named Brig McKenzie— well, make that any white male around thirty named McKenzie. Check accident reports and titles of cars through whatever agency they've got up there."

"Could be quite a list. McKenzie's a common name."

"I know, I know, but humor me, would you?"

"You think the John Doe is McKenzie?" Gonzales clearly didn't believe it.

"Nah." Wilson cracked his knuckles in frustration. "I said it was a long shot, a million-to-one. Oh, Christ, it's probably nothing more than a wild-goose chase. But just to make sure, let's check it out."

Twenty-nine

Sunny was waiting for her. Dressed in a long black gown, her gray-streaked hair pinned into a tight knot at the base of her skull, she sat on the edge of her bed, purse plopped in her lap. "Cassidy," she said warmly, extending her hand. Her skin was dark and smooth, without a wrinkle, but one eye was clouded by a cataract she refused to have removed. She didn't trust doctors with knives or lasers or whatever it was they used.

"I thought you'd like to visit Chase," Cassidy said, walking up to her and taking her hand. She'd never felt comfortable around her mother-in-law and hated to think Sunny had been her father's mistress, but it was still hard to see her here away from the home she loved.

"Been looking forward to it." Sunny stood with difficulty. Though her skin was as supple as that of a woman half her age, her joints were becoming arthritic—a condition which had worsened, she'd confided in Cassidy years before, because she wasn't able to get out to the woods to find the proper herbs. Even when she requested them from a local health-food store, her doctor wouldn't allow her to take anything other than what he prescribed—store-bought pills, synthetic chemicals dispensed by huge corporations. Sunny didn't have faith in man-made drugs and often refused medication.

Her old fingers tightened over Cassidy's hand. "Something's wrong."

"Yes, the fire and—"

"No, there's something else," she insisted and Cassidy's stomach clenched. Sliding her fingers from the old woman's grip, she didn't want to believe in the power of her mother-in-law's visions despite the fact that she, regardless of her own arguments against it, had married the man Sunny had predicted she would wed.

"Here's your cane." She offered the walking stick made of smooth dark wood, the handle carved in the shape of a mallard's head.

"You might not recognize Chase," Cassidy warned as they walked down the carpeted hall past smooth, almond-colored walls where pastel watercolors had been bolted to the plaster.

"I know my boys."

"But his face—"

"I can touch him, can't I?" Sunny waited for the electronic door to be opened by the smiling blond receptionist who had only to press a button beneath her desk. With a buzz, the lock was disengaged and Cassidy shoved open the glass door.

"He's covered in bandages and he might not want you to—"

"He's my son. I can touch him," she said stubbornly. "Chase is a good boy." She said it too quickly, as if to convince herself. Cassidy wondered how often Sunny had argued with her conscience so that she could still keep faith in a son who had committed her to an institution she detested.

They walked slowly down the steps to the curb where Cassidy's Jeep was parked. Cassidy held the passenger door open while her mother-in-law settled into the bucket seat.

Within minutes they were passing through open gates, Sunny waving to the guard. "What is it you want to ask me?" she asked.

So she'd sensed the questions racing through Cassidy's mind. With one brief touch. It was damned weird. "It's—it's nothing." This wasn't really the time or place to ask her about her old lovers, about Rex Buchanan.

"Don't lie to me." Smiling sadly, Sunny brushed a stray hair from her face. "You want to know about your father."

It was uncanny, almost as if she could read Cassidy's mind.

"You found out we were lovers," Sunny said and the air in the Jeep seemed to grow stale.

"Yes," Cassidy said, unnerved as she eased the rig into the flow of traffic.

"He told you?"

For God's sake, how did she know? Cassidy's hands were suddenly clammy against the wheel. She cleared her throat. "I, uh, I don't think he meant to."

"It was time."

Cassidy's heart was knocking wildly, so hard she could barely breathe. "I should have known, before I married Chase. I should have known that you were involved with my father."

"Chase knew."

Cassidy nearly lost control of the Jeep. She swore under her breath. "He knew?"

"Well, suspected. I never admitted it."

"For the love of God, he *knew?*" Her mind screamed the truth at her. Why hadn't he confided in her? Why?

"I think he saw your father once when Rex visited. Chase was just a boy at the time, and after that we were more careful."

Cassidy's brain was thudding wildly with questions she didn't dare speak, suspicions that should never see the light of day. "I don't understand—"

"Lucretia was a cold woman."

"But you could have gotten preg . . . I mean—"

"I did." Sunny cast her a dark look. "It's time you knew the truth."

"The truth," she repeated. How many lies had she lived with, unaware? Cassidy's heart sank and she drove without thinking, automatically slowing for corners, avoiding oncoming traffic by habit, though her mind was disengaged, her actions rote.

"Buddy was your father's son," she said flatly.

"Buddy?" Cassidy repeated, stunned. "Not Brig—?"

Sunny sighed softly. "Brig was Frank's boy. As is Chase."

"But how could you be sure?"

With a superior expression reserved for women who've conceived and borne children, Sunny glared at Cassidy. "I know."

"Oh, God." Cassidy tried to breathe deeply, to think rationally. So Sunny and Rex had been lovers, so what? It didn't change things. She wasn't married to her half brother, hadn't made love to someone related to her. Her stomach, so volatile these days, clenched and spewed acid to her throat.

"I would never have allowed you to marry Chase if he'd been your brother."

"Sweet Jesus!" Cassidy whispered as the town of Prosperity came into view. She rolled down her window hoping fresh air would clear her head. "What happened to Buddy?" she asked, but she wasn't sure she wanted to know the answer. He could be dead, he could be stashed in a mental institution, a vegetable who knew no one, wouldn't even recognize his own mother.

"Buddy's safe." She touched Cassidy on the arm with her soft fingers. "He lives with his father."

"What—?"

Sunny chuckled deep in her chest, as if she was pleased that she'd pulled the wool over her daughter-in-law's eyes. "You grew up with Buddy, Cassidy."

"But—" Then it hit her, like a lightning bolt that exploded in her brain. "Willie," she whispered, her stomach tying itself in ever tightening knots. Why hadn't she guessed? Why hadn't anyone in town put two and two together?

"Yes," Sunny said, relief making her voice quiver slightly. "Finally, after all these years, I can go to him."

"But why—why hide him?"

She stared out the window. "It was your father's idea. After the accident where Buddy nearly drowned in the creek, it was obvious that Buddy would never be . . . well, normal again. Too much brain damage from lack of oxygen. Rex offered to take care of him, to see that he was put in the best facility available. He would pay all the bills, and since Frank and I couldn't afford . . . well, that's when Frank left. Not because of Brig, but because of Buddy."

She seemed so lucid, so clear about the past. "How did you find out that Buddy was Willie?"

"Rex told me; oh, it was years later, when Buddy was nearly grown. The private hospital where Willie—that was the name Rex had given him after paying off the doctor in charge . . . anyway, the institution was closing, the hospital sold to a group of investors who had plans to tear it down and put in a strip mall or something—" She waved her fingers as if it didn't matter. "Rex decided Willie would come to live with them. He wasn't all that old, about ten or twelve, I think—you were just a little girl. At first he lived with the family of that foreman of yours, Mac something or other, then Rex gave him a room above the stable. I believe he's been there ever since."

Cassidy didn't recall Willie coming to live at her parents' home. For as long as she could remember, he'd been there, hanging around the stable or the barns or the pool.

"Does my mother know?"

Sunny shook her head. "No one knows. Just Rex and me. Not even Buddy."

This was too much to handle. "I don't think you should say anything to Chase. Not until he's better."

Sunny shot her a disdainful glance. "I would never do anything to hurt any of my sons," she said, as if Cassidy should understand her. "Never."

"Good." Cassidy shifted down and nosed the Jeep through the rounded corners of the tree-lined street leading to Northwest General. She wondered if the story about Buddy McKenzie and Willie Ventura was complete—or if there were holes left for her benefit. Sunny seemed remarkably clearheaded and yet her thoughts were known to wander; fact and fiction sometimes interwoven. How many times had

Chase worried aloud about his mother's sanity? Before he'd had Sunny committed, he'd always been concerned for her safety.

She dropped her mother-in-law off near the front doors, parked, then joined her in the reception area.

Together they took the elevator to the second floor, and at the door to her husband's room, Cassidy paused knowing that he would be furious with her for openly defying him and bringing his mother to the hospital.

"Chase?" she called softly and entered the room where her husband lay unmoving.

Sunny tensed as she saw her boy, but she walked forward steadily. "Can you hear me?" Sunny asked and the unbandaged eye that had been closed opened suddenly. "I thought so."

The eye narrowed up at her before shifting to Cassidy and accusing her of horrid things. "She wanted to see you," Cassidy offered.

"Are they treating you well?" Sunny reached forward, and though Chase tried to pull away, she touched his swollen fingers with her gentle probing hands.

He blinked rapidly as she closed her eyes and whispered something in Cherokee. Cassidy couldn't understand a word, but Chase seemed to. His eye focused on his mother and some of the anger disappeared from his face. "You will be well," she said. "It will take time, but you will heal." Tears filled the older woman's eyes as she released his fingers. "I've been worried about you."

Chase looked away, staring past Sunny to the wall behind her, and there appeared to be a tensing of the muscles in his face, though with the discoloration and swelling it was hard to tell.

Cassidy opened the door. "I'll just be down the hall," she said, understanding that she shouldn't interfere between mother and son. Not that she ever had. Chase had never allowed it. "I'll deal with my mother, you deal with yours," he'd always said when there was some problem with Sunny.

It was as if he considered her his personal burden; but he'd always felt that way, even before Brig had left. She walked past the nurses' station and took a seat in the small waiting area near a picture window. From her vantage point she could look outside or at the door to Chase's room, so that she'd see Sunny when she emerged. Later, she'd talk to Chase herself, tell him that T. John was about to identify the man in CCU.

As she glanced out the window, she noticed a cruiser from the Sheriff's Department rolling into the parking lot. Lights flashed as it was parked near the front door. Detectives Wilson and Gonzales threw open the doors of the vehicle, kicked them shut and strode quickly into the hospital. Sunglasses firmly in place, faces grim, they disappeared from her view. Cassidy's insides jelled. She told herself to remain calm, that even if they did come up to interview Chase, she could handle it. She'd wanted to warn Chase that they knew he could speak, that she'd told them he was stonewalling them, but she'd hoped to tell him when they were alone, without Sunny overhearing.

Now, it didn't matter. She braced herself for the worst, expecting two determined detectives to storm past the nurses' station and throw her hate-filled glances. With a soft chime, the elevator landed and an elderly couple emerged, a gray-haired man helping a stooped woman who shuffled slowly down the corridor.

Five minutes passed, then ten. Maybe Wilson was stopping at CCU, she thought. There was also a chance he was at the hospital for another reason—there were certainly other accidents to be investigated—but she couldn't stop the restless feeling that something was wrong.

She glanced to the door to Chase's room, still closed, then looked out to the parking lot again where the cruiser was parked at the front door. She licked her lips and told herself that she was just edgy, that she had no reason to be nervous, and yet . . . her reporter's instincts were on overdrive. *Something* was happening. Something big. And she'd bet all the money in her checking account that it was about the fire. The elevator landed again. This time a doctor emerged, his face masked in a scowl.

Cassidy couldn't stand the suspense a second longer. She walked to the nurses' station. "I'm going to run back to my car for a minute," she said, lying easily to the portly blond nurse at the desk. "Would you mind seeing that my mother-in-law—she's in room 212 with Chase McKenzie—that she waits for me here? I'll only be gone a second."

"No problem." The nurse didn't bother looking up.

"Thanks." Cassidy walked down the hall and into the waiting elevator car. Within seconds she was in the hallway in front of CCU, wondering how she could get inside without a police escort.

Reaching for the phone that connected directly with the Critical Care Unit's nurses' station, she heard voices, angry voices, then the doors burst open. Detective Wilson, chewing gum furiously, his features drawn together in a severe grimace, strode through. Gonzales was on his heels.

Wilson's sunglasses had been shoved into a front pocket of his shirt, and his eyes, dark and ominous, landed on Cassidy with such intensity she backed up a step and hung up the phone.

"Well, well, look who's here," Wilson drawled, unable to hide his sarcasm. "Seems like you're always around when there's trouble."

"Trouble?" she repeated, feeling the floor beneath her start to buckle.

T. John swiped a hand through his short hair and sighed. "Our man in there," he hooked his thumb to the doors swinging shut behind him, "didn't make it. John Doe, or whoever the hell he is, just died twenty minutes ago."

Thirty

No! No! No!

Cassidy wouldn't believe that Brig was dead. Though she'd lived for years telling herself that he'd left this world, deep in her heart, she'd always believed that he was alive somewhere and that someday she would see him again. Then, when she'd learned of the John Doe, when he'd been holding on to a St. Christopher's medal, she'd let her imagination run away from her and convinced herself that he was Brig.

"Oh, God," she whispered, tears threatening her eyes. He *can't* be dead! *Cannot* be dead!

"Hey, you all right?" the detective said. He sounded far away, his voice muted. "You're not going to faint on me, are you?"

"No—" Her own voice was displaced. She ran a hand over her forehead and steadied herself against the wall. Blackness threatened the edges of her vision.

"I could call a nurse."

"I'll be fine," she snapped, still reeling.

Wilson studied her. "You gonna tell me what you know about him?"

"The man in CCU?" She shook her head. "Nothing."

"Yet when I tell you he died, you look as if you've seen a ghost. What is it?"

"I—uh, I just hoped he would make it. So he could talk to me, to you, to explain what happened," she said, her mind still filled with a kaleidoscope of images of Brig. It had been so many years, and yet she remembered him as clearly as if she'd been with him only yesterday.

"I think we should tell your husband."

Oh, God!

"He's not talking to us, you know. Hasn't so much as said a word, but I can tell he's listening. Maybe this will loosen his tongue."

"He's with his mother now . . ." Impulsively she touched the officer's arm. "Don't say anything until you talk to the doctor, please. I don't want Chase to take a turn for the worse."

"It's not him I'm worried about. But you."

"I'll be all right," she lied, blinking against tears. "It was just such a shock . . . if you'll excuse me."

T. John watched as she pulled herself together. It was amazing how quickly she could transform. A second ago he was certain she would fall in a heap, but she managed to square her shoulders, dash away any sign of tears and offer him a sad smile before she disappeared into the elevator.

"She's hiding something," he said to Gonzales. Reaching into his pocket, he found the first pack of Camels he'd bought in months.

"But what?"

"Unless I miss my guess, she knows who the John Doe is."

"And you don't?"

"Can't prove it. Not until we hear back from Alaska." In frustration, T. John opened the cellophane wrapper from his cigarettes and even got so far as to shake one out. But he didn't light it, just rolled it in his fingers as he stared at the elevator doors. Nurses, doctors, visitors passed him, but T. John didn't notice; his mind was too focused on Cassidy Buchanan McKenzie and the secrets she so jealously guarded.

He'd find out what they were. Oh, it would take a little time and a lot of digging, but as sure as Elvis was dead and buried, T. John would find them.

"Call Chase McKenzie's doctor—Rick, er Richard Okano, I think the guy's name is—find out when we can talk to his patient." He lifted the cigarette to his nostrils and smelled the fresh tobacco, then caught the eye of a nurse who stared pointedly at his hands, almost daring him to light up. He noticed the obnoxious no-smoking sign posted near the nurses' station. Yeah, well, it seemed like you couldn't light up anywhere around here anymore. Good thing he'd quit.

"Keep the John Doe on ice until someone claims him and check with Alaska—see what the hang-up is."

"You got it," Gonzales said.

"And pictures. I want every picture you can find of Brig McKenzie." He thought for a minute. "I want to talk to every old-timer in town, find out what the gossip around here was seventeen years ago." His eyes narrowed on the elevator, and he imagined Cassidy as a gawky teenager, a tomboy, pale in comparison to her older half sister. "See what the family dynamics of the Buchanans and the McKenzies were. I want to know why Lucretia Buchanan offed herself, why Frank McKenzie took a hike and how Brig McKenzie fits in with Angie and Cassidy Buchanan. There was friction between him and the Baker boy who got killed. Check that out as well."

"Anything else?" Gonzales asked.

"Yeah. Find out where Chase McKenzie was during all this time. He was supposed to be the good McKenzie boy, always looking after Mom, toeing the line, going to school and working his butt off. But it just doesn't wash with me."

"You think he's lying?"

"He's not talking at all, but yeah, he's lying. The whole damned lot of them are lying. But the trouble with lies is that when one starts to unravel, the entire web starts falling apart. All we have to do is pull one thread and my guess is we should start with Willie Ventura. He's the one who'll have the most trouble holding his lies together."

Cassidy walked on legs made of rubber. There was no proof that Brig was the man in CCU, no reason to believe that he was dead, yet her stomach was sour and an emptiness stole through her heart as she found her way back to Chase's room.

"Mrs. McKenzie—" The nurse at the station seemed worried. "Mrs. McKenzie, I've been trying to locate you."

Oh God, what now? Cassidy hesitated. "Yes? Is something wrong?" she said, reading the concern in the woman's dark eyes. "My husband—"

"Is stable. It's not him. It's your mother-in-law."

"Sunny?" Dread was a needle pricking deep into her heart.

"Yes." The nurse lifted her hands. "She's not with you?"

"No, I left her here, remember?"

"Oh, dear. I'm afraid she must've slipped out of the room while I was making rounds of medication and the other nurse was attending someone else—"

"Wait a minute." Cassidy's foggy mind instantly cleared. "You mean to tell me that she's not here. Not in the hospital?"

"I don't know about the rest of the hospital." The sallow-faced nurse started to get defensive. "But she's not in this wing on this floor."

"You're certain?"

The woman's mouth became a formidable line. "Yes, Mrs. McKenzie, but I'm sure she's around here somewhere."

"Has anyone checked the bathrooms?"

"No, but—"

Cassidy's heart was pumping wildly. Sunny wouldn't have taken off, would she? She couldn't get very far. She used a cane, for crying out loud. "Look, my mother-in-law needs to be found. I'll check my car and the restrooms. If you would have someone look elsewhere, in case she's confused—" Cassidy was already running down the hallway toward the front doors. She didn't believe for a minute that Sunny had gone to the Jeep, but she couldn't be certain.

Outside the sun was blazing. Hot rays burned across the pavement, softening the tar in the asphalt. The Jeep was where Cassidy had left it, and she was just about to turn back to the hospital when she spied a note, tucked beneath the wiper blade of the driver's side.

She snatched it up and saw the penciled scrawl:

Don't worry—the spirits are with me in my quest. Love, Sunny.

No!

Cassidy sagged against the fender and stared at the blinding white paper, the back of which was soiled and advertised yard work—a flyer that had apparently just blown across the parking lot.

"God help her," she said, shading her eyes as she swept her gaze across a sea of vehicles. Where would Sunny have gone? And why? What the devil was her quest? Chase was right, she was getting worse. Now she'd fantasized that she was off on some vision quest, the kind her ancestors followed.

Chase would be furious. He hadn't wanted Sunny to visit him, and now she was running loose, capable of inflicting pain on herself or others. Cassidy kicked at her tire in frustration, then slowly walked down each and every row of parked cars, making sure Sunny wasn't crouching behind a station wagon or lying in the bed of a pickup. She wasn't. Not a sign of her. How had she left? Called a cab from the hospital? Hitchhiked? Stolen a car? Found a bus? Hobbled off with her cane for God's sake? *How?*

Sweat beaded on Cassidy's scalp as she made her way back to the hospital. She didn't know how to break the news to Chase. Any of the news. Not only was it likely that his one brother was dead, but his half brother was very much alive, though Chase didn't know they were related. On top of that, his mother was missing. All Cassidy's fault. One more reason for their already crumbling marriage to fall more quickly apart.

"I knew she should never have come here," Chase growled, once Cassidy had told him the news about Sunny.

"I thought she needed to see her son."

"Well, she didn't stay here long."

"Did you talk to her?"

"No."

"Oh, Chase—" She walked to the bed and stared down at him. His angry eye followed her. "She'll be all right."

"I wouldn't count on it."

She grabbed the rails of his bed and swallowed hard. "I'm sorry."

He didn't respond.

Calming herself, she slowly let out her breath. "There's something else you should know."

"More good news?" he mocked, his words barely distinguishable through the wires in his jaw.

"No. It's bad." She took in a shuddering breath. "The man in CCU died today. That's where I was; I saw the detectives come in and I had this feeling and . . ."

The eye closed and the room grew incredibly still. If possible, he seemed to stop breathing, his lips tense, the bruises on his face green and garish. Noises through the door were muted—phones ringing and carts rattling and voices speaking—all seemed so far away and unimportant.

She plunged on. "They still don't know who he is, Chase, but they'll be here, asking questions again as soon as Dr. Okano says it's okay. You . . . you should think about what you're going to tell them."

"I'll tell them the truth."

"Which is?"

He stared at her so hard, she nearly cried out. Though he didn't say a word, she understood that the dead man was Brig. "This will be hard, Cass," he said with the first trace of tenderness she'd heard from him in a long, long while. "On you. On me. On everyone."

Sunny thanked the farmer and climbed out of the dusty pickup. The floor was littered with tools. Dust covered every interior space, and the glove box was tied together with bailing twine, but the man was good and wholesome and had offered her a ride and she'd accepted. She'd turned down two before him, one was a bunch of kids in a beat-up Chrysler. They'd rolled to a stop, offered easy smiles with devilment in their teenaged eyes. A cloud of marijuana smoke had billowed out when one of the boys had said, "Hey, Grandma? How about a trip to heaven?" The other kids, packed in like sardines, had snickered.

"Already there," Sunny had replied with a smile.

"You don't need a ride? Come on, old lady, you've got a cane."

"Thank you, but I'd rather walk."

"Ain't that a pisser?" The boy's sunny disposition had disappeared, and Sunny realized that her first instinct, that the kids were only picking her up to make sport of her, was correct. She saw their auras, knew that the ringleader, the one talking to her, was a bad seed. No conscience. Out for a good time, and if it meant frightening little old ladies, all the better. The other kids were just along for the ride. Two girls— they were nervous—and another boy, the driver, who seemed worried and kept checking the rearview mirror.

"I'm meeting my son," she said.

"And who's he?" the ringleader snarled. "Jesus Christ?"

"His name is T—that stands for Thomas—John Wilson," she lied. "You may have heard of him."

"Shit, man, let's get out of here," the driver said. "T. John Wilson's with the Sheriff's Department. He's thrown my old man in jail a couple of times."

"I know." The ringleader's eyes glittered like hard, cold stones. "You're making a mistake, lady."

"I don't think so." Suddenly, she reached forward, grabbed his arm and her fingers wrapped around the small bones. Closing her eyes, she began chanting in her mother's native tongue, over and over again, her voice high and reedy.

"What the fuck?" the boy screamed, startled.

"I don't like this," one of the girls exclaimed.

"She's crazy, man." The driver stomped on the throttle, Sunny let go of the boy's arm and the car sped away, swerving over the center line before straightening.

The next people that pulled over were a young couple with a baby strapped into a car seat. Sunny didn't take the ride because she recognized the woman—Mary Beth Spears, recently married and now a mother. Mary Beth was angry, her lips drawn into a tight little pout, and though she didn't seem to recall Sunny, she was in a bad mood.

"Need a ride?" Her husband, a sandy-haired fellow with trusting eyes, craned his neck to look past the stiff profile of his wife.

"I'm enjoying my walk."

"Mighty hot."

"There's a breeze."

"We'll be glad to take you back to Prosperity or wherever you want to go."

Mary Beth shot her husband a hate-filled glance, and whispered something out of the corner of her mouth—something about heathens and the devil.

"No reason, I'm fine."

"She's fine, Larry," Mary Beth said just as the baby in the backseat started to fuss. "Now let's just get going. Mama and Daddy are waiting."

"Just trying to be a Good Samaritan," he said, then looked at Sunny again. "You're sure, lady?"

"I'm sure."

"Come on, Larry." Mary Beth's fingers drummed on the worn copy of the Bible spread open on her lap.

"Well, good day to ya," Larry said, as the baby started crying in earnest.

"Same to you."

"May Jesus be with you," Mary Beth said, evoking a perfect and pious smile.

"And you."

The car roared away and Sunny was grateful that Chase had never gotten involved with Mary Beth. They'd only dated once at the Caldwell party, the night Angie Buchanan had died, but that one date had struck fear into Sunny's heart.

Several motorists passed, sending clouds of dust toward the ditch before the farmer, a muscular man named Dave Dickey stopped. She sensed immediately that he was a good man as he'd leaned over and opened the door to the cab. He was an honest man, his eyes clear brown behind photogray glasses that had darkened in the sun.

"Need a ride?" His smile was genuine, a slash of white against skin tanned from days in the sun, his hands callused from hours of labor.

"Looks as such."

"Well, hop in." He came around to help her and tucked her cane under her legs.

The old Ford—a '66, Dave had boasted—wheezed and clanked over potholes in the road. Dave muttered something about replacing the drive line someday. He'd gladly taken her all the way to Rex Buchanan's house, and now she stood here with the sun lowering over the horizon, the last rays gilding the gray stones of the house that looked like it belonged in the English countryside rather than nestled in the foothills of the Cascade Mountains.

She hadn't been here in years, not since the week of Angie Buchanan's funeral.

Thirty-one

Rex Buchanan was alone in the house. He finished one drink and carried a second upstairs, where he paused at the door of Angie's room. Biting his lip, he hesitated.

Go on. You're alone. Who's going to find out? It's your house, damn it. All of it.

Slowly he opened the door and stepped over the threshold. A guilty thought pierced his brain, but he ignored it. Dena had driven into town to visit Chase and run a few errands; she wouldn't be back for hours. His wife would never know.

The room hadn't changed in seventeen years—he wouldn't allow it. Though Dena had insisted it would make a wonderful guest room, Rex had refused. Forever it would belong to Angie. He stared longingly at the picture of Lucretia and their little girl, then set his drink on the nightstand and stretched out on Angie's bed. The room still smelled of her; he paid the maid a little extra in cash to sprinkle her favorite perfume, which he also bought on the sly, over the bed.

Tears filled his eyes. God, he missed them both. His fingers curled in the bedclothes, and his mind was filled with images of his daughter and his wife. Sometimes the images blurred, their blue eyes, shimmering dark hair, full lips were nearly identical, and even now thinking of Lucretia—he felt an erection begin and he touched himself, imagining her hands, light and feathery, her mouth moist, her breasts—he fought the image for a second, then gave in to it. In his mind's eye she was always playful and sexy—more like their daughter. He rewrote his own history and gave it a delicious, sensual spin where Lucretia was eager for him, anxious to make love to him, wet and warm and ready, writhing and bucking beneath him.

His hips moved reflexively. Sweat made his skin clammy.

"Rex?" A voice, a soft feminine voice that was good and kind. Lucretia's voice . . .

"Rex?"

Again she called. His eyes flew open and he realized where he was. Alone. On Angie's bed. Half-drunk and humping an imaginary wife—a woman who had been dead for decades. He scrambled off the mattress, hitting the night-stand with his knee. *Crash!* Glass shattered against the floor. Aged Kentucky whiskey splashed onto the wall, the bed, the nightstand.

He was on his knees, trying to right himself, wondering how he could explain himself, when he saw her. "Oh, God," he whispered, lifting his head. Somehow Sunny had broken into his house, into his private life, and was standing in the doorway. She was plumper than he remembered, her face beginning to sag, her hair gray, but she still had the uncanny ability to see into the darkest reaches of his soul. "What're you doing here?" he whispered, still kneeling.

"I came to see you."

"Why?"

She stood proudly in the doorway. "I told Cassidy all about Buddy—who he is and how he's related to her."

"Oh, my God, Sunny, why?" he nearly yelled, startled, his hand scraping across the floor. Glass sliced into his palm. "Are you crazy?"

Dark, bold eyes held his. "You, of all people, know how sane I am."

"But you promised—"

"Cassidy guessed the truth anyway, from what you'd already told her." She let out a slow breath. "She's searching, Rex, searching for answers to her life, to her marriage, to the fires. It was time."

"And Dena," he said, his lies falling apart one by one.

Blood dripped to the floor, mingling with the whiskey and dust motes that collected near the skirt of the bed.

"Dena knew about us."

"But she doesn't know that Willie is Buddy."

"It will be all right, Rex," Sunny assured him. Leaving her cane at the door, she walked stiffly into the room and gathered tissues from a box on the night table. Taking his hand in hers, she cleaned the jagged wound, deftly plucking shards of glass from the heel of his palm. "I think we've lived with lies long enough." Slowly she lifted his hand to her lips and pressed a kiss into his palm, tasting his blood. A kiss of old passion, of new trust, of reassurance. "Don't be afraid, Rex," she said in her soothing voice. She glanced at the rumpled bedcovers, and pain shadowed her eyes before she looked at him again. "It's going to be all right. But you have to help me . . ."

"All I'm saying is that it looks bad." Felicity clasped her gold bracelet over her wrist and surveyed herself in the mirror. The first hint of wrinkles showed near her eyes, and she had to touch up her hair every other week. If the tiny webbing of crow's-feet got much worse, she'd call a plastic surgeon. She worked hard to keep her body in shape, her face perfect, though she thought it might be a futile battle. Her husband, smelling of brandy and leaning insolently against the doorjamb, barely noticed her anymore.

"I don't care how it looks," Derrick grumbled. "I've never given a rat's ass about Chase McKenzie so why should I start pretending now?" He fished into his pocket for his pack of Marlboros and lit up. Smoke curled lazily over his eyes.

"He's your brother-in-law."

"My half-brother-in-law or some such crap. The family's so fucked up I can't keep it straight."

"Watch your mouth. Linnie's just down the hall."

"You used to like it when I talked dirty."

"In bed. Whispered, not shouted like a drunken sailor."

"You knew how I was when you married me. No, I take

that back"—he lifted his drink and cigarette in one hand—
"when you tricked me into marrying you."

"I didn't—"

"Sure you did, Felicity. You didn't have to get pregnant.
Remember? You had before and we took care of it. But not
this time, no way, you went running to Daddy."

"I wanted a baby," she said, her back stiffening with
pride.

"You wanted to be Mrs. Derrick Buchanan."

"And it worked out, didn't it? We both love the girls."

He didn't respond, and Felicity experienced the dull ache
she always felt when it came to her daughters. She loved
them both desperately, wildly. They were beautiful, clever,
witty and smart enough to know that their father didn't love
them. She tamped down the old pain. Angela had turned bitter toward Derrick, her sarcasm as cutting as his own. With
no respect for her father, she had begun disobeying and become outwardly defiant. Just like her aunt and namesake at
sixteen. But Belinda—sweet Linnie—still adored Derrick and
believed that he loved her. She'd created her own fantasy
family, enhanced by Felicity's lies—and couldn't understand
Angela's sarcasm. Linnie had a good but fragile heart. One
that Derrick was certain to break. "You . . . you need to show
the girls some attention."

Derrick snorted. "Attention?"

"You know, take them to a movie, or to a play, or just sit
down and talk with them, act interested."

His nostrils flared. "I'm not, okay? And I never will be. I
saw the kind of 'attention' my father gave to my sister and it
made me sick." He shot a stream of smoke into the direction
of the master bath.

"Just because your father was a . . ."

"*Is*, Felicity, he *is* a sicko. A pervert. He's never gotten
over Angie's death and you know why."

"I don't want to hear it."

"Shit." He drew on his cigarette hard, then shook his head
in a cloud of smoke. "I need a drink."

"You've had enough."

"So who appointed you my mother—" As soon as he'd said the words, he paled. He rarely mentioned his mother, didn't allow Felicity to bring up Lucretia's name.

Felicity grabbed her sweater, a cardigan woven in strands of cream and gold, off the foot of the bed. Her bed. Derrick rarely slept with her anymore. "You're too drunk to drive and we have to be at the Alonzos' in ten minutes."

"I don't give a shit. Isn't it enough we live together and work together, do we have to go out to see a bunch of fuckin' bores? I can't figure out why you drag me to these stupid little get-togethers."

"Because they're necessary," she snapped back, tired of her husband's lack of ambition. Both she and Derrick had been born privileged, but she was also fired with a competitive streak that wouldn't quit. When she saw something she wanted, she put it squarely in her sights and went after it. She'd grown up as the only child of The Judge, and as such, she'd been given anything she wanted. Except for Derrick; she'd had to work to nail him. She'd gotten pregnant once and he'd insisted she have an abortion. Agreeing in order to appease him, thinking that he'd love her more, she'd had the procedure, then regretted it as he'd lost his respect for her. So she'd kept up their affair, gotten pregnant again, and this time insisted he marry her. He still hadn't respected her, but she'd married him, which had been, at the time, her primary objective.

Now, she still did whatever was necessary, including working a couple of days a week at the office, just to check up on her husband and Chase. God, he was slippery. She also made sure that she and Derrick were included in all the right social circles in Prosperity and Portland. Her father's connections didn't hurt.

"Bobby Alonzo's an asshole." Derrick dropped his cigarette into his empty drink glass. It sizzled before dying.

"But a banker; his father owns one of the few independent banks in the region."

"He was also Jed Baker's best friend." Derrick left his glass on the bureau.

"Jed's dead."

"Yeah, well, tell it to Bobby. He still brings him up. Like he's some kind of god because he died screwing Angie. Christ I need a drink."

Felicity's patience snapped. "You don't know what they were doing together. We've gone over this a dozen times, so what's gotten into you tonight?"

"Everything. Hell, Chase is going home tomorrow, probably planning to start in with the company again."

"You could stop him."

"He's like a damned freight train once he gets rolling."

"Buy him out." She was tired of the argument. Tired of Derrick's incompetence. Tired of being the one who held things together.

"He won't sell, at least not to me." He scratched his jaw and swayed a little as he reached for his jacket. "You know they've never found his mother. She just walked out of the hospital on the day the John Doe died, and no one's seen her since. Weird, isn't it?"

"That's nothing new. Sunny McKenzie's always been weird. Now, come on, we're late."

Derrick snorted in disgust, but followed her out of the bedroom they barely shared. Hers had been a hollow victory, Felicity thought as Derrick reached into his pocket and had trouble retrieving his keys. His drinking was worse than ever, and she suspected he was cheating on her again. Oh, if she could only turn back the clock . . .

But she couldn't. And she had the girls to think about. And damn it, she loved Derrick Buchanan, loved being his wife. But it would be a helluva lot better if he'd return the favor someday.

Thirty-two

Cassidy had forgotten how stubborn Chase could be, how downright bullheaded when his pride was in the way. She parked near the front door of the house, and before the Jeep had completely stopped, Chase threw open the door, propped the rubber tips of his crutches on the asphalt and hauled himself to his feet. He was sweating, his still-discolored face twisted with the effort, but he wouldn't take her hand, just as he hadn't let her push him out of the hospital in a wheelchair and just as he hadn't spoken a word to her in the car.

She made excuses for him. He didn't like the feeling of not being in power. He was still angry that she'd gone against his wishes and brought his mother to see him and that Sunny had taken off. He was adjusting to the fact that he might limp for the rest of his life. He'd been through incredible trauma, nearly losing his life. And he had a secret, the only one who knew for certain that his brother was dead.

However, she was tired of his attitude. It rankled her. No two ways about it. She tried to be considerate and empathetic, but right now her empathy was running thin. Real thin.

"Let me get the door," she said as he balanced on his good leg and started for the house.

He didn't reply and she marched by him, reminding herself that he couldn't speak well. His jaw would still be wired together for another week, his leg still casted.

She unlocked the front door, threw it open and waited just

inside. He passed by her on the way to his den. "I'll get your bag."

Again, no response.

Counting silently to ten, she walked back to the Jeep and reminded herself once again that speaking was difficult for him. His face was still swollen and discolored, and a patch covered his bad eye. Fortunately his cornea was nearly healed and soon he'd be able to use both eyes again.

She grabbed the small nylon bag from the backseat, carried it into the house and left it in his room near the back hall. She returned to the den and found him trying to manipulate the phone.

"What're you doing?"

He didn't reply.

"Chase—"

"Leave me the hell alone," he finally said in his raspy, mumbled voice. His single-eyed gaze swung to her and bore into her with such hatred she nearly took a step back. At the sound on the other end of the line he turned his back to her. "Yeah I'd like to order a cab," he said.

"For the love of God, Chase, don't—" She walked quickly across the room.

"I live outside of the city—about four miles—" Without thinking she pressed the button on the phone and cut him off.

"What the hell? For Christ's sake, Cassidy—"

"You're not going anywhere. Not tonight."

"I can't stay here."

"Why not—I thought you couldn't wait to get out of the hospital."

He dropped the receiver and hobbled to the bar. "You know why not."

"Because we're supposed to be separated?"

"Amen." He reached for a bottle of Scotch and fumbled in the cupboard for a tumbler.

"You shouldn't drink. The pain medication—"

"You're not my mother now, are you?" he said, ignoring

her. "My mother's missing, remember?" She stiffened. "And you're certainly not my boss—"

"Chase, please—"

"And the last time I looked, you weren't Jesus Christ, so I guess you can't tell me what to do."

"I'm just trying to help."

"Then leave me alone," he bit out. "If I remember right, that's what you wanted."

"You're hurt—"

"And you're making me sick with this charade of concern. Everyone knows it's a joke, so why don't you give it up?" Balancing against the wall, he splashed liquor into his tumbler, spilling some onto the glass counter. Picking up his drink, he caught her gaze in the mirror mounted above the sink. "Cheers," he mocked and tossed back the Scotch.

"What're you planning to do? Drink yourself to death?"

"Haven't got a clue."

She took a step closer to him. "Why are you treating me like this?"

Every muscle stiffened in his body, and he slammed his empty glass down so hard she thought the counter might shatter. "Why do you think?"

"This is about the divorce."

He glared at her so hard her breath stopped. "Bingo."

"Chase, if we could just talk this out—"

"We talked. You want out. So go. Walk out the door. I really don't give a good goddamn." He turned and poured another drink. The cords in the back of his neck stood out and his hand shook as he held the glass.

"I think it would be best if I stuck around, helped you get back on your feet, made sure that you're okay."

"So you could do your duty and salve your conscience? Forget it." With a flourish, he held his drink up as if he were a king holding a sword in the act of knighting his finest soldier. "I release you. You owe me nothing."

"You want me to leave?"

"No, Cassidy. The truth of the matter is that I don't care what you do." He swayed a little and she took a step toward him, reaching out, before he drew away from her so quickly he stumbled and fell against the wall. "Don't touch me, Cassidy," he warned. his voice lowering an octave. "Don't do me any favors, don't try to fawn all over me like the loving, dutiful wife, and for God's sake, don't touch me."

With a crash, his crutches hit the floor. Cassidy jumped. Chase grabbed the back of the couch. Half-bent, the muscles of his good arm supporting him, he slowly inched so close to her that she could smell the liquor on his breath. His gaze focused on her with such intensity her throat caught. Was there a fleeting glimmer of passion in his eye, the old fire that had drawn them together, or was it just her imagination? "Let's get one thing straight, wife," he said in a harsh, low whisper. "The fire didn't change anything. You don't love me and I sure as hell don't love you, so we're only going to live through this sham of a marriage until I'm on my feet, my part of the company is sold for the price I want, and you and I can split the sheets forever. Got it?"

Reeling away from her, he seized his crutches, threw them under his arms and jabbed them angrily against the floor. Cassidy's fingers coiled into fists. Anger and despair filled her heart and yet she knew he was right. They'd already decided to divorce. The fire was only a complication that would slow the process. But she was surprised that he wanted to sell part of the company. For years, work had been his mistress, the buildings, properties and assets of Buchanan Industries his only interest.

Her throat dry, she said, "Listen, Chase. There's something you should know . . . something I probably should have told you in the hospital, but I didn't want to upset you."

She saw his shoulder muscles flex beneath his shirt but he didn't turn around to face her. "You've found a lover," he said, defeat edging his words.

"A lover?" If the situation weren't so tragic, she would have laughed. She forced her fingers to straighten, then pressed her palms together. "I've never been with anyone but you."

"That's a lie."

"Not since we married," she insisted. They'd been over this territory a hundred times. "But whether you believe me or not, it really doesn't matter at this point. What I think you should know is that your mother told me about Buddy."

"Buddy?"

"Yes, your brother—well, half brother. Half yours, half mine."

"What the devil are you talking about?" Whirling on his crutches, the veins in his neck standing out, he glared at her with such venom she recoiled.

"Buddy—Willie—is my father's son. Dad and Sunny had an affair for years."

"Lies!"

"Sunny said you knew, that you caught them together once."

"I—I don't remember," he said, his throat working. "I can't believe—"

"Buddy's alive, Chase! He's the reason your father left town. It wasn't because he thought Brig wasn't his son." He stiffened, and she added quickly, "I know the rumors, I heard the town gossip for years."

"Ancient history," he growled, his fingers grabbing the handles of the crutches in a death grip. "Jesus, I don't believe we're having this conversation. What the hell kind of incest are you peddling?"

"Ask Sunny. Ask Rex. It's true, Chase. Why would I lie?"

"God only knows," he said, and there was a trace of regret in his words.

"You're impossible!"

"Try hard to be."

"Buddy's your brother!"

"And yours."

"Yes!"

Beneath the wires, his jaw seemed to clench, and his furious eye bored straight to her soul. A whistle of air passed through his teeth. "Why should I believe you?"

She lifted her hands skyward. "Why would I make it up?"

"I don't know." Emotions played across his face. Emotions

she couldn't name. His eye shut for a second, and suddenly he seemed dangerous and volatile and utterly unreachable.

"It's the truth, Chase, and really, doesn't it make sense? Didn't you admit to me that you thought Buddy was probably alive and in some institution? Haven't you always wondered about him? And Dad's been so adamant about him keeping a job—"

"Where is he?" he demanded, his voice low, his eye narrowing suspiciously. "Where?"

"He was in jail, but he's out now."

"Jail? Why?"

"Because of the fire. He's the one who found the wallet in the ashes at the sawmill." He still seemed skeptical. "It's Willie, Chase. Willie Ventura is Buddy. He's your brother and he's my brother and—"

"Enough!" he thundered. "What wallet?"

"The wallet everyone, including the police, is presuming belonged to the John Doe—the man you were meeting that night. How Willie got it, no one knows. He's staying up at the house with Mom and Dad. Mom called. She's pretty shaken up about it. About everything."

"Jesus."

"But Detective Wilson wants to talk to you. I imagine he'll be here soon. He's interrogated Willie already and I don't know what he found out. I don't even know if Willie was at the mill that night. But Wilson will. He'll piece it all together and he'll expect you to tell him the truth."

Chase stared at her long and hard, and even though his face had changed—was nearly grotesque—the look was pure male arrogance and reached a feminine part of her she'd hoped no longer existed. She could barely breathe for a second.

"Of course he expects the truth. Why in God's name would I tell him anything else?"

Dena watched as her husband and Willie climbed out of Rex's car. Something was wrong; she could tell it in the nervous glances Rex shot at the house as he guided Willie past the planters overflowing with red and white petunias and held open the screen door.

Dena reached for her cigarettes and tried not to grimace as Willie, head hanging like a wounded puppy, hay and dust and God-only-knew what else clinging to his shirt and jeans and shoes, followed Rex inside.

Her gaze fell to the grimy duffel bag in one of Willie's big hands.

"I've decided that it's time for Willie to move up to the main house," Rex announced.

Good manners kept her from saying what she thought. She clicked her lighter and lit up.

"We've got plenty of room and . . . well, Dena, I finally told Willie the truth, that his name is really Buddy McKenzie and that I'm his father."

"His *what?*" She choked on a lungful of smoke and her eyes filled with tears. Certainly she hadn't heard correctly.

"Willie's my son."

"Oh my God." She glared at the half-wit boy. "But how— why?" She must be dreaming. Surely there was some mistake . . .

"You remember the accident where Buddy McKenzie nearly drowned. You were working for me then. Lucretia was still alive and—"

"You . . . and Sunny had a child?" she cut in, trying to make sense of his ramblings. "Buddy is—" Her voice failed her and she thought she might pass out for a second before she leaned heavily against the counter. "Look, Rex, I know this is rough, but I don't think, I mean, to have him live here, as if . . . as if . . . well, it's just not done. People will talk . . . my God, what're you thinking?"

Rex's expression was stern. "Let me get Willie settled, then we'll discuss this."

Willie was blushing, staring at the floor and shifting from one foot to the other. "I don't want to cause no trouble, Mrs. Buchanan. Really I don't. Maybe I should just stay down at the stable—"

"Nonsense." Rex clapped him on the back. "Derrick's old room has been empty for years."

Willie cringed and shook his head. "Derrick. He won't like it none."

"He'll get over it," Rex offered his son a smile as they headed for the back stairs.

Dena smoked anxiously, her mind spinning ahead. She could hear the gossip in town now—starting out as a few lone whispers and growing into a curious rumble. Eyes would be cast in her direction, smiles covered with polite hands, evil eyes twinkling that the Buchanans were finally getting theirs. More scandal. More pain.

Dena had known of Rex's affair with Sunny McKenzie, realized that it had begun long before Lucretia died and had continued after Rex's first wife's death. But she had never understood his fascination with the palm-reading supposed psychic and had hoped once they were married he would give up his mistress. She'd convinced herself that Rex had strayed only because his first wife was a cold-hearted bitch who couldn't satisfy him, but even after she and Rex had married, he hadn't stopped seeing Sunny—not for a long, long time, until just before Chase had the good sense to have her committed. The crazy woman had some kind of hold on Rex—some kind of voodoo or black magic. It was spooky.

But she hadn't suspected that he'd fathered a son—even though rumors had abounded when Brig had been born and Frank had left. Dena hadn't listened. It was so obvious that Brig had been a McKenzie; he looked so much like his father and older brother . . . but now . . . Finally she understood. For years she'd begged Rex to get rid of Willie and had just assumed that his philanthropic nature had made him want to keep the boy. But it had gone deeper than that. Much deeper. Sick inside, she heard footsteps in the rooms overhead. Willie moving in. Willie living with them, eating at the dining-room table, sleeping right down the hall, creeping through the house. She shivered at the thought. The boy wasn't right. Everyone knew it.

Everyone but Rex.

The town would be buzzing with the news. As if it wasn't enough that Chase was involved in something underhanded with the man who had died in the fire. As if it wasn't enough that Derrick was a drunk and Felicity a jealous shrew. As if it wasn't enough that Sunny McKenzie was on the loose somewhere. Dena drew hard on her cigarette, trying to calm herself before letting out a long breath of smoke.

She could handle this. She could. She reached for the phone and punched out her daughter's telephone number.

Cassidy found Willie in the stable. He was working hard, sweat soaking the shoulders and armpits of his shirt. He offered her a weak grin as she walked through the open door.

"Hi, Willie."

"You haven't been here in a long time."

"Too long," she admitted, watching as each horse buried a velvet-soft nose into the loose hay. Teeth ground, dust swirled, and the familiar scents of horsehide, dung, sweat and dry hay brought back memories of her youth.

"Dena called you."

"Yes."

"She don't like me livin' in Derrick's house."

"It's not Derrick's house."

"His room." Willie shrugged and threw his shoulders into his task, forking hay into the manger.

She reached forward and petted a black nose. The horse snorted and shook his head, dark eyes bright with an inner fire.

"I should be down here. With the horses."

"Would you like that better?"

He nodded, held her gaze a second longer than was comfortable and began working again. She remembered how often she'd found him staring. At her. At Angie. "I'm sure Dad would reconsider. He just wants you to be happy." And Dena would be relieved. She'd already bent Cassidy's ear, sounded nearly hysterical at the thought of Willie being in the house.

"Derrick won't like me in his room. Uh-uh." He worried his lip between his teeth.

"Derrick moved out a long time ago. He lives with Felicity and the girls on the other side of the property. He won't bother you."

Willie didn't seem convinced, and Cassidy leaned against one of the support beams. "You found a wallet in the ashes of the fire."

Willie bit his lip harder and scooped up the loose strands of hay with a pitchfork.

"Whose wallet was it?"

"I didn't steal it!"

"I know, but it belonged to someone."

Willie looked at the floor, but his eyes were restless, his gaze moving quickly over the dusty cement, as if trailing swift little rats scurrying through the shadows.

"Whose was it?" she repeated.

"The man's," he said, worrying his lip.

"What man?"

"They call him John."

"The man who died in the fire?"

Nodding, Willie turned away from Cassidy and hung the pitchfork on the wall next to the shovel. Horses shifted and chewed, rustling hay, grinding teeth, snorting loudly. The stable was hot and flies buzzed near the windows. Higher up in the rafters, wasps were busy crawling into their paper nests.

Cassidy's heart was pounding so loudly she was certain Willie could hear it. Running the fingers of both hands through his hair, he leaned against the wall and blinked rapidly.

"You know who the guy was, don't you?" Cassidy whispered.

Willie shook his head so violently spittle was flung from his mouth.

"You do."

"No!"

Slowly she advanced on him. "Willie?"

His jaw worked and his eyes bulged. "It weren't nobody from around here and it weren't Brig. Swear to God, Cassidy, it weren't Brig."

Despair and certainty touched her heart with cold, cruel fingers. "I didn't ask you if it was Brig," she said, her insides trembling as Willie half-ran out of the barn. The sun was intense, heat waves rising from the earth, no breath of a breeze offering any kind of relief.

Willie headed through a gate to the curve of Lost Dog Creek to the willow tree where Cassidy had played as a child, where she'd seen Derrick making out with a dark-haired girl, where Brig had caught her beneath the leafy swaying branches.

Plopping down on a flat rock, Willie stared into the thin stream of water that wandered down an otherwise bone-dry chasm. He didn't look over his shoulder when he sensed her presence. "It happened here. In this creek," he said suddenly, his voice choked. "That's why I got stupid."

"You're not—"

"I am! I know what they say. 'Dumb as a doornail . . . doesn't know his ass from a hole in the ground . . . half-brain . . . stupid son of a bitch . . . retard.' I know, Cassidy."

An ache burned deep in her heart. She reached for his shoulder, but he shrugged her off.

"You know I'm your sister."

"I don't see how."

"Our father is the same."

"I'm too *stupid* to know."

"It's . . . it's like the horses, Willie. You know that one stallion can be with a lot of different mares and—"

"People aren't horses, Cassidy. I'm not that dumb!"

"It doesn't matter how it works anyway. And don't believe what everyone says. They're the stupid ones."

She knelt beside him and he sniffed loudly, his eyes red and blinking, though he wouldn't cry. He'd learned long ago to keep his emotions deep inside.

"Tell me about Brig. Why was he here with Chase?"

Willie shook his head. "Don't know."

"But you saw him?"

"I—I was at the mill." He swallowed hard. "I saw Chase and a man."

"Brig?"

Rubbing his nose furiously, as if the motion might make him concentrate, Willie scowled. "It was dark."

"But you saw him."

Willie quit moving altogether as he thought.

"What were you doing there?"

"Watchin'."

"For what?"

"Dunno." Turning to face her, he said, "I always watch. I watch you. I watch Chase. I watched Angie." Standing, he strode to the tree and pointed upward, past the first split of branches to an old limb. "See here—I seen this, too."

"What?" she asked, squinting against the sun as the drooping branches rustled in the breeze. Shadows played upon the ground and her eyes adjusted slowly. Then she saw it—a heart carved deep into the bark of the tree. Angie's name was hewn across the heart and Cassidy remembered sitting here beneath this very tree while Brig, fingering a jackknife, had talked to her. With a tug on her heart, she wondered if he'd chiseled her sister's name into the thick branch.

"Didn't know it was there, did ya?"

"No—I've never noticed it."

" 'Cause you ain't been watchin'."

"What else did you see, Willie?" she asked and he just stared at her, his blue eyes blank.

When he smiled, she felt the wind pick up. "Everything." He stared at her so long goose bumps rose on her flesh. She saw shadows race through his eyes. Dark, knowing shadows. Finally he looked away then turned and started back to the stable. "I see everything," he repeated, and his whisper was like the soft knell of doom.

* * *

The rest of the afternoon Cassidy worked at the paper. Half the time she'd spent avoiding Bill Laszlo, who had called her several times at home and cornered her twice in the office. Currently, he was hovering again.

" 'No comment' won't do," he warned.

"I have nothing more to say."

"Even though our friendly John Doe died?" He leaned a slim hip against the edge of her desk.

"I'm sorry he's dead."

"Your husband didn't say anything."

"He barely talks. His jaw is still wired shut. At least for a few more days."

"Isn't that convenient?"

"Painful is what it is."

"Well, what can you say about Sunny McKenzie taking a hike right out of the lobby of Northwest General?"

"I was with her and I'm worried about her and anyone who has seen her should contact me. I assume you'll put that in your piece, won't you? Where to call if she's located?"

He clucked his tongue and looked up at the ceiling. "You're stonewalling me, Cassidy."

"I don't have any more to give."

He scratched his arm and frowned at the ceiling tiles. "You know, I've been pretty patient with you. Because we're really on the same team."

"Same team? Save that speech for someone who hasn't heard it a million times, will ya, Bill?"

"Give it a rest, Laszlo." Selma fished into the bottom of her purse and dug out a pack of Virginia Slims. "You know you were a lot more friendly when you smoked. Want to join me on the back porch with the rest of the gang?"

"You're killing yourself."

"I'll quit someday. Maybe I'll take up running, too, and tell everyone else what they should do with their lives."

"I'll come with you," Cassidy said.

"You don't smoke!" Bill was aghast.

"Not yet, but maybe I'll have to take it up so that you'll quit badgering me."

"Badgering you?" A wounded expression converged over his even features. "Hey—you know all about this job."

Selma threw out a hip, and the gauzy fabric of her skirt swung just above her knees. "Look, I need a hit. Are we going to argue here or go outside and have a laugh or two?"

Cassidy needed a laugh. Or two. Or six hundred. Ever since the fire she'd been wound tighter than a watch spring, her nerves so tight she could barely sleep at night. Grabbing her purse, she left her computer humming and Bill muttering under his breath. They stopped at the machine for a couple of sodas, then continued on their mission.

Outside, the sun was still beating down, and a few other employees were enjoying a break. "The Coke and smoke crowd," Selma said as she offered Cassidy a cigarette.

Cassidy shook her head and flipped the top of her Diet Coke. "I don't think this is the time to take up another vice."

"Didn't know you had any." Selma struck a match and drew on her filter tip.

"Secret vices."

"Don't tell Bill. They'll all be exposed in the next edition."

"And I'll get a sermon."

"Amen," Selma said, laughing. Other employees joined them and the talk covered the next election, baseball, complaints about married life, jokes about single life and inevitably the fire. By the time they returned to their desks, Bill had given up his vigil and Cassidy finished two articles, one on possible new funding measures for schools, the other on one of the gubernatorial candidates.

She hurried out of the office, glad to be able to go home for the evening. Except she had to face Chase. At the thought, her stomach churned. How much longer could she keep up the charade? How long before the inevitable, that one of them moved out, occurred? She hoped to hold the marriage together until Chase was recovered, until the mystery surrounding the fire was solved, until she was certain that there was no chance for them.

Had there ever been one?

Had they ever truly loved each other?

A part of her cried out to be his wife, but then she remembered their last argument, the one that had simmered for days, then sparked on the day of the fire, and she knew that it was only a matter of time until they agreed to part company forever. And then what?

She climbed into the Jeep, rolled down the windows and started driving. Her future stretched out before her like an empty road across a desert—endless pavement leading to an unknown destination, the mirage of wedded bliss an illusion, the ribbon of highway desolate and lonely.

"Oh, stop it," she told herself. This was no way to act. Like a maudlin fool. She needed to find some answers, that was all—to get to the bottom of this fire as well as the last one. And the first person she had to deal with would help her, whether he wanted to or not.

It was time to have it out with her husband.

Thirty-three

Chase wasn't inside. She called for him and walked through each room, her heart racing as the stillness of the house swept over her. Aside from the hum of the refrigerator, the tick of the clock, the soft whir of the air-conditioning system, the house was silent. Empty. Her footsteps rang out against the tile and wood floor then were muffled when she crossed carpeting.

His crutches were missing, but as she threw open his closet, she saw his clothes, all neatly pressed and hanging where they had been. So he hadn't been foolish enough to move out. But where was he? His car, a green Jaguar, was still in the garage. The truck he'd taken to the sawmill had burned in the fire.

She walked back to the den, searched for a note, some clue, when she looked out the window in the back and found him leaning against a rock in the shade of a walnut tree near the lake he'd had dug the second summer they lived in the house.

He'd only been home a day, was still on pain medication, and though he could walk with crutches, he was, for the most part, dependent upon her. And he hated it. Each time she talked to him, she saw the anger in his good eye, the silent fury that seemed to radiate from him. There had been other emotions as well, hot and simmering under the surface, an electric current that neither one of them wanted to examine too closely.

The sun was beginning to set and he looked more at ease

than he had since returning home. She thought about leaving him be, starting dinner and waiting for him, but decided instead to join him. Maybe it was time to heal some old wounds.

The argument they'd had before the fire still clamored in her ears.

"You never loved me," she'd accused, tears building behind her eyes. "You married me just to be a part of this . . . this empire of my father's."

"And you married me because I was the closest thing to Brig."

"That's a lie."

"Is it?" he'd snarled, a big hand curling over the lapels of her jacket.

"I married you because I thought I loved you, because I wanted to settle down and have children, but all you wanted was to come back here and make a name for yourself. Prove that you were as good as the people with money, show how smart you were. And you did it, didn't you? Even convinced my father. Well, you've made your point, Chase, and you've got what you always wanted—a pile of money and a piece of the Buchanan fortune."

"And one of the richest women in the county for my wife."

"That was it, wasn't it? All along. It wasn't me you wanted," she said, her fists curling in frustration while she strove to keep her composure, refusing to break down into sobs. "It was my name and social status."

"You'd understand, if you hadn't been born with more money than you could ever spend in a lifetime. If you'd had to work two jobs to help support your nutcase of a mother, if you had to hold your head high even though your ears burned with the gossip that the town was whispering about her, about your brother, about a father who had just walked away one day." His anger had seeped away and he'd stared at her with pained eyes. "So you want a divorce."

"I want us to have a life. You don't have to work eighty-hour weeks. You don't have to leave town on business trips that last for days. You don't have to prove anything to me or the rest of the damned town."

"Why? So I can be home more nights? So we can start a family?"

"Yes, I think—"

"It would be a mistake, Cassidy. I don't want children. I've never wanted kids."

Her heart had cracked at that point. "I thought you'd change your mind, you said that it was possible—"

"Stop twisting my words around. Kids ruined my mother's life. Kids ruined your father's life. Kids are only trouble."

"And joy."

"Not enough," he said with feeling, and as she'd stared into his blue eyes, she'd finally understood.

"You won't be happy until you have it all, will you? The company. The subsidiaries. The property."

"The respect, damn it! Don't you understand? That's all I want, all I've ever wanted. I'd sell it all if it bought me one iota of respect."

"And you thought it could be bought by marrying the right woman or owning the right things . . ."

"I know it can."

All her dreams had shattered. The illusions she'd held so dear so foolishly, were instantly destroyed. "Then I want a divorce, Chase."

"Over my dead body."

"But—"

"Listen, Cassidy," he'd threatened, a vein throbbing at his temple. "Listen hard and good. I'll never let you divorce me, and if you try, I'll do everything and anything to force you to stop. I'll hire lawyers, private investigators, whatever it takes and I'll be sure that if you do finally get rid of me, you'll end up without a dime."

She'd recoiled at the thought, her face twisted in pain. "Why?"

A vein ticked angrily in his forehead. "Because, whether you believe it or not, I love you and I'd rather die than lose you." The fire in his eyes had frightened her but made her believe him.

And now he wanted a divorce. And was willing to sell his shares of the company. A complete turnaround. Because of what he'd been through? Because of the fire? Because he'd finally faced the truth that they could never make their marriage work? Just when she was willing to try again. Ironic, wasn't it? They never seemed to put out the effort at the same time.

She walked outside—past hanging pots of fuchsias with their dripping petals, and heavy-bloomed roses—following a brick and cement path to long grass and wildflowers that grew near the water's edge. When he'd dug out the lake, he'd refused to have it landscaped, insisted that the old walnut tree be left standing and let nature decide what would grow on the sandy shores.

Hearing her approach, he lifted his head. Slowly, his bruised face was becoming more recognizable.

"You worried me," she said, sitting down on the beach near the tall grass and staring across the smooth water. "When I couldn't find you in the house."

"Can't stand being cooped up."

"I know." Shoving off her shoe, she dug a bare toe into the white sand he'd had trucked in from the beach years ago. She'd always thought she would watch her children build sand castles here, splash and swim in the clear water, fish and hunt for crawdads and periwinkles where the water lapped beneath the trees. But she'd been a fool. A silly, hopelessly romantic fool.

"You should have told me about Willie as soon as you found out."

"Probably. I was just trying to—"

"Protect me?" he mocked, his words and voice still muffled from the wires. "I don't need you to save me from the truth."

"Do you need me at all?"

He didn't answer, just picked up a flat rock with his good

hand and, flipping his wrist, sent the stone sailing over the water, making it skip four times, causing rippling circles to play on the glassy surface of the lake.

"Look, I've been thinking . . ." She gazed across the water to the horizon where the smoky ridge of the Cascades met the sky. "Maybe we should try harder."

"To what?"

"Save our marriage."

His jaw worked and his eye trained over the water seemed even more distant. Geese flew across the sky, reminding her that summer would soon end. A breeze ruffled the drying leaves in the walnut tree and teased at her hair. "Why?"

Why. "Because it was good once."

"Was it?"

"In the beginning," she reminded him. "Once we'd settled the past, it was good. Even after we moved here, for a while . . ." She let her voice trail off.

Geese honked in the distance and the scent of dying roses perfumed the air. Somewhere far away a tractor's engine rumbled, and high in the sky the wake of a jet billowed fluffy white against the blue sky.

"You don't have to feel obligated. Just because of what I said about not letting you divorce me—"

"I don't. Well, maybe I do a little, but not because of what you said, but because I want it, Chase. I want it to work for us."

He considered, his eye narrowing at some inner vision. "And if we fail?"

"We're no worse off." She reached for his hand and his reaction was swift.

Drawing away, he turned and glared at her. "I don't want your pity, Cass."

"I don't pity you."

"And I don't want you to feel duty-bound to a crippled, half-blind man. You don't have to pretend to love me."

"I would never—"

"Of course you would. You already have. Don't lie, Cass.

Whatever you do, don't lie to me." The words seemed to reach back to another time and place, a distant, fuzzy place she couldn't remember.

"Look, Chase, I don't fake feelings. And most importantly, I don't lie." She stared him straight in that ugly, healing eye. "I just want to start from square one—a clean slate, okay? Neither one of us will pretend anything. Everything's on the up and up. We'll try to work this out together, and if things fall apart, then we'll talk."

He snorted, as if the outcome had already been determined.

"Just tell me you'll try, Chase."

"If it makes you happy."

"Say it." She stood and her skirt whipped around her legs with the breeze that blew sand over the tops of her feet and caused the branches overhead to sigh. "Say it."

He hesitated for a second, then lifted a shoulder. "Okay. Fine. I'll try."

"Good." Relief washed through her. There was a chance they could put together their lives again, find what they'd lost.

"But I think we should keep things on an even keel, so I'll be staying in one of the guest rooms, for now." He must've seen the pain in her eyes, and his throat worked as he dragged his gaze away from her again. "Considering the circumstances, it would be best."

"This is temporary?" she asked, remembering his aversion to touching her. Since the fire he'd not reached for her once, wanted no physical contact whatsoever, insisted that she keep her distance from him.

"Yes." He took in a long breath. "Just until we see which way the wind blows."

"Meaning you don't trust me."

He planted his crutches into the sand and stood, staring down at her. "Meaning that neither one of us really trusts the other."

* * *

They ate together, though most of what Chase could put down was blended and sucked through a straw. Fortunately the wires holding his jaw together were scheduled to come off in a couple of days. He was still on pain medication and he wasn't much interested in thin mashed potatoes and pureed meat. "Feel like a damned baby," he complained.

"Things'll get better."

"Will they?" he asked from his chair near the window, and she knew he wasn't talking about the food. Behind him, in the fading sunlight, a hummingbird hovered near a feeder.

"Sure. You'll be in physical therapy starting tomorrow, the wires off in a few days, your casts will be off before you know it and—"

"And we'll still be here. In limbo."

She picked up the dishes and carried them to the sink. She'd planned to come home and have it out with him, demand answers, ask him questions he'd refused to answer, but she'd backed down. Why? Because she was afraid of the truth?

"There's no reason to rush things, is there?" he asked.

She nearly dropped a plate because he was so wrong. Ever since the fire, she'd felt that time was running out, like sand passing through the neck of an hourglass, slipping away forever. As it had for Brig. Her heart squeezed.

Chase settled back in his chair, his leg stretched out to the side of the table, his eye regarding her silently. "I thought you wanted out so badly."

Frowning, she set dirty plates and bowls in the dishwasher. "I didn't want to go on treading water," she admitted. "I know that you said you loved me the night of the fire, but before that . . . well, you remember. We drifted apart."

"And you had an affair," he said quietly.

She shook her head. "Never. I've never cheated on you Chase, and I never will. As long as we're married, I'll be faithful." She slammed the dishwasher door shut, turned and, resting her hips against the counter, wiped her hands on a towel. "I expect the same from you. If you can't trust me, then you'd better let me know now."

He muttered something under his breath as the phone rang. They looked at each other and let the answering machine pick up in the den. Reporters had been calling and Cassidy hadn't been interested in dealing with them. She would listen to the messages later, and together they would decide whom they would call back.

"Tomorrow," Chase said, straightening, "I'll need to talk with the insurance people, Derrick and the cops. The mill's been shut down too long. Those men need to get back to work, the records are going to have to be reconstructed, a new—temporary office found near the mill, or maybe we can have one of those modular things brought in." He rubbed his eye, then stood and stared out the window as if he were searching for something or someone.

"Let Derrick handle it," Cassidy advised. "You can't do much now. Until you're on your feet and—"

He swung his crutches under his arms, and stood. "I am on my feet, in complete control of my faculties, and as long as I don't take too many of Doc Okano's horse pills, I'm reasonably able to function."

"You should rest."

"While Derrick runs the company down the tubes?"

"He's not—"

"Your brother is a liar and a cheat and he's been skimming money from the corporation."

"You have proof?" she asked, not really surprised. Chase had hinted that Derrick was embezzling before, but he'd never pursued it.

"What do you think?" He glared at her and she swallowed hard.

"Is that why you were at the mill that night? To check something?" When he didn't answer, she let out her breath. "You—you think he started the fire to destroy the records?"

"I don't know what to think. There're copies of everything in the main office, on the computer, unless that's been screwed around with. But the books were at the mill."

"I can't believe that Derrick would—"

"I'm not saying he did. I'm just not taking any chances

with the company. Or my life." Squinting through the window again, he scowled, then hobbled into the den with Cassidy on his heels. Her mind was spinning ahead to possibilities. What Chase was suggesting was that Derrick may have started the fire to destroy the books . . . or to kill him. Or both. She remembered how cruel Derrick had become as a teenager, but arson? Attempted murder?

She paused at the doorway to the den and watched as Chase rewound the tape on the recorder. He waited impatiently, then listened as reporter after reporter left a message. There was another one from Dena and one from Felicity but none from the person he was waiting for. None from his mother. "Where the hell is she?" he growled as Detective T. John Wilson's voice filled the room and he announced that he'd be stopping by later.

Chase's scowl deepened and he jerked his way out of the room as the tape player clicked off. *Great,* she thought sarcastically. Just what they needed. Another interrogation from the inimitable T. John Wilson.

Thirty-four

"The detective's here." Cassidy paused at the doorway to the den where Chase was propped up on a recliner. He'd never said a word to the police in the hospital, only answered questions with a nod or shake of his head.

"Well, by all means, show him in," Chase said.

A few minutes later T. John was declining Cassidy's offer of coffee and balancing himself on the arm of a leather sofa. "You may as well stick around," he said to Cassidy, "this might interest you as well."

"What?"

"Our John Doe finally got himself a name. Postmortem, but a name nonetheless."

Cassidy ignored the hammering of her heart and braced herself for the truth. "Did he?"

"Marshall Baldwin." Chase's voice was the clearest it had been since the accident, though he was still speaking through a wired jaw.

T. John grinned. "Thought you might have known him."

"Who is he?" Cassidy asked.

"Well, now, that appears to be the million-dollar question. Ol' Marsh, he seems to be some kind of enigma."

"He's a developer and lumber broker from Alaska."

"That's right; a self-made millionaire."

"What was he doing here?" Cassidy asked, her eyes rounding on her husband. How many secrets had he hidden from her over the years? She'd been so certain the dead man was Brig. Relief swept through her blood.

"Interested in selling me raw lumber. Even talked about buying out our mill, or some other one down here."

Cassidy couldn't believe her ears. "Now? In Oregon? When mills are shutting down all over the state? That doesn't make much sense—"

"I know. Told him as much. But he said the prices were right. He could get a helluva deal."

"Why were you meeting him at night?" She couldn't help being suspicious.

"Isn't it obvious?"

"No."

He cleared his throat. "I didn't want you or Derrick to find out. I suggested we meet in Portland, but he wanted to see the operation firsthand, so we settled on meeting at the mill, then going into town."

"You were hiding this from me?" she asked, a trace of bitterness in her words. She shouldn't have been surprised—she'd learned over the years that Chase ran his life by his own rules. Still, she felt betrayed.

"I just wanted to get all the facts straight. Then, if I'd decided we should sell—"

"If *you* decided? Don't I have a voice in this? For God's sake, Chase—" She caught the warning look in Chase's eye and stopped cold. This wasn't the time or place. He seemed to be silently warning her, telling her not to make a scene in front of the detective.

"Baldwin was interested. That's all."

"And so you met at the mill and then what?" Wilson asked.

"We'd just left the office and were walking up the ramp to building one when there was a blast—so loud it sounded like dynamite exploding in a tunnel. The walls started to collapse and we tried to run."

"Was Marshall holding anything in his hand?"

"I don't remember."

T. John shifted. "Was he wearing a chain with a St. Christopher's medal?"

"I didn't notice."

"What was he wearing?"

"Hell, I don't remember."

"A suit?"

"I don't know."

"Sport jacket and slacks?"

"Jeans maybe, but it was too hot for a jacket. I left mine in the office."

"Why wasn't his wallet in his pocket?" Wilson demanded.

"I don't have any idea."

Wilson slowly unwrapped a piece of chewing gum and frowned, his gaze centering on the fireplace, though Cassidy suspected he was watching Chase's reaction in his peripheral vision. "Let me get this straight. You planned to meet a guy you'd never seen before late at night at the mill to talk about the possibility of selling it."

"Or buying his lumber. Either way."

"The way I heard it, you were like a son to Rex Buchanan, put in eighty—maybe ninety-hour weeks. Some people around here think that mill meant more to you than anything, even your family, but all of a sudden, out of the clear damned blue, you were thinking of selling?"

"I'm always thinking of selling if the price is right."

"What would your father-in-law say?"

"Hadn't gotten that far."

"But he'd taken you under his wing, loaned you money for your education, let you work your way into being the corporate attorney and then senior vice president. Above his own son."

"Not above. Not even equal to. But almost. Rex has great faith in my abilities."

"And for that you sneak around, thinking about selling out your share without telling him."

"Yes." Chase's glare was cold as ice.

"Well, why's that? Hell, I'm no businessman, just a po-dunk policeman with a badge, but it don't make a helluva lot of sense."

Cassidy went cold inside. She never would have thought

Chase would have entertained the idea of selling. Not the night of their last fight.

"You were thinking of getting out, maybe?" the detective persisted. "Leaving town because of marital problems?"

"Wait a minute—" Cassidy interrupted but Chase held up a hand to stop her protests.

"That's personal, and has nothing to do with the mills."

Rage poured through her blood. He had no right to discuss this with anyone! Not even the police.

"All patched up, I hope."

"All patched up," Chase said without inflection.

T. John thought about it, lifted a shoulder as if to ask, *Who could understand love?* "Okay. Whatever."

Cassidy knew he wouldn't give up on it, he was just appeasing them both. He stretched out his leg before bending it and clasping his hands over his knee. "So you and Baldwin, you're both two big corporate execs—hell, you're a goddamned lawyer and neither one of you remembered your button-down shirts, suits, or briefcases for a meeting that might result in some major corporate changes."

"It wasn't that kind of business meeting."

"What kind was it?"

"Casual."

Wilson's eyebrows drew together. "So you said. Just strikes me as kind of funny, that's all."

"We're not talking Wall Street, for Christ's sake. Major deals are struck every day on tennis courts or on golf courses. It isn't always necessary to get the board together—not until something's been decided, and this was preliminary, very preliminary. As I already said, I might have ended up just milling some of his lumber."

Cassidy stared at her husband, looking for perspiration or any sign of nervousness. There was none. His face was impassive, nearly bored, one arm in a sling, the other resting on the arm of the chair. No fingers drummed, no sweat dampened his hair, no nervous tick gave a clue to the level of his anxiety.

Wilson scratched a day's growth of beard. "So what did you discuss that night?"

"Not much. He'd barely gotten there when I started to show him the layout."

"Wouldn't he want to see the mill up and running, you know—check the equipment, make sure it was in working order, keep track of the employees to find out if they showed up on time or cut out early? Watch the men working together and see how you bring in log trucks and empty them, how you cut your boards, all that shit?"

"That would come later—if he decided to buy and I was willing to sell. It wouldn't matter much if he was just trying to sell me some raw lumber, though. All he'd be interested in would be the terms and the price." Chase leveled the detective a single-eyed gaze meant to cut through granite. "It wasn't such a big deal."

Wilson considered. "You think whoever set the fire was trying to kill Baldwin?"

"I have no idea."

"Otherwise the timing seems a little coincidental, wouldn't you say?"

"I couldn't even venture a guess."

Cassidy watched the detective try and bully Chase into saying something he didn't want to, into slipping up. "Chase, maybe we should call a lawyer—"

"I am a lawyer," he said swiftly.

"I know; I mean a criminal lawyer." Things were moving too quickly; she needed time to think. "Besides, Detective, my husband's just gotten out of the hospital and he tires easily—"

"I'm not tired," Chase snapped. "And I don't think Detective Wilson is here to charge me with anything." He leaned forward in the chair. "Or am I wrong?"

" 'Course not." The good-old-boy grin slid across the detective's jaw. "Just lookin' for information about the crime."

"That I can't tell you; I don't know who set the fire or why. I wouldn't have any idea if the explosion was a means used to kill someone or just an expensive prank. Obviously someone wanted to do some damage. I'm just not sure how much."

"You didn't see anyone else at the mill that night?"

"No one."

Cassidy rubbed her hands on her jeans. Her palms were sweaty, her insides shaking. *What about Willie? He'd been there.*

T. John crossed one leg over the other and popped his gum. "You know, I was a little disappointed when we finally pieced together Baldwin's ID."

"Why's that?" Chase asked.

"Because up to that point, I would've bet my badge that the John Doe was your brother."

Cassidy didn't move.

"My brother?" Chase repeated, again without so much as a hint of emotion.

"Yep. I had myself a notion—call it gut instinct—that Brig had come back to town and met with you."

"Late at night at the mill?" Chase said, his voice filled with derision.

"Why not? He's still a fugitive. Wouldn't chance prancin' through the streets of Prosperity in broad daylight, now, would he?"

Chase didn't even glance at his wife. "Brig's dead."

"You know that?"

"He's dead to me. Never showed his face around here after the first fire."

"That first fire; that's what got me thinkin'," T. John said. "I was of the mind that the two fires were connected, and it's a damned shame I couldn't have talked to Baldwin to find out why he was down here."

"I told you why."

"Yeah, yeah." T. John stopped chewing. "But did it ever occur to you that Baldwin might be your brother?"

Chase snorted. "Don't you think I would've recognized him?"

"Well, that's just it; I don't know."

Cassidy could barely breathe. It was one thing to have her

private fears, another to have them voiced. "You're saying that you think Baldwin is Brig?"

"He wasn't Brig. I was there," Chase cut in.

T. John rubbed his chin. "I'm saying nothin's for sure. Not yet. See, Marshall Baldwin doesn't have any family, none that either we or the boys up in Alaska can find. He claims he's from California and we're checking birth certificates and such, from somewhere around L.A. All government records show that he was never married, no brothers and sisters, parents dead. Not even an uncle or a third cousin is crawling out of the woodwork and you'd think that someone would want to lay claim to his money. I told you he had himself a pile, didn't I?"

"You mentioned it, yes," Cassidy said, knowing that the detective was sharp enough to remember everything he'd said.

"Yep. Showed up in Alaska, near as anyone can tell, as early as 1977. Not a dime to his name. He got himself a job working on the trans-Alaska pipeline, maintenance. I think it was already built—finished the year before. Worked for three or four years before he bought out a guy who owned a sawmill and worked round the clock to get that mill on its feet—kind of like you," he said to Chase. "The man had no social life, just sixteen-hour days, seven days a week. It worked, too; pretty soon he bought himself another mill and another. Invested in a fishery or two, a mining operation and even some kind of farm . . ." He screwed up his face, then snapped his fingers as if the thought finally struck him. "Potato farm, I think it was. Don't that beat all?"

"Don't it just?" Chase mocked.

"Anyway, most of the time Baldwin kept a low profile, but he was suspected of being an anonymous donor to quite a few charities up there—especially saving the wilderness, that kind of crap."

Chase let out a sound of disgust. "I know you don't remember him, but Brig . . . well, he was never what you'd call a philanthropist."

"He was just a kid when he took off."

"Well, he used to laugh at Cassidy's father, claiming old man Buchanan was always trying to save the world by donating to good causes just to ease his guilty conscience."

"No—" Cassidy said.

Chase ignored her. "Brig also had no ambition. And he was always in trouble with the law. I think you can find records that prove it."

"Not our friend Baldwin," T. John said, placing his hands on his knees as he straightened. "The man was lily white. Not so much as a speeding ticket according to the authorities in Alaska. Can you believe it? A man lives up there nearly twenty years, makes a shit-load of money and remains practically invisible."

"But you think he's Brig."

"Could be."

Cassidy felt a trickle of sweat slide down her spine.

"How about dental records?" T. John asked as he walked to the fireplace and leaned against the cool stones. "I can't find any record of you or your brother going to the dentist."

"We didn't. No money and good, strong teeth."

"Funny, Baldwin didn't have a dentist up in Anchorage, either. Or Juneau or Ketchikan or anywhere else, near as we can figure. Can't believe a guy can live over thirty years without a toothache. Ah, well, we're still lookin'. Too bad his mouth was so busted up. Teeth broken. Kinda like yours."

"What about fingerprints?"

"We took what we could, his hands were pretty burned. So far, no match."

Cassidy could barely think straight. "Brig—he was arrested; here in Prosperity, there should be some record."

"Well, now, that's interesting, Mrs. Buchanan, because Brig never was printed. Not once. Oh, he was dragged in, talked to a lot, scolded and slapped on the hands, but never once did he have to put his fingertips in ink. Because of your daddy and some fancy lawyer always steppin' in. Ain't that convenient?"

"And Baldwin?" she asked.

"No military record. No criminal record. No prints. Like

I said, damned convenient. No kin to claim his body or peti-
tion for his money, a will that leaves a provision for the employees to buy out the sawmill and fishery if they want, and
the rest of his money is to be given to a nonprofit organiza-
tion dedicated to preserving the Alaskan wilderness, an orga-
nization that Baldwin helped found. He kept his name and
face out of the papers, but spent money, lots of it, on causes
he cared about."

"That's not my brother."

Wilson shrugged. "Maybe he was a changed man.
Trauma can do that."

Chase made a sound of disgust in the back of his throat.

T. John ignored it. "I thought maybe you might recognize
him, so I brought along some snapshots, the few that we've
got." He dug into the inside pocket of his jacket and withdrew a manila envelope. Cassidy's heart began to knock, as,
one by one, the glossy prints fell onto the desk. Were they
Brig? She tried to keep her hands from trembling as she
picked up one picture and studied it carefully. A bearded,
dark-haired man stared back at her, his eyes deep set and
brooding, his demeanor one of complete and utter distrust.

"I guess the man looks a little like Brig," Chase admitted.

"Dead ringer, I'd say."

"But Baldwin didn't have a beard."

"Ain't that strange? Been wearing one up in Alaska for
seventeen years, then shaves it off to meet with you." T. John
smiled and shook his head, then he pulled out another piece
of paper, an artist's sketch. "We had one of our boys draw the
guy without a beard and we're trying to reconstruct his face
by computer, then compare it with photos of your brother.
Trouble is all we've got is a couple of shots from a high
school yearbook."

"You're serious?" Chase glared at the detective.

"Damned straight." For the first time Cassidy got a glimpse
into T. John's soul. No cocky grin. No twinkle in his eye. No
good-old-boy laughter. Just blind ambition glinted in his eye.

"Why is it so important that Marshall Baldwin be Brig?"

"Well, that's interesting. Your brother, he takes off after one of the worst fires in the history of Prosperity, then shows up again seventeen years later at a fire just like the other one. Nearly the same incendiary device used. Helluva coincidence. Lots of 'em." T. John flipped through the pictures and scowled.

"I'd know Brig." Chase picked up a grainy snapshot of Marshall Baldwin and stared at the black and white image.

"You ever talked to Baldwin before?"

"Just on the phone."

"How'd he get your name?"

"He was interested in the mill, called and asked for me."

"Not Rex Buchanan, even though he's the CEO or whatever fancy name you want to put on president these days."

"Baldwin had heard at a convention that I run the company; Rex is semiretired and Derrick's just a figurehead."

"Even though he's Rex's son." T. John tugged at his lower lip. "So you never once suspected this guy was Brig?"

"He wasn't."

"Sure." T. John scooped up the pictures, straightened and cast a smile in Cassidy's direction. His eyes silently called them both liars as he popped his gum and started for the door. "Here—you might want one of these. I got more at the office." He handed Cassidy a picture of Marshall Baldwin, one where he was squinting against the sun as he stood on some rocky cliff. "I know you're both tired. It's been a helluva week. If you can tell me anything more about Marshall, I'd appreciate hearing from you."

Chase struggled to his feet. "And when you hear anything about my mother, I'd like a call."

Wilson clucked his tongue. "Now that's odd, don't you think? Seems as if she up and disappeared into thin air. Thought you might know where she was."

Chase's jaw clenched hard. "Find her, Wilson," he ordered.

"Doin' my best," the detective said with a cold smile. "Doin' my level best."

Thirty-five

"What do you know about Baldwin?" Cassidy demanded when Chase hobbled into the kitchen the next morning. He'd refused to talk to her last night, just left her in the den and headed for his bedroom, but she wasn't going to be put off again. The *Times* was open, a picture of Marshall Baldwin on the front page next to Bill Laszlo's column.

"You were there. You heard me." Chase glanced at the newspaper and scowled. "So the vultures are already circling."

"Bill's just doing his job."

"Right. It's just a piss-poor way to make a living."

"The same way I do."

He ignored that and leaning on one crutch, he poured a cup of coffee and found a straw.

"I heard what you told the detective. Now I want to know the truth."

"You think I'm lying? God, Cass, give it a rest."

"Not just me. The detective thinks it, too. Knows it. He may talk like some country boy who just fell off the hay wagon, but he's sharp, Chase. Sharp, dedicated and relentless. Rumor has it that he wants Floyd Dodds's job as county sheriff. All he needs is the right kind of publicity—*this* kind."

"Well, he's not getting it from me." Ignoring his coffee, he tried to pass but she lodged her body firmly in the door. Her chin thrust out, determination stiffening her back, she glared up at him. "Move, Cass," he ordered.

Trembling inside, she tried to rein in her emotions. *Be professional. Take yourself out of this. Keep your distance and study the situation objectively. Without emotion. As if you were on camera reporting a story.* Impossible. With Chase, she was always riding the gut-wrenching back of emotion. "Look, Chase, if we're going to start over, we'll need to begin by telling the truth."

"Like you've always done with me."

"I've tried—"

"Like hell, Cassidy." He tried to swing by her, but she wouldn't budge. His chest was rising and falling, his skin flushed with rage. "Besides, I never said a word about starting over. I think I agreed to cohabit with you as long as you left me alone. I believe I agreed to 'try again.' No promises. No strings attached."

"We can't do that unless you're honest."

"That goes two ways, Cass. You haven't exactly been straight with me."

"What do you—"

"I know you've been conducting your own little investigation. Calling around, collecting seventeen-year-old information about the fire at the gristmill. About Angie's death. About Brig's sudden disappearance. That's what this all boils down to, isn't it? Brig." He spat his brother's name as if it tasted foul. His nostrils flared in rage. "Don't try and act so innocent. I know why you're trying to solve this damned mystery; so that you can have the scoop of the century."

She felt as if he'd kicked her. "I never—"

"I've seen the file, Cassidy. Read your notes on the computer. I'm starting to wonder if you wanted us to 'work things out' so that you could spend your days trying to drag information out of me and end up the town hero by solving the crime."

"You're crazy. I'm not working on a story. Laszlo's been assigned to the fire." She hitched her chin toward the open newspaper.

"And you'd love to show him up, wouldn't you? This should be your story. It's about your family. I can see it in your eyes, Cassidy. You're pissed that Laszlo, just because he's a man, got this little plum."

"For the love of God, Chase, you can't really believe that I'm in this for the glory." He didn't respond, just looked down his broken nose at her. Sick inside, she whispered, "You think I wanted you to stay here so I could further my career."

"Why else?"

"Because . . ." She stopped just short of saying the dangerous words that wanted to fall from the tip of her tongue. "Because . . ." *I want to fall in love with you* screamed through her brain though she wasn't certain she could ever love him or that he would love her. They'd become so used to wounding each other, to expecting another emotional blow, that they couldn't trust each other, not even a little.

"By the way, he called."

"Who?"

"Laszlo. Early. While you were out swimming," he said and she was surprised that he'd known her whereabouts at six in the morning. "Sounded desperate to talk to me. It was almost as if my wife had egged him into it. I didn't pick up, just let him blabber into the recorder, but he's anxious to get some facts for his next column."

"I told him to stop trying to pump me for information. If he wanted answers from you, he'd have to call you himself."

"Great." He didn't make a move for the door, just stared at her with such an intensity that she could barely breathe, hardly think. Close enough that his breath was warm against her face. "Anything else you want to discuss, or are we going to stand here all day?"

She asked him the question that had been nagging at her ever since the fire—something about his attitude. "What is it you're afraid of, Chase?"

He hesitated.

"What is it?" The seconds ticked by and she refused to wither under his stare. His chest rose and fell as quickly as hers and she heard the soft rush of air as it escaped his lungs.

"You," he whispered and she barely heard the single, damning word. "I'm afraid of you, Cassidy."

"Me? Why?"

"I don't want to get too close to you again," he admitted. "It's just not safe."

She gazed at him silently, heart thudding.

The muscles tightened in his neck and he looked away. "Damn it, Cass."

"You're going to leave, aren't you?" she guessed, aching a little.

A flicker of regret crossed his face. "I won't have a choice. Now, get out of the way, Cassidy. Don't make me a prisoner."

"Chase . . ."

He pushed past her. "Stop trying to make something out of nothing. I agreed to your charade. To live with you. Stay in the same house. Hell, I even decided I could *pretend* that we were happy. For your parents. For the police. For the whole damned town, if that's what you want. But when we're alone, I expect you to leave me the hell alone."

Her reflex was instant. She raised her arm, wanting to hit, to scream, to kick her way past the shield he'd put up between them.

He laughed. A dark, sarcastic sound that rippled wickedly through the room as she slowly dropped her hand. "Can't hit a cripple, Cass?"

"You self-pitying bastard!"

"Now, that's more like it."

"I don't really know what happened to us," she said, refusing to back down, "but I believe it can be fixed."

"Marriage isn't like an old broken-down Pontiac, Cassidy. Both parties have to want it to work."

"Fight me all you want, Chase McKenzie, but I'm not giving up on us."

"You did once," he charged, and she cringed inside. He was right.

"And for that you'll never forgive me."

"There are so many things between us we couldn't start forgiving them all."

"We could try."

"Yeah, well, you know what they say about hell freezing over." He plunged his crutches ahead of him and swept past her, moving quickly, but awkwardly, through the house.

Despair stole into her heart, but she refused to give up hope. Damn it, she could be as stubborn as he. And she'd find a chink in his emotional armor if it killed her, though she was afraid that it was guilt, not love, that drove her.

"Tell me about Marshall Baldwin." Bill Laszlo caught up with Cassidy in the kitchen as she was pouring herself a cup of coffee. She glanced at an early copy of the *Times,* identical to the one she'd seen on the kitchen table at home. Chase had left the house immediately after their fight, refusing to let her drive him, taking an automatic pickup that he somehow managed to maneuver into town.

"Baldwin died in the fire."

"I know that much. Hell, I wrote that story," he said, motioning to the short article headlined ALASKAN BUSINESSMAN IDENTIFIED. "But who was he, really?"

Cassidy stirred powdered cream substitute into her coffee. "I don't know."

"Sure you do. Hey, watch out, that stuff will kill you. It's loaded with preservatives and crap like that. Notice the word 'nondairy.' "

"Thanks for the tip," she said, dropping her stir stick in the waste can.

"So come on. You must know something about Baldwin."

"All I know is what I read in the papers, what you wrote. He's an Alaskan industrialist. He owns some sawmills, a farm—potatoes, I think, a fishery and land. Gives a lot of money away to charitable causes."

"That's just his publicist talking."

"Did he have one?"

Laszlo was undeterred. "What I want to know is the man below the surface. Who was he really? The way I hear it, he has no family; isn't that a hoot? All that money and not an heir—not even a will?"

"Someone will claim his money."

"I hope so; I'd like to know more about him." He reached for a cup on an upper shelf. "What's Chase say?"

Cassidy was cautious, but it didn't hurt to tell Bill what she'd learned from Chase. "Just that Baldwin came down here to talk about having some lumber milled here."

"You believe that? When we're shipping lumber to Japan? Don't they have mills in Alaska? Doesn't he own his own?" Laszlo poured himself some hot water and dunked a bag of herbal tea into his cup.

He was asking the same questions she'd asked herself, but she wasn't about to tell him about Chase selling out his interest in Buchanan Industries. Not yet.

"Come on, Cassidy. Don't kid a kidder. I know that before the fire you were ready to walk. Chase is married to the Buchanan fortune, not to you. Now, all of a sudden, everything's hunky-dory, your marriage is back on track, and you're trying to protect him."

Irritation edged her voice. "If you don't believe me, call Chase."

"I have," Bill said. "He's not particularly chatty."

"Maybe it's because his jaw is still wired together."

"And maybe it's because he's got something to hide."

She picked up her coffee and headed back to her desk. He started to follow. "Leave me alone, Bill, I've got work to do."

"So do I."

"Then do it, and stop pumping me for information I don't have."

He ignored her as she wove through the partitions to her own desk. Selma wasn't in yet. Wheeling his chair over, Bill plopped down next to Cassidy as she turned her attention to her computer screen and tried to tune him out. Damn the man. He wasn't a bad reporter and persistence seemed to be his middle name. Picking up her cup, she sipped the coffee—a little stronger than she liked—and pulled up a story she'd started the day before.

Bill dropped his wet tea bag in her trash. "Marshall shows up in Alaska in the fall of 1977."

"So?"

"Less than two months after the fire here."

"I'm still not following you," she said, her heart hammering so loudly she was afraid he could hear the wild knocks.

"No family. No friends. Nothing. As far as I can tell, he didn't have a dime to his name, not even a decent coat and he's in friggin' Alaska. Do you know how cold it is up there in November? He lands a job, gets credit at some company store so that he can buy some warm clothes and stays in the cheapest dive available. At the time he claims he's twenty-two, but no one knows for sure. He could have been younger."

"Or older, if he's lying."

"Don't be obtuse."

"What're you getting at, Bill?"

"I'm working on the theory that Marshall Baldwin might have been Brig McKenzie."

Isn't everyone?

He watched her reaction, his gaze never leaving her face as he took a swallow of his tea.

"That's a big leap."

"I'd like to talk to Chase, face-to-face, and then to his mother. You know they think she was spotted up in the foothills?"

"What?" Cassidy nearly spilled her coffee. "Someone's found Sunny?"

"Unconfirmed as yet, but two kids who'd been camping in the woods came home and told their mother they'd seen a witch; a gray-haired woman chanting in a small clearing. Now the kids could be lying, of course. I'm going to interview them when the police are through. And then there's a farmer—Dave Dickey, lives out on his family's homestead a few miles out of town. He admits to giving a woman with a cane—probably your missing mother-in-law—a ride. And guess where she ended up?"

"I can't."

"At your Mom and Dad's place. That was the day she escaped; the day Marshall Baldwin died. I'm going to have a chat with Farmer Dave, too. Sooner or later the truth's gonna come out, Cassidy, and the *Times* is gonna report it under my byline. So"—he stood—"if you find out anything, I'd appreciate it if you'd let me know."

Thirty-six

"Where's Sunny McKenzie?" Dena's voice shook as she demanded answers of her husband. Rex was in the stable watching as Mac, the foreman who had been with Rex for as long as Dena could remember, drove his old truck away from the ranch. Dust and the smell of diesel filled the air.

"I don't know where she is."

"Like hell." Dena's anger was out of control. She felt the heat in her face, knew her lip was trembling in rage. For over a week she'd felt as if she were walking a tightrope, her stomach in knots. The pills her doctor had prescribed, little capsules that were supposed to "calm her nerves," didn't help much. She was already upping the dosage. "Look, Rex, I've put up with a lot over the years. I knew about you and Sunny—"

He scowled defensively, his eyes sliding away, as if he were suddenly interested in the mares and foals grazing in a far pasture.

She brazened on. This was her life, too, damn it. "For the most part, I turned my head, even though it hurt me, but I won't allow you to harbor her around here somewhere. She's an escapee from a mental hospital, for God's sake!"

Rex rubbed the back of his neck as he stared across fields dotted with the most expensive horses in the county. "Sunny's the most sane person I know."

"Oh, for the love of St. Mary. Will you listen to yourself Rex? Sane? A woman who made her living reading palms, and listening to voices or seeing visions or whatever it was? Sane? She tried to slash her own wrists, for God's sake! Why do you think Willie is a half-wit?"

" 'Cause he nearly drowned, that's why," Rex said, his cheeks reddening as he faced her. "And it's my fault."

"Your fault?"

"I should've claimed him from the beginning, or at least paid Frank McKenzie enough so that he could keep a decent place for his family." Rex closed his eyes. "I've been a coward, Dena, afraid to tarnish my reputation, but no longer. I'm going to call Cassidy at the *Times*. Let her print the story."

"Oh, Rex, no—"

"It's time, Dena," he said, offering her a kind, patient smile—the one he reserved for hotheads and neurotics. Oh, he'd changed from the man she'd married over thirty years before. He'd been strong, then. Forceful. The most powerful man in three counties and now in his old age he seemed to be weakening, trying to make his peace, forever trekking up to the cemetery and reliving the past.

"God's punished me for my cowardice," he said. "First Lucretia, then Buddy's accident, then . . . then Angie." His voice cracked.

"God isn't punishing you."

"Of course He is." Rex lifted his hat, smoothed his hair and frowned as he squared the cap back on his head.

"I won't let you ruin my life. Or Cassidy's," she said.

"The truth won't ruin anything."

"The truth is that your first wife was a cold bitch who decided to end it all in the garage. As for Sunny McKenzie, she's nothing better than a half-crazed whore—"

"Stop it!" he hissed, startling a spindly-legged colt in the next paddock. The colt let out a frightened neigh and bolted. Rex's big hands curled into fists. "Never, and I mean never, will you denigrate Lucretia, Sunny or Angie." He stepped closer to her, his rage evident in the flare of his nostrils, his body stiff and seeming four inches taller than it had been only seconds before. Some of the old fire blazed in his eyes.

"If I ever catch you badmouthing any of them, I'll personally come at you with a belt and after that, by God, I'll divorce you."

"But you couldn't. Your faith—"

His lips curled into a sneer. "Okay. If divorce won't work, then I'll kill you, Dena. It's that simple. Somehow, I think God would forgive me." He turned and strode into the stable and Dena, barely able to control her bladder, watched as he picked up the telephone extension. She leaned against the fence and, horror-stricken, overheard his part of the conversation as he spoke with Cassidy—their daughter—the one he'd barely noticed when Angie was alive—and told her to print everything about Sunny McKenzie and the fact that she'd borne Rex Buchanan a son, Buddy McKenzie, known as Willie Ventura, who from this day forward would be recognized as Rex's son. He'd be called Willie "Buddy" Buchanan.

"Oh, God, no," Dena whispered, her knees weakening. She imagined the hidden smiles she would notice from the corner of her eyes as she slid onto her knees during mass; the whispers that would be just loud enough for her to hear Sunny's name over and over again as she walked through town, the quiet little coughs and sniggers at the social functions she and Rex planned to attend. A part of her died in that instant. She would be mortified, humiliated, reminded that she was only Rex's secretary who had been blessed with the good sense to get herself pregnant after Lucretia—sacred Lucretia—had died so that she could become the next Mrs. Rex Buchanan. But she'd always been second-best. Wife number two. She'd never had the hold over her husband that Lucretia still held, even after being dead for decades. Nor did she fascinate Rex as Sunny McKenzie, a half-breed palm reader, did.

She heard him slam down the phone and then he was beside her again, squinting against the bright sunlight. All of his rage had disappeared. It was as if he'd just come from the confessional, or given a fifty-thousand-dollar check to a charity. "I'm relieved, Dena," he admitted, smiling benignly again, no trace of the man who had threatened to kill her just minutes before. "This was long overdue."

He's a simpleton. Somewhere along the road, he had lost that razor-sharp edge that had made him so successful. "Oh, God, Rex, you don't know what you've done."

"I've cleared my conscience, dear," he said tenderly, almost as if he meant it. "I've made my peace."

"And now what?"

He glanced at the sky, clear and blue and still holding fast to summer. "I can die anytime God decides to take me."

Sometimes the tension in the house was more than Cassidy could take. The glowering glances, the short responses, the ever-present feeling that there was a storm brewing, right under the surface, whenever she and Chase were in the room together. The wires holding his jaw together had been removed. He buried himself in the work that a messenger brought from the office or in his physical therapy, which was twice daily now, the therapist coming each morning and late afternoon. Chase had insisted that he wanted to improve as quickly as possible. He'd push himself to be whole again.

He avoided being alone with Cassidy and yet there were times when she was certain he'd been staring at her, not in hostility, but as if he were trying to figure her out. And he wasn't as immune to her being a woman as he'd like to let on. She'd felt the heat of his gaze on her back when she swam in the lake, part of her daily ritual.

Early each summer morning, when the sun was barely up, the water ice cold, the stars just beginning to fade, she'd carry her towel to the edge of the pond, let her robe fall into the sand and swim naked as she had for as many summers as they'd had the lake. When they had first moved back here, Chase would often sneak out to the water's edge, watch her for a few minutes, then join her. They'd make love in the water or later, when he would carry her laughing back to the house and drop her, wet and chilled, onto the bed.

Over the years, he'd stopped following after her, stopped showing any interest in her at all, stopped making love to her. She'd wondered if he'd taken a lover, but it didn't seem his style and she never found any evidence nor heard any rumors to suggest he was involved with anyone else. She'd even asked him once, and he'd laughed at her. That night he'd made love to her. Not tenderly, but roughly, angrily, as if he were trying to exorcise some inner demons that he kept secret from her.

Now he was interested again, she thought as she cinched the belt of her robe tight around her waist and hurried out the back door, letting the screen door bang shut. Her feet were bare as she followed the flagstone path that cut through the gardens and lawn before the stones gave way to a sandy trail curving through sun-bleached grass that brushed her calves and knees and bent in the breeze.

As she had since the weather had turned hot, she dropped her robe under the tree, took three steps across the sandy strip of beach and ran into the water. Cold as an arctic storm, it nearly burned her skin. She dived deep, following the contour of the bottom of the lake, feeling her body tingle in the frigid depths before she rose to the surface, flinging her hair from her eyes and gasping with the cold.

"Feel good?" Chase's voice seemed to reverberate through the morning. He was standing at the edge of the water, wearing faded jeans with one leg cut out for his cast, no shirt and propped on one crutch. He'd given up his eye patch two weeks before.

"Great." She was treading water, aware that her breasts were white in the darkness, her nipples round and visible through the ripples. *Just like Angie had been aware when she'd lured Brig to the pool all those years ago.* "You should join me."

"I don't think so. With the cast, I could drown."

"I wouldn't let you," she said breathlessly, and his face relaxed a little.

"You don't have to be my savior, Cass. You don't owe me anything."

The wind whispered across the lake, stirring up the water as the gray light of dawn was fast turning golden over the ridge of mountains to the east. "I'm your wife."

He pinned her with his harsh glare. His face was beginning to take shape again. Though not the same, he was starting to resemble himself, the man she'd vowed to live with forever. "I shouldn't have come out here."

"Why did you?" she asked, swimming close to the shore.

"Couldn't sleep." His gaze never left her, and even in the cool water, she felt his heat. Her skin tingled as her toes found the sandy bottom of the lake. This attraction was something neither could deny, but they'd both ignored it. It was safer that way.

"Neither could I." She walked out of the water, twisting the moisture from her hair and acting as if it was nothing out of the ordinary to stand naked before him.

"You haven't had your swim."

"It's okay." Her robe was on the ground, but she ignored it. She studied him a moment and her throat caught, aware of the changes inside her, the feelings that she couldn't tamp down and didn't begin to fathom. Her skin tingled when he didn't look away.

"Chase—"

He closed his eyes.

She wrapped chilled arms around his middle and he quivered, the touch of her wet skin against his warm flesh sending a tremor through him.

"Get dressed, Cassidy," he muttered, though he didn't say it with much conviction. "I've got coffee started."

"I don't want coffee, at least not yet." She angled her face up to his and saw the flare of interest in his eyes.

"What do you want?"

She didn't have an answer. She just waited.

His newly mended jaw, still partially wired, seemed to clamp down harder. "I can't—"

She kissed him then. Pressed her wet lips to the bare skin of his chest. There were scars on his skin, burn marks, scratches that had healed, but he didn't flinch.

"Oh, God." The sound was torn from his throat. "No—"

She didn't stop and her tongue found his nipple.

With a dry, desperate gasp, he wound his fingers in her wet hair and pulled her head back angrily. "Don't start something you can't finish," he warned. "Cass, I—"

Her fingers found the top button of his fly. With a loud pop his waistband opened and a series of snaps resounded like the ripple of muted gunfire ricocheting across water.

"Don't—I told you I don't want you to touch me." Rasping, painful words. Lies.

"Chase, please, let me—"

"No!" But she felt him surrender. The steely resolve wavered, and the crutch fell with a thud to the sand. Leaning against her, he balanced as his good arm surrounded her shoulders. Strong muscles dragged her close. "You're dangerous," he growled.

"So are you."

They tumbled to the ground and she kissed his battered face feeling his lips against her own, tasting of him and losing all control. He was warm and hard and hot on this shimmering summer morning. While dawn chased the stars away, she held him close, loving him, feeling his hand touch her already-stiff nipple, sighing into his mouth.

Her fingers explored the surface of his skin, taut skin over ribs and firm muscle, sinewy flesh that seemed to grow more taut with her touch.

"You don't know what you're doing—oh, God." She slid her hands into his pants, her fingers grazing the hard texture of one thigh as she delved into his boxer shorts, and surrounded his erection with cool fingers.

His abdomen retracted, giving her more access. A groan escaped his lips and he closed his eyes, holding her close, dragging her body over his until she lay atop him, naked and straddling, her breasts plump and poised over him. He touched her, gently at first, then more roughly as he held her with his casted arm and fondled her with his free hand. Her back arched of its own accord and she offered herself to him, two proud peaks, with stiff little nipples hovering above his face.

Shuddering at the touch of his tongue, she let out a sigh as soft as the wind and felt the first burst of sunlight touch her back. "Cassidy," he said, his voice filled with emotions she couldn't begin to understand. "We can't—"

She quieted him with a kiss. The words were too desolate, destroying the beauty of the morning. Closing her eyes, she listened to her body, to the desire singing through her veins, the rapture being murmured in her heart.

He suckled gently at first, kissing and tasting, then more ardently, holding her fast, causing her heart to thrum, her breath to be quick, shallow whispers. "Sweet Cassidy," he said, his voice rough and needy as her fingers worked their magic. She stroked him and kissed him and loved him, knowing that while his leg cast was in place, she would have to be satisfied with touching. He didn't try to stop her, just succumbed to the magic of her touch, straining, writhing, fighting the inevitable, and when at last he let go, his release was quick—a convulsion that caused him to lift from the ground before settling down again.

He grabbed her and held her close. "You didn't have to—"

"Shh," she whispered against his chest. "It was time, Chase."

"But you didn't—"

"It's all right."

He stared deep into her eyes. His own a determined shade of blue. "Roll onto your back."

"What—?"

"It's your turn."

She laughed. "Hey, I'm not keeping score." She reached for her robe. "This doesn't have to be even."

"Of course it does." He clasped a strong hand over her forearm, causing the terry cloth to drift from her fingers.

"Chase—" But he was relentless. He moved quickly, forcing her onto her back, and then holding her down with his casted leg, he began his ministrations. Slowly he touched her. One finger tickling her spine, while his lips found soft crevices and valleys she'd forgotten existed.

He explored her with experienced fingers and a tongue

that caused liquid heat to burn deep within her soul. Her body, so long ignored, turned torrid. Sweat clung to her skin as he slowly parted her legs and his fingers delved deep, sliding easily to her warmth, causing her mind to spin in wild, erotic circles. She twisted on the sand, gasping for breath, bucking anxiously as he kissed her belly, her breasts, her thighs. She couldn't stop herself, felt the first rush as he whispered her name. "Cassidy, oh, love—"

The world collided.

Lights exploded behind her eyes, sending sparks of vibrant colors that melded somewhere deep in her heart and far away to the ends of the universe. She lay gasping, drinking in the sight of him and wondering about their future. Together? Apart? Her throat ached with the need to know, the desire to trust him and love him and close her eyes to the rest of the world.

"Satisfied?" he asked in a voice devoid of emotion. Sitting on the sand beside her, he'd somehow managed to button his pants. Regret shaded his eyes.

"Yes, but—"

"This is what you wanted, isn't it?" The words cut like the bite of a whip, and yet there was more than anger etched in the lines of his face. "Or at least the best I can offer right now."

"I don't understand—"

He stared across the lake. "You wanted to seduce me and you did."

"Me—seduce you?" she said, her senses suddenly clear again, anger chasing away any lingering hint of afterglow. "You followed me out here."

"Just like you expected me to. You knew that I couldn't stay away, didn't you?"

"I didn't—"

"Don't lie, Cassidy," he said, pulling himself upright by his crutch and staring down at her. His mouth, so warm and loving only minutes before, had flattened into a thin, unforgiving line. "It doesn't become you."

The spell of the morning was shattered. "Get dressed," he

said, ramming his crutch into the sand. "Someone else might see you, and you could get more than you bargained for."

"You arrogant, self-serving son of a bitch," she cried. "You think I'd—"

"I don't know what to think, Cassidy. Because I really don't know you anymore."

"Chase—"

"And you don't know me."

He staggered away and she was left staring at the smooth muscles of his back. Seamless and fluid, they served to remind her just how much she wanted his touch, how anxious she was for him to make love to her, how desperate she'd become. "Fool," she ground out, kicking at the sand and throwing her robe over her shoulders. Cinching the belt, she watched as he disappeared around a bend near the patio. She felt a nagging little thought—something more than her fury—something deeper and worrisome, but she couldn't, for the life of her, understand what it was.

Thirty-seven

Cassidy tossed her purse onto the couch in the den and kicked off her shoes. She was alone. Again. Just like before the fire.

Chase was keeping his distance. Away from her. Away from the house. He spent hours in the office downtown, or at the physical therapist's, or anywhere other than home. Oftentimes he'd be gone by the time she got up in the morning and didn't return until midnight or later.

She felt him slipping farther away from her and tried to communicate with him, but he was evasive, just confiding that there was a lot of work to do to try and get the sawmill rebuilt and functioning at full capacity. There were plans to build a new on-site office and replace the metal drying sheds that had crumpled in the blaze. The accounting department was trying to reconstruct the payables, receivables, general ledger and profit-and-loss statements, searching through the old records that remained, and any computer files they had, then calling logging firms, trucking companies and lumber brokers, trying to piece together their inventory. The work was endless, he told her, but she suspected he was using any excuse to avoid her.

Maybe it was just too late for them.

Though she swam every morning, he never followed her again, and when she touched him, he always reacted swiftly, pulling away and breaking contact. He wouldn't talk about what they'd shared that morning by the lake, and if she ever brought up the subject, he would leave the room or say tersely, "It was a mistake. Don't make a big deal of it."

Once in a while, he seemed to let down his guard, and when he did, she saw another side to him—one with humor, one with humility, one that felt regret.

Physically, he was improving. Bit by bit. He was free of his casts. He could drive to town easily now, move around the house freely, and see out of both eyes. He looked like he would survive. The scars to his face were still visible, the skin not yet healed, but in time he would look nearly the same, walk without crutches, be the man she had decided to divorce.

And when he was finally completely healed, there would be no reason for him to stay in the house. There would be no reason to be married. Why that suddenly mattered so much, she didn't know. She'd been so close to divorcing him before the fire, before she'd faced the loss of him from her life, before she'd been convinced that his brother had given up his life in that horrid blaze.

A headache thundered behind her eyes and she took two aspirins before carrying a cup of coffee back to the den. She didn't bother starting dinner; she'd waited too many nights without so much as a phone call, her meal simmering to rubbery nothing on the stove, her appetite waning as the hours passed and the candles burned down.

Massaging the kinks from her neck, she selected several of her favorite compact discs and slid them into the player. As music filled the room, she opened her briefcase and slipped a computer disk into her station in the den, then hummed along with Paul McCartney while printing out the information she'd gathered at work. Information about the fire at the sawmill, information on the burned gristmill and information on Marshall Baldwin. She'd spent the past few days at the office, linking up electronically with news agencies across the country, especially in the Los Angeles area and all around the state of Alaska. She'd hoped to find some information about Baldwin before he'd moved north, but so far had come up with nothing. It was as if the man hadn't existed.

But he'd sure become visible once he'd started working on the pipeline. She tapped her pen on the edge of the desk and scanned her notes. Though she hadn't known much about Marshall Baldwin when Bill Laszlo had asked her about him, she was learning more and more each day. She'd called a colleague whom she'd worked with in Denver before he'd transferred to a Juneau television station. She'd called papers, the police, the DMV and even a man she'd heard about who located people. Michael Foster, working from a wheelchair and a computer system linked up with agencies around the United States and the globe, had the reputation of locating people even when they didn't want to be found. Cassidy didn't know if he'd tapped into the computers of the IRS or the Social Security Administration or the telephone company, but Foster, a paraplegic, was phenomenal. She'd learned of him about five years ago and had thought of phoning him to help her locate Brig, but decided it would be a mistake considering the declining state of her marriage. Now, however, she had no qualms about placing the call, asking about Brig as well as anyone remotely related to Marshall Baldwin.

She'd also hired a private investigator, a man who now lived in Anchorage who was willing to look into every aspect of Baldwin's life, checking out his story from the beginning when he was a nobody working on the pipeline and following him through the years. The private detective, Oswald Sweeny, was a little on the sleazy side, but he was thorough and had recently lived in Oregon, helping find a missing heiress. Sweeny had assured Cassidy that he would spare no expense and "leave no stone unturned in this whole damned tundra" to find out anything and everything about Alaska's reclusive millionaire.

No one, not even Chase, knew how deep she was digging. Because no one really understood her motives. It wasn't idle curiosity that kept her going; it wasn't even the fact that a mystery had plopped itself right in front of her and nearly taken her husband's life. It was that she felt compelled to find out the truth because she was convinced that, without the answers to the questions that had haunted them for seventeen years, without the complete story on this latest fire and the enigma of Marshall Baldwin, she and Chase would never be able to step forward, never be able to find each other again.

It was as if their marriage had been built on quicksand. Not rock-steady to begin with and now slowly and inevitably sinking. They'd never be able to trust each other, to climb out of the muck, until they faced the truth.

As she scanned her notes, the fax machine whirred to life and pages started filling the tray. Frowning thoughtfully, Cassidy read the report. Sweeny was slowly unraveling Marshall Baldwin's life, thread by secretive thread. He'd managed to dig up a woman Baldwin had spent time with in Fairbanks. She was willing to spill her guts—for five thousand dollars. A retired foreman from the crew hired to keep the pipeline running remembered Marshall—a fine, hard-working kind of quiet, good-looking boy who'd had to fight off the women. There were other statements, for the most part vague and disappointing because it seemed that no one had really gotten to know Baldwin, but Sweeny was still looking.

With a sigh she tapped the pages together and stuffed them into the growing file she kept locked in the drawer of her desk. She withdrew the thick sheaf of papers—newspaper clippings, police and fire reports, pictures, anything she could locate about the fire that had killed Angie and Jed. She still couldn't look at pictures of Angie without feeling an overwhelming sense of sadness, and though she'd never liked Jed Baker, she hadn't wished him dead. His family had never gotten over the loss of their son. When no culprit had been found in Jed's murder, the Bakers had made scathing comments about the inadequacies of the Sheriff's Department, then moved from Oregon, relocating somewhere in the Midwest, far away from the memories and the pain. Cassidy would hate to contact them and bring up all the agony again, but she would if she had to. If it meant finding the guilty party responsible for either or both fires and if it meant that she'd know more about Marshall Baldwin. Or Brig.

Chewing on the end of her pen, she flipped through the papers until her fingers came to the picture of Marshall Baldwin, brooding and dark. Who was he? Maybe he wasn't Brig. Maybe he was a man who resembled the McKenzies, a man who had his own personal reasons for hiding his past. He could have experienced an abusive childhood, or been running from the law, or avoiding the responsibilities of a wife and kids he didn't want to deal with. He could have been involved in something illegal and was running from a deadly partner or the mob or a million other things.

Or he could have been Brig McKenzie, and Chase was lying. Again.

She closed her eyes for a second and listened as McCartney sang an old Beatles tune and her throat thickened.

Yesterday. Love was such an easy game to play . . .

What was Baldwin's purpose? Why, of all the sawmills in the Northwest, did he choose the Buchanan mill, and why, if he wanted to deal with Buchanan Industries, didn't he call Derrick or her father? There was more to the story, more than Chase, who'd met with Baldwin, was willing to tell.

Oh, I believe in yesterday.

"Stop it," she muttered and changed the CD to something less melancholy.

She made a few notes on the legal pad, questions for which she needed answers, then rewrote them on the computer, her fingers moving easily over the keys. Was there a connection between the two fires? Was Marshall Baldwin the guilty party or a victim? What about Chase? Willie? Other members of her family and Chase's? Where was Sunny? Was her escape from the hospital planned? As far as Cassidy knew, Sunny had left the hospital, hitched a ride with a farmer and ended up at the Buchanan estate, though Dena and Rex had denied ever seeing her. Had she gone to visit

Willie? Cassidy doodled, her mind turning over the information only to end up back where she started.

Felicity's words echoed through her mind. What was it she'd said? Cassidy concentrated. Something about hoping the guy in the hospital died so that they didn't have to worry about any more fires. If Marshall Baldwin had been the arsonist and if he'd acted alone. But what if he had an accomplice? What if he came back to harm Chase . . . But why?

She was so wrapped up in her work, she didn't hear him come in. The music was loud enough over the hum of her computer that she missed the rumble of an engine, the crunch of tires on gravel and the creak of the screen door. Before she knew what was happening she saw a ghostlike image in her computer screen. Chase's reflection. Her heart jolted as she turned and found him eyeing her notes.

"Been busy, haven't you?" he asked, contempt edging his words. "So now you're an investigative reporter again. I knew it."

He was spoiling for a fight; she could see it in the tense lines of his face, the way his fingers wrapped over the hand hold of his crutch.

"This isn't for the paper."

"Sure." He didn't believe her.

"When you married me, I was a reporter."

"And you regretted giving up your job in front of a camera to come back here and work for the newspaper."

"That's never been a problem."

Making a sound of disgust, he shook his head. "I've always wondered how you went from a tomboy who spent more time with horses than she did kids her own age, to reporter."

"You know the story, I needed to leave home. Life after Angie died was . . . well, it was hard." Why was she explaining everything to him all over again? Defensively, she said, "Look, I'm just trying to piece together what happened." She punched a button on the keyboard, saved her notes and switched off the computer.

One of his shoulders was propped against the door casing, and he was still using a solitary crutch. His shirt was open at the throat, and each day he was healing, he more closely resembled the man she'd married. Dr. Okano had warned her that he'd never look the same, that he'd require extensive plastic surgery to repair the flesh over his broken nose, shattered cheekbones and jaw, but that he'd still be a decent-enough-looking man. So far, the doctor seemed to have called that one. Chase was still handsome, despite the redness and scars.

He cocked his head toward her computer. "Can't you leave it to the police? Old T. John seems pretty determined to catch his man."

"That's what bothers me about this, Chase. I'd think you'd want to know what happened—that you wouldn't rest easy until you found the son of a bitch who did this to you."

"I do. But I'm not going to become obsessed with it. Look at this," he said, gesturing to her desk, covered with notes and articles and a barely touched cup of coffee. "It's like you can't think of anything else." His gaze landed on the picture of Marshall Baldwin and his lips flattened. "I don't know what you're hoping to find, Cassidy, but I'm afraid you're going to be disappointed."

"Why?"

His eyebrows slammed together and his gaze was unforgiving. "You're still trying to find Brig, aren't you?"

She shook her head. "No, but—"

"Aren't you?" he demanded again, his voice rough, his expression hard to read.

"I just want to know the truth."

"Do you?" He arched a dark brow. "And if you find out that Baldwin was Brig and now he's dead? What then?"

"At least I'll know."

"You're hopeless!" Was there a hint of wistfulness beneath the harshness of his words? "Grasping at straws."

"The man was clutching a St. Christopher's medal when he died."

"So?"

"I—I gave Brig a medal like that on the night that he left." Inside she was shaking, her heart beginning to pound as she finally admitted what she'd never breathed to another living soul—not even her own husband. He'd suspected that she'd given her virginity to his brother, but he'd never really asked, and they'd both avoided the subject. Past loves were, for the most part, a taboo conversation. Off-limits. "I was with him that night, Chase. He'd been at the fire and swore he didn't set it. I believed him, talked him into taking Remmington and . . . and gave him the chain and medal."

"Jesus." He hobbled to the bar, reaching for a bottle. "I don't want to hear any more."

"I thought I loved him."

"This just gets better and better," he mocked. "I suppose he loved you, too." Chase splashed some liquor into a glass.

"I don't think so."

"You don't think he loved you, but you clung to his memory for all these years? You're unbelievable, Cassidy. Damned unbelievable." He took a long swallow, then wiped his mouth with his sleeve. His face was twisted and pale, as if fighting a losing battle with long-buried feelings.

"Look, I know I made a mistake. I know that you and I have this unwritten rule that we don't discuss our sex lives before our marriage, but—"

"You slept with him." The statement was flat, without any condemnation.

"Yes."

"Christ." His gaze met hers in the mirror over the bar.

"You suspected."

"I don't want to hear the sordid little details, okay?"

"Look," she said, walking up to him, seeing him stiffen. "All of this has got to end, Chase. Even though I believe T. John has the best intentions, I'm not sure he'll be able to sort it all out." She reached for his glass. Lifting it from his fingers she took a sip. Scotch hit the back of her throat and drizzled a burning path to her stomach. "I'm just trying to put it all to rest. For us."

His eyes darkened a shade. "Us?"

"Is that so hard to believe?"

"Damned impossible," he said, but his words lacked conviction. He stared at her long and hard, his eyes studying the contours of her face as if seeing her for the first time in years. Reaching forward, he touched her cheek slowly. Tenderly. With fingers that trembled slightly. She leaned into his open hand.

"A lot of people wear religious necklaces—chains, crosses, stars, medals," he argued. His breath was irregular.

"I know."

His thumb traced her cheekbone. "You can't pin your hopes and dreams on a piece of tarnished medal."

"I don't." His hand lowered to rest at the curve of her neck and he scrutinized her so intently, she was certain he would kiss her. Her throat worked. His gaze centered on her mouth. Her heart began to thud in anticipation. It had been so long since he'd looked at her with such yearning. So long . . .

Throat thick, she turned her face up to him. "We can work this out."

"Why do you want to?"

"Because . . . I love you." She stumbled over the words earning her a cold stare.

"Don't turn this around, Cassidy. I don't believe . . . I can't believe . . . oh, hell! I can't do this anymore!" Abruptly he grabbed the drink from her hands and took a long swallow before throwing his glass in the sink. It crashed against the porcelain, chipping a fixture for which he'd paid thousands of dollars. He didn't seem to notice—didn't so much as blink. "I should be done using this damned crutch in one week—two at the latest," he said, stepping away from her and ignoring what had just transpired.

Cassidy couldn't let it go. She reached for his arm. "Chase—"

"Don't, Cass—" he warned, but there was no anger in his voice, only pain.

She bit her lip. "How long are you going to shut me out?"

Shoving his crutch forward, he hobbled to the door. "Leave it alone, Cassidy. For both our sakes. For now, it's best if we just leave it the hell alone."

Thirty-eight

Derrick shouldered open the glass doors to the lobby floor of Buchanan Industries. This was it. His empire. He'd grown up being groomed to be heir, being told that one day he'd own it all. It didn't matter that Rex Buchanan had two daughters—his *son* would become the next czar.

Except that Chase McKenzie had muscled his way into a spot of power. Not only that, but the old man respected that piece of white trash with his self-earned law degree. Derrick had never planned on having to deal with a brother-in-law who had aspirations of his own. Well, maybe he was lucky. He had only one social-climbing, ass-kissing in-law to deal with. If Angie had lived, he might have had to deal with another.

Angie.

A pain settled deep in his soul when he thought of her, which, thankfully, he did less and less over the years. It didn't do to dwell on the past. Instead, he concentrated on the present and his birthright—Buchanan Industries.

This main office building was unique, and even though it wasn't as grand as a big-city skyscraper, it served its purpose well. Built in the late sixties of concrete and steel, the building wasn't much to look at from the outside, little more than four stories of glass walls reflecting the sun of the late summer afternoon, but inside it was impressive: leather furniture arranged around marble-topped desks; trees in planters that grew a full two stories and were rewarded by sunlight filtering through a skylight high overhead; brass fixtures and a polished brick floor.

Ignoring the no-smoking signs, he lit up as he took the elevator to the fourth floor, where the executive offices were housed. His father's suite of connecting rooms occupied one end, Derrick's the other. Derrick had been awarded the same setup as his father when he was appointed senior vice president. His suite of offices was a mirror image of Rex Buchanan's, with an identical reception area, inner office, executive bath, dressing room and bedroom at his disposal. Wedged between the two suites were the board room on one side of the bank of elevators and Chase's office on the other. Chase was the only other employee whose office was on the executive floor, and the fact that he was there bothered Derrick a lot. Like a burr under a saddle, Chase's presence continually irritated Derrick.

Too bad he hadn't bit it in the fire.

Flicking his cigarette into the sand of an ashtray, Derrick was nearly past Chase's doorway when he heard his name.

"Derrick." That raspy drawl he'd learned to hate over the past few weeks. "I was hoping you'd show up today."

Chase's voice had that same old mocking ring to it Derrick despised. But then he hated just about everything associated with the McKenzies. Low-life bastards, that's what they were, and Willie or Buddy, or whatever the hell his name was, wasn't any better. But now they were blood kin. It made his stomach turn over to think he was related to a retard.

Silently cursing the son of a bitch who was his brother-in-law, he walked into Chase's domain. Huge desk, neat piles, law degrees mounted on one wall, leather-bound volumes stuffed into a ceiling-high bookcase on the other. A window with a view of the street and potted plants with wide fronds open to the sun. On a corner of the desk was a color portrait of Cassidy—not one of those glamour shots like Felicity had given him last Christmas, just a natural pose of Cassidy astride a horse. "You want something?" Derrick asked, glancing to the corner of the sectional, beside which Chase's crutch was tucked away.

"Just a chat."

Warning bells clanged in Derrick's head. Chase looked like shit. It had been six weeks since the fire, but he still wasn't healed. His face wasn't as swollen, but it sure as hell was discolored where the wires in his jaw had been removed. His eyes, however, were clear and blue and mocking. Chase had always been arrogant enough to look down his broken nose at his brother-in-law. Derrick didn't understand it. He was the rich one—the one born to privilege. Chase was just a hick with a crazy half-breed witch for a mother and a father who'd taken a hike. What right, what goddamned right, did he have not appreciating the fact that Derrick was and always would be his superior?

Chase motioned toward the sofa tucked in a corner and leveled Derrick with that same damning gaze that made him want to cringe. "Have a seat."

Derrick eased into one of the overstuffed cushions. He didn't like the feeling he was getting; that Chase was holding something over him. Just as always. Christ, the man who had nearly been blown up was now staring at him from a face that looked like yesterday's garbage while twiddling a pen in the fingers of one good hand. Despite his injuries, Chase had the goddamned audacity to lord something— Derrick didn't know what yet—over him.

"I was just going over the books. It took a little while to put them all back together what with the fire and trouble with the backup disks," Chase told him.

"And?" Derrick asked, waiting for the bomb to drop.

"Looks like we're a little behind. You've taken a few personal draws to the tune of . . . let's see here. What? Forty-five, maybe fifty thousand dollars? And that's just in the past few months."

Derrick began to sweat. "You know Felicity's into remodeling. What's a few grand?" Derrick's nerves were strung tight, his muscles flexing a little as he crossed one leg over the other, resting his ankle on his knee.

"Ah, right. The never-ending renovation. She's mentioned it a couple of times when she came in to work." Chase was playing with him now, a regular cat-and-mouse game. His smile on that discolored face was hideous. Gave Derrick the creeps. "You know, if the money isn't in your account, or hasn't been paid to the contractor, some people might begin to wonder."

"Wonder what?" Derrick asked, but he knew where this was leading. "Felicity checks everything. You know she does. She works in accounting—"

Chase lifted a hand, as if warding off any more feeble excuses. "Felicity's your wife. And she doesn't work every day. Only when the spirit moves her."

"She's the daughter of one of the most respected judges in the damned state."

"And my mother reads cards. Big deal. What old Ira does—whether it's sitting on the bench or playing golf with his cronies—doesn't mean a thing when it comes to covering up payoffs."

"Payoffs?" Derrick wasn't following, but he could tell from the quiet anger in Chase's eyes that it was bad.

Chase leaned forward. "To the schmuck who did it."

"Did what?"

"Set the fire for you."

"Are you nuts? Why would I set fire to the mill?" Derrick demanded, scared spitless. What the hell did Chase have on him?

"I can think of lots of reasons. Let's start with insurance money—since that's the one the Sheriff's Department is so keen on. You'd end up with over three million in cash if the mill burned down, wouldn't you?"

"The mill's worth a lot more as long as it's running!"

"Yeah, but that might not be forever, what with all the restrictions on federal land, and the depletion of Buchanan forests. And hell, we could sell Buchanan lumber to other milling operations and let them take the risk."

"As well as the profit," Derrick blustered.

"It's the old bird-in-the-hand theory," Chase said, his lips barely moving.

"No way."

"Well, what about for revenge?"

"Against my own mill? Shit, you've flipped."

"Against me." Chase's eyes were as cold as the North Sea. "You've never hidden the fact that you hated my family—Brig and me—that you didn't like me marrying your sister, that you weren't crazy about me working for your old man, and now that I've got a little power, it would be a whole lot simpler for you if I was out of the picture."

Derrick leaned on the small of his back and dug in his jacket pocket for a pack of Marlboros. "Hell, Chase, if I wanted to kill you—'specially if I was gonna hire it done, then I wouldn't bother with burnin' down the mill. I'd take you out and no one would be the wiser and I'd still have the damned mill."

"But no cash."

"You really are a nutcase. Probably runs in the family. Your mom—she still missing?" Derrick flicked his lighter to the end of his cigarette and sucked hard, dragging calming smoke into his lungs. Where was Chase going with all this? He was surprised at the face-to-face approach. Chase was usually the sly, move-when-your-back's-turned type, a real kiss-ass to your face.

"My mother has nothing to do with us."

"Doesn't she? Hell, she's been screwin' my old man for years. We end up with the same moron for a brother and you're married to the only sister I got left. This involves both of us. I just hope the cops find her soon and lock her up."

"I wouldn't count on it," Chase said, his eyes glinting as if he had one helluva secret. "She'll be found when she wants to be."

The way he was staring gave Derrick the creeps. Sometimes he wondered if Chase had inherited Sunny's E.S.P. or whatever the hell it was. Shit, maybe Willie had it, too. Derrick thought of all the times he'd been cruel to the half-

wit and decided that Willie, had he been the least bit clairvoyant, would have gotten out of his way or chanted a curse
at him or something. Still, it was sick. This whole incestuous
damn family made him sick. And he was part of it. Caught in
the middle.

"I think you should put the money back," Chase was saying. "Otherwise the police might get suspicious."

"They know what I did with it."

"Do they? Do they know you were at the mill that night?"

"Me? Man, you're really reaching. I have an alibi!"

"Your wife, I know." Chase dropped his pen and clasped
his good hand with his bad. "But I saw you at the sawmill.
Just about a half hour before the whole thing blew."

"I wasn't there," Derrick said, hoping he sounded convincing as the sweat trickled down his back. He'd been careful; no one had seen him and it was long before the explosion.

"Sure you were. The only reason I didn't tell our friend T.
John Wilson is that I wanted to gather the evidence against
you and see you face-to-face first and let you know that, when
the police come knocking, I'm the one who sent them."

Derrick's lungs seemed to freeze. Even when he took a
drag from his cigarette, he didn't feel any warmth from the
smoke, no sense of calm from the nicotine. "You set me up,"
he said.

"You set yourself up."

"No way. I'll deny it. My alibi is ironclad."

"Is it?" Chase lifted a dark eyebrow. "Your wife would
stand up for you no matter what? Lie for you? Why?
Because you treat her so well?"

Derrick's mouth was suddenly dry. He couldn't suck in a
bit of saliva. Chase was going to screw him over. Big-time.
Somehow, some way, the bastard was going to make it look
like he was behind the fire! It wasn't enough that he'd caught
him skimming a little off the top of the books, but he was
going to make him the fall guy for the blaze as well. "I won't
let you get away with it, McKenzie," he said, calling up the
bravado that had bluffed him out of more fights than he could

count. Use the right words and most men backed down, but
then, Chase wasn't most men. "Fuck with me and I'll see to
it that your neck snaps."

"You don't scare me."

"No? Think about it." Derrick jabbed his cigarette out in
the soil of a potted plant. "Maybe you don't care about yourself anymore, maybe you don't give a shit about anything,
but Cassidy does and your mother does, and the way I see it,
they're sitting ducks for, say . . . another attack."

Chase, despite his injuries, leaped over his desk in an instant. The plant turned over, the picture of Cassidy tumbled
to the carpet, pencils and books scattered. Chase didn't appear to notice. He shoved Derrick against the wall.

"You think about it," he warned, throwing Derrick's
words back at him, his arm rammed hard against his brother-
in-law's throat. "Think long and hard." His body, tense and
lean, pressed so tight against Derrick's that Derrick could
barely breathe. "Try anything and I swear, Buchanan, you'll
regret it for as long as you live." Chase's breath was hot as it
fanned Derrick's face, his eyes blazing with a livid fire. "I
promise that whatever pain you think you'll inflict, I'll pay it
back to you a hundred times over. This is between you and
me. No one else."

"Don't push it, man." Derrick reminded himself Chase
was still a cripple, still hobbling around on a crutch and seeing a damned physical therapist. Why then did he feel fear—
cold and gnawing and deep in the middle of him? Ice seeped
into his blood. With all his strength, he pushed Chase out of
the way, kicking at his bad leg.

Chase's face turned white as a sudden jab of pain ripped
through his body. Good.

"Don't ever threaten me, McKenzie. You're scum and
you'd better remember it. I know that your mother's a half-
breed whore and your old man a spineless wimp who left his
family. You've worked hard, smiled a lot, and licked more
asses than I can count to get where you are, but you're still a
poor, white-trash sonuvabitch in an expensive leather jacket

that cost more than your mother made all those years of lying on her back and spreading her legs for my old man."

Chase lunged, his fingers at Derrick's throat. Derrick kicked his good leg away from him. Chase crashed against the wall and Derrick sidestepped him easily, leaving him writhing. "Pathetic, McKenzie. That's what you are and all you'll ever be. Pathetic." To make his point he spat, a wad of spittle hitting Chase square on his forehead.

Cassidy worked most of the afternoon. Her routine with Chase had become familiar in the past couple of weeks. While he was at physical therapy or doctor's appointments or the office, she would work at the *Times*. Ever since their argument in the den they'd settled into an uneasy peace, the past still between them, the future nebulous and fuzzy.

There were no endearments. No soft little touches. No quiet jokes. But there hadn't been in a long, long while. Not because of the fire, but because they'd drifted apart, gone separate ways, reached for separate goals. Now, by outward appearances, they were together.

At home they were civil to each other, learning to trust again, though there were always undercurrents of tension. Unstated, but humming beneath the surface, charges that were ready to explode. She'd caught him staring at her when he thought she didn't notice, felt his gaze following her. And he was checking up on her, rummaging through her desk when she wasn't home. She was sure of it. He would never trust her.

But the nights were the worst. Knowing he was just down the hall, probably as restless as she. Wanting. Aching. Remembering. Pretending. To her family. To the world. To each other.

"I'm so glad you're trying to work things out," Dena had said just the other morning when she'd stopped by. "Marriage is never easy."

"I guess not."

"Things haven't been the same for us, either," she admitted. "Ever since Rex told that Willie-character that he was his father. You know, of course, that he gave him a room upstairs in our house. Derrick's old room. I'm telling you it makes my skin crawl when I'm in the house alone with him."

"Willie's harmless."

"Is he? I don't know. I remember when you girls were growing up, he was always sneaking around, hiding in the bushes, watching. Lord knows what he was doing, but I caught him several times, in the hemlocks and rhododendrons behind the pool, staring up at Angie's room—probably trying to catch a glimpse of her in her bra and panties. Lord, it's sick." She shuddered and reached in her gold case for a cigarette. "And to think they were half brother and half sister. It's . . . well it's beyond my comprehension. Not decent." She pulled out a Viceroy. "Everyone seems to have forgotten that Willie was at both fires."

"You know that?"

Dena lit up and blew smoke to the ceiling. "It only makes sense. He saw the first one, singed his eyebrows, remember? And as for the second, well, it's common knowledge that Willie found that Marshall Baldwin's wallet there. The police missed it and he found it? I don't think so. Sounds like he was there before the cops."

"You think he started the fires? Willie? He's too . . . too kind and gentle. Mom, are you serious?" Cassidy had been incredulous.

"Dead serious. And I'm not the only one. A lot of people in this town think he's capable of it. A regular firebug. Face it, honey, the man's got no brains to speak of. He . . . well, he's just not right. It's a shame, I'll be the first to admit it. That drowning incident was a tragedy. I'm not vengeful enough to think that it was God trying to teach Sunny a lesson, but . . . well, it seems like more than a coincidence that he was at both fires, doesn't it? I think your father would be doing the family and the entire town a favor by sending Willie to an institution, where he'd be with people like him— his own kind. He wouldn't feel like such a freak."

"He's not a freak, Mom. He's—"

"Creepy." She fiddled with the strand of pearls at her throat. "Think about it. Living in the same house with him? I hate to say it, but it's time I put my foot down. It's my house, too, and the way I look at it, he goes or I go."

"Mom—"

Dena's cigarette quivered in her mouth. Ashes dropped to the floor, and she bent down quickly to brush them aside. "I—I don't know what else to do," she admitted, and when she straightened, tears shimmered in her eyes. "Your father has become so unreasonable lately."

"Calm down. It's not so bad—"

"It is, Cassidy," she finally said, her voice breaking, her fingers dabbing at the corners of her eyes to catch her tears without streaking her mascara. "Being married to Rex Buchanan is a living hell. For the first time I'm beginning to understand why Lucretia took her own life."

Thirty-nine

T. John cut the engine of his cruiser and kicked a clod of dirt from his boot. He'd spent parts of the last two weeks chasing down leads of Sunny McKenzie sightings. It was getting old. He was beginning to believe that he had as much chance of catching her as of running across the alien spaceship old man Pederson claimed landed in the middle of his field, scorching the grass and scaring the hell out of his herd of black-faced sheep. In T. John's opinion, Pederson tugged a little too much at his own moonshine—some kind of beer he made himself—but moonshine just the same.

His back muscles popped as he stretched and stepped over the curb in front of the 7-Eleven. Inside, a couple of kids played arcade games. Another boy was trying to eye the girlie magazines tucked beneath the counter, and a woman with a squawking baby was buying a package of disposable diapers.

Same old. Same old.

He smiled at the clerk, Dorie Reader, a fiftyish woman with a mean pair of legs, barrel body, and frizzy blond over-permed hair. As he slathered up a sausage dog, he asked about Dijon mustard.

"I already told you, T. John, if you want somethin' fancy and sophisticated, go across the street to Burley's." T. John snickered. It was their running gag because Burley's, a local strip bar, had been shut down as many times as it had been open. Before working homicide, T. John had often as not done the closing.

Two scoops of onions, some pickle relish, a glob of yellow mustard, and he had lunch. Since he couldn't have a beer, he settled on a super-sized Coke and ordered a pack of Camels along with a roll of antacids.

"Bon appetite," Dorie said as he used his butt to open the door.

"Same to ya." Outside in the glare of midday sun he noticed a few teens loitering around the door of Burley's and knew it was only a matter of time before the department would have to get another injunction against the place. Too bad. Burley was an okay guy, trying to pay off alimony and child support to three wives and providing Prosperity with a little honest entertainment. The girls got up on stage and danced, jiggling their tits and twitching their fannies, but the customers were kept at bay and the dancers used disguises and assumed names. Burley made sure no one was hurt or insulted and the girls were paid well for their trouble.

But despite Burley's honest intentions, there was always trouble. A lot of liquor, too much testosterone, naked girls and the invariable handgun; add to the mix, the overactive and judgmental sermons of the Reverend Spears, and Burley never seemed to get a break. If it wasn't the customers acting up, it was the religious nuts. In T. John's opinion, Burley should give it up, but the man seemed to think it was his God-given mission to provide T & A to the locals.

Spears could spew his rage from the pulpit, march against the place and condemn its patrons all to hell, but T. John knew some of the reverend's most devout members of the congregation were probably nursing hangovers on Sunday morning from downing a few and watching the near-naked dancers bump and grind on Saturday night.

He eyed the surroundings through his aviator sunglasses and chewed on his sausage dog slowly. Today his trouble wasn't Burley's. Nope. Today he was tied in knots, as he had been for nearly two months, over the damned Buchanan sawmill fire. Floyd Dodds was on his case, wanting a solution, hoping that T. John could scare him up a culprit or at the very least a scapegoat, and as yet, T. John hadn't turned up a damned thing.

Couldn't even locate a crazy old woman. That bothered
him. Hell, even the dogs had been fooled. They had taken a
pair of hounds out into the woods where the kids had sworn
they'd seen the "witch woman," let the dogs get a good whiff
of an old nightgown of Sunny's from that fancy "home"
where Chase had committed her, then let the dogs run free.
They'd started baying immediately, running around in confused circles, howling up a storm. But they never left the
clearing, couldn't be prodded into the woods. It was as if
Sunny had just disappeared. Like the witch she was rumored
to be. Maybe one of old man Pederson's aliens had dropped
down and scooped her up before hightailing her to the other
side of the universe.

Or maybe she wasn't crazy after all. Just a whole lot
smarter than anyone trying to find her.

And so the sawmill arson and murder was still unsolved.

No alibis had cracked. The older Buchanans had been in
California, Derrick and Felicity at home with each other and
the kids, Sunny had been locked up in a mental hospital, and
Willie had been in town drinking. Lots of people had seen
him before he went out snooping in the ashes. Only Cassidy
had been alone at home, working on the computer, or so she
claimed.

But she seemed an unlikely suspect. T. John told himself
it wasn't because she was so pretty with those gold eyes and
all that loose hair; she just wasn't the type to torch her old
man's property.

"You're losing your touch, Wilson," he muttered, finish-
ing his dog. Wiping his mouth with a napkin, he tossed the
greasy paper tray into an overflowing garbage can and slid
into the warm interior of his county-owned car. Things were
clicking along, but slowly, too slowly for Dodds. Too slowly
for T. John.

Every week he got a little more info from Alaska about
Marshall Baldwin, and he was watching all of the Buchanans
and McKenzies, hoping they'd trip up. But the tails he'd placed
on the family had turned up nothing, and all of his talking

hadn't produced one lie that he could prove. His men were scouring all the local hospitals and clinics looking for some kind of injury that would have scarred Brig McKenzie's body while he was growing up—a kid like that had to have broken some bones or cut himself and been stitched up a time or two. When T. John found the old records, he'd compare the injuries to Baldwin's autopsy report. So far, no one had found any records to help him out. Other than a nose broken once or twice and a couple of lacerations, Brig didn't seem to have much medical history at all.

"Damn it all anyway." At one point in his life he'd envied the wealthy. As the son of a farmer always in jeopardy of losing his few dusty acres and a wife who worked from sunup to sunset to scratch out a living, T. John, the oldest of six, had always thought money would solve most of his personal problems. Now he wasn't so sure. The closer he got to the Buchanans and their money, the more he was certain that he'd never met a sorrier, unhappier lot of people in his life.

He took a big gulp of Coke, downed two antacids and opened his pack of Camel straights. He'd had a feeling this case would drive him right back to his nicotine habit, and he didn't feel one bit guilty as he lit up and sucked in a deep lungful of smoke and settled behind the wheel. He'd gained five pounds since he'd last quit, and he knew that he'd lose the weight and think more clearly if he smoked. Once the case was solved, he'd quit again. Give his lungs a rest.

Cigarette clamped firmly in the corner of his mouth, he twisted on the ignition and backed out of his parking space. Gonzales had called with more information on Marshall Baldwin. Maybe they'd finally catch a break.

Cassidy walked into the house. It was quiet except for the sound of running water coming from the guest room. Chase's room. She imagined him trying to clean off with limited use of his healing arm and leg. As often as she'd offered to help him, he'd refused, never so much as letting her have a glimpse of his bare torso or hips or buttocks, as if he were afraid that allowing themselves to be too intimate again was an irretrievable mistake.

She dropped her purse and keys on the kitchen counter and started down the hall. She was his wife, damn it. She had a right to stare at him and touch his body as much as she wanted. She was tired of the silly games they were playing, the feeling that she was always taking the chance of violating his privacy.

She didn't even bother knocking, just turned the knob of his door and smiled inwardly when it wasn't locked. She didn't stop for a second. The window was open, letting in a hot summer breeze. The door to the bathroom was cracked, and through it she saw steam clinging to the mirror over the sink. There were noises coming from the shower: the continuous spray of water, the soft thud of a bar of soap being dropped and quiet cursing as he attempted to retrieve it.

He'd probably read her the riot act when he found her. Fine. She didn't give a damn. Heart racing, she sat on a corner of the bed. His bed. The one he refused to share with her. For a second she considered taking off her clothes and slipping between the sheets, waiting for him to hobble from the bathroom and find her lying naked on his turf, ready to give herself to him, but she controlled herself. No telling how he'd react.

The drizzle stopped suddenly. She barely dared breathe, her eyes trained on the door. When it opened abruptly, she felt instant regret. Chase, a towel slung around his waist, stopped in the doorway. His hair was black and curling over his ears, his skin stretched tight over smooth, sleek muscles of a hard abdomen, dark hair swirling around his flat nipples.

"What the hell are you doing here?" he asked, when she stared in amazement at his body.

"What's it look like?" she fired right back, her voice a little too breathless for her taste. "Waiting for you."

"I thought we had an agreement. This room is off-limits—"

"I'm your wife, Chase," she said, impatience coloring her words. "There are no locks and prison doors in this house. No gates and keys. No lines on the floor separating yours from mine. We live here together."

"An arrangement you weren't too thrilled with recently."

"Maybe I've changed my mind." Her heart was drumming wildly, beating a frantic cadence, and she felt that she had to make this stand, to fight him. Or lose him. And for the first time in years she couldn't bear the thought.

"Maybe I haven't changed mine. This isn't a good idea."

But she remembered his lovemaking by the lake. He was lying. She walked toward him. "I've never had to pursue you," she said, gaze holding his steadily. "Never. You were the persistent one. When we were first married, you couldn't get enough of me."

His lips tightened. "I don't want to hear it."

"Don't you remember?"

"It was a long time ago."

"Not that long," she reminded him, throwing out a hip with her challenge.

He sucked in his breath. "A lot has changed."

"No, Chase, we changed. You and me. You got involved with your work and I—I let it happen. I'm as much to blame as you are for the . . . apathy of our marriage, but I'm willing to change that."

"Right here? Now?"

"Yes." Angling her head upward, she defied him, her eyes daring him, her body only an arm's length from his. "I think it's time."

"I'm a cripple," he reminded her, and a darkness crossed his eyes. "And even if you don't remember, your brother does."

"You're not a cripple. You're my husband." Boldly she stepped up to him, so close she could smell the soap still clinging to his skin. "Chase—" Closing her eyes, she touched his bare arm.

He didn't draw away.

"Just hold me," she whispered, leaning into him. His

muscles flexed as if he were fighting the impulses racing through his body.

"I can't," he whispered, his voice raw.

"Please."

"Oh, God, Cassidy." His arms surrounded her, strong and comforting. "This is so wrong."

"No." She pressed a kiss to his neck and he groaned. A tremor passed from his body to hers. The corded muscles surrounding her flexed and he lowered his head with unerring precision, catching her lips with his, kissing her with an intensity that stole the breath from her lungs. Yearning, long denied, uncoiled within her belly, reaching out, flowing through her blood and limbs. Her arms wound around his neck and she kissed him with all the pent-up emotion that had been gnawing at her for days.

"Cass, think—"

"No, Chase, don't think. Just feel." She caught his lips with hers, and her mouth parted in open invitation. His tongue slipped between her teeth, and his hands moved slowly upward, scaling her ribs through the silk of her blouse, the fabric rustling as he surrounded her breasts.

Nipples erect, she rubbed against him, moaning as he kissed her eyes, her cheeks, her neck, aware that her blouse was being unbuttoned and tossed from her body, that the strap of her slip was being lowered, that her breasts, encased in sheer lace, were suddenly free and he was touching them, tracing the sculpted edge of the lace with his rough fingers, picking her up and holding her, his back braced against the wall as his tongue circled the delicate bones at the base of her throat.

"Cassidy, Cassidy."

She kissed him harder, sensing his resistance. "Just love me."

With a groan, he dropped her onto the bed—his bed. Dark emotions shadowed his eyes. "I can't. Not yet."

Disappointment and humiliation burned through her. "Are we on some kind of timetable that I don't know about?"

she demanded, her voice shaking. "For God's sake Chase, don't shut me out—"

But he'd already turned away from her, giving her a brief glimpse of his back before ramming angry hands through the sleeves of a shirt. The towel dropped and he stepped quickly into a pair of boxer shorts, allowing her a small view of his bare buttocks for a second before he clumsily found his jeans, growled as he nearly fell over stepping into them and balanced against the wall. "Hell," he ground out, trying to force his bad leg to bend.

"You don't have to get dressed."

"Can't walk around the place naked, can I?"

He snapped his fly and drilled her with an unforgiving stare. "I've got something for you."

"What?" she asked warily.

"Protection."

"What kind of protection?"

"Serious protection. From your family."

"My family? Oh, come on—"

Chase yanked a belt through the loops of his jeans and buckled it quickly. He seemed angry at her, angry at himself, angry at the whole damned world. "I guess you haven't heard the latest."

"Which is?"

He made a noise of disgust and, if possible, he seemed to blush while he forced his feet into running shoes. "I thought the way Felicity spreads rumors she would have called you the minute she heard. Maybe she hasn't talked to Derrick yet. Your brother and I got into it yesterday. At the office. To make a long story short, he threatened you and me."

"Derrick? He wouldn't—"

"He would, Cassidy, and he has. I made the mistake of calling him into my office yesterday. Intended to browbeat him into confessing that he was involved in the fire."

"Derrick? But he was with Felicity that night—"

"Maybe for part of it. But he was at the mill, Cassidy. I saw him about a half hour before the fire."

Her mind reeled ahead. "Did you tell Wilson?"

"Not yet. It's something I didn't remember—I don't know why, but the doctor said I might have trouble sorting everything out. Maybe I didn't think it was significant enough to recall."

"Your memory seems fine to me," she said suspiciously.

"I thought so, too. Until yesterday. I can't go to Wilson yet, because, so far, it's just my word against Derrick's, even if I can finally prove that he's been embezzling."

Cassidy could hardly believe her ears.

"You've got to call the police."

"I will," he said, his eyes holding hers. "When the timing's right."

"But—"

"Don't worry, Cass. I'll deal with it," he promised.

"What did Derrick say?" She couldn't believe he was capable of burning the sawmill or killing a man or . . . *Why not? He's always had a cruel streak and thought the world owed him a living—a good living—and Felicity would do anything for him. Even lie to cover up the fact that he was a murderer.* She shivered at the thought.

"Derrick turned things around. Did all the beating himself, for now. Mistook my face for a spittoon."

She let out a gasp of protest.

"And there wasn't a damned thing I could do about it."

"And now you think he might . . . what? Attack us here?"

"I don't know. But I'm not going down without a fight. Come on, I'll show you what we've got." He threw her one of his sweatshirts and she scrambled into it. Then she followed him out to his truck. He opened the door and a sleek black German shepherd bounded to the ground.

"Stay!" Chase commanded and the dog froze. "Cassidy, meet Ruskin."

She laughed at the sight of the animal, sitting and staring at her with clear gold eyes.

"You two are going to get to know each other real well, and Ruskin will make sure that no one comes sneaking around here without thinking about it twice."

Forty

Checking her watch and silently cursing her husband, Felicity pushed open the door of her daughter's room. Angela was there, sleeping like a baby, her breathing deep and regular. But the bedroom window was open, blinds rustling in the breeze. Something wasn't quite right, she decided, and though she felt like a traitor, she tiptoed across the carpet and lifted the coverlet to find her firstborn completely clothed in skin-tight jeans, black sleeveless T-shirt and sneakers. "I know you're awake," she said, though Angela didn't respond, still feigning sleep. "And I know you plan to sneak out of this house and meet that Cutler boy." She settled into the chair by the window. "Go ahead and pretend, but I'll sit here all night to make sure you stay in this house."

"For Christ's sake, Mom—"

"Don't you ever swear at me."

Angela pushed herself into a sitting position and tossed her dark hair out of her eyes. "Then don't call Jeremy 'that Cutler boy,' like he's not good enough or somethin'."

"He isn't good enough. Not for you. You're a Buchanan."

"Big fuckin' deal."

"That's it! You use that kind of filthy language one more time and you'll be so grounded you'll never see the light of day, much less any more of that Cutler—Jeremy."

Beneath the fringe of her bangs, Angela glowered at her mother. "You can't stop me!"

"No?" Felicity wasn't going to let a sixteen-year-old girl push her around. "I'll have you followed by a private investigator if I have to and I'll make sure he takes pictures, and if that boy lays one finger on you, I'll go straight to the police and cry rape so loud that it will echo all the way to New York."

"You wouldn't!"

"Oh, yes I would, Angela. I'd do anything to protect you and keep you from making a mistake."

"Jeremy isn't a mistake."

Felicity understood her daughter's naïve rationale. Hadn't she felt the same way about Derrick when she was Angela's age? The difference was that Derrick was a Buchanan and socially correct. She'd at least made the right choices.

"What if I decide to go to the police?"

Felicity's heart nearly stopped. "Why would you do that?"

Her daughter's smile was a catty little grin, flashing white in the gloom of the dark room. "Because I know about Daddy," she said in that superior way that bugged the hell out of Felicity.

"What about him?" Dread leaked into her blood.

"Uh-uh." Angela shook her head. "I'm not trading secrets, Mom. Just understand this. If you say one word against Jeremy to anyone, I'll pay you back in kind."

"You little—"

"Ah, ah, ah, Mom. Careful, now," she mocked, enjoying the fact that she had Felicity over a barrel.

"I don't know what you're talking about."

"Sure you do, Mom. Think about it. Now, why don't you just run along? Pretend I'm in here sleeping and getting a good night's rest for school tomorrow."

"You're not meeting that boy."

"Sure," Angie said. "Whatever you want to think. But if you don't leave me alone right now, Daddy takes the fall. The big one. Think what that would do to your precious reputation?"

"I won't be blackmailed, Angela."

"Sure you will. You have been for years."

Felicity stood swiftly and crossed the room. She grabbed her daughter by the shoulders, then slapped her soundly across the cheek. Angela's head snapped backward, hitting the headboard.

"You bitch!" Angela cried. "You fucking bitch!"

Another well-aimed slap. Felicity's hand hurt and she cringed as Angela's head slammed hard against the headboard. Angela burst into tears. Felicity pretended she didn't see the horror in her daughter's eyes or witness her sixteen-year-old bravado drain away.

"Don't push me, Angela," she said through lips that barely moved. "You have no idea what you're up against. You're not to see that boy again, and that's final. And come September, you're going to St. Therese's in Portland. They still have a few nuns teaching there; maybe they'll be able to show you how to behave." Back stiff, she left the room and felt as if she might throw up. She'd never struck her daughter before and she hated the thought of it now.

She'd grown up in a home where her father adored her, but he'd thought nothing of spanking her with the flat side of a hairbrush. It hadn't stopped until she'd married Derrick, because The Judge intended that his headstrong daughter learn respect and learn it early.

But those blows with the brush had backfired and Felicity had sworn nothing her children ever did would force her to use violence against them. Not her children. But sometimes a woman had to take charge. Sometimes the rules had to be bent. Like tonight. And if Angela ever tried sneaking out with that horrid little lump of pimply flesh again, then Jeremy Cutler would find himself in a fight he couldn't hope to win.

Felicity knew all too well to what lengths a woman would go for a man. She'd done them all. She'd been humiliated, felt abject terror, pain, jealousy and a rage so deep it burned. But she'd survived. She could handle a nerdy little twit like Jeremy Cutler. It would be child's play.

"You'll call?" a soft female voice asked Derrick as he hurried to his truck. Glancing over his shoulder, he spied her standing in the doorway of a cheap motel overlooking the Willamette River. Barefoot. A black silk teddy her only clothing. She was barely sixteen, with thick dark hair and blue eyes and a smile that reminded him of Angie, his sister. Her name was Dawn.

"I'll think about it."

"Come on, Derrick, you said you'd call."

"You got paid, didn't you?" He climbed into the cab of his truck, and the air inside was stale.

"I don't do it for money," she pouted as he rolled down the window.

"Sure."

"I do it 'cause I love you."

Christ! Every insomniac in this fleabag of a motel could hear her. Windows were open, and it was after one in the morning. He jabbed his keys in the ignition, and the engine started. "That's good. You've got a ride, right?"

"Don't worry about it. Just call me." Dawn tossed her hair in a way that was damned sexy. An open invitation. The teddy fell off her shoulder and showed off one firm little tit.

"I will," he promised, knowing that Felicity would kill him if she ever found out he was banging a girl who was about the same age as their daughter, a girl who reminded him of his sister, a girl who could run to the police and get him in big, big trouble. But she wouldn't. She liked jewelry and nice clothes and her new little convertible too much to spoil a good thing.

Her mother was in on the deal, and once in a while, when Dawn wasn't available, Lorna came on to him. He never actually initiated the action, but he didn't stop it either. She wasn't as young and nubile as her daughter, but she was quick with her tongue and a dirty phrase. If he didn't show much interest, Lorna became real inventive, dressing up in all kinds of getups—bras with holes for her nipples, crotchless panties and a leather garter belt decorated with metal studs. She'd tease him and whip him with some kind of feather and rawhide thing that tickled and cut, teased and gave pain.

But still, Lorna's skin wasn't supple, she was running to fat, her waist thick, and though her breasts were much bigger than her daughter's—huge mountains decorated with a tattoo of a hummingbird—he preferred the firm solid flesh of a young butt and thighs that could wrap around his waist for hours. Even Dawn's small breasts were a turn-on as long as she rouged them up and danced in front of him, letting her nipples hover near his mouth only to drag them away. He could play rough with Dawn and he loved it when she called him "Daddy," begging him to spank her until she cried, then making him kiss her welts.

One night when Dawn had said she wanted to stay home rather than go to a motel, Derrick had agreed. Though the apartment was seedy and he thought she enjoyed going to an upscale hotel where they could order room service, he reluctantly agreed. The rooms smelled of stale cigarette smoke and some kind of grease that hadn't been cleaned from the kitchen stove, but Dawn was such a turn-on that night, dressed in a little girl outfit, her hair in pigtails, that he didn't argue. She led him into her mother's room and he threw her on the bed. Then, while he was fucking the hell out of her, Lorna came in and watched. Right in the middle of the action, she leaned over him, holding her breasts, offering those huge pillows with nipples the size of half dollars. "Lick these, sweetie," she'd said and he'd rubbed his tongue over them only to taste something different. "It's coke, honey, and I'm not talking soda pop, here. You'll love it."

He suckled hard, humping upward while Dawn, naked except for ribbons around her pigtails and ankles, rode him. "Come on, baby," she cried, beginning to scream in a higher pitch than he'd ever remembered. He thought his back might give out or he might suffocate as Lorna forced more tit into his mouth. With a cry, he finally bucked upward, sucking huge nipples as he came into a fresh young body. He hadn't been so turned on in years. He'd done it again then, with both mother and daughter—the coke heightening his senses. So much pussy, coke and tits his bourbon-soaked brain could barely function and his erection had given out.

Afterward, Lorna had offered him more blow. For years he'd avoided drugs, but he was on such a rush already. He snorted just a little, but from that night on they'd gotten high together and oftentimes they'd done a three-way. Always in Lorna's king-sized four-poster bed. Jesus, he was getting hard just thinking about it even though he'd driven away from Oregon City and was heading toward Prosperity.

Tonight had been different. Dawn had agreed to leave with him and she'd given him what he'd wanted and more, but he'd sensed a restlessness about her, as if she were keeping a secret.

You're sick, Buchanan. Sick. The things you're into are perverted. She's just a kid.

Angry with himself, he flipped on the radio hoping to hear some news or country music that would drown away the silent scoldings he inflicted upon himself. But someone, probably Felicity, had changed the station to old rock and roll.

His bones turned to ice as the words of the song wafted through the speakers and filtered into his mind, a song from a night a long time ago, an old Elvis tune he'd tried to forget.

Love me tender, love me true
All my dreams fulfill . . .

He'd been seven at the time and woken up from a nightmare. When he'd called out for his mother, Lucretia hadn't responded. Sniffing and trying to hide his tears, he walked to her room in the dark, but when he knocked on her door, she didn't answer.

"Mommy, Mommy," he wailed, trying the door and finding it unlocked. The bed was still made, and though it was late at night, she wasn't in the bedroom or bathroom or dressing room. He started for his father's room down the hall when he heard it, her favorite song by Elvis, and he followed the music, not to the living room where it was usually played but down a hallway leading to the garage. An extension cord ran the length of the hallway, a brown snake that wasn't supposed to be there.

For my darling I love you . . .

Taking several deep breaths, he inched forward slowly, the sound of Elvis's deep, comforting voice luring him.

"Mommy?" he called, beginning to worry, walking with his back pressed against the wall, knowing that the snake was evil. The song was suddenly over and the house was silent, except for the sound of a car's engine rumbling evenly. "Mommy."

Elvis began again, the same song, and Derrick saw that there was a hole in the bottom of the door leading to the garage. Just big enough for the extension cord to slide through.

"Mommy? Daddy?" His mouth was dry and tasted like vomit. He pushed hard on the door and it swung open, letting a cloud of blue smoke through the house. His heart was pounding and the smell was horrible. Through the veil of exhaust he saw their new stereo, sitting on its roll-away cart, the speakers on the bottom shelf as if Mommy had wanted the entire system in the garage. Heart thudding, he walked to the car and saw her inside, her head resting on the steering wheel of the shiny new car she'd gotten for her birthday, a hose hooked up from the exhaust pipe to the cracked window of the passenger side of the car. He tried to open the driver's door, but it was locked. Crying out to her, he pounded on the windows and began to choke.

The music was so loud he could barely scream above it, and when he did, foul-tasting smoke rushed down his windpipe. "Mommy!" Why was she sleeping in her car? "Wake up! Wake up, Mommy!" She didn't move and his eyes began to water from the exhaust fumes that leaked from the car into the garage and the fact that he was suddenly more scared than he'd ever been in his life. Something was wrong. Horribly wrong. His fists banged on the windows just as one of the garage doors opened and he looked up to find his father, tie askew, usually smooth hair rumpled, face ashen, staring in disbelief. "What's going on?" he said. "Derrick, what're you doing—? Lucretia?"

Rex's face slackened in horror. "Oh, for the love of God, no!" He ran to the car, tried to open the door, fiddled with his keys, and when he couldn't find one that fit, grabbed a hammer from the rack on the wall and began pounding at the passenger-side window, smashing the glass, sending shards into the car, onto the cement floor, flying through the air.

And I always will.

"Lucretia! Oh, baby, what have you done? What have I done?" He managed to smash enough glass to force his hand inside and lift the latch. Flinging open the door, he cut the engine and dragged his wife from the birthday gift that had become her hearse. "No! No! No!" he cried, as Elvis crooned in the background. Yanking her outside and laying her gently on the grass near the garage, he leaned over her, trying to force air through her parted lips, pressing on her chest.

"Call the police!"

Derrick stood rooted to the spot.

"Damn it, Derrick, call the police."

"I—I don't know how," he said, his chin trembling, fear making him shake and cry. "Daddy, I don't—"

"Call the operator, for God's sake! Tell her to call an ambulance and send it to the Buchanan place on Buchanan Lane."

Derrick swallowed hard. "I—I—Daddy, is Mommy gonna die?"

Rex's face was suddenly slack. "Not if you call the ambulance right now! Do it!"

Somehow he'd managed to run into the house and stand on a chair to reach the wall phone in the kitchen. He dialed zero and felt pee trickle down his leg. "You've got to have the ambulance come and save Mommy," he cried, sobbing so loudly the woman on the other end of the line could barely hear what he was saying. "She's dying! She's dying!"

Even now, decades later, the memory of that night brought an anxiety in him like no other. Everyone had told him it wasn't his fault, he couldn't be blamed for not remembering their address, he was, after all, just a little kid, but he'd never forgiven himself. Nor had his father forgiven him. From that day forward, Derrick had sensed a change in Rex Buchanan, and his son was no longer the best and brightest. All of his fatherly attentions were shifted to his tiny daughter—the spitting image of her mother.

Derrick, misunderstanding, had done anything to get Rex's attention—good deeds and bad. The bad seemed to work better and they were a helluva lot more fun. Even though he'd been groomed to be Rex Buchanan's heir, he'd never been loved again—not the way he had been before. Not with the adoration of both Lucretia and Rex. The night God had taken his mother, Derrick Buchanan had lost his father as well.

Forty-one

Oswald Sweeny confirmed what Cassidy already knew. Marshall Baldwin didn't have a past. No childhood, no adolescence, no first love, no damned history whatsoever. No kindly grandmother responded to any inquiries, no forgotten sister who called for more information, no grade school teacher who remembered him.

"Yep," Sweeny said, his voice clear though he was still in Alaska, "looks as if our boy just appeared at age nineteen or so. I checked California records and guess what? There was a Marshall Baldwin born in Glendale in 1958, but when I checked further, I found out he'd died six months later. Sudden infant death syndrome. Talked to his mother myself; she lives in Fresno now."

Cassidy's stomach tightened. This wasn't surprising news—she'd heard basically the same thing from Michael Foster, but it meant that Bill Laszlo and his sources would have the same information soon.

"There weren't any other boys by that name?"

"Quite a few—but I checked 'em all out and they're living or dead, but can be accounted for. But the baby from Glendale—now there's an identity that could be easily assumed."

Oh, God!

"Can't help but wonder if Baldwin was Brig McKenzie," Sweeny said, as if divining her thoughts.

"Seems possible," she said, her mouth as dry as dust.

"He wouldn't have looked all that much the same, considering the accident."

"Accident?" she repeated.

"Yeah, Baldwin was in kind of a freak milling accident. Something backfired in one of the chippers, a piece of wood flew out and hit him on the left side of his face. Had to have surgery. Anyway, doesn't mean the guy isn't McKenzie. Want me to look into it?" He sounded anxious, as if he had finally found something to set his teeth into.

"No, thanks . . ." She could barely concentrate on the conversation. "You've done more than enough. If you could just send me a bill . . . here, to the office."

"No problem."

She hung up the phone and glanced up from her desk to find Bill Laszlo leaning against the partition, his eyes centered on her. "Bad news?" he asked, his cocksure grin in place.

"Just you." Selma rolled her desk chair around the corner of the partition. Bill had to move quickly to avoid being hit. Finger-combing her springy curls, she said, "You know if you don't quit bugging her, she really will have to take up smoking."

Laszlo ignored her and picked up a paperweight from Cassidy's desk. "Looks like you just saw a ghost."

"What is it you want, Bill?" Cassidy asked.

"Confirmation."

"Of?"

"That Marshall Baldwin was really Brig McKenzie."

"I don't know that."

"That McKenzie was the arsonist in fire one"—he held up a finger—"and fire two." Another finger popped up.

"You're creating news now, not reporting it."

"More than a coincidence that he was here for both of them, wouldn't you say?"

"I wouldn't say anything. You don't have any facts, Bill. Just pure conjecture and last I heard the *Times* doesn't print speculation."

"This isn't something you haven't thought about, nor the police. Everyone thought John Doe was Brig, then he turned up with this identity of Baldwin, but I think it's all just a smoke screen. The real question is why your husband's lying."

"You don't know that he's—"

"Just tell him I'll be stopping by."

"He won't talk to you."

"He'll talk."

"How? Gestapo tactics?"

"Get a life," Selma muttered. "Come on, Cassidy. It's time for a little lung-cancer break." Bracelets rattled as she hiked her purse over her shoulder.

Bill's irritation showed in the tight little corners of his mouth. "You can't avoid me, you know. The way I look at it, you can work with me or against me. You could make a name for yourself or just be another source in the paper."

"I'll pass. On both." Cassidy flipped off her computer and reached for her briefcase and purse. "I'm taking the next couple of days off." She couldn't stand being in the building another minute, didn't want to try and avoid the hard-edged questions in Bill's eyes, knew that attempting to concentrate on some story she didn't care about would be useless.

All she could think about was that Brig was dead and Chase had lied. How many times had she asked him about Brig? How often had she suggested that the John Doe might be his brother? And he'd lied. Because he'd known. He'd had to have known.

As she drove home, her thoughts spun as rapidly as the tires of her Jeep. If Brig had been living in Alaska under an assumed name, with a new identity, why did he return to Prosperity? When did he get back? How long had Chase known the truth about a brother he'd pretended was dead? Had they planned Brig's reunion? Did Sunny know?

Her head was throbbing by the time she parked the Jeep in the garage. She didn't bother calming herself, didn't stop to count to ten. She wanted answers and she wanted them now. No more lies. No more games.

"Chase!" she yelled, storming through the back door, her stomach in knots, fury racing through her blood. Ruskin, lying under the kitchen table, bounded to greet her. She patted him on the head a second, then continued through the house. "Chase?"

She found him just hobbling out of the door of his room. Stripped to the waist, he was wearing gray sweatpants, wet near the waistband, his chest bare and soaked in sweat. His face was flushed, his hair damp as if he'd been working out, doing the painful physical therapy exercises to strengthen his muscles. Ever since his run-in with Derrick, he'd pushed himself to the limit each day. Now, he braced himself against the side of the wall.

"Marshall Baldwin didn't exist." She launched right in, pinning him with her harsh glare.

"What're you raving about?"

"I checked, the Sheriff's Department has checked, Bill Laszlo and Oswald Sweeny have checked."

"Sweeny—the detective you hired?"

"Sweeny used to live in Portland but moved to Anchorage." She took two steps closer to her husband. "Before Marshall was nineteen and working on some kind of maintenance for the pipeline, Marshall Baldwin had no life. Not in Alaska, not in California. And guess what? The only Marshall Baldwin that could possibly have been born at the right time age-wise in California died as a baby. SIDS."

"Who said Baldwin was born in California?"

"Don't lie to me, Chase!" she nearly screamed. "I know." She hit his chest with the flat of her hand, fingers splayed. "I *know* that the John Doe, or Marshall Baldwin, or whoever you want to call him was Brig. It's just a matter of time before it's proved."

"Christ, Cassidy! Listen to you—"

"I know, damn it!" So angry she was shaking, she grabbed him by the forearms, her fingernails digging deep into his muscles. "I deserve the truth!"

His jaw clenched and relaxed, and his eyes turned the color of midnight. With the look of a condemned man, he sighed and closed his eyes. "All right. You want to hear it so badly. Brig was Baldwin."

Her world collapsed. The truth, hidden so long, crushed her with its weight. "Oh, God," she whispered, her arms falling from his as if weighted. She nearly stumbled as she tried to step away from him, to face her grief. Strong arms surrounded her. "You *knew.*" Her throat caught and a wave of emotions tumbled over her. "Why didn't you tell me? How could you lie?"

The arms tightened and she struggled, trying to break free.

"Why, Chase?" she cried, tears tumbling from her eyes. She'd promised herself that she would never cry another tear for Brig McKenzie, would consider him dead years ago, but always there had been a tiny ray of hope that had lingered in her heart.

"He wanted it that way."

"I don't understand—"

"He knew that if you thought he was still alive, you might never get on with your own life, never find yourself."

"You knew all along?" Her voice was a whisper, her lips moving against his chest as he crushed her to him.

"For a long time."

"Before we were married?"

He hesitated. His breath rushed out. "Yes."

"Oh, God."

"He swore me to secrecy."

"Chase—" She tilted her head up and felt his lips against hers. She tasted the salt of her tears and smelled the perspiration clinging to him. Warmth invaded her, and despite the pain, or because of it, she surrendered to the pure physical yearnings that swelled deep within her.

Instinctively her arms wound around his neck, and when his tongue pressed urgently against her teeth, she willingly opened to him. Distant thoughts flitted through her mind, treacherous ideas that she was making love to the wrong man, that giving herself to him would be condoning his lies, but she closed her mind to everything but the feel of his hard muscles against her body, the male smell that tickled her nostrils, the taste of his skin. Lifting her from her feet, he struggled to carry her into his bedroom, where he dropped her onto the bed.

Still kissing her, he lay beside her, his fingers anxiously shoving buttons through unwilling holes. "Cassidy." He murmured her name across her skin. Spreading open her blouse, he kissed the center of her chest, lips wet and hot, as if feeling the beat of her heart pounding fast beneath her breast bone.

She could barely breathe, and when she heard the soft hiss of her zipper being lowered, she closed her eyes. It had been so long. She touched him all over, feeling flesh that was firm, muscles hard, hips lean.

He opened her bra and nuzzled at her breasts, his breath whispering across her nipples. His tongue teased, his lips suckled, his teeth nipped and desire was a warm and welcome whirlpool that began to spin in ever-widening circles, enveloping her.

"I'd forgotten how beautiful you are." He kissed her again, and his hands clamped over her bare buttocks, fingers grazing her inner thighs. Shivering in anticipation, she writhed beneath him, felt him spread her legs with his knees, noticed vaguely that he shifted so that his weight was on his strong leg.

"Do you want me, Cass?" he asked.

"Yes." She could barely speak.

"For how long?"

"Forever."

A shadow passed over his eyes as she stared up at him. "If only—" Clamping his jaw shut, he moved suddenly, entering her. Fiercely. Hungrily. As if in so doing he could thrust away the past, the pain, the lies. As if he were branding her from the inside out, and her body responded in kind, moist and hot, a willing partner.

Fingers digging into his shoulders, she clung to him as her blood ran hot, her back arched and she wrapped her legs around his waist. The room seemed to fade away, the house no longer existed and they were alone in the universe. One man. One woman. One love.

Chase. Brig. Love. Images spun and whirled behind her eyes.

"Oh, God, I can't stop—" he cried as his body became rigid and he gave out a desperate yell.

She convulsed beneath him, the world exploding, the stars colliding, the air so hot she couldn't breathe.

Gasping, he fell against her and she welcomed his weight, her arms surrounding his sweat-slickened torso, her fingers lacing over the strong muscles of his back. "I've missed you," she whispered, tears stinging her eyes.

"And I missed you. If you only knew." He was still breathing with difficulty, his words edged in a hopelessness she couldn't understand.

"Just hold me."

"As long as I can, darlin'," he whispered against the damp strands of her hair. "As long as I possibly can."

Sunny felt a jolt. As if the earth had cracked. Her old heart hammered and she looked up at the threatening sky. Clouds blocked the sun. The wind was angry, and though the temperature was sweltering, reaching high into the nineties every afternoon, Sunny felt a chill as cold as death. It crept through her bones each morning, then settled back down like a dog circling before lying down. Restless. Unsatisfied.

She was tired of being a prisoner. It seemed wherever she went, there were guards. The hospital was the worst, but after that, Rex had insisted she stay on his grounds. There was a little house in the foothills where he'd harbored her. Where Willie had come to visit her. Where she'd almost felt safe. Until she'd seen Rex's weakness and knew that he would eventually be forced to tell the authorities where she was.

She'd left then and began wandering through the woods. Her boys needed her. She knew that much. The images of fire and water had risen behind her eyes again. There was trouble. The worst kind. She looked to the moon and the stars, but they were hidden and darkness covered the forest.

She wasn't afraid, she tried to convince herself. And she was patient. She'd wait for a sign.

Cassidy stretched on the bed and found it empty. Chase had already left, but it didn't matter. They'd spent the night making up for lost time, making love and dozing only to make love again. She tingled all over and felt sore between her legs.

She threw on one of his shirts, buttoning it as she walked barefoot into the kitchen, where coffee was already brewed. Staring through the back window, she saw him standing by the lake, staring across the water. Waiting for her.

She didn't disappoint him, but hurried outside, the tails of his shirt flapping around her bare legs, the soft caress of morning cool against her skin. He glanced her way, but didn't smile. She wondered if all the old barriers they'd torn down last night were being resurrected.

"Last one in's a rotten egg," she said as he turned to face her. For a minute her heart stopped. He looked so much like Brig, she didn't dare breathe.

"Something wrong?"

"No—I—" She was being silly, of course. Too many emotions all at once. "Come on." She ripped the buttons through their holes, let the shirt fall on the sand and ran into the icy water. Before she could let her traitorous mind wander dangerously, she submerged, diving low, skimming the bottom, only to resurface and let the breath out of her straining lungs.

Chase wasn't standing beneath the tree. He wasn't—

She saw a movement and suddenly he was beside her, treading water, arms outstretched. "This is insane," he said, drops clinging to his beard shadow as he took her into his arms.

"Hey, wait! I'll drown."

"No way. I'd save you." His lips found hers. His arms and

legs surrounded her, and she felt his body hardening despite the cold, her blood heating in the frigid lake, her passion rising instantly.

She closed her eyes and let go of the doubts, gave herself to this man, her husband, a new beginning.

It wasn't until later, when they were sitting on the back porch, cradling steaming cups of coffee, watching the few horses Cassidy had raised graze in the fields beyond the lake, that she realized her mistake. Rays of sun pierced the clouds and burnished the hides of the mares and geldings as they swatted at flies with their tails and plucked at the dry grass.

She'd never bought a colt or a stallion. Remmington had been her last.

Wrapped in a robe, she sat on one chair, her feet propped on the table, Ruskin lying on the floorboards beside her. Chase stretched out on a lounge, his injured leg raised slightly, his faded jeans slung low on his hips. He wore the shirt she'd pulled on when she'd climbed out of bed. It was still wet in places and he hadn't bothered with the buttons.

"You're waiting," he finally said as he finished a swallow. "For me to tell you about Brig."

"I think I deserve to know."

He trained his blue eyes on hers, then glanced far away to the horizon. "Fair enough, I guess." Hesitating a second, he rubbed the back of his neck before beginning. "Brig contacted me about four or five years after he left. Tracked me down in Seattle. Told me he was living in Anchorage, had spent a few years working on the pipeline, then worked in a sawmill and finally was buying one. He wanted everyone— you, Mom, the whole damned town—to think he was missing in action or dead or whatever you want to call it. He was never coming back."

"This was before or after I met you again?"

"Before. But I didn't hear from him again for a long time. We were dating then and . . . he told me to tell you he was dead."

"He said that?" she whispered, trying to ignore the old pain in her heart.

"Thought it would be best."

Her thoughts were unraveling. Chase had lied from the beginning. To everyone. "He—he didn't care that we were seeing each other?"

His eyes turned cruel. "No."

"He didn't try to talk you out of it, to—"

"I said he didn't give a damn, Cassidy. Can't you accept that?"

Something wasn't right about this. She could feel it in her bones. Her reporter's instincts warned her that he was altering the truth. Again. Her hands shook a little and coffee sloshed over to burn her hand.

"He told me he didn't set fire to the gristmill."

"I know that."

"But you don't know what happened."

"Do you?" she whispered, her heart beating frantically. Who was this man who knew so much and kept so quiet—this man who was her husband, to whom she'd made love? How many secrets had he harbored over the years? How many thoughts had he kept to himself?

"Brig had gone to the gristmill to have it out with Jed Baker. They'd already fought at our place, but Brig was convinced that Jed was up to no good. And Brig knew that Jed had set up a meeting with Angie. She'd told him so earlier. So he rode his motorcycle to the mill. But it was too late. By the time he got to the mill, it was in flames. He saw Willie there and ran inside, pulling Willie to safety before he went back in and tried to get Jed, to save him." His eyes seemed suddenly dead, his voice barely a whisper. "He couldn't, though—a wall of fire was between them."

"And Angie—?"

Chase's gaze drifted to a distance she couldn't see. "He was too late for her, too."

"Oh, God." Cassidy felt suddenly cold, as if she'd stepped into a dark, frigid lake. She remembered the fire, the bank of flames that had reached for the sky, the stench of smoke, the ugly, blinding fear . . .

Chase's gaze returned to hers. "He said you helped him escape. Insisted he take your horse."

She nodded mutely.

"And you gave him your St. Christopher's medal." He was staring at her with such intensity that she couldn't look away. "I think he kept it with him all the time. He was wearing it the night he came back."

Tears filled her eyes, and she clamped her teeth together to keep from crying. Her cup dropped to the porch and rolled off the edge into the sword ferns and azaleas. "He never forgot you, Cass."

"Why did he come back now?"

He glanced away.

"Chase—? What did he say?"

Chase rolled off the lounge and sat on the coffee table, where she'd braced her bare feet. He straddled her legs and held her ankles, his hands warm and comforting against her skin. "That it was time. He was back because he wanted to find out who set the fire; he felt that he'd been framed, and now that he had the money and what he thought was the perfect disguise, he wanted to start looking for answers. He asked me to help him. Buying lumber and all, that was just a cover-up."

"But wouldn't people have recognized him? He didn't have the beard anymore—"

"No one else would see him for a while and he looked different. His nose had been broken again and he'd been in some kind of accident while he was working in one of the mills. His face had changed quite a bit."

"Did you recognize him?"

He swallowed, the tips of his fingers grazing her calves before he stood and drew her to her feet. "Of course."

"Would I?"

He stared down at her for endless seconds. When he spoke, his voice was low, filled with emotions she didn't begin to understand. "I don't think so, Cass."

Clouds shifted, blotting out the sun.

"I would have liked to say good-bye."

His arms tightened around her, pulling her close. "Me, too."

She slid her hands around his waist and held on tight. "I—I'm sorry for all the pain I caused you. Because of Brig—"

"Shh. It's over." His breath stirred her hair.

Tears slid down her cheeks. "Is it?" She wondered if it ever would be, or if the ghost of Brig McKenzie would haunt them forever.

"If we let it die."

"How can we? Until we find out who burned the mill, who killed Angie, who—" She shuddered and her hands splayed over the back of his shirt, feeling the sinewy strength of his muscles beneath the cotton fabric. "Who was the father of her baby?"

"You think it was his?" Chase asked, not moving, his body suddenly rigid.

"I don't know, oh, God, I don't know." She clung to him desperately, her hands creeping up against the smooth skin of his shoulders. He kissed her then, his lips full, his eyes bright from his own emotions.

"Cass, I love you," he said, blinking hard, as if the admission were deplorable, as if uttering those three little words would alter the course of their lives.

And then it hit her. Like a lightning bolt thrust from the sky by angry gods. Oh, God, no. Not now! "What?" she whispered in a voice so low it was barely audible. "What did you call me?"

"Cassidy—"

"No—no—" The porch seemed to shift and buckle beneath her bare feet. "You've been calling me Cass ever since the fire and you never used to . . . oh, God . . ." Pictures spun in her mind. Chase stepping out of the shower, with only a towel slung around his waist, dressed in his sweatpants, his shirt off, naked in bed last night, in the water swimming this morning. She began to shake.

"What—?"

Her hands moved over his shoulders, fingertips searching, finding nothing. *Nothing!*

"Cassidy?"

"Let me go!" She wrenched away, staring at him in horror. Her palms were sweaty with dread, her heart pumping out of control. "Take it off," she ordered.

"What?"

"Your shirt, take it off!" she nearly screamed, afraid she was going out of her mind.

"Why?"

"You know why."

His blue eyes fixed to hers, he slid his arms through the sleeves and held the crumpled shirt in one big fist.

"Turn around."

"Are you out of your mind?"

"Turn around, damn it!" she said, and he did, lifting his hands over his head as if he had nothing to hide, and there was his back, smooth and perfect, a few scars from his recent accident visible, but the old injury, the bullet hole in his shoulder, the one Brig had inflicted on Chase by accident when they were children, the one she'd traced dozens of times before, was missing.

"How could you?" she said as he spun slowly and faced her. His eyes held hers for a second that seemed to last forever. She could barely stand, and a noise as loud as the sea roared in her ears. Disbelieving, she watched his chin harden and his shoulders straighten, and all of a sudden the truth was so clear to her—so damned evident she couldn't believe she hadn't seen it before—that everyone who'd met him hadn't seen it. "You're not my husband . . . not Chase . . ." Her knees gave way, and she sagged against the wall for support. Her bones felt heavy, and darkness teased the corners of her eyes.

"Cass—"

"Don't. Don't call me that!" Hysteria welled up in her throat, blinding her to anything but the damning truth. How could she have been so blind? The intensity of his gaze, the line of his jaw, the arrogance of his lips, the way his shirts stretched across his shoulders. "Chase is dead, isn't he?" she said, tears filling her eyes. "My husband. He's dead!"

He reached for her and she shrank away, afraid of his touch, of his gaze, of him. "Don't!"

"Cass, listen—please, just try and understand—"

"Understand? *Understand?* Listen to what you're asking, for God's sake!"

His fingers closed into a fist. "I didn't mean to—"

"Like hell! This was all part of your plan! Oh, God, I've been such a fool, such a damned fool!" Her voice rose an octave, and her breath was tight in her lungs. She couldn't breathe, couldn't move, couldn't think. "Of course you meant to. You've known the truth all along and you kept it from me—from your mother. From everyone." Her voice broke and she felt her lips tremble. "I can't believe I was so stupid, so damned blind."

Again he stepped forward, and she nearly tripped as she scrambled away from him. "Don't you ever touch me again," she warned, her voice threatening, her hands feeling along the wall as she inched toward the door, the skin of her palms scraping against the rough siding.

"If you'll just stop for a minute and listen—"

"I don't want to hear it."

"You have to!"

She halted then, stopped dead in her tracks. He was right, though she was loath to admit it. She couldn't run away, and so there, in the shadows of the porch, she paused, lifting her chin, damning him with her gaze. "For the love of God, Brig McKenzie, what have you done?"

Forty-two

He should have told her in the beginning. Hell, he'd meant to. Planned to. He'd never intended to deceive her, not this way, but he'd had no choice. His back was to the wall. And now she detested him. Standing defiantly in front of him, trembling, afraid to take a step nearer, she didn't move.

"Why did you lie?" she demanded.

"I didn't. You all assumed that I was Chase."

"Your identification—the medal . . ." Her voice was stronger now, filled with new, conflicting emotions.

"Switched. Chase was pinned, I tried to get him free but couldn't, and it was his idea," Brig admitted, the horror of that night haunting him as it had since the fire . . .

Bang!

Brig was thrown across the large room as an explosion boomed through the mill. He landed on the floor, a dozen feet from where he and Chase had stood.

Beams broke and fell, bringing the ceiling with them.

Supports buckled.

Flames crackled skyward.

Brig scrambled to his feet. He had to get out. Now.

Smoke billowed through the hole in the roof. "Chase!" he yelled, his voice already raw. "Where the hell are you?" He squinted, eyes searching the rubble, burning from the acrid smoke. "Chase!"

"Here! Get out. Now!" Chase was heading toward him, dragging a leg.

Bam! The second explosion ripped through the mill and the roof above Chase tumbled downward, old wooden beams, steel roof, metal girders, collapsing.

"Chase, run!"

But it was too late.

One of the beams slammed across Chase's body. With a wail of pain, he went down, the beam pinning him to the floor.

"No!" Brig dashed through the smoke and dust, finding his brother bleeding, half-conscious, the lower part of his body crushed. "Come on, come on," he said to his brother as Chase moaned. "I'll get you out of here."

And he meant it. Despite the wall of flames, the blistering heat and the smoke that burned his lungs, making him cough and retch, he was going to pull his brother from this inferno.

He tried to lift the beam. On his knees, wedging his body beneath the heavy timber. "I'll push up, you crawl out!" he ordered.

"I can't, man. I can't move." Chase's voice was panicked.

"Sure you can, it's the beam."

"No, Brig, I can't feel anything down there. Oh, God."

Brig pushed the beam with all his strength, his muscles quivering, sweat running in his eyes. "Damn it, Chase, move!" he yelled, willing his brother out of this funeral pyre.

"I'm telling you, I can't!"

"Get out now!" Brig's muscles were straining, bulging, his teeth bared with the effort, searing, smoky air burning through his lungs. "Chase, *now,* dammit!"

"Brig, stop. Just take my wallet," Chase said. "I can't move."

"I'll get help."

The fire roared around them in hot, wild waves.

"It'll be too late. Hell, Brig, take the damned wallet!" Chase yelled, his voice a rasp as he lay pinned to the floor, his face bloody, his back crushed. "Leave yours with me!"

he insisted as the smoke billowed to the sky and fire roared all around them.

"No way, I'm getting you out of here!" The heat blistered, the fire raged, and when Brig threw all of his strength into moving the beam again, Chase screamed in pain.

"Get out! Now." Blue eyes looked up desperately through the smoke. Somehow, he'd been able to pull his wallet from his pants. "Take my ID, leave yours with me," he pleaded, coughing . . . "say you're me. For God's sake, save yourself!"

"No. You'll be fine." *You've got to be!*

"For Christ's sake, Brig, it's over!"

"I'll get help!"

"Switch the damn wallets! And take my ring. Do it for Cassidy!"

"No, Chase, I'll get—"

"Shut up and do this. For Cassidy and me!" Chase was breathing hard, blood running from his nose and mouth, his teeth bared against the pain. "For once in your life don't be so damned selfish!"

He'd done it. Quickly, taking the wallet from Chase's out-stretched hand and yanking off Chase's wedding ring before placing his billfold into Chase's palm and curling his fingers over the worn leather.

"Good." Chase's voice was frail. His eyes rolled back in his head as Brig jerked the chain from his neck and threaded it through Chase's fingers.

"Hang in there! I'll be right back." Scared witless, Brig ran back to the office. Flames crackled and hissed, devouring sawdust, chips, lumber, anything in their path and licking to the night-black sky. Heart drumming, Brig coughed as black, cloying smoke billowed toward the heavens and filled his lungs. "Please God—"

This couldn't be happening! Not again! He yanked the door to the office open. Heat seared his lungs. The door was wrenched from his hand as another explosion rocked the mill. Sparks spewed upward in a geyser of fiery embers. His feet were blasted off the ground. He flew backward. The sky was a blur—black and orange, alive with flames and so damned hot! He tried to break his fall. His wrist snapped as he smacked against the ground and his leg twisted back on itself. Pain ripped up his arm and knee and he screamed. A flying piece of metal slammed against the back of his head. "Chase!" he yelled as the lights behind his eyes nearly blinded him. Pain exploded in his temple near his right eye. Screaming, he felt the blackness surround him. Just before he lost consciousness he was thankful that he wouldn't feel the agony of the flames that were sure to devour him body and soul.

Days later he awoke in the hospital and everyone was calling him by his brother's name.

Now, it was time to come clean. Just as he'd told himself he would, once he was out of the hospital and on his feet again.

"Who did this?" Cassidy demanded. "Who set the fires? Derrick?" She blinked rapidly and he saw that she was holding on to her composure by a thin, unraveling thread.

"I don't know," he admitted. "But I'm going to find out. I promised Chase."

"Lies, Brig," she accused, white and shaking and staring at him as if he were Satan incarnate. "You were there! Both times!"

"I didn't start either of the fires. Swear to God."

She stared at him as if she wanted desperately to believe him. "Who would want to kill Chase?"

Guilt settled over him like lead, weighing his shoulders, squeezing his insides. "Lots of people, I think. He knew that Derrick was skimming money, knew about Rex and Sunny, knew way too much. He'd made his share of enemies over the years, but in the beginning, when the first fire was set, no one would want him dead." He shoved his hands deep into his pockets. "I think they were trying to kill me in the fire in the gristmill that killed Angie. I think whoever was behind the first fire mistook Jed Baker for me. They expected me to be with Angie that night. I'd been her date at the Caldwells' party."

"You think they were trying to kill you," she repeated, as if a light were dawning in her mind.

"Maybe this time, too."

"Then—and now? But who? No one knew you were back—"

"Someone did."

"Who?" she repeated as she thought of all the enemies Brig had made in the years he'd been in Prosperity.

"Willie knew. He was at both fires. He saw me."

Her eyes turned dull. "You're not going to blame this on a poor man who can't—"

"My mother knew, too. She sensed it, I think. That day in the hospital, she knew who I was. Touched my hand and didn't even blink, just said she'd been waiting to see me again for a long time. Called me by name." Brig was moving slowly toward Cassidy, closing the distance, dying a little as she shrank away from him and surveyed him with wild, frightened eyes.

"Sunny didn't set fire to the mill. For God's sake, Brig, listen to you!"

"Of course she didn't. But if Sunny and Willie knew, others did, too."

"Or else someone was trying to kill Chase," she whispered, "and when they find out they missed, they'll try again." She looked up at him, fear shining in her eyes. "They'll murder you, too."

"Unless we stop them." He touched the side of her face with a finger and she closed her eyes for a second. He felt her quiver, then she yanked backward, repulsed.

"I . . . I can't . . . Brig . . . I . . . for God's sake, *please* don't touch me. I can't even believe that we're having this conversation." But she'd known. Part of her had sensed that he wasn't the same, wasn't her husband. Though she'd denied it consciously, she'd felt a difference, not only in him, but in her response as well. Why else had she decided against the divorce that she was so adamant about before the fire, why else had she pleaded for a second chance, why else had she clung desperately to him when he'd so callously tried to keep her at arm's length? Because of some skewed sense of loyalty? Because the fire had made her see how much she loved her husband? Because her faith prevented her from divorcing him? Or because some sixth sense had told her that he was Brig?

Sick with herself, with him, guilt riding heavy on her shoulders, she walked past him and into the den to Chase's private stock of Scotch, but as she retrieved the bottle, she saw herself in the mirror over the bar and Brig's reflection as he stood in the doorway.

"You want a drink?" she asked.

"Yeah, but I don't think it's the time."

"Wh—what are you going to do?" Her hands were unsteady and she forced them deep into the pockets of her robe. Dear God, what now? She was married to Chase and he was dead; she'd slept with Brig, given herself to him, closed her eyes to the blatant lies, just as she had in the past.

She was angry with him for deceiving her, angry with herself for falling for him again and scared out of her mind. There was a lunatic on the loose. Someone who wanted Chase or Brig dead.

"What am I going to do?" he repeated. "I'm going to figure out who did this. Wait here." He hurried down the hall with his uneven gait, and Cassidy collapsed in a corner of a couch. She held her head in her hands, hoping that the throbbing in her head and the ache deep in her soul would disappear. She'd always been in love with Brig, but now it seemed vile, a schoolgirl fantasy turned the work of the devil.

As much as she'd loved Brig, she'd never, ever wanted to sacrifice Chase—one brother for the other. Her stomach convulsed and she ran to the bathroom, locking the door and throwing up over and over again until there was nothing left but stomach acid. She scooted back on the cold tile floor, shaking as she wiped her mouth with the back of her hand, tears splashing down her cheeks. Had she ever cried more in her life?

"Cass?" He rapped on the door with his knuckles, and her heart knocked wildly. *Brig! Oh, Brig!* Squeezing her eyes shut, she tried to block out the feelings of betrayal—her betrayal to her husband. "Hey, are you all right, darlin'?"

Sweet Jesus, don't let him be kind to me. I can't take any tenderness right now.

"Cassidy." His voice was stronger now. How had she not known? Her insides quivered, her hands shook, she couldn't think straight . . .

"If you don't answer me, I'm going to break down this damned door and—"

"Leave me alone!"

"I swear, Cass, you come out of there now, or I'll bust it."

"Just leave me the hell alone, Brig!" Again she retched over the toilet and she heard him swearing under his breath, the words indistinguishable, the meaning clear.

Standing, she felt the pain between her legs, reminding her of their lovemaking, how long, how furious, how hot it had run. "Oh, God, Chase, I'm sorry," she whispered, then bent over the sink and washed out her mouth. Her reflection, ghostly pale with condemning gold eyes, glared at her, silently accusing her of horrid crimes of the heart. "Oh, just go away," she told her image and splashed cold water on her face. She could wallow in self-recriminations and guilt for the rest of her life, and it wouldn't do one bit of good. No, the only way she could atone for her unwitting indiscretion—the sin of not loving her husband as much as she should have—was to find Chase's killer.

And what if it's Brig? What if it's the man who's been posing as your husband for weeks? The man who left you? Who deceived you? Who betrayed himself, his mother, and his brother? The man who made love to you and turned you inside out? What do you really know about him? Nothing! Nothing!

But she wasn't afraid. No matter what, she would never be afraid of Brig McKenzie. She just wasn't certain that she could trust him.

*   *   *

He was in the den, waiting, a drink in one hand. She glanced at the glass of amber liquid and he said, "I figured I owed myself. Already gave up the other kind of crutch."

"You said you wanted to show me something."

"While you've done your investigation of Marshall Baldwin—including all the information you've gotten from Oswald Sweeny and your connections in the business, I've done some digging myself. And while I was at it, I've thrown some information Sweeny's way, so he could report back to you. He didn't know it, of course."

"Of course," she said dryly. What kind of man was she dealing with?

"I called some people in Anchorage, Fairbanks and every place I lived as Baldwin. Just the people I trust. People who trust me. They gave Sweeny and Wilson and Laszlo the information I wanted them to have."

"You are a true bastard."

His smile was positively wicked. "No doubt. But I couldn't have you or the detective or Billy-boy Laszlo find out too much before I was ready, could I?"

"That's why you didn't tell anyone that you saw Derrick at the sawmill—because sooner or later someone would recognize you and you're still a suspect in Angie's death." Her heart was pounding loudly in her ears and the conversation felt surreal. After all these years. All these damned years.

Nodding, he swirled his drink. "Anyway, while you were all on your wild-goose chases checking out Baldwin, I've been doing research of my own."

"Have you?" She sat in a chair and watched him, listening to the cadence of his voice, wondering why she'd taken so long in discovering the truth. There was an energy that surrounded Brig McKenzie that hadn't been a part of Chase. She tucked her feet beneath her and accepted a glass of Scotch without any argument.

"Obviously whoever set the first fire, if it's the same culprit and not some copycat, lived here then as well as now. And—"

"And Angie was pregnant." Why she blurted this out now, she didn't know, but it was important, had been nagging at her for years. Cassidy's heart seemed to stop as she stared at him and her fingers clenched so tightly around her glass they hurt.

"I heard." His blue eyes were steady. "I wasn't the father, Cass."

"How do you know?"

"I didn't—"

"As if I can trust you! You've lied to me. Over and over. Each day you didn't call or write or try to reach me and tell me that you were alive and well and . . . you lied, damn it. So why should I believe that—"

"I wasn't the father," he repeated, fury snapping in his eyes.

"But—"

Drink falling to the floor, he crossed the room in three long, cumbersome strides. His hands grabbed her shoulders. "I didn't do it, Cass, and you can believe anything you want, but I never made love to your sister. Oh, I came close a couple of times, damned close, but I didn't go through with it, and do you know why?"

She couldn't answer. Couldn't move.

"Do you?"

Her throat was cotton, her heart a snare drum.

"Because of you, damn it. The hottest number in the county was wagging her pretty little ass in my face, trying like hell to seduce me, and I couldn't think of anything but her scrawny, beautiful tomboy of a sister!"

"I don't believe—"

"Oh, hell." He jerked her close to him, his mouth fitting over hers perfectly, his taste, his smell, his feel so achingly familiar. She felt her body sagging against him, kissing him feverishly, hungrily as one of his hands slid lower to untie the knot at her waist and part her robe. Strong fingers cupped the bend of her waist, touching skin already inflamed, leaving a brand as real as it had been so many years before. "Cass," he whispered. "Sweet, sweet, Cass."

She sighed loudly, her voice thin and breathy, filled with a need so great it scared her. Her fingers linked around his neck and she was kissing him again, opening her mouth to him, feeling the tingle deep between her legs. His fingers tangled in her hair and his lips were hot, wanting, searing. His tongue plundered her mouth and she moaned deep in her throat before the horror of what she was doing sank into her passion-dazed brain. "Oh, my God!" She slapped him then, her flat palm smacking hard against his cheek, making him wince from pain in a jaw not completely healed.

"Shit!" He sucked in his breath, held his face and stamped a foot to counter the pain.

"Chase—Brig—oh, God, I didn't mean to—" She stumbled away from him.

He glared at her for a frightening moment, then turned, walked to the window and, fists clenched in fury, swore again. "No more rules, okay, Cass? I won't tell you what to do and you sure as hell won't order me around. I'll call you whatever I want to and you can do the same, but we won't sleep together, we won't touch each other and we won't pretend like we're married."

His fingers flexed and stretched, as if he were physically trying to hold on to his patience. "Just bear with me for a few days until I clear this up, then . . . then we'll put everything straight and I'll leave."

Leave? Again? A horrid ache spread through her. From the pit of her stomach to the tips of her fingers. She felt suddenly dead inside and knew she couldn't face the thought of never seeing him alive again. "I don't know if I want you to leave," she said, and when he faced her again, his features were hard and set.

"You don't know what you want. While you were married to Chase, you wanted me. Now that he's gone, you want him back."

A squeak of protest passed her lips.

"All I need is a week, maybe more—"

"For a crime that hasn't been solved in seventeen years? You can figure it out in a week? Come on—"

One side of his mouth lifted. "I've been working on this a long time. Why do you think I came back when I did?"

"You know who started the fires?"

"Not yet, but I'm getting close, I think. I've got someone nervous." He sighed and his eyes narrowed on her. He paused, as if considering his words.

Now what? She couldn't stand another emotional battle.

"There was another reason I showed up at the mill that night," he admitted.

Steeling herself, she asked, "What was that?"

"I came back for you."

"What?"

Leaning on his good leg he scrutinized her reactions. "Chase had told me, and I believed him, that you wanted out of the marriage. That you were hell-bent on divorcing him. He knew that it was over and . . . and he was going to stand aside, Cassidy. If I wanted you, and you wanted me, he was going to give you up."

"You expect me to believe that?" She shook her head. This was too much.

"Well, there was a little hitch. He wasn't just going to walk away, not when he'd worked so hard. He wanted all the rest." Brig waved one arm expansively toward the windows. "The mills, the land, the timber, the offices."

"I can't believe he bargained for me," she said, though the words held a ring of truth. Hadn't she always known that Chase was more interested in the Buchanan fortune than her?

"It wasn't easy for him. He wasn't even being particularly noble, I think. But he knew that he could never possess you, that you didn't love him, that you never would, and it killed him a little more each day, so he became indifferent, throwing himself into his work." He rubbed the back of his neck and avoided her eyes.

"There's something else," Cassidy guessed.

He sighed.

"Brig—?"

"Shit!" He leaned against the windowsill and tipped back his head. "The truth of the matter is that you weren't his first choice."

"Wh–What?" Cymbals seemed to crash in her head.

"That's the irony of it, Cass," he said, turning to face her again. "Chase married you because you were the only Buchanan woman left. A long time ago, he was in love with Angie, too. Just like everybody else in this damned town."

Angie! Angie! Always Angie!

Couldn't anyone forget that bitch? I felt a tic at one side of my left eye and I could barely breathe as I listened to the argument between Cassidy and her husband. I heard only a little of the conversation, but they were both pissed, their words blurred. Their anger was seething, and it had something to do with Angie.

Seventeen years! The slut had been buried in the ground for seventeen years! So why was it people in Prosperity treated her as if she were a saint—a damned martyred saint!

My blood boiled when I thought of it. Would she never die? Never?

I eased away from my side of the window and slunk through the rhododendrons. If Angie was a saint, then her younger sister was a certifiable idiot. First Brig McKenzie and then Chase had walked all over her from day one.

What kind of a moron was she?

She was so damned pathetic. Always had been. Not ever in the same league with her older sister.

But then few were, I reminded myself and hated the turn of my thoughts. Quickly, I slipped away from this monstrosity of a house Chase McKenzie had built.

Thank God his brother had finally died. Maybe no one else had figured out the truth, but I knew that the John Doe now known as Marshall Baldwin had been Brig. Who else? That's probably what Chase and Cassidy had been discussing. I'd heard Brig's name a couple of times and I'd strained to hear Chase's side of the story, but the air-conditioning unit had been humming and I hadn't been able to piece everything together.

But I had enough.

My frown gave way to a smile as I remembered how I'd finally been able to get Brig to give up the ghost.

I'd slipped into the hospital several times and, on the fourth try, had been able to sneak into his room and make sure an air bubble reached his heart. Quick. Simple. In and out. By the time the monitors had started squawking, I was in the bathroom downstairs, stripping off my gloves, lab coat and scrubs. Any camera or witness would never recognize me.

At least I hoped.

I had seen one person I recognized in my escape. A reporter from the *Times*, someone who worked with Cassidy, but she'd looked through me, as if I weren't there.

For the most part I'd been invisible all of my life. It had been a pain in the backside as a teenager. Until I'd learned how to use my adeptness at fading into the background to my advantage. I knew I could have the limelight when I wanted, but it was better to plot and plan, appear not as bright or good-looking, keep my mouth shut and carefully and methodically make things work.

I didn't have much time.

If things were going to work out the way I'd been planning, both Cassidy and that damned husband of hers would have to die. As soon as possible.

I eased away from the house, down a path near the lake and through the surrounding trees. My truck was parked on federal land on the other side of a barbed-wire fence.

If I played my cards right, no one would ever know that I'd been here. No one would guess that I'd been behind it all.

Forty-three

"I should have your badge!" Rex Buchanan was livid as he walked into the kitchen and found T. John Wilson drinking coffee with his wife. "You and the rest of the department. What have you done besides swill coffee, shoot the damned breeze and mutter 'no comment' to the press! Who burned down the mill? Who tried to kill my son-in-law? Where is Sunny McKenzie? And who the hell is Marshall Baldwin?"

T. John sighed loudly. "We're working on all those things. Let's start with Mrs. McKenzie. We've had dogs tracking her, but she's a slippery one. Just the other night the dogs went crazy, started howling and carrying on somethin' fierce. I thought we'd found her in a cabin not far from Hayden Lake, you know, up on some of that property you own in the foothills."

"I know the cabin. I used to go fishing there when I was a kid."

"Been there lately?" T. John asked.

"Well—" Rex glanced nervously at his wife.

"Oh, Rex, no." Dena reached for her cigarettes.

"She needed somewhere to live, damn it. If she turned herself in, Chase would have her locked up again and she's the mother of Willie—"

"And your mistress!" Dena said, puffing up, not caring any longer what anyone thought. She was at the center of all the town gossip as it was.

T. John pushed himself upright. "Well, she's not at the cabin anymore."

"I know. That's why I'm here." Rex leaned against the table, then sat down heavily in one of the kitchen chairs. He stared out the window to the grounds and the pool. For years he'd tried to recapture a fleeting youth when Lucretia had been alive and he'd failed. Miserably.

"Thought you might know where she is."

Pulling off his driving cap, Rex worried it between his meaty fingers. "No," he admitted. "She left me."

"Oh, Rex." Dena fought a losing battle with tears.

"Just like Lucretia."

"You know, I've been wondering about that. Your first wife, I mean. I wasn't around then."

"She left me."

"Left you? But I thought—"

"Left me for heaven," Rex clarified, the lines in his face becoming deep chasms of age. "Couldn't take it anymore. Because of Sunny."

"That's always puzzled me," T. John admitted as he stared across the table at the man who had once been the most powerful force in Clackamas County. "Why, if you were so in love with your first wife, you fooled around with another woman?"

"Because Lucretia was a cold-hearted bitch who locked him out of her bedroom."

"Dena!" Rex stood, but she sent him a look that could curdle cream.

"It's true. I know. I had to have the locks removed when I moved in. I don't know what happened, Rex, or how you managed to father two children with her, but I know she ruined you, treated you like a leper, and then, when you turned to another woman, she got her ultimate glory by sitting in her damned Thunderbird, turning on the engine and listening to Elvis!"

"It wasn't like that."

"And she didn't even care enough about her kids to worry about them. Derrick found her, you know, and little Angie was upstairs in her crib. What would have happened if there was a fire, or Angie had fallen out of her bed and started down the stairs? Have you ever wondered what it was like for Derrick to find his mother dead behind the wheel of her damned birthday present?"

"Dena!"

"No wonder he's screwed up. Anyone would be. Lucretia deserved to die, Rex. Any decent woman would have taken care of her children first before she turned on the damned record player and the car. She was selfish in life and selfish in death and you've spent the last thirty-odd years feeling guilty about it!"

Rex's face had gone blank. He felt nothing inside, just a growing numbness. "Lucretia was an angel."

"For God's sake, Rex, open your eyes!"

"Find Sunny," he said to T. John. He ignored his wife and her ravings as he had for over thirty years. "I can't lose her, too."

T. John reached for his aviator glasses and slid them onto the bridge of his nose. "Where's Willie Ventura?"

"His name is Buchanan, now."

"Well, whatever he calls himself these days, he's missing. You know anything about that?"

"Dena threw him out."

T. John stared at the second Mrs. Rex Buchanan.

Dena rubbed her arms as if suddenly cold, then found her lighter and lit her cigarette. The flame trembled. "He gave me the creeps, okay? Him padding around here. He got into Rex's liquor a couple of times, one of the rifles is missing from the gun case, and I found him in Angie's room, just staring at that damned portrait of Lucretia. I know everyone thinks he's harmless, but that boy is evil. Pure evil. And he's not as dumb as he lets on."

"Shut up, Dena! He's my boy." Thrusting out his chin, Rex glared at the detective. "Find him, too. If you're successful, I'll donate money to your campaign, Wilson. I know you're planning to run for sheriff, and it's time Floyd Dodds had some decent competition. You find my boy and Sunny and I'll bankroll you. Legally or illegally. I don't care. I just can't lose any more of my family."

"But they're not your family," Dena cried.

Rex smiled weakly at his wife. "That's where you're wrong, Dena. That's where you've always been wrong."

Cassidy didn't know how much longer she could keep up the charade. She'd spoken little to Brig since she'd discovered his true identity a few days ago. They'd agreed on a plan of action, but she didn't know how much longer she could pretend that nothing had changed when her entire life was turned inside out. As for her personal life with Brig, it didn't exist. They lived in the same house, were dedicated to the same cause of finding out the truth about the two fires, but they had little personal contact. It was safer that way. He hadn't shown up at her morning swims, though he'd insisted that Ruskin accompany her and she'd purposely avoided Brig whenever he was in the house. But she couldn't keep up the masquerade. Not when her life was unraveling.

Her mother was upset. Willie and Sunny were missing. Rex was in a foul mood. Felicity and Derrick were fighting again and she was pretending to be married to her supposedly dead brother-in-law while her husband was the one who had died, his body already shipped to Alaska.

"Give me strength," she said as she walked into the newspaper office and headed straight for Bill Laszlo's desk. "I have something for you," she said to his bent head as he pounded furiously on the keys of his computer. He hadn't heard her approach and he nearly jumped out of his chair.

"What?"

"I think we should talk it over with Mike first." She didn't wait, just headed for their editor's office.

Gillespie was ecstatic. For once the *Times* would scoop all the other state papers, including the *Oregonian*. Hooking his thumbs in his suspenders, he beamed as proudly as if he'd been the first man on earth to give birth. "So Chase is willing to give a statement about Marshall Baldwin being Brig McKenzie."

"Yes."

"The town will breathe a sigh of relief, let me tell you," Laszlo said. "From what I can dig up, no one much liked Brig. Big trouble with the law, with girls, with everything and everybody—the ultimate town bad boy."

Cassidy managed a thin smile. "He was my brother-in-law," she reminded him. "I wouldn't lay all that bad-boy garbage on too thick with Chase. He might not like it."

" 'Course not," Mike said, shooting Bill a warning glance. "Just 'cause a kid gets a little reputation—"

"A legendary reputation," Bill countered. "You should hear the Reverend Spears. He hates the guy—well, he's not too fond of your husband, either."

"Or me," Cassidy said, the hackles of her back rising.

"Called Brig a heathen."

"Well, Brig probably called him a few choice names as well," Mike said. "Okay, let's not let this get cold. Chase is willing to give a statement today?"

"That's right. At the company offices. One o'clock. He should be done talking to the Sheriff's Department then."

"We should be down there! Getting a statement from Sheriff Dodds and Detective Wilson! Christ, why didn't you call me sooner?" Bill said, scooting out his chair.

Cassidy wouldn't be pushed around. "At the office. One o'clock. You blow it at the sheriff's office and there's no exclusive."

"But—"

"It's all right," Mike said, though his face was red and he looked angry enough to spit nails. "This is Cassidy's game, Bill. We'll play it her way."

"Christ, Mike—"

"Can it!" the editor growled.

Bill kicked a trash basket in frustration, sending it reeling against the wall.

"And no other news agency will be there?" Gillespie clarified.

"Not unless you call them," Cassidy promised.

"You sure took your sweet time comin' forward," T. John said, eyeing Brig suspiciously. He pulled out his lower lip and studied the contours of Brig's face as if searching for a lie. "I've been badgering you about John-Doe-slash-Marshall-Baldwin's identity from day one."

"I know. I was protecting him."

"From the law?"

"He was still under suspicion for the deaths of Angie Buchanan and Jed Baker, wasn't he?"

"True enough." T. John leaned back in his chair, tenting his hands, not seeming to buy one word of Brig's story.

"He came back to try and square things. Yes, he wanted to do business with me, but—"

"That was just a cover."

"Yeah."

"You shoulda come forward a lot sooner."

"My mistake." Brig leaned back in his chair. He was sweating a little because he sensed in T. John a deep-seated hunger, not unlike his own. The detective would go to any lengths to get what he wanted.

"Could be construed as withholding evidence."

"Could."

"And you knew where he was?"

"Not really. He'd call occasionally and I guessed he was either in Canada or Alaska."

"Why?" T. John was still watching his every reaction.

"Infrequent references to the seasons."

"But you didn't ask, nor did you check out the phone bills from the telephone company to see where he was calling from."

"Nope."

"Why not?"

"I wasn't too interested in seeing him again."

"And why's that?"

"Because he was in love with my wife."

T. John seemed to stop breathing. "Your wife. Cassidy?"

"Yes."

"But I thought he was involved with the other girl, her older half sister."

Brig lifted a shoulder, a gesture he'd seen Chase do often. He felt as if a noose had been thrown over his neck whenever he thought of Chase, and there was a spot in his soul that had died with his brother. Guilt, rage and vengeance burned through his blood, but he managed to display no emotions. "Brig got around."

"Had himself quite a reputation, I'll grant you that. I've talked to some of the women who were involved with him. They're all married now, have kids, don't want to say too much but from what I can piece together he was one helluva ladies' man."

Brig's stomach turned sour at the thought. The noose seemed to tighten a notch. "He was young."

"And randy."

"Right. And randy."

"And your wife, she took a shine to him, too?"

The detective was pushing it. "Yes." Talking about Cassidy bothered him. He hated dragging her into this mess, but had no choice.

"But you married her."

"She thought Brig was dead."

"And you knew different?"

"Yeah."

"Did she ever stop loving him?"

Brig looked the detective squarely in the eye. "Yes," he said for certain, though he knew that he'd killed that love himself, only days before.

Derrick hung up the phone with shaking fingers. His life was over. Lorna had just called—told him about the video-tapes she'd made of his little sessions with her daughter, who, she happened to mention, wasn't eighteen, sixteen or even fifteen, just a fourteen-year-old who looked older than her age.

The contents of his stomach threatened to rise up his neck. *Fourteen! Christ, she was younger than his daughter. You're a pervert, Buchanan, just like your old man.*

As he sat at his desk, god of the Buchanan empire, he saw it all crumbling away. He would be ruined, shamed, exposed. Felicity would divorce him, the girls would refuse to see him and his father would disinherit him. No matter that the old man had been banging other women for years, or that he'd been attracted to his own daughter. God, it was sick.

Again Derrick's stomach rumbled and he pushed himself up from the desk. Forty-eight hours. That's all she'd given him, then copies of the video taken in her big four-poster would be delivered to news stations, his wife, and the fucking Sheriff's Department.

He didn't doubt Lorna for a minute. She'd marked him from the beginning. She wanted a million, but she wasn't greedy—or so she'd told him—she'd take payments. Fifty thousand a month for a couple of years when you threw in interest. And just for kickers, if he was willing to risk the utter humiliation and ruin of his reputation and family, Lorna had friends, including Dawn's father, an ex-con with a nasty temper.

"Shit," he growled, staring out the window, sick with himself and the lust that burned through his blood and always led him into trouble. What could he do? He was backed into a corner. And his family—oh God, what would happen to his daughters? He may not have paid them the kind of attention Felicity had expected, but he loved them. In his own way. He kept his distance for their safety. After seeing his old man lust after Angie, he wasn't going to put himself in temptation's way—not again.

"Derrick?"

He visibly started. Felicity's voice jolted him out of his reverie. She was standing in front of his desk, staring at him, looking as if she could kill. *Oh God, she knows!* The inside of his mouth turned to sand.

"Something's going on." Felicity saw the nervous tick in Derrick's cheek and she steeled herself for the worst. "What is it?"

"Nothing. Nothing's going on."

She didn't believe him. He'd been acting secretive again, as he had at various times over the years. She suspected that he had affairs and she wasn't stupid enough to think she didn't care. Each time he stepped out on her, it hurt. It hurt like hell. She'd given him everything, risked everything. *Everything.* And still he didn't want her. He never really had, but, she decided, the least he could do was be faithful. That seemed to be too much to ask these days.

She was usually comfortable in the building, or any other piece of property bearing the Buchanan name, but this afternoon something wasn't right. She glanced at her watch and then her husband again. He was sweating and trying his best to seem casual. Something was up.

The trouble involved Chase. As she'd hurried past the open door of Chase's office, she'd seen him from the corner of her eye and he'd offered her the hint of a smile—his first since the fire—the kind of chilling grin that made her blood run cold.

"You sure there's nothing I should know about?" She stared through the reception area and down the short hallway to Chase's open door.

"What is it, Felicity?" Derrick didn't bother hiding his irritation. "Look, I'm busy. If you've got something you want to talk about—"

Felicity dragged her eyes away from Chase's door and faced her husband. Derrick had the nerve to check his watch as he snapped a lighter to the end of his cigarette. "I wanted to talk to you about Angela."

"Here? Now? At work?"

"She's refusing to go to St. Therese's. Wants to stay here because of that boy she's been seeing . . ."

"What boy?"

"Jeremy Cutler. He's a nobody, just a horny kid who—what the hell is *she* doing here?" Felicity saw Cassidy, along with that other reporter—the tall guy who'd hit on her a couple of times at the athletic club—Bill Laszlo—saunter into Chase's office.

Derrick was following her gaze. "Cassidy is Chase's wife. She's also a Buchanan. She belongs here. As much as you do."

She turned sharply, pinning her husband with a glare that could cut through steel. "But Laszlo doesn't. I'm telling you, something's up. Something big. It has to do with Chase and Brig. And I'm going to find out what it is. You might want to come along since it probably has something to do with the fire."

"Why would I care?"

She crossed to the door and shut it, then leaned against the cool panels. "We both know that you weren't home the night of the fire, and I don't think we want Detective Wilson getting any ideas that you might have been down at the mill."

"I wasn't there." He slipped his lighter into his pants pocket.

"Then where were you, baby, hmm?" she said, crossing her arms over her chest and drumming the fingers of one hand against her forearm. "And where were you when the fire was set at the gristmill the night Angie died? Everyone thinks you were with me. That's twice that I covered for you." Holding up two fingers, she tried to keep her rage under control, but years of lying, nights worrying, days praying she could keep her straying husband under control, erupted. Anger seared through her gut and now these problems with Angela . . . "I've never asked you where you were that night seventeen years ago, just gladly lied for you even though I knew you were in love with your sister."

"My what—?"

"Don't act so innocent. Don't you think I know who the father of Angie's child was?"

"Jesus, Felicity, listen to you! I don't know what you're talking about." Derrick had the decency to look shocked. God, he was good at lies, at deception. Almost as good as she was. But she knew better than to trust him and there wasn't any time left for pretending. She'd done enough of that to last her a lifetime.

"I saw you with her, you know," she said, advancing on her husband and keeping him in her cold glare. "I know you were screwing your sister . . . your own damned sister!"

His face was the color of chalk. "You're crazy! I never—"

"Save it for someone who'll believe it, Derrick," she hissed, afraid that someone might overhear their conversation. "I figured you were the father of her child and so I covered for you on the night she was killed."

"Oh, Christ, you think that I did it . . . that I started the fire and murdered her . . . burned her?" Now she had his full attention. His throat worked and his color had returned. Oh, God, she thought he might actually cry. Well, tough.

"I know it, baby. What I don't know is why you started the fire at the sawmill a few months ago. Unless you were jealous of Chase because of Cassidy."

"That's sick!"

"Are you trying to tell me you haven't been balling your half sister—or been attracted to her?"

"Where do you get this?" he said, his eyes incredulous, but she saw it then, that little spark of guilt. He'd always been as perverted as his father. She'd thought once Angie was dead that he'd change, but he hadn't.

"Pull yourself together," she said, though inside she was dying a thousand deaths. She'd never called him on it before, never felt so threatened. "We'll deal with this later, but right now I think we'd better find out what your brother-in-law is saying so that we can adjust our stories accordingly."

"I didn't—"

"Just shut up! We don't have time for any more lies!"

Derrick glowered through a cloud of smoke. "Chase doesn't know anything."

"I hope you're right, Derrick. I hope to God that you're right, but considering your track record, I think I'll just go down and check."

Darkness shrouded the forest. Only the thin light from a handful of stars and a sliver of a moon cast any glow on the trickle of water running through the ravine of Lost Dog Creek. Sunny closed her eyes and felt the night close in on her. A breeze riffled her hair, causing trees to sway, branches to dance and stir up the dust of the rocky shore. An owl hooted his lonely song and soft footsteps crept through the forest. Night creatures. Not humans. Not dogs. She'd been careless before, let those kids see her—and the Sheriff's Department had called in the hounds. So easy to fool.

Her visions were strong, getting more powerful, and she knew that the time had come for the truth, as ugly as it might be. Her sons' lives depended upon it. She had no other choice. All deception had to end. She felt a tremor deep within the earth and smelled the scent of a distant thunderstorm approaching as she laid the dead twigs and dry leaves in a circle of rocks. Then she reached into the voluminous folds of her skirt and found her matchbook and the front page of yesterday's edition of the *Times:* ALASKAN INDUSTRIALIST MARSHALL BALDWIN IDENTIFIED AS BRIG MCKENZIE. Grainy black and white pictures of Brig as a boy and Marshall Baldwin surrounded the article that described the fire years ago in parallel to the most recent blaze that took Brig's life.

But the article was a lie.

Brig was alive.

Chase was dead.

She ached from the inside out, felt the pain of losing her firstborn as if a knife had been thrust into her heart. She let out a long, keening moan that caught on the wind. Chase had been so good to her for so many years.

She swore in her mother's native tongue that she would wreak her own savage vengeance upon her son's murderer.

He would not go unpunished. "Death to you and those you love," she whispered, as if she could speak to her son's killer. She pulled out a match. With a scratch and the smell of phosphorous, flame sizzled to life, shifting in the hot air, casting the ground golden as she dropped the match.

Tinder-dry leaves sparked and the flame was born.

The wind rose in the trees, fanning the small fire. Staring at the hungry flames, Sunny reached into her pocket once more. Pulling out her bone-handled knife, she held it aloft to the heavens, then swiftly sliced her own hand, letting drops of blood drizzle from her palm onto the fire, where they sizzled and spat.

Chase would not be forgotten.

She closed her eyes and drew up the vision.

Her three sons stood at a wall of flames, smoke billowing skyward, their bodies bronzed and sweating. They faced the flames, their arms raised to the heavens.

Rain fell from the dark sky and yet the fire continued to rise in the sky, growing and feeding, casting out its evil heat, consuming everything in its wake, and yet her sons didn't move.

Run! She tried to yell. *Get away!* Her voice was still. *Save yourselves!*

When they didn't move, she walked forward. *Take me,* she silently cried to the fire. *Take me and leave my boys!*

She felt the heat. The flames touching her legs.

Her sons turned to face her.

She gasped.

Buddy's face was blue, his hair wet, and he staggered, gasping as the rain drenched him, forcing him to the ground, where he flopped like a fish on the land.

She cried out.

Chase's features were burned off his face, his eyebrows gone, his skin charred, his hair aflame. His body buckled and he fell, the scent of burning flesh filling her nostrils.

Brig, leaning on a crutch, faced her. Then the crutch changed, morphing into a woman, Cassidy Buchanan, who stood beside her husband's brother, her shoulders holding him up, as if she belonged with him. Brig leaned hard against her.

"You did this!" he yelled at his mother, his voice booming through the heavens. He pointed an accusing finger at her. "You killed my brother!"

Tears fell from Sunny's eyes. Fell to the flames at her feet. *Fire and water.*

I loved my boys. I would not hurt them. Nor you, son, she tried to say, but her tongue wouldn't move, and to her horror, appearing in the smoke and flames was Chase's killer, a dark shadow on the prowl, a person she recognized, moving silently, determinedly, ever closer to Brig.

Sunny's heart froze.

The murderer's face was horrible, lips pulled into a cruel smile, eyes that glittered like a snake's, features that were the embodiment of evil.

No! Sunny tried to scream as terror ripped through her soul, but her lips were mute, her tongue unable to form words, and she shuddered with a fear so cold she didn't realize the flames from her small campfire had caught on the hem of her dress. She dropped to the ground and rolled, her legs burned, her heart heavy.

There was little she could do.

She was considered crazy. A lunatic. A witch.

The police wouldn't believe her.

Rex would dismiss her notions.

Even Brig would doubt her if she told him the truth.

It seemed that all of her sons were doomed.

Forty-four

"I can't live a lie." Cassidy stood in the doorway, her suitcase packed, the keys to her Jeep clutched in fingers that didn't seem to feel. The news conference had been an ordeal, telling her parents had been worse. All the while she knew that she was lying about Brig. And Chase. Upon learning that Marshall Baldwin was really Brig McKenzie and that Brig was dead, Rex had sworn, Dena had made comments about good riddance to bad news and Cassidy had felt the biggest hypocrite on earth. Since first talking to Laszlo two days before, she'd told more lies than she could count to the police, her family, her peers and her friends.

She needed time to think. Time to put her life back together. Time to grieve for Chase and time to accept Brig as . . . what? He couldn't pretend to be her husband forever. Someday, and soon, they would have to come clean and then the truth would be out: she'd been living with her brother-in-law, been his lover, while hiding the fact that her husband was dead.

Life with Brig was far beyond complicated. The future seemed murky—her goals confused. He'd lied to her. Over and over again. He'd used her. Pretended he was her husband. Made love to her.

Angry and hurt, she reached for the handle of the door.

"So you're really leaving." Brig's voice stopped her cold. She turned and found him walking toward her, his limp still noticeable, his jaw set and firm. Clean shaven, with only trace lines of his scars, Brig was rugged and handsome, as strong and unapproachable as the mountains in Alaska where he'd lived in his own private hell for seventeen years.

The phone rang, but they ignored it. More reporters. She laughed at the irony of it. How many times had she been on the other end, fingers crossed, praying that her source would pick up so that she could confirm or deny? It seemed so impersonal now.

"Why?" he asked, motioning to the suitcase in her hand.

"I feel like a prisoner here."

"With me?"

"With the lies."

"It won't be much longer," he said, his eyes as clear as a summer's day.

"How do you know?"

His gaze shifted from her face to the corner of her mouth. "I know."

"Brig—" She caught herself. She'd tried hard to keep referring to him as her husband, rarely by the name *Chase*—that was too deceitful and somehow disrespectful to him—but she was afraid that she would slip. It was so obvious to her that he was Brig, the differences between him and his brother weren't so much physical as mental, but sooner or later someone would guess the truth.

His jaw worked. His hands opened and closed. His voice, when he spoke, was rough—raw with the internal battle he waged within himself. "I want you to stay."

The house seemed close and silent. The heat from the day had settled in and his gaze shifted to the pulse at her neck—the same pulse that was pounding through her brain.

No! Living with him, under the same roof, would be impossible. She had to get away. While she still could. "I won't tell anyone, if that's what you're worried about. No one will suspect anything anyway. It was pretty much common knowledge that my marriage to Chase was falling apart. This will look only natural, that I stuck by you until you were healed and then we decided to split up."

"Except that we're not married, that part will come out as well."

"Eventually."

"Soon."

She stared into his eyes and wished their lives weren't so complicated—so wrapped in lies. There was a part of her that still loved him, had always loved him, would probably love him until the day she died, and there was a part of her, a purely female part, that responded to him as a man, in the most primal of ways. That part couldn't be trusted. Staying with him would be begging for disaster. She had no choice but to leave. "I just need to sort things out."

"You'll be back?" He didn't bother hiding the hope in his voice.

Her heart nearly broke. "I don't know. I hope so."

She opened the door, intent on leaving for . . . where? Her parents' home? A fleabag of a motel in a big city where she could rethink her life and stare at the ceiling? An old friend's home in Seattle? Selma's apartment by the river? One of the houses her father owned on the West Coast? She didn't know. Because, for the second time in her life, she didn't belong. Not in Prosperity. Not with Brig. Now without him.

Somewhere in the distance a dog barked loudly, and farther away a siren wailed.

"Good-bye, Brig." She shouldered open the door, but he caught her arm.

"No!" Whirling her to face him, he held her fast. "Don't go, Cass." His throat worked. Emotions from long ago filled his eyes. "I lost you once, I don't want it to happen again."

"But—"

"Oh Jesus. Don't you get it? I love you."

The words ricocheted through the house and reverberated through her mind. *Love.* How long had she waited to hear him say that he cared? A lifetime. "You don't even know me," she whispered.

His fingers clamped down hard. The suitcase tumbled from her hand and thudded against the floor. "I love you as I've never loved a woman, as I never could love another. I love you as no man has a right to love a woman."

"Oh, Brig, you don't mean—"

The look in his eyes was dark and serious. Determined. "I do, Cass. I mean it. I've loved you forever and I'll never stop." Pride angled his chin. "Oh, hell—" Yanking her close, he kissed her roughly. Refusing to be denied. His arms surrounded her and dragged her close, and any protest she felt died on her tongue. Firm, sensual lips, filled with purpose, molded over hers. His hard body felt so right, rigid angles and planes pressed unyielding to hers as he backed her against the wall. Their hips fit snugly. Through the denim of his jeans his erection pressed anxiously against her mound. Her breasts were crushed, the air lost in her lungs as his fingers yanked out the band holding her hair away from her face.

Her keys clattered against hardwood, and she wrapped her arms around him. His kiss deepened and the sensual beast deep in the most feminine part of her stirred and awakened, sending out pulses of heat, creating a moist, hot whirlpool between her legs.

It had always been like this between them. Hot. Needful. Lusty.

With a groan, he lifted his head and stared deep into her eyes. His smoky gaze burned to her very soul. "Don't leave me," he whispered roughly, his thumb tracing her jaw. "Cass, please, don't ever leave me."

"Brig—" She couldn't think as he kissed her again, over and over again. She couldn't see, couldn't breathe, couldn't hear, all she could do was feel. Dear God, she was weak where he was concerned. So damned weak.

With a groan, he lifted his head. "Damn it, Cass," he whispered, "I can't, I won't lose you again. Ever." His fingers curled in her hair, drawing her head back and he brushed his lips against her throat and lower still. She shivered with want as he kissed her between her breasts, on the front of her blouse, leaving a wet impression. She arched closer to him, her body so willing, her mind losing hold fast.

"Stay with me forever." He lifted her from her feet.

Damning herself for her weakness, she clung to him, kissing and touching, exploring and knowing that this time, she was making love to Brig.

With trembling fingers, he stripped her quickly, laid her on the bed she'd shared with Chase and came to her. He kissed her breasts, her navel, her thighs, and she writhed for more, crying out his name, wanting more . . . so much more. All doubts fled as his fingers played magic upon her skin and she welcomed him—into her bed and into her heart. *This is right,* her body screamed. Giving in to the feel of him, she knew that this night was theirs, but as soon as this one ultimate act of lovemaking was complete, she'd walk out of the door, closing it on this man pretending to be her husband.

"I'll be back late," Derrick said. Felicity and the girls were in the family room, watching television—though, from the looks of it, they weren't too interested in the program. Felicity was studying the newspaper in her lap so intently that a deep furrow marred the space between her perfectly plucked brows. Linnie was on the phone, yakking with a friend as always, and Angela, her black thick-soled boots tucked beneath her long legs, was curled in the corner of the couch and wearing a pouty look that he'd seen too many times before. Alternately glancing at a rerun of *Roseanne* or sending a hate-filled look at her mother, Angela sent out vibes that she'd rather be anywhere other than trapped in the house. She and Felicity weren't getting along these days, but then no one was. Felicity had been in one bitch of a mood ever since the interview between Bill Laszlo and Chase.

"Where ya goin'?" Angela asked, arching a dark brow that reminded him of her namesake

"To meet with a client." He shrugged into a jacket and Felicity didn't bother looking up, just gnawed at her lower lip thoughtfully.

Angela leaned forward, suddenly interested. "How old is this client?"

What kind of a question was that? "Hell, I don't know," Derrick replied, patting his pocket to make sure he had his cigarettes.

"What sex?"

"Excuse me?" Derrick said, then caught the mean little glimmer in his daughter's eyes. So much like Angie.

"Is your client male or female?"

"Last I heard, Oscar Leonetti was decidedly male. I don't think he's had an operation to change that."

"So where's the meeting?" she asked innocently.

Felicity looked up from the paper she'd been reading and stared at her husband.

Derrick wanted to squirm under his daughter's calculating stare. "In Portland. At the Heritage Club."

"I can reach you there?" Felicity asked, and Derrick nodded. The members and staff of the Heritage Club always covered for him—as they did for everyone. If anyone in the family was bold enough to phone him, the staff would call him on his mobile and he'd get back to his wife within fifteen minutes. She'd never suspect a thing.

"Does Lorna work for the Heritage Club?" Angela asked.

Felicity's face was suddenly pale.

Derrick's heart jolted. *Don't panic.* "Don't know. She could be a waitress or a hostess. They come and go." How the hell did Angela know about Lorna? Coincidence? He didn't think so—not if the nasty little gleam in his daughter's eye could be believed.

"Oh. Well, you might want to look her up, 'cause she called earlier today. Said she had a package for you."

"A delivery?" Derrick said, thinking fast. Lorna was getting desperate. And bolder. Calling the house was dangerous, stupidly so.

"Photographic equipment, I think she said." Angela smiled at her father then tossed her hair from her eyes. She knew what she was doing and it made him sick inside. Somehow his daughter had found out about him.

"I'll be damned." Felicity's eyes closed for a second and she shook her head.

Derrick was in a panic. She knew, too.

"I can't believe no one else has figured it out." Felicity's face was taut, white lines of rage rimming her lips.

"What?" Angela asked, delight etched in her pretty young features. "Figured out what?"

"Nothing." But Felicity, newspaper in hand, was on her feet and she headed for the den. "I think you should see this," she said out of the corner of her mouth and Derrick had no choice but to follow. That was the problem with his marriage. Felicity insisted on running the show and she was forever leading him around, nagging and telling him what to do. Calling him spineless. Forcing him to go to boring parties. Inviting friends of her father's and his over for dinner and a rousing political discussion which he hated. It was as if he had a damned ring in his nose attached to a chain that Felicity could yank at her whim. He thought of Lorna with her big, soft tits. Right now they were a turn-off, and he realized she'd been setting him up for months, offering up her daughter as bait, planning his seduction and videotaping it. And he'd fallen for it.

Felicity closed the door to the den behind her and Derrick waited, knowing the bomb was about to be dropped. Maybe that was for the best. It was time to quit hiding and lying.

"Chase isn't Chase," she whispered, her eyes bright.

"What?" Now what was she talking about? Again his heart threatened to give out on him. He rubbed his thumb nervously against his index finger.

"I knew something was wrong," she said, almost to herself, as if she were plotting again. Her eyes narrowed slightly. "I picked up on it right away during that damned interview. Cassidy looked like she'd seen a ghost and Chase . . . well, he wasn't himself. Chase is dead. He's got to be."

"Hey—wait a minute," Derrick said, not following her reasoning, but relieved, that for now, she didn't appear to know his dirty little secret. "You're talking in circles. What do you mean Chase isn't Chase?"

"I can't believe you're so blind. Everyone's so damned blind!" Shoving the newspaper under his nose, she said,

"See for yourself. Marshall Baldwin might have been an alias for Brig McKenzie, but now he's got a new one. That bastard is impersonating his brother."

He was starting to understand. "You think Chase is really Brig?" God, she'd really flipped.

"Yes! Yes! Just look!" She wagged the paper under his nose. "I knew it!" A smug smile crossed her lips. "Damn but it's good to be vindicated."

Derrick snatched the newspaper from her outstretched fingers and stared at the pictures in disbelief. Of course there was a resemblance, but it seemed she was making one helluva leap. "How would you know? They looked so much alike."

"But they weren't twins, for God's sake. Sure they looked the same, and their speech patterns and voices were similar, but their *attitude* was different. The way they walked or looked at you or the rest of the world for that matter. At first I thought it was because of the fire—that Chase was talking a little differently because of all the surgery to his face or seeing things in a new perspective because he had a near-death experience that really shook him up, but that didn't explain the attitude. That cocksure son-of-a-bitching attitude that I've noticed lately.

"And Cassidy. She'd done a one-eighty. Remember, right before the fire, she was going to walk, divorce Chase and never look back? Remember how Chase never gave her the time of day in the last couple of years? At first I thought that your dear little sister had a change of heart or felt some guilty feelings of obligation because her husband nearly bought it—or it was possible that she was just trying to save face so the whole town wouldn't think she was just a cold-hearted rich bitch who would divorce a cripple. That explained why she was sticking around. But it's more than that. She's not filing for divorce because she's with Brig and I told you she always had a thing for him. I'm surprised I didn't see it right away," she added angrily, obviously furious with herself.

Derrick stared at the pictures in the paper. Deep in his

bones, he felt it—that tiny drop of dread that told him Felicity was right.

"I just wish I'd figured it out earlier," she rambled on, "but I didn't really understand what was going on until I saw him talking with Laszlo. He was too cool. Too relaxed. Not even bothering with a tie. That wasn't Chase—not pinstripe and button-down Chase McKenzie. I knew it, damn it!" She seemed pleased with herself for her cleverness, and Derrick had to hand it to her, she'd always been sly and perceptive. Hadn't she managed to trap him? "Why do you think Baldwin is always pictured with a full beard, hmm? It was a damned disguise—just in case!"

"I'm not sure—" Derrick lied, sick to his stomach. If what Felicity was saying were true, all hell was about to break loose.

"Look, for Christ's sake!" she said, ripping the newspaper from his hands and placing it on the desk. She pointed a brightly tipped nail at the picture of Baldwin. "It's Brig, god-damn it! And Cassidy's protecting him. Just like before."

"She didn't—"

"Oh, Derrick, grow up. Of course she did. She was the last one to see him all those years ago, wasn't she?"

"Yes, but—"

"And he took off on her horse, her precious Winchester."

"Remmington," Derrick said automatically.

"Whatever. It doesn't matter. He's back. He's with your sister. And he's up to no good. That lying piece of white trash is up to no damned good." She should have still been furious, but she grinned, as if she had a secret.

For the first time in months, Derrick agreed with his bitch of a wife. He hated Chase McKenzie, true, but Chase was smart enough to know his place. Always scratching and climbing and pursuing the damned American dream, but deep in his heart Chase knew, realized, that there was the inevitable fact of birthright. He could go to the finest schools, become a lawyer, marry a rich man's daughter, and bullshit his way up the ladder, but there were rungs unavailable to him by virtue of his poor background that included being born to a trampy half-breed mind reader and a flake of a father. But Brig. He was different. The muscles in the back of Derrick's neck cramped. Brig didn't know the rules. He didn't give a shit about the privileges awarded at birth.

"Do you know what this means?" Felicity said, her eyes gleaming.

"No—I—"

"He's back for only one reason, Derrick. To clear his name."

"But he can't. He killed Angie." His confidence faltered though he'd said it so often that he almost believed it. Almost. The old jealousy burned through Derrick's blood. When he thought of Angie and Brig, a hot rage blistered his mind. But Felicity knew something. "Didn't he?"

"So all we have to do is turn him in to the police," she said though he could tell by the way her eyes narrowed she was looking at the problem from all sides. He admired Felicity for her shrewdness. She was a thinker, always considering the big picture and his future—their future. "He is a fugitive, you know."

"If he killed Angie."

"Not only killed Angie, Derrick, but her baby as well." The smile fell off her face and her mouth worked.

"You don't know—"

"That the kid could have been yours? Give me some credit, will you? The baby was either Brig McKenzie's, your father's, Jed Baker's or yours." She frowned because she didn't have a sure answer. "My guess, because I know you so well, my love, was that the child was yours."

"Are you crazy? What the hell are you saying? That Angie slept with Brig—"

"Yes! She was slumming. For a purpose. I couldn't figure it out at first, but eventually, I got the picture."

"What picture—?" he asked, not really wanting to hear her explanation.

"She needed a patsy. Someone she could blame. And not someone upstanding and certainly not her own brother or father . . ." Felicity's face twisted in an old, painful rage. "She was pregnant and she couldn't let anyone know, so she had to seduce someone of less than high moral standards, someone whose reputation was already so black no one would believe him if she cried rape."

Derrick just stared at her, stunned. "She was setting Brig up, you think."

"Oh, she was attracted to Brig, who wouldn't have been? He was a sexy son of a gun, the sexiest man in this town. He attracted everyone."

"Including you?" Derrick asked, not wanting to hear this. For years he'd hated Brig and had thought he was out of his life forever. But he'd always been nearby, teasing the edges of Derrick's conscience, and when Cassidy had married Brig's brother, Derrick had seen his old nemesis again. But Chase knew his place and . . . Shit—Felicity was right. Just recently hadn't Chase leaped over his desk and tried to beat the living tar out of him when provoked? Derrick had thought it odd at the time. Chase wasn't known for his temper, at least not in recent years. He always handled things civilly, through words and the courts, his anger honed to do more damage than just the physical. But Brig, he'd always been a hothead, unafraid of jumping in over his head as long as his fists were flying. Cold certainty settled in Derrick's guts. What the fuck was Brig McKenzie doing back in Prosperity? Felicity was talking again . . . what was she saying?

"Attracted to Brig? Me? Only in a purely primal way, and that's never been enough for me. Remember, darling, I had you. I didn't mess with Brig McKenzie or Jed Baker or Bobby Alonzo or any of the boys who would have been glad to score with me. Because I was faithful. Always have been, always will be. The daughter of one of the most respected judges in this state!" Her face showed lines of age and despair. "Unlike you, I don't need to rut like a goddamned animal. You've never been true to me."

He didn't argue; there was no point.

"Anyway," she went on, fighting tears, "for some reason,

Angie was hell-bent on getting laid by Brig. I could never figure out why she was so anxious. Any boy in the county would have gladly humped—"

"Don't!" Derrick grabbed her roughly and threw her up against the wall, her head slamming against the plaster. "Don't talk like that about her!"

"And don't you hit me!"

"You're belittling Angie and—"

"For the love of God, Derrick, can't you face the truth?" Her breath was shaking and she sniffed loudly. "I'm just explaining that Angie needed a man she could name as the father of her baby." Felicity's face was red, her eyes bright. "Unless it really was Brig's."

Derrick closed his eyes. He nearly passed out, but he shook his head. "No."

"Your father's?"

"I—I don't think so. Much as he wanted her, I think Rex never . . . I really don't think he touched her. Ever. Even though he wanted to. He, uh, he . . . he found other women." He dropped his arm, and Felicity slumped against the wall.

"But not you, huh, baby? Tell me the truth, Angie was pregnant with your child, wasn't she?" she asked in a little voice, a voice hoping that he would deny the truth, even though she seemed certain of it.

He blinked hard. "Maybe." His voice was rough. "She was scared. So scared. The baby—well, it might not be right and she didn't believe in abortion and . . ."

Felicity's jaw trembled and scorn curled her lip. "I thought so!" Tears spilled from the corners of her eyes. "You bastard," she whispered. "You fucking bastard! You were two-timing me, cheating on me, so that you could ball your own sister!" She recoiled from him as if he were suddenly vile. "The least you could have done was deny it. Blame it on your father! Or blame it on Brig! Blame it on anyone!"

"I have. For seventeen years," he said, and then he knew what he had to do. He turned, heard her cry out, but ignored her. With renewed determination he retraced his steps—taking the same path as he had seventeen years before. True, he was in a different house, but the gun closet stood near the back door and he only stopped for shells before unlocking the cabinet and pulling out his favorite rifle—the one that had felled so many bucks and does and fawns.

"No!" Felicity, following him, saw the Winchester and shook her head. "You can't—"

"I've got no choice."

"Don't do this, Derrick. I've handled it—it's already taken care of—" She threw herself at him, but he flung her off easily. She was sly but small and he liked that about her, that he could push her around. She hit the wall, but was back on her feet. "You don't know what you're doing."

He slid the shells into the chamber, slammed the rifle closed with a loud click.

"Derrick, please, don't do anything rash." She was panicking now and he liked the frantic look that came to her green eyes whenever she was scared—for in those moments he had absolute power over her, over everyone who cringed before him.

"I've had it in for that bastard for years."

"But you can't—think of the girls." She scrabbled for the gun, but he yanked it away and heard her yelp as one of her acrylic nails ripped off.

"Mommy?" Linnie was suddenly in the hall. Derrick froze. "What's—Daddy, oh no—"

"Honey, it's all right," Felicity said as Derrick saw his older daughter, the spitting image of his dead sister, round the corner.

"Oh, my God, what's going on?" Angela stared at the rifle and her throat worked.

"Nothing—Daddy's just a little upset," Felicity said, sniffing and smoothing her hair. "Come on, Derrick, you're scaring the girls, put the gun away and—"

"You mean he beat you. Again." Angela's face showed her contempt. "You're disgusting," she said to her father, echoing the same words he'd told himself after the first time he'd been with his sister, down by the creek, so intent on feeling her heat surround him that he hadn't noticed the figure on the other side of the willow fronds—Cassidy? Willie? At the time he hadn't cared, all he'd wanted to do was lose himself in the seductive moist warmth of Angie. Her big breasts, her tiny waist, her triangular thatch of dark curling hairs at the apex of gorgeously formed legs and eyes so blue and round that when he thrust into her they widened in ecstasy and horror at the forbidden passion of the act. He'd taken her virginity roughly and she'd given it, oh, so sweetly. Even now, thinking about that, when they'd both crossed over the line together, he got hard.

He'd told himself that it would only happen once, that the vodka he'd stolen from his father's liquor cabinet had confused him, that he was messed up because he'd seen his mother as she'd died and Angie looked so much like her and was sexy as hell to boot. But he hadn't been able to stay away and she'd wanted it—hell, she'd practically begged for it, holding him, kissing away his tears, loving him as no other woman had . . .

He sniffed and realized that he was crying, deep tears of shame trickling from his eyes. Angie had made a fool of him in the end, flirting with every boy, trying like hell to seduce Brig McKenzie—oh, she threw that in his face often enough. She'd grown tired of Derrick and was looking for new blood and there was this problem with the baby . . . as soon as she could name someone else as the father, she was going to walk away from him. Leave him. When he loved her, with all of his heart. He couldn't let her go . . . couldn't. She was his.

"Don't," Felicity begged, bringing him sharply back to the here and now. Felicity's face was already starting to bruise where he'd slammed her up against the wall. "Derrick, it's all taken care of." She lifted a hand and glanced at her daughters. "Just don't."

He didn't hear another word, just curled his fist over the stock of his Winchester. He slammed out of the house, his mind on Brig and how Angie had suddenly fixated on the boy from the wrong side of the tracks, how she'd flirted with him, pranced around in nothing, hoping to seduce the bastard. Hoping to find an escape from her possessive brother.

Throwing his rifle onto the seat, he climbed into his truck.

Felicity ran from the house, yelling at him, hanging on by her fingers to his door. "Don't, Derrick. Please. You don't have to do anything. He won't bother you anymore; no one will—"

He flicked on the ignition, slammed his rig into reverse and tromped on the accelerator. She was flung from the truck, stumbling against the asphalt.

"Derrick!" she screamed.

The gears clicked again, tires squealed as he found first and roared past her, so close that she jumped back. Her face was white as the moon overhead, her eyes frantic. But he didn't give a good goddamn. Not now. Not when McKenzie was finally in his sights. Scowling darkly, intent on doing serious, permanent damage, he reached for his cigarettes and shook one out. He slapped at the lighter and flicked on the radio.

". . . and now, in our continuing tribute to Elvis, one of his chart busters . . ." the announcer said before the first notes of "Love Me Tender" sifted through the speakers. *It was fitting somehow*, Derrick thought, as the lighter clicked and he took a long, lung-burning drag from his Marlboro. As Elvis crooned the very song that had been playing when his mother had taken her last breaths, the barrel of his rifle gleamed in the green reflection of the lights from the dash.

Derrick smoked and thought about the night ahead of him. He'd teach that white-trash prick a thing or two and he'd deal with Lorna the same way. Maybe, if he was lucky, he'd run into his half brother, the retard, and scare the shit out of him again.

Derrick chuckled deep in his throat while tears stood in his eyes. It was time they all learned that no one, *no* one, fucked with Derrick Buchanan.

* * *

I had to work fast. Things were spinning out of control and that would never do, not after everything I'd worked for, everything I'd planned.

I drove to the old garage and, after donning surgical gloves, held a flashlight in my mouth and used my key to open the rusted dead bolt. There was a combination lock as well, clipped to old brackets. I dialed the numbers that no one thought I knew, and the old door swung open. The smell of dust, old rubber and oil filled my nostrils as I hurried past the car—once considered a classic—Lucretia's Thunderbird— the one Rex had never had the heart to sell and had sequestered in this old, unused, hundred-year-old garage, out of Dena's sight and, apparently, her mind as well. I glanced at the once-gleaming machine in which Lucretia had died and bile climbed up the back of my throat. Lucretia. Just one more beautiful, self-serving bitch.

The car was covered in a thick layer of dust, and as far as I knew, no one had paid it any attention since the police had released it. The odometer reading was the same as when Lucretia had died, and I wondered if the old Elvis tape was still in the player. *Love me tender,* my ass.

I made my way past the old T-Bird and ignored it. I didn't have time for any ridiculous, maudlin memories, not when everything was falling apart. No, no, not falling apart, I thought desperately. It would be all right. I would make it all right. Didn't I always?

At the back of the garage, under what had once been a workbench, I bent down and opened a cupboard. I heard the scrape of tiny claws. Beady eyes caught in the flashlight's glare, then a scrawny rat scurried out of the cabinet and across the floor to hide beneath the car. "Shit," I swore, nearly dropping the flashlight, then bit my tongue and counted to ten to calm my jittery nerves.

The rat was a good sign. It was obviously not used to being disturbed. No one had been here since the last time I'd visited. I was safe. I took a deep breath and went to work.

Using the thin beam of the flashlight for illumination, I peered past the tools that had been long forgotten in the cupboard. Everything was as I'd left it. Tucked behind a box of ancient wrenches, wrapped in old newspaper, I found the device I'd put together less than a week ago, a simple little bomb with a detonator, timer and short fuse.

Just like me, I thought. I was self-aware enough to know that I could be mercurial, like the detonator, ready to go off at a second's notice; I was as patient as the timer, waiting for everything to be set; and I had a short fuse, my temper legendary. But I could control it.

As I could control everything.

As I would take care of things tonight.

I stashed the unassembled bomb in my athletic bag, then walked out of the old garage. Using a broom by the door, I swept away my path, just in case my boots made any impressions in the dust and grit upon the floor.

Flipping off the flashlight and placing it into the bag, I slunk outside, spent a minute making certain no one was nearby and cast one look up the hill, over the tops of the tall fir trees to the Buchanan house, nearly half a mile away. A few lights still glowed in Rex's castle. The security lamps.

Carefully, I hid my bag under the seat of the pickup and slid behind the steering wheel. My hands were sweaty in the gloves, my hair damp, adrenaline firing my blood.

Everything I'd worked for had come to this.

I imagined the coming explosion. The deadly flames. The intense, hellish flames. And the screams. The final screams that came with imminent, painful death.

Yes!

My skin tingled and I glanced in the rearview mirror to see the glint of excitement in my reflection. *At last,* I thought, conjuring up images of burned, seared flesh, faces twisted in agony, secrets dying with those who had burned.

I licked my lips in anticipation and jammed the truck into gear.

I couldn't wait.

Forty-five

The woman looked like hell. Leaves and dirt stuck in her hair and skirt, and she looked like she'd been wandering around the woods for weeks. "So, let me get this straight," T. John said as Sunny sat in his office cradling a cup of herbal-friggin' tea and waiting for the meal the detective had ordered for her. "You started the fire to contact me. And that's why you lit the other little campfires we've found in the woods."

"Yes." She sipped from her cup and looked as if she might pass out. She'd refused medical treatment despite the burns on her legs.

"Next time use a phone. AT&T is a lot safer than a forest fire."

She wasn't going to listen to a lecture, he could see it in her eyes. She was babbling again, half in some kind of Native American tongue, the rest in English. What he could make from it was that she was afraid.

"He'll be hurt, maybe even killed," she said, her voice shaking, her dark eyes scored with pain.

"Who? Your son."

"Both of them! Buddy and Brig."

"Now, wait a minute, I thought you understood that Brig was already dead," he said and knew he was going to have to call the doctors over at her hospital and have her committed again. She was completely out of touch with reality and though she didn't seem in pain, her legs looked like hell. She dropped her cup, the hot tea spilled on her lap and she didn't seem to notice, just closed her eyes and rocked back and forth as if in some kind of trance. It gave T. John the willies. He reached for his smokes. He'd seen a lot of charlatans in his time. Fakes who bilked people out of their money by saying they were psychics, but only a few had been clairvoyant and those guys were scary—damned scary. He didn't like the thought of anyone seeing into his damned future. Sunny might just be one of those. Or she was nuts—certifiably crazy.

The high-pitched chanting was more than he could take. He lit up and felt the smoke curl comfortingly in his lungs.

A knock on the door announced the arrival of food from the deli next door, ham sandwiches and potato chips, but Sunny didn't appear to notice, just kept chanting. Brig's name and Buddy's name kept coming up. Over and over again. But never Chase. Never once Chase.

"What's this?" Gonzales asked, staring at her.

"She's out of it. Thinks there's big trouble for her sons, but get this, she's not worried about Chase. Just Buddy and Brig."

"I thought Brig was Baldwin."

"He was." T. John picked up half a sandwich and took a bite, but he barely tasted the ham, mustard or onions because his mind was turning, like stripped gears running faster and faster. For the first time he understood. "Hell!" He felt a shiver, as if an icy finger had slid down his spine. "You don't think we gave the wrong McKenzie brother a death certificate, do you?"

"What? Are you crazy?" Gonzales said, but then stared at the old woman.

T. John was on his feet. "Have Doris come in and stay with her and we'll go chat with McKenzie."

The chanting stopped. "I'm coming with you." Sunny was instantly as lucid as he was. Hell, was the whole psychic mumbo jumbo chanting thing some kind of an act?

"No way."

"These are my sons we're talking about, Detective. *My* sons. Their lives are in danger and I'm coming with you.

Now, let's not waste any more time." She grabbed her damned cane and stuffed a whole sandwich into her pocket before she headed through the door. In the hallway, she stopped short. "Oh, God," she whispered, leaning heavily against the wall. "It's . . . it's too late." She stared blankly ahead and her face was twisted in horror. "Oh no, no, no! Brig! Brig!" She began screaming wildly and T. John called for help. "Get her to the hospital, pronto," he yelled as Officer Doris Rawlings hurried from her desk.

"No! Oh, God no! They're burning. *Burning!*" She was sobbing and screaming hysterically. T. John felt as if pure evil had oozed into the room.

"Take care of her!" he ordered Doris as he pointed at Sunny. "We're going out to Chase McKenzie's. Might need a backup. I'll call."

"Gotcha." Doris approached Sunny, who was wailing, scratching at the walls and herself as if she were in physical pain.

"Death . . . he's going to die. My baby is going to die!"

T. John left her and ran down the hall. His boots rang loudly and he was already breathing hard, his usually tough as old leather insides turning to water. God, she was creepy with all that singsong nonsense, burnt dress, silver hair and eyes as horrified as if she'd seen the very devil himself. T. John Wilson was as scared as he'd ever been in his life. Flinging open the door, he headed for his cruiser with Gonzales on his heels. He caught the first plaintive scream of a siren.

"Shit, man, the fire engines!" Gonzales said, and T. John heard it then, the low honk of horns, rumble of engines, scream of tires and as he looked to the east, toward the mountains, he saw a glow of orange light in the darkness.

"Get in!" he barked and started the engine, throwing the car into reverse before Gonzales even shut his door. With a sinking feeling, he wheeled out of the lot, the cruiser's siren howling, its lights flashing.

No doubt Sunny was right. He was already too late.

* * *

Creeping between the bushes, aided only by moonlight, I set the timer on the detonator, then slunk back to the lake. Chase Buchanan's house was about to be history. I looked around the grounds, so perfectly manicured, and that stupid man-made lake that he'd dug shimmered in the moonlight.

From beneath a fir tree I gazed over the entire compound . . . the house, stable, farm, garage, tended acres as well as the lake, as if he deserved all of this, as if by marrying Cassidy Buchanan he could become a rightful heir, a pretender to the throne.

Well, he got his, didn't he, just as Angie had. I smiled when I thought of that fire and Angie's terror and Jed's; the blowhard deserved his fate. As had Chase McKenzie . . . and now Brig and Cassidy. I'd even taken care of the stupid dog.

In a few minutes' time . . . but it wasn't enough for me to drive away as the explosion rocked through this fake, sorry little estate. I wanted to see. To watch.

Why not start now?

The grass was summer dry . . .

Smiling to myself, I took out my lighter and, as the wind picked up, flicked it. A tiny flame shot upward and I bent down, touching it to the white blades of grass near the lake, seeing that the flames, blocked by the water, would creep, crackle and grow toward the house.

Pushed by a west-blowing breeze, they spread hungrily over the ground, heading toward the house.

Toward Brig.

Toward Cassidy.

Cassidy's heart was heavy. She'd left Brig in bed. Asleep. With only a quick note of explanation. She'd kissed his temple, then tried to say good-bye to Ruskin, but the dog had wandered off. Strange—he'd always stuck around before, lying on the porch near the front door. It bothered her a little, but she really didn't know what his nocturnal habits were yet.

She drove by instinct, not really knowing where she was going, just that she had to get away. The ring on her finger seemed to wink in the darkness, mocking her. "Oh, Chase," she whispered, feeling every bit the betrayer. She'd cared for him, yes, and been faithful to him but she'd never loved him, not like she loved Brig. "Fool." Her fingers tightened over the wheel and she turned toward town. Toward Prosperity.

Why are you leaving? Brig's the man you always wanted and now he's yours. He loves you. He said he loves you. Why are you leaving?

"Because I have to. I'm Chase's wife."

Not anymore. Chase is dead. You didn't kill him. Brig didn't kill him. It just happened. You love Brig! Why the hell are you leaving?

"I have to." She looked in the rearview mirror, saw her own eyes and eased up on the gas pedal.

You're leaving because you're scared, Cassidy Buchanan. Scared of loving too much, scared of admitting that Brig has always owned your heart, scared of a future that you've never dared dream about. Face it, Cass, you're a chicken-shit!

"Oh, God!" She stood on the brakes and the Jeep swerved, tires skidding and screeching sideways over the center line. With a shudder the rig stopped and she looked into the rearview mirror again, staring into her own eyes. *You've never run away from a fight in your life, Cassidy McKenzie, and you're not going to start now.*

She loved Brig. He loved her. Nothing should come between them. Whatever fate threw their way, however they felt about Chase's death, they could deal with it. Resolve the past. Face the future. Together! Joy touched her heart, then held on tight. She'd get back before he opened an eye, and when he did, when dawn shone on their faces, she'd tell him how much she loved him. And then she'd show him.

Cranking on the wheel, she rammed her foot hard on the accelerator. With a lurch, the Jeep turned back toward her house, and that's when she noticed it, the orange glimmer on the horizon, the sickening golden light that shouldn't exist at this time of night.

Her heart froze and her breathing stopped for a second. No! It couldn't be! "Please God, no."

She knew in her heart that something was horribly wrong, but she wouldn't believe that another fire was burning, raging at her house . . . oh, God, please not Brig!

"Get out of bed, you bastard." The click of a rifle being cocked filled the stillness of the room.

Cassidy? Where was Cassidy?

Brig lifted his head, and fear curled like a fist in his gut. He was staring down the barrel of a high-powered rifle, and Derrick Buchanan was at the other end, his finger curled over the trigger. "I should've done this a long time ago."

"What are you talking about?" All of Brig's senses snapped to life. The room was warm but cold fear slid down his spine, and all he could see was the rifle pointed at his head. But Cassidy wasn't with him. Thank God. Unless . . . unless Derrick had already found her.

"Put your pants on, McKenzie," Derrick spat, his face twisted in a hatred so intense that Brig recoiled. His mouth was dry as sand and he could barely breathe and the room, though dark with the curtains drawn, seemed brighter than it should be. Hotter. Smelling of fear. Where was the dog? Slowly, so as not to disturb Cassidy's brother, Brig stepped into his jeans, but stayed on the balls of his feet, ready to move if he had to.

"Where's Cassidy?" he demanded.

Derrick lifted a shoulder. "Never could keep track of your women, could you?"

"She was here." She had to be safe. She had to. The burning fear increased.

"Well, she isn't anymore. Her Jeep's gone. Shit, loverboy, you ain't got no one to call for help."

Relief flooded through him. If Cassidy was safe, he didn't

care. Nothing else mattered and he didn't think Derrick was lying, not now. He was too focused on his hatred of Brig and would have loved to make Brig think he'd already harmed her.

"And as for that dog of yours, he must've found himself some rat poison or taken off with Cassidy, 'cause he's not around. Lucky for me. I hate mongrels. Especially half-breeds."

His eyes turned dark, and Brig felt his muscles tense. He wanted to grab the gun and ram the barrel against Derrick's throat and strangle the bastard, but it was a no-win situation; Derrick would blow him away first, so he held back, thinking, trying to buy himself some time.

Cocking his head toward the door, Derrick, sweating, snarled, "How's it feel, screwing both my sisters?" His eyes were slits, and a black, deadly fury radiated from him.

"What?"

Derrick waved the gun toward the doorway, and Brig got the message. He understood that he was supposed to lead Derrick out of the bedroom. Heart pumping, adrenaline spurting through his veins, he entered the hall.

"Why don't you tell me who's better—Angie or Cassidy? I always wondered. Never had a piece of Cassidy myself."

"Shut up!"

"You're not giving orders, McKenzie." The end of the rifle, cold steel against warm skin, pressed into his bare torso, reminding him who was in charge.

Brig's mind was whirling. There wasn't a sign of Cassidy except for the note that was propped on the nightstand. The note Derrick hadn't seen. So maybe Derrick was telling the truth and she was safe. Sending up a prayer to a God he hadn't believed in for years, Brig hoped that Cassidy had decided to take off and was far away.

"Move it!"

Hands over his head, he walked barefoot along the corridor. The floor, usually cool, was warm. He heard horses neighing as if in fear. Something was wrong, out of sync. More than Derrick's rifle . . . "What's this all about?"

"I know who you are, Brig. Well, Felicity figured it out, really."

Brig's bones turned to ice, but still he was sweating, and he saw the first flickering shadows of orange light beyond the drawn curtains.

"She thinks that we should wait for the police, let them arrest you for Angie and Jed's murder, but I'm not sure that would be such a good idea."

"Because you set the fire that killed Angie?" *Fire!* That was it! Oh, Christ, another fire! Derrick had already lit another blaze—outside the house. So what was he doing inside?

"Hell, no. I didn't kill her. Believe it or not, McKenzie, you'll be my first, and I gotta tell you, I'm lookin' forward to it." The barrel of the gun slammed into his bare back and Brig stumbled slightly before catching his balance. "I'd never do anything to hurt Angie. Even if she was ballin' every boy in town."

"Including you?"

"She was mine, damn it!" Derrick's voice was rough. "Mine. We lost our mother, got shut away from our father when he married that bitch Dena. Angie and me. We were a couple."

Smoke curled through an open window, but Derrick didn't seem to notice. Brig coughed.

"What about you and Felicity?"

Again the gun prodded into his back. Brig was sweating now. It was so damned hot. Heat seared in through the windows, and as they rounded a corner and faced the back of the house, he saw it—in all its crackling, satanic fury. Angry flames whipped by the wind, racing through the grass near the lake, charring the bark of the old walnut tree, creeping steadily forward toward the house and the stable. "What the devil are you trying to pull, Buchanan?" he said, trying to sound calm, when inside he was panicking. "Call the fire department."

"The what?" Derrick must have finally seen the blaze, smelled the scent of smoke. The high squeal of terrified horses, thudding hooves and the distant cry of a siren swept into the room finally and pierced his brain. "Holy shit. What the hell's going on?" he said, as if mesmerized by the flames. "I didn't see—"

Brig, feeling the barrel move slightly, a slackening between cold metal and his sweat-soaked back, dived to the side. He scrambled on the floor, moving through the darkness, running as fast as his feet would carry him.

"Hey! Stop!" Derrick yelled, stumbling slightly. "You fucking bastard, I'm gonna kill you—"

Crouching, Brig sprinted through the house, toward the front door, but he was slow. His bad leg was like a dead weight and pain screamed up his thigh.

He reached the knob and pulled, but Derrick caught up with him. Yanked him back inside. Brig was ready. His fist doubled and he smashed Derrick in the face, hitting him square in the nose. Blood spurted. "Son of a bitch—" Derrick clamped a hand over the squash that had been his nose.

Brig nailed him again. A left cross that crunched bones and snapped Derrick's head back. Blood sprayed on the walls and splattered Brig's chest.

The rifle clattered to the floor. A window in the back of the house burst from the heat. Glass shattered and sprayed, and all around the house hot flames crackled and roared.

Brig hurtled through the open door and started running, his bare feet hitting the asphalt that was already warm.

"You can't run away this time, you dumb fuck!" Derrick's voice was hysterical.

Brig dived. The rifle cracked. His body jolted. Pain seared through his side. He slammed hard against the pavement, the skin of his face scraping, blood pouring from his abdomen. The air was hot, unbreathable, and his side burned.

"Ha! Nailed you, you bastard."

Stunned, fighting to stay conscious, Brig started crawling, moving forward, away from the inferno and his brother-in-law.

"Help Brig." Willie's voice was close by. Suddenly, he

was lifted to his feet and dragged toward the woods on the far side of the property. Only fifty yards, but it seemed like a million.

Flames and smoke were everywhere. Heat so intense it waved, seared the breath from his lungs.

"Got to run. Brig. You run." Willie was insistent, propelling him forward, big hands dragging him away from his attacker, away from the fire toward trees not yet devoured by the flames.

"Derrick's mad and it's gonna burn. Gonna burn."

"Two for the price of one," Derrick yelled.

Agilely, Willie dropped to the ground, taking Brig with him. Pain scorched up Brig's leg. The Winchester cracked again and a bullet whizzed above their heads.

"Come on! Hurry!" Willie, his eyes wide with fear, was desperate, yanking on Brig. The woods were closer now, only thirty yards. They could make it. Brig forced his feet to move. A rifle report split the night. With a squeal, Willie fell. His body smacked against the pavement, his head cracking.

"No!" Brig cried.

Air whistled through Willie's lungs.

"Nooooo!" Brig screamed, turning to see Derrick standing on the front porch, the house a burning backdrop of living flames. "It's okay," he said to the dying man. "It's okay, you just hang in there." But blood gurgled from Willie's mouth and nose and drained from the wound in his chest. Brig tried to help him, stanching the flow, but there was just so much blood everywhere. "Willie, hang on!"

Willie's eyes were wide. He stared upward as Brig held him. "Brig," he whispered, blood and spittle spraying.

"Don't talk—"

"Brother. Good."

"Yes, good, Willie."

"She burned."

Cassidy? Oh, God no! "Willie—"

"Felicity—she burned Angie. She burned Chase. She burned you—"

"No, Willie, you don't know what you're saying," Brig whispered. "Don't say anything, okay? Now, hold on. Help will be here—oh, shit no!"

A horrid rattling breath wheezed through Willie's lungs and his blue eyes glazed.

I couldn't tear myself away. God, it was beautiful, the flames crackling through the house, the windows breaking . . . and then I saw Derrick with his rifle. God, no! Not after all I'd been through. He was going to mess things up. Again. He was there with Brig and Willie and . . . and . . . no, this wasn't right. Not after all my planning. All the time I'd put in to see that he inherited everything, that he and I and our girls were the rightful heirs to all the Buchanan holdings . . . Rage tore through me and I started toward the blaze that was roaring wildly, white-hot flames licking the heavens.

"Don't!" I yelled. "Get away . . . Derrick, don't!"

A rifle cracked and everything I'd worked for, all the plans I'd made, died in that horrifying instant.

"No, no, no, you damned fool. Don't!"

But it was too late. Willie Ventura was spitting up blood and Brig McKenzie looked like he would kill Derrick with his bare hands, and Derrick, the fool, stood beneath a burning roof that was about to collapse. "Oh, God, no," I whispered. This couldn't be happening. Not to Derrick. "Run!" I screamed but he just stood there, as if rooted to the porch. If I didn't do something and fast, he too would die a grisly horrid death!

"No!" Brig cried. He held his half brother's head, denying the inevitable. "No!" He glared up at the heavens, at the furious inferno devouring Chase's land, and then his rage turned black and deadly. Fury and vengeance drew an ungodly pact in his mind. "I'll get him," he swore to Willie. "If it's the last thing I ever do, Willie, I'll get him and I'll get him good—"

Coughing, blood pouring from his side, Brig struggled to his feet. Derrick hadn't moved from the porch, seeming unaware or unconcerned about the flames devouring the roof above his head, the ugly smoke surrounding him, the glass spraying as windows shattered. Tinder-dry grass ignited and the fire moved swiftly, demolishing everything in its gruesome path, heading toward the stable and sheds. Somewhere nearby sirens shrieked and deep, bellowing horns honked.

The fire department.

But it was too late. Too damned late.

Deliberately taking his time, Derrick stepped off the porch, the rifle pointed squarely at Brig's chest.

"I think it's time you went directly to hell, McKenzie," Derrick yelled, coughing but fearless and stupidly proud. "And I want you to know that I'm proud to be the one to send you there."

"You murdering bastard, I'll take you with me," Brig growled. He rushed forward. Horses screamed. Tires screeched. Horns blasted and men started running.

"Hey—you!"

"Stop!"

"What the fuck's going on here? Oh, Christ, he's got a gun!"

Derrick squeezed the trigger.

An explosion roared in his ears. Brig took one step forward before the blast hit him, throwing him off his feet, causing fire to spew into the sky and rain down from the heavens. Boards and glass, metal and chunks of concrete flew out from the house.

Brig knew that he was going to die. Blood flowed sticky and hot from his side, and he couldn't get enough air. Smoke clogged his lungs and billowed upward, blotting out the moon. Blackness threatened to take him. He reached up to his neck, his fingers searching for the chain and medal he'd worn so many years and finding nothing.

"Cassidy," he whispered hoarsely. "Oh, God, Cassidy, I'm so sorry." He closed his eyes and her beautiful face swam in his vision. "I love you. I've always loved you . . ."

* * *

As she pulled the Jeep around a huge fire truck, Cassidy stood on the brakes and gazed in horror at the fire, at the house, at Brig. And Derrick on the porch with a gun . . . Oh God.

"Stop!" she yelled, flinging open the door as a blast knocked her back. "Brig!" He flew through the air and landed near the base of an old apple tree. Limp as a rag he slammed into the earth. "No!" she yelled. "Brig, no!"

"Hey, lady, stand back!"

Ignoring one of the firemen, she ran to Brig, heard the final words torn from his lungs over the scream of sirens. "Brig! Brig! I love you!" she cried, falling on her knees beneath the tree and cradling his head in her lap. She kissed him, tasting his blood and sweat, willing life into him. "I love you. I've always loved you. You can't die, damn it, you can't!"

Her voice was drowned by the sirens and engines of a truck that ground to a stop only inches from where she knelt, holding him, praying that he was alive, knowing that she'd loved him all her life. Tears rained from her eyes, despair clutched her soul. "I love you . . . oh, God, I've always loved you."

Men scrambled around her. Firemen, paramedics, policemen and women. Even Felicity, who had appeared and was raving and screaming about Derrick.

"I didn't mean to do it!" Felicity yelled, searching for her husband as a fireman restrained her. "I didn't want to kill him. Not Derrick. Just Brig. He needs to die. Just like Angie! Oh, Christ, please, someone save Derrick!"

"Hold on there. Someone call a policeman over here. Her husband—"

"It doesn't look good. Probably dead."

"No! He can't die! He can't! Just Brig. Oh, God, what have I done?" Felicity screamed. "What have I done?!"

Cassidy glared at this monster of a woman. "I hope you get everything you deserve, and believe me, if the justice system doesn't take care of you, I will!"

"Enough," a policeman intervened. "I think we'd better read this woman her rights."

"Save him—save Derrick. He's—oh, God!"

The fire chief paid her no mind. "Get the number two truck hooked up and spray the stable, three can start on the house—what the hell? Where'd this dog come from?"

"Found him locked up in the stable—looks like he's been drugged or something—"

"You have the right to remain silent—"

The words were dull and fuzzy, other sounds—horses and a dog barking and men shouting—all muted against the dull roar of the fire and the fear that took hold of her heart as she held Brig to her. Brig, the only man she'd ever loved. The man she'd left . . .

Cassidy didn't move, couldn't. Just held him tight.

"Hey, there—" Detective T. John Wilson's hand was heavy on her shoulder. "Let's take a look at him."

Lifting her head, she stared up at the man she'd considered her enemy so long and blinked through her tears. "Save him," she begged. "Please, you've got to save him—"

"The boys in the ambulance, they'll do their best."

"I love him."

"I know you do, darlin'."

"He's—"

"I know that, too. Come on now. We have to work fast. Get him to a doctor." She climbed to her feet though she couldn't feel her legs, or anything else for that matter, and watched as he was placed on a stretcher and carried into the ambulance.

"She's in shock," someone said. "Better get her to the hospital." But she threw off the gentle arm over her shoulders and ignored the stench of smoke and yelling, stepping over hoses and around men as they pumped gallons of water onto the house that Chase had built for her. Instead she insisted on being with Brig, knowing that she might never see him alive again. The ambulance, siren howling, took off. She held his hands in hers, lacing her fingers through his. She couldn't stop her tears, just stared at him, wishing she could relive the last twenty-four hours. "Please, Brig. Wake up and love me." But he was motionless, blood soaking through the bandage they'd wrapped over his side, dirt and sweat covering his face that was again scraped raw of skin from the asphalt where he'd landed.

Tears slid down her face, and the ambulance roared through the night. Couldn't they go any faster? Brig was so pale, looked so near death.

"I love you. Don't you dare die on me, Brig McKenzie," she added, her voice catching. "Swear to God, if you do, I'll never forgive you!"

He moved. Just slightly, but he moved. His eyes blinked open for a minute and he looked at her—straight in the face. "Wouldn't dream of it, Cass," he whispered, his tongue thick.

"Brig!" Her heart leaped.

His hand tightened over hers, giving her strength.

Hot tears spilled from her eyes all over again, and she leaned forward to kiss his scratched cheek. "Don't ever leave me."

"Never," he vowed. "From here on in, it's you and me, kid."

"Promise?"

His gaze held hers before his lids lowered again. "Promise."

Derrick . . . oh, God, not Derrick! I felt tears run down my face and my heart squeezed painfully. This was wrong. So wrong! I was sobbing, unaware of the men shouting, the hoses streaming water, the smell of charred wood. All I could think about was Derrick. "No, no, no!" I railed to the heavens and fell to my knees.

Someone, I didn't know who, pulled me to my feet. Roughly. I blinked and stared into the face of a dark-eyed man with a sharp nose. "Felicity Buchanan, you're under arrest."

"What?" Dazed, the words didn't really sink in.

"For the murder of Angie Buchanan, her unborn child, Jed Baker and Chase McKenzie."

"What?" I finally screamed, trying to pull away. "Are you out of your mind?" The oaf of an officer yanked my arms behind my back and snapped on the cuffs. "Do you know who I am? Who my father is?" I forced some starch into my spine as I felt my world crumbling, the world I'd been born to, the world I'd only tried to improve.

"Yep." He stared at me. "I'm Detective Steven Gonzales with the Sheriff's Department."

I stared him down. "You have no proof."

"What were you doing here?"

Think, Felicity, I told myself, trying to regain some composure. "I . . . I followed my husband. I saw him take the gun and I followed him here." *Yes, that was the story I'd use.*

"I just happened to hear your confession," he said, a smile sliding across his steely jaw. "And I found your truck . . . it's got some interesting things inside. Disguises and electrical equipment. I'm having it impounded."

"Why? No!" I thought of everything in the truck and felt sick inside. "It's registered to my husband!"

"But you were driving it. He came in another vehicle."

"No . . . you've got it all wrong. I . . . I drive a Mercedes."

"Which isn't here."

"But . . ." With me standing, shivering in rage, he slowly pulled out his wallet and began reading from a card.

"You have the right to remain silent . . ."

"You're serious about this?" I screamed, my face flushing. Why hadn't I driven away? Why had I been so fascinated with the fire I'd set . . . because of Derrick. Everything I'd done was for him and now . . . now, he was dead . . . oh, God . . . I think I let out a long, horrid wail of grief. For a brief, painful second I thought of my girls . . . precious babies. I squeezed my eyes closed and shut out the images of my children, of my husband. "Look, you're making a huge mistake here," I said, fighting a rising tide of panic that crept up my spine. "My father is Judge Caldwell. I assume you've heard of him. He'll have your job, your badge and your gun. You'll be railroaded out of Prosperity . . ."

The stupid detective just kept reading, and when he was finished, he looked up at me with dark eyes that glittered in victory.

Fear squeezed my heart and then I saw another man hurry up. Him, I recognized. Detective T. John Wilson.

"You got her," he said to Gonzales.

"Standin' here, watching the whole thing. Screamin' that she didn't mean to kill her husband. Already got her truck, parked on the federal land." He nodded in the direction where I'd hidden the pickup. A sick, horrible sensation swept over me and I thought I might puke.

"We got her," Gonzales said and he grinned.

"What? No," I said, panic taking hold of me. What had I said? I had to backtrack to fix things. "I didn't know what I was saying. I'd just seen my husband die and . . . and . . . I was telling the officer here—"

"He's a detective," T. John said.

"Yes, well, he's making a huge, career-ending mistake." I was blinking back tears, trying to keep my mind on the conversation while grief was ripping me apart. How could Derrick have been so stupid? How could he have died?

"Gonzales doesn't make mistakes," T. John said and his eyes were even colder than his partner's. "It took us a long time to catch you, Mrs. Buchanan, but we've got you, dead to rights. You can tell us all about how you arranged the murders of your best friend, Angie Buchanan, and her baby."

I cringed at the thought of that little unborn bastard. Derrick's bastard.

"And Jed Baker, Chase McKenzie, just to begin with. We were already piecing it together, but your confession a few minutes ago helped a lot."

"My confession? No . . . I was out of my mind with grief. I . . . I didn't know what I was saying . . ."

"Tell it to The Judge," T. John said and I thought for a second it was his pitiful attempt at humor but his face was hard and cold as granite.

"You can't do this!" I yelled as they herded me to a police cruiser and T. John opened the door.

"We're doing it."

"No, you can't." I saw the future then, not the bright, beautiful life I'd planned with Derrick, but years ahead of living in a small cell, alone, or with dozens of women who were criminals . . . oh, no . . . no . . . "You can't," I said, my voice betraying my fear.

Finally T. John smiled. "No?" he mocked as Gonzales protected my head and pushed me inside the car. "Just watch."

Epilogue

Squinting against a lowering sun, Brig pounded a nail into place and listened as a car approached, but the engine wasn't the familiar rumble of Cassidy's Jeep. He waited and a cruiser from the Sheriff's Department slid to a stop in the old lane that his mother had used for years. Sliding the hammer into his tool belt, he cracked his back and walked stiffly to what would eventually be the door of his new house. It was just an open space now, a wider opening between the walls framed with fresh two-by-fours.

T. John stretched out of his car, and Brig steeled himself. He hadn't been able to shake off his distrust of the authorities. After a lifetime of running, his instincts were still on alert every time he saw a uniform. T. John scaled the board that bridged the chasm around the foundation of the new house—his house for Cassidy.

"I thought you might want to see a couple of things." T. John smiled as he surveyed the newly framed walls of a permanent dwelling at the site of Sunny's old trailer. He handed Brig an envelope and black cassette case. Sawdust and nails littered the plywood floors and the roof was half completed, while the joists smelled of freshly cut wood.

"Why—what're they?"

"You might want to return 'em to their rightful owners."

Inside the envelope were two checks, each for a hundred thousand dollars made out to T. J. Wilson. One from Rex Buchanan. One from The Judge.

"Bribes?"

T. John lifted a shoulder. "Could be construed as such."

Cassidy drove up just then and climbed out of the Jeep. Brig couldn't help but smile each time he saw her. She was slim and tanned, no visible evidence yet of the child she was carrying. Their child. His smile widened as she joined them and set a paper bag and small cooler in what would someday be the front hall.

Brig fanned the checks out for her to see.

"I was told to use them for my election campaign or my retirement. Whatever I wanted. But the county takes care of one, and I'm not too worried about the other. Since I solved the two fires and murders, looks like I've become the local hero. Imagine that." T. John smiled as Cassidy glanced at the checks, then handed him a beer.

"I'm on duty."

"It's lunchtime," she said. "And you may as well celebrate, hero."

"Fair enough."

"What's this?" Brig asked, fingering the plastic case.

"Pornography. With Derrick as the star."

"Great." Cassidy sighed. "What're you going to do with it?"

"Give it to The Judge. He wants it, you know. Since Felicity's already serving time, and Derrick's not around anymore, he'd like to destroy all copies. We already nailed the woman who owns it with attempted blackmail, but The Judge, he's afraid there might be more copies around and he doesn't think it would be good for his granddaughters to see it."

"They're doing remarkably well," Cassidy said. "Angela's spending as much time as possible with that boyfriend of hers and Linnie—well, Linnie reads a lot. I told her she could come and live with us, but she seems okay with the Caldwells." Sighing, she said, "She keeps talking about Felicity coming home."

"I don't think so. She's got a crackerjack of an attorney, but it'll be a long time, probably never," T. John said, and Cassidy understood. The evidence against Felicity was overwhelming. She'd learned about incendiary devices from books in the library and years ago, afraid of losing Derrick to his sister, had decided to kill Angie and Brig while they were together to prove to Derrick that his sister was unfaithful, but she'd ended up killing Jed instead.

Cassidy hated to think about it, but she assumed that after Brig wouldn't fall for Angie's attempts at seduction, she needed another man to name as her baby's father. Jed was the choice and happened to be at the wrong place at the wrong time. Years later, the prosecution was presuming, Felicity not only tried to kill Chase, but the company records as well, hoping to hide the fact that Derrick had been embezzling. She hadn't known of Brig then, hadn't realized that Chase was going to meet someone. So she wanted both McKenzie boys killed and had nearly succeeded. She had to set the third fire to finish the job, hoping to kill Chase, but then, realizing he was Brig, thankful that she could get rid of him as well. If the McKenzie boys died, so would all of Derrick's sordid secrets.

"I'm afraid Felicity will never get out, which is fine by me," T. John said. "And she's not the only one. We got Lorna and her ex-husband on some drug charges, so I think they'll willingly cough up the copies of the tape and cop a plea. The Judge won't have to worry. Then he can raise his granddaughters the way he wants."

Brig opened his beer and took a swallow. Cold against the hot of early October. Some of the leaves had already fallen and he worried a little about building the house in the winter, but the roof would be on soon and he didn't really give a damn if the rain and winds tore the whole place apart.

He wondered about Felicity. Though he'd never trusted her, he hadn't considered her as a suspect, not really. Probably because she was so outwardly submissive to Derrick. Brig had been fooled; hadn't expected her to go to such lengths to protect what was hers. How could a woman who was slapped around by her husband commit murder to save her relationship with him? Crazy, that's what it was. Crazy.

"How's your mother?" T. John asked Brig as Cassidy unscrewed the cap of a bottle of iced tea.

"She's gonna live here."

"With you?" T. John's eyebrows shot over the rims of his aviator shades.

"In the guest house. We're building it, too—see over there—" He pointed to a bridge and an excavation site on the other side of the creek.

T. John took a long swallow from his can. "You sure she shouldn't be back in a hospital—"

"She'll be fine," Brig cut in. "Losing Chase was tough, but Ma believes in all things spiritual, seems to think she'll see him in an afterlife or two. Besides, she's got Buddy to take care of."

"He was lucky. We all were," Cassidy said, smiling at Brig.

"Thank God." He rubbed his chin. "Ma also wants to be close to Rex since Dena finally left him."

Cassidy ran her fingers through her hair. "My mother was convinced that he was involved with Angie."

"Jesus," T. John whispered.

"Lots of people thought so," Brig agreed.

"He swears he never touched her, and Sunny backed him up," Cassidy said, staring at the hills in the distance. Her emotions were still jumbled. It was strange to think of her parents divorced and yet she'd known their marriage had never been rock-solid. She only hoped they would be happier now that the ghost of Angie had been laid to rest. "I don't think Dad ever touched Angie, not inappropriately—at least not that I remember. Dad loved her, yes, but his one true love was Lucretia. He just mixed Angie up with her, but not so far as to . . ." She couldn't even say it. Incest. So ugly. Surely if it had happened, she would have known. But then she hadn't guessed about Angie and Derrick—though Rex had. The confirmation of their affair had nearly destroyed him. Thankfully he had Sunny to see him through. At the thought of her half brother and Angie together, Cassidy's stomach turned and she took a quick swallow of tea. Now that she was pregnant, her stomach was often anxious to rid itself of its contents. She noticed that both men were still looking at her, expecting her to say more. "Dad, he was just like every other male in town—half in love with Angie."

"Not every male," Brig reminded her, his grin nearly wicked.

"Okay, not *every* male, but the majority. Anyway, Mom's a lot happier in Palm Springs—away from the scandal and away from all the gossip. No one down there really knows what happened."

Brig winked at his wife. "I think she was afraid that Ma might curse her."

"Oh, you!" Cassidy made a face, but laughed.

The detective's grin stretched to cover the lower half of his face. "I don't really blame Dena. Sunny's different and . . . well . . . that gift of hers—"

"Could come in handy for the next sheriff if he learned to work with her rather than against her," Brig said.

"Humph." T. John downed the rest of his beer and crushed the can in his fist. "I'll think on it."

"Do that."

"Take care." With a wave, he was off, and Brig stared at the videocassette and checks. As the cruiser pulled out of the drive, he winked at his wife, proud that she finally bore his name—Mrs. Brig McKenzie.

She touched her abdomen; they'd already decided on names if their baby was a boy. Chase William McKenzie—sometimes known as Buddy. If they had a girl, she'd probably still bear the nickname of Buddy. It was the least they could do, as Buddy had saved Brig's life.

So much pain, but now, so much happiness. She stared into her husband's devilish gaze and couldn't let grief pull her down. She felt the corners of her lips twitch upward.

"You know, I have a great idea," Brig said, pulling her gently against him.

"Oh?" Cassidy looked at him with those gold eyes that

had touched his soul so many years ago. "Something dangerous?"

"Of course."

"Does it involve disrobing?"

"Definitely." He pulled on her hand and led her down to the basin of Lost Dog Creek, where Buddy had nearly drowned so many years ago. Now, in late autumn, the creek was barely a trickle. Brig kicked some dry leaves and sticks onto the muddy bank, then knelt down. With a wicked glint in his eye, he set the checks and videocassette on his makeshift pyre, adding a couple of squirts of lighter fluid.

"What're you doing?"

"Getting rid of garbage." He flicked his lighter and a flame shot skyward, then he watched as the lighter fluid ignited. Small flames crackled and hissed, devouring the checks. Paper and wood went up in smoke, and the videotape melted from the heat. The smell was ugly, but the fire died a quick death as he kicked dirt over the ashes.

It was over. Finally. His heart ached for Chase, for the years lost in Alaska, but now he was home. With Cassidy. Where he belonged. Forever. A horrid weight had been lifted from his shoulders.

Standing, he slipped his arms possessively around her waist. "Now, wife," he said, savoring the word as the fire smoldered to ashes, "what do you say to initiating our bedroom?"

"It's hardly a room." She turned to look at the framed structure and the opening where French doors would eventually open to a veranda overlooking the creek.

"Do you care?"

Laughing deep in her throat, she asked, "What do you think?"

He stared at her so hard a pink flush stole up her neck. Then he scooped her off the ground and carried her to their house—the home where they would raise their family and live proudly, heads raised over the ugly rumors of their past. Their love had sustained them; their lives would be blessed.

He wouldn't have it any other way. Finally, their lives would be complete.

Brig's lips brushed over hers, and desire sparked to life. "What I think, lady," he whispered against her ear as he dragged her to the floor, "is that I'm the luckiest man on earth."

"Mmmm. Does that make me the luckiest woman?"

He grinned wickedly. "Damned straight."

Dear Reader,

When my publisher asked me to rewrite *Intimacies,* I was delighted, but a little worried. Why? I loved the book in its original form, and I especially loved the characters. The two heroes in the book, Brig and Chase McKenzie, were both very real, complicated, and sexy men. The heroine, Cassidy Buchanan, was a woman I could relate to.

Because I loved this story so much, I wasn't certain it needed rewriting. It was strong as it was. However, once I had sunk my teeth into the project, injecting more suspense into the pages, creating new scenes, adding a deeper understanding of the characters, giving the story a new perspective, I had a blast.

I was raised in a small town in Oregon, so it was a natural to return to Prosperity, a timber town nestled in the foothills of the Cascade Mountains. Though I didn't know anyone like the Buchanans or the McKenzies, I did own a horse and I did run him on the flats of an abandoned, drained pond at an old logging camp, and I did swim him in the river against my parents' warnings.

So, rewriting *Final Scream* was nostalgic for me on two levels. I think the book turned out well.

I hope you enjoyed reading *Final Scream* as much as I did writing it. Let me know what you think of this new, updated version and especially how you feel about the McKenzie boys! Visit me at *www.lisajackson.com.*

And now that you've finished *Final Scream,* I'd like to tell you about my next thriller from Zebra books. *Fatal Burn* will be on the stands in March 2006, and it's the follow-up book to *Deep Freeze,* my March 2005 release.

Fatal Burn is a whirlwind! It starts with the kidnapping of Dani Settler, a clever tomboy of a girl. Dani is at the heart of a deadly scheme. Her abductor is using her as bait, to flush out her biological mother.

Shannon Flannery gave up her baby thirteen years earlier and now she learns that her child is in dire jeopardy. The baby's adoptive father, Travis Settler, has tracked Shannon down, demanded answers, and let her know that he'll do anything to get his daughter back. He's suspicious, worried, and sexy as hell.

The man behind the abduction, a cruel killer, has his own agenda, one that involves Shannon, her brothers, and a secret so dark it's been buried for years.

What the kidnapper doesn't count on is the tenacity, brains, and slyness of Dani Settler. She's not about to sit around meekly while some creep decides her fate.

Fatal Burn is an exciting, roller-coaster of a story with characters that have stayed with me for months after writing the book. I think you'll like them. Visit *www.lisajackson.com* for more information about the book. While you're at my website, e-mail me and let me know what you think of *Final Scream,* enter contests, play games, and read excerpts from my other books.

Keep Reading!

Lisa Jackson

**Here is an exciting peek at
Lisa Jackson's
next new thriller
FATAL BURN
coming in March 2006!**

He stood before the fire, feeling its heat, listening to the crackle of flames as they devoured the tinder-dry kindling. With all the shades drawn, he slowly unbuttoned his shirt, the crisp white cotton falling off his shoulders as moss ignited, hissing. Sparking.

Above the mantel was a mirror and he watched himself undress, looked at his perfectly honed body, muscles moving easily, flexing and sliding beneath the taut skin of an athlete.

He glanced at his eyes. Blue. Icy. Described by one woman as "bedroom eyes," by another as "cold eyes," by yet another unsuspecting woman as "eyes that had seen too much."

They'd all been right, he thought and flashed a smile.

A "killer smile," he'd heard.

Bingo.

The women had no idea how close to the truth they'd all been. He was handsome and he knew it. Not good-looking enough to turn heads on the street, but so interesting that women, once they noticed him, had trouble looking away.

There had been a time when he'd been so flattered that he'd rarely turn in the other direction, a time when he'd picked and chosen and rarely been denied.

He unbuckled his leather belt, let it fall to the hardwood floor. His slacks slid easily off his butt, down his legs, and pooled at his feet. He hadn't bothered with boxers or jockeys. Who cared? It was all about outward appearances.

Always.

His smile fell away as he walked closer to the mantel, feeling the heat already radiating from the old bricks. Pictures in frames stood at attention upon the smooth fir. Images he'd caught when his subject didn't realize he or she was on camera. People who knew him. Or of him. People who had to pay.

His eyes fixated on one photograph, slightly larger than the others, and he stared into her gorgeous face. He traced a finger along her hairline, his guts churning as he noticed her hazel eyes, slightly freckled nose, thick waves of unruly reddish curls. Her skin was pale, her eyes alive, her smile tenuous, as if she'd sensed him hiding in the shadowy trees, his lens poised at her heart-shaped face.

The dog, some kind of scraggly mutt, had appeared from the other side of the woods, lifted his nose in the air as he'd reached her, trembled, growled, and nearly given him away. Shannon had given the cur a short command and peered into the woods.

By that time, he'd been slipping away. Silently moving through the dark woods, putting distance between them, heading upwind. He'd gotten his snapshots. He'd needed nothing more.

Then.

Because the timing hadn't been right.

But now . . .

The fire glowed bright, seemed to pulse with life as it grew, giving the bare room a warm, rosy glow. He stared again at his image. So perfect in the mirror.

He turned, facing away from the reflection.

Looking over his shoulder, he gritted those perfect white teeth, gnashing them together as he saw the mirror's cruel image of his back, the skin scarred and shiny, looking as if it had melted from his body.

He remembered the fire.

The agony of his flesh being burned from his bones.

He'd never forget.

Not for as long as he drew a breath on this godforsaken planet.

And those who had done this to him would pay.

From the corner of his eye, he saw the picture of Shannon again. Beautiful and wary, as if she knew her life was about to change forever.

Lookout, he thought, smiling evilly. *I'm coming, Shannon, oh, yes, I'm coming. And this time I'll have more than a camera with me.*

"Move over, Stephanie Plum! Jane Kelly has arrived!"
—Lisa Jackson

Romance is thin on the ground in Lake Chinook. But the bodies are just beginning to pile up . . .

Jane Kelly is through with following men anywhere. Last time she did, she left Southern California for the dubious charms of Lake Chinook, Oregon, where she's traded in bartending for the much more glamorous trade of process serving. (Well, she can tell herself it's glamorous, anyway.) And the boyfriend, of course, is long gone.

So she's thirty, she's single, she's living in a town where fishing is more important than fashion, and one of her closest friends is an "information specialist"—which is a fancy way of saying private detective. Odder still, she's been helping him out, which makes the criminology courses she took a few years back with her ex at least worth the tuition. She's not making any lifetime commitments, but when Portland divorce attorney Marta Cornell calls with a P.I. job, the money involved sounds like the answer to her dwindling bank account—until she learns Tess Bradbury wants her to investigate the disappearance of Bobby Reynolds.

Four years ago, without warning, Bobby murdered his young family and promptly vanished. No one disputed that he'd slaughtered his own flesh and blood except Tim Murphy, his best friend—and Jane's ex—the one guy she's never quite gotten over. The murders had driven a wedge between him and Jane, and finally drove him right out of town. Now he's on his way back, to attend a Lake Chinook Historical Society benefit that Cotton Reynolds, Bobby's father, is hosting.

Every alarm bell in Jane's head is clanging, but before she can say "Not on your life," Marta has convinced her to accept Tess's assignment—an interview with Tess's ex-husband,

Cotton, who she believes has been in contact with Bobby. It looks like Jane's going to be following men around again— this time with a tape recorder and a camera.

To top it off, an only vaguely remembered aunt has left her a homely pug named Binky, and her mother is once again threatening to head north and settle in Oregon. With a brand-new job she's learning as she goes along and the man who broke her heart into a million pathetic little pieces back in town, Jane's life just went from stress-free to completely stressed-out. And that's before she finds the dead body in the lake . . .

**The following is
an exciting sneak peek at
Candy Apple Red
by Nancy Bush
coming in October 2005!**

If I'd known they were about to find a body at the bottom of Lake Chinook, I never would have gotten myself into the whole mess. The lake's deep in places, and the Lake Corporation only drains it every couple of years to check the sewer lines running along its muddy bottom. The thought of the little fishy things trolling the waters, chewing off teensy nibbles of human flesh, would have been enough for me to say, *"Hasta la vista,* baby," and I would have exerted great haste in making tracks.

But I didn't know. And I also didn't know my whole life was about to change. The day I spoke with *uber*-bitch/lawyer Marta Cornell I was blissfully ignorant of the events in store for me, which was just as well. Don't ever tell yourself you're happy with the way things are because that's when everything changes in seconds flat. And not necessarily for the better.

"Jane!" Marta boomed over the phone. The woman was over six feet tall with a voice to match. She could deafen with one word. I yanked the phone from my ear and hoped I still possessed my hearing. "I have a client who has an un-usual request and I think you're just the person to help."

"What unusual request?" I asked.

"It's about Cotton Reynolds."

My heart leapt. Christ, I thought a bit shakily. I'd just been thinking about my ex-boyfriend, Tim Murphy, who knew Cotton well. Had thoughts of Murphy actually triggered the past? "What about him?" I asked, trying to hold my voice steady.

"My client wants some follow-up on . . . Bobby Reynolds." Marta had hesitated, unlike her to the extreme. "She wants you to interview Cotton."

I stared at my office door and, instead of its scarred, paneled wood, saw the white-haired man who happened to be one of the wealthiest in the state of Oregon. Cotton Reynolds lived on the only island in Lake Chinook, less than a mile from my bungalow. By boat, I could be there in ten minutes, if I wanted to. By car, it would be trickier. The island was private and Cotton's was the only house on its three acres. If I dropped in to say hello, I wouldn't get past the huge, wrought-iron gate nor the island's guard dogs, two ill-tempered Dobermans.

But interviewing Cotton wasn't what was on my mind. Following up on Bobby Reynolds was. Murphy's close, high school friend. His best buddy.

I almost hung up right then. I probably should have. A shiver slid coldly down my spine; someone walking on my grave.

Bobby Reynolds had murdered his family and left their bodies lined up in a row—wife Laura; Aaron, eight; Jenny, three; and infant Kit—somewhere in the Tillamook State Forest, just off the Oregon coast. Bobby Reynolds was a "family annihilator:" a man apparently overwhelmed with the responsibility of his family so he chose to send them to a "better place." He shot them each once in the back of the head, then drove away. He dumped his Dodge Caravan on a turnout off Highway 101, which meanders along the West Coast throughout Washington, Oregon, and into California, then disappeared without a trace, though he'd been rumored to have been seen as far north as the Canadian border and as far south as Puerto Vallarta. To date, after four years, he was still very much a fugitive. The murders—disputed by Murphy, who simply could not believe his friend capable of cold-blooded homicide—had driven Murphy away from Lake Chinook, the tragedy, and me.

I cleared my throat and asked, "Who is this client?"

"Tess Reynolds Bradbury."

"Bobby's *mother?*"

"Cotton won't talk to her about Bobby or anything else. They haven't spoken civilly in years. When it was all over the news, they had words, but it wasn't exactly what I would call communication."

"I remember," I said, recalling how Cotton's ex, with her blond bob, hard eyes, and angry mouth, had been bleeped out by the local news, time and again. Cotton had been silent and stony, although my impression was that it was a mask for deep, deep pain and shock. I'd tried to talk to Murphy but he'd gone to a place inside himself, as distant as a cold moon, before he'd left for good.

"Why does she want me to talk to him?" I asked, baffled. "The police and FBI and every news channel around have been on this since it happened. What could I learn? I don't even know Cotton."

"You've met. You were Tim Murphy's girlfriend."

"I wouldn't call myself his girlfriend," I said carefully. "I knew him." Not as well as I thought I did, as it turned out.

"Murphy was close to Bobby and Cotton. Tess thinks you can use that connection—"

"No," I said again, with more force. "I'm outta this. I'd be useless."

"She stopped by my office the other day, and we started talking about Bobby, a little. She never could before. But it's like she's suddenly gotta get it out. Along the line, your name came up. She remembered you."

If I hadn't been so overwhelmed, I would have been surprised. Tess had barely seen me. She'd been divorced from Cotton in those few months before Bobby's deadly deed was discovered. I hadn't known Bobby very well, as he and his family had moved to Astoria. I mostly knew about them through Murphy. I'd met Bobby and his wife Laura exactly once, so when their pictures were in the papers, they'd looked like the strangers they were to me. I said, "It would be a miracle if Cotton remembered me."

"He knows Murphy. That's all that matters."

I didn't like it. It was sneaky and wrong. Oh, sure, I can be a snoop, but this tragedy was epic in size. I felt small and mean even talking about it with Marta. "What kind of information does she expect?" I asked. "I don't get it."

"Whether she's right or wrong, she thinks Cotton's been in touch with Bobby. I know the police and FBI have wrung him dry, and he's been more than cooperative. I'm just telling you what she wants. And she's willing to pay well."

"I'm not a private investigator."

"As good as," Marta dismissed, but then she was always saying things like that when she wanted something.

"How much is she willing to pay?" I asked cautiously, lured in spite of myself. I inwardly shuddered. It was like dipping a toe in cold, cold water.

"An initial five hundred dollars and then whatever you work out. She wants you to develop some kind of relationship, Jane," Marta went on. "She says Cotton always admired you when you were there with Murphy. She thinks you could . . . have some sway."

"I doubt it."

"Are you saying you won't do it?"

I didn't know what I was saying. I was out of my depth and I knew it. I'm not all that hot at self-delusion. If I were really thinking about taking the jump to information specialist/private investigator, I'd sure as hell like to start with something smaller. Like grand larceny. Or . . . corporate tax fraud. Or that Erin Brockovich deadly chemical thing. I did not want to be personally involved in the investigation, no matter how distantly, as I was in this one.

"Cotton does remember you," Marta insisted. "Bobby told Tess how his dad liked you."

"Bobby told his mother that his dad liked me? That's just great. When was that, Marta? I was only here for a few months before it happened."

Marta sighed at my obstinacy. "Are you going to do it, or not?"

"All signs point to 'not.'" I paused, belatedly hearing some innuendo between the lines. Why did Tess want me to get close to Cotton? My thoughts took a turn toward the salacious. "I'm not going to sleep with him."

"Oh, for God's sake, Jane. Tess just wants you to suck up to him a little, show some interest in the guy. He's been living like a hermit with his young wife ever since Bobby slaughtered his family and ran." I cringed at her words. "Tess thinks this is the perfect time to lend a sympathetic ear."

"I won't get any results the police haven't."

"Five hundred dollars plus, whether you learn anything or not," Marta coerced.

Five hundred dollars plus. My brain started calculating, taking a trip of its own, as I wondered how many "sessions" I could squeeze out of the deal. It's hard to turn down pure, cold cash. My mentor Dwayne Durbin would be proud of my way of thinking.

"Cotton's having a party next Saturday night." Marta sweetened the pot. "I can get you an invitation."

"How?"

"Well . . . Murphy's been invited. He's coming into town this week."

I swore beneath my breath, loud enough for Marta to hear. *Murphy?* "What a setup. I'm not interested, Marta. Not one little bit."

"He knows you might be there. He wants to see you."

"Not a chance." Marta knows what she's doing at all times. She's an operator, someone who sees what she wants and goes after it, no matter how many souls she grinds into the pavement along the way. I almost admired her.

"Murphy still talks to Tess," Marta went on. "He mentioned you the other day. That's what got Tess thinking."

"Murphy and I don't talk."

"Jane, Tess is going to be in my office at three today. She'd really like to meet you."

"You're railroading me. I can hear the train whistle."

"I thought you might want to see him."

"Bullshit. You thought of a new way to squeeze money out of a client. How much is Tess paying you for this setup?"

"Plenty," was her equable answer. "Tess is a grateful client."

I almost laughed. I could imagine how well Marta had put the squeeze on Cotton as Tess's representative in their divorce. Her unabashed greed appealed to me, maybe because deep inside I'm a kindred spirit. Okay, maybe it's just that I'm not that deep inside.

She seemed to sense my lessening fury. "Is that a yes?"

I had an instant memory of a hot midnight on Murphy's boat, illegally docked in the shelter of Phantom's Cove, the deepest part of Lake Chinook, two hundred feet beneath the houses perched on the bluff above, hidden by the canopies of oaks and firs which kept the cove under shadow most of the time. I remembered fevered bodies wrapped tightly together, sweat and silent laughter that remained caught in the back of my throat. And pleasure.

An ache filled me inside. I'd fallen in love once in college, but Murphy was the next, and last, man who'd ever filled my senses so completely. I half believed now that it would never happen to me again. Maybe it would, but right now it felt impossible.

The thought that he might actually be at this party was enough to send me into the kind of female panic I loathed seeing in others. I couldn't go. Even if I met with Cotton, I couldn't go to this party if Murphy was going to be there.

I said as much to Marta. At least I think I did. But she responded with a quick overview of how much income this could provide me. I turned her down over and over again, I swear. Yes, dollar signs danced in front of my eyes, but the thought of clapping eyes on Tim Murphy again was something my system couldn't take. I told myself I would rather live in destitution for a thousand lifetimes than go another round with Murphy.

"We'll see you at three, then," Marta said happily and hung up.

I was left staring into space, my jaw hanging open. Slowly, I brought my lips together again and clicked off my cell phone. There was no memory in my mind of my agreement to meet with Tess, but somehow I'd managed to say yes.